SEE SADIE JANE Run

FOUND FAMILIES BOOK FOUR

KELLY ELIZABETH HUSTON

PRAISE FOR SEE SADIE JANE RUN

SEE SADIE JANE RUN, 2024 NYC Big Book Awards Distinguished Favorite for Women's Fiction**

"_See Sadie Jane Run_ is a briskly-paced, character-focused romantic thriller that doesn't let its foot off the gas for a second. Written in a confident and accessible manner, Huston's energetic storyline is sure to have widespread appeal." —**Publishers Weekly, Booklife Prize**

"_See Sadie Jane Run_ has it all: mystery, romance and wit...Amidst the backdrop of a small town with lingering secrets and vibrant characters, Sadie confronts her past while navigating corporate intrigue and a chance at redemption. A highly recommended read you'll be thanking me for!" —**Kyle Ann Robertson**, author of _No So Little Things_

"If you enjoy sweet-with-some-heat stories set in small Southern towns featuring quirky characters—including a leading lady who's smart and funny and refuses to suffer fools—check out Kelly Elizabeth Huston's _SEE SADIE JANE RUN_." —Jan Heidrich-Rice, author of _Secrets of the Blue Moon_

To the women who struggle to give themselves grace and the ones who love them anyway. Everyone is worthy.

One

SADIE JANE KLEIN

present day

I CUSSED WHEN MY head snapped back—the ridiculous veil caught in the door I'd just slammed closed. Not one of the more genteel profanities my long-ago college boyfriend's mother informed me was appropriate for a *lady* to let slip from her lips, mind you. Polite society *might* abide the occasional "damn" or even "shit," but beyond that, no one would approve of such a mouth. Naturally, I made it worse when, with a wink, I informed her that her son liked my mouth just fine.

I didn't even want to wear a veil—certainly not anything that long. Hell, I didn't want to wear a dress. *Shoot*, I didn't even want to get *married*. Then again, neither did Tristan. Right? So, we didn't. But there I stood, in a pitch-black room I didn't know, on *The Sapphire Selkie*, a riverboat casino I *never* would have chosen, with my *chapel-length* veil stuck in the door I just banged shut, trying to escape a banquet hall and the shocked faces of hundreds of wedding guests left in my wake. Wait, what was that look on Tristan's face? And where the heck was he? He should have been here by now.

Nope. I dropped a full-on *F*-bomb and ripped the veil's hair comb free from my tight curls.

Out of the dark, a chuckling snort startled me. My eyes adjusted to the lack of light with the help of the dim glow that snuck through a round side scuttle on the boat's starboard.

Forgetting the headdress left dangling in the door jamb, I hoisted my organza gown to my knees, ready to make another run for it.

"Is that an invitation?" By the sounds of it, my hideaway pal had enjoyed the open bar before the ceremony. Tristan, playing the role of "groom," called it pre-gaming, and since it was a midnight ceremony on a gambling vessel, somehow that tracked.

"Excuse me?" The southern drawl I tend to keep buttoned up doubles when I get frazzled or happy or drunk or... "Is that any way to talk to a bride on her would-be wedding day?"

"Shit." Chair legs screeched across the floor when the silhouette of a tall man pushed to his feet. "Sadie? Sadie Klein?" A faceless twang met mine.

I stepped deeper into the dark.

"Apologies. I didn't mean to—"

"Do I know you? Hard to imagine since I know all of ten people on the pages-long guest list—and I only like two of them."

The stranger laughed again. "It's Ellis, Ellis Holland."

I didn't speak, stunned to learn he was, in fact, *not* a stranger, but relieved the nighttime light helped hide my shock.

"We went to high school together," he continued.

Still, no words came from my side of the cabin.

"I was a couple years ahead of you in your brother's class. Leo?"

"I know my brother's name, Ellis." Reining in my bark, I played dense while desperate to keep calm. "Your name's—Ellis?"

"You tutored me. In Calculus. How do you not remember? People call me Dutch because my last name's Holland—"

"Yes," I interrupted. "How clever." Having little interest in any sort of small world reunion, I pushed ahead, knowing I needed help, seeing as my rogue bridegroom appeared to be a no-show. And I had no plans to stick around. But of all the people... "Two questions." I zeroed in on a Plan B.

"Ask away, Sadie," he sighed, but I ignored the dismay.

"How drunk are you?"

He didn't slur his speech, but what self-respecting southern boy did, no matter how inebriated he got? "Just drunk enough, I s'pose."

"Great. One floor down, at the aft of this too tall river barge, there are three twelve-foot, inflatable pontoon rescue dinghies equipped with 10.0 short shaft outboard electrical motors." I met silence. "They're red," I offered when I realized my error. I have a tendency to focus on details few others find interesting or important or at all necessary.

He cocked his head in the shadows. "Again, apologies. Imma little drunk. Was the second question hidden in all of that?"

With my eyes adjusting to the environment, I'd swear I could see enough to register the handsome man's quirked lip. "Oh. No. Right. Think you could help me get off this hell-boat and pilot one of those puppies the two miles back to dry land, Mr. Holland?"

"Captain."

"O-kay. I'll call you whatever you'd like."

"No, it's *captain* one of those puppies, not pilot. You captain a boat, pilot a plane."

I waited a beat. "Ellis? Dutch? Oh, Captain, my Captain? Could you help out a runaway bride?"

"It'd be my privilege, Sadie Jane Klein." If he'd worn a hat, he'd have tipped it. Memories of small-town-living where everyone knew everything about you, including your middle name, washed over me and struck me dumb. A rare condition. Neither of us moved for a full three seconds.

"*Ahem*, I'm assuming you mean *now*, darlin'?"

"Yes, Ellis. Now'd be good, but *never* call me that again."

Dutch rushed past me, opening the door a crack to see if the corridor was clear. Hall sconces highlighted his sea green eyes and days-old beard. Sandy-brown curls, I recalled from our younger days, were gone, and now he wore his hair quite short, if not an all-out buzz cut. Unfastening his top button, he loosened his necktie while I stared at his chiseled profile. The man had aged well.

"Sadie?" It might have been the *second* time he beckoned me from the door.

"Yes?" I jolted out of the chaos ruling my brain but couldn't pull my gaze from his lips. The new light also revealed a faint scar, almost silver, at one corner of his mouth. I winced with the sudden memory of how it bled all those years ago. And why.

"Isn't this boat gonna move again soon?"

"Yes, out twelve nautical miles for the gambling to begin." Another unnecessary detail.

"So, we should probably hurry."

"Yes." My feet wouldn't move. Tristan should have been here by now. Hell, Tristan and I shouldn't have ever been here at all. *Son-of-a-*

"You sure, Sadie Jane?"

That name, said just that way, was all the encouragement I needed. I met Dutch's bloodshot eyes. "Let's do this," I spat, and hitched up my skirt again, grabbed the crook of his arm, and we bolted for the nearest stairwell, leaving behind the ludicrous veil.

I knew better. *Everybody* knows better. But as we fled the party at sea, buzzing through the humid night air, I couldn't help myself. "That was easier than I thought it'd be." I didn't say it *to* anyone. The high-pitch whine of the electric motor, splashing surf, and blustery wind demanded a near-yelled conversation, and that wasn't happening.

Nevertheless—I said it, even though I knew better.

Under the perceived circumstances, one might think our great escape should have included more than the uneventful run-in with an on-a-break busboy, a ladder that was a bit too narrow and a bit too steep for my bridal get-up, and a couple of troublesome sailor knots that slowed our freeing the dinghy. I'd never admit it aloud, but I couldn't have made it without help. It seemed my debt to Ellis "Dutch" Holland continued to grow.

Of course, the old chestnut about perception versus reality—well, it played a regular theme in my life. It wasn't a surprise no one had launched an all-hands-on-deck search for me. Dollars to dumplings, Tristan created some distraction to give me a head start, and as soon as I figured out how it all went so wrong, how I allowed that dumbass to get me into this mess—wait. Who was the dumbass?

My fellow fugitive and I sped toward socket string lights that seemed to twinkle along the faraway dock landing. They didn't, really. The sea breeze made them oscillate, and the undulating tide beat out a rhythmic *clank* as moor chains assailed the buoyed channel markers. For people who grew up in a coastal town, those markers, the lights, those sounds make finding your way, even at night, something like automatic. And I had no doubt Dutch would get me to shore. What would happen then? I hadn't a clue.

Halfway between the anchored riverboat and the berth, we found ourselves in the darkest part of the journey. Lights glimmered ahead and behind us, but out in the waterway, I could barely see my hand in front of my face. Barely.

Looking back at the *Sapphire Selkie* and the near-mistake I'd dodged didn't seem prudent, nor did staring at the man who looked like a mistake I might *enjoy* making. While I chastised myself for that impudent notion, the engine's whine, the wind, the splash of the surf—*everything* went quiet. Yep, I knew better.

My head hung low. "Ellis?"

The glow from the distant casino-at-sea outlined the movement of the figure at the rear of the rescue craft. That figure didn't reply. I repeated his name, but my question was obvious.

"Can't say for sure, Sadie, because it's darker than the Devil's—I can't read the digital display, but I imagine the battery died."

"Yeah. I figured," I sighed. "Two things."

"You're big on that."

"On what?"

"Twos."

"What?"

"*Two* questions, *two* things."

You'd think my distress in the thorniest of run-ins at the most untimely moment might encourage a milder manner—a less knee-jerk reaction toward the man who'd volunteered to be my liberator, but no. "Stick around, Ellis. Sometimes there's *three*."

"Careful. I just might," he mumbled, but I caught it.

"Might what?"

"Stick around."

I faced the shore, hiding my smile. Not that it mattered on a moonless night. The choppy water lapped on the boat's bow, and I kept my eyes on the far-off marina. A chill racked my frame, and my grin nearly morphed into a laugh. I stifled it.

Finally, he spoke again. "You were saying. Two things?"

I paused to be sure I wouldn't let slip the unhinged howl building in me, brought on by the absurd circumstance: dressed in a $15,000 gown, stranded on an out-of-battery rescue dinghy in the middle of Booby Creek at o' dark thirty with the wrong man, a man I hadn't seen in fifteen years. A booby is a sea bird, by the way, and don't let the term "creek" fool you. It was big. I shivered again. "Please tell me this thing came equipped with paddles, and, more importantly, that you are carrying—a flask."

The raft jostled, and I grabbed the nylon rope laced around the boat's hull. Dutch removed his dark suit coat and leaned to hand it to me. "Here. Put it on."

"That's not necessary but thank you." Hard-headed, I refused his kind gesture, already too indebted to the man.

"The flask is in the inside pocket."

"Oh." That changed things. I reached for the jacket, honestly eager for some warmth. "Aren't you the gentleman?"

"We'll see," came his quick reply.

I stopped short while slipping into the refined fresco blazer. Someone had expensive taste, and not just me. The sterling silver flask full of top-shelf Scotch further proved the point. I took my second healthy swig.

"And yes, we have paddles. Your favorite number. Two."

I stowed the booze in the breast pocket and extended my hand. "Well, hand me one, and let's get to shore."

"I will not. You're wearing a wedding gown, an expensive one, I'd guess. Not that I've taken much notice in our rush, but if I know Tristan Pembroke—and I do—it's pricey. No, you will not be rowing ashore, Miss Klein."

I opened my mouth to correct him. I was *Dr.* Klein, a Ph.D. in geotechnical engineering, but Dutch interjected before I could get the words out.

"Let me guess. Two things."

Damn, I wish he didn't make me smile like that. More stubbornness bloomed. "Three things, actually. I couldn't give a flying ferret about the dress, and how do you know Tristan?"

"That's only two things."

"Don't be an ass."

"But you said *three*—"

"No, that's the third thing, Ellis. Don't be an ass. Now how do you know my fiancé?"

"*Oof.* Hate to be the one to tell you this, but I'm pretty sure he's your *ex*-fiancé now. And I work with his father. That's why I was on the boat tonight. Work."

"Work? What kind of work?"

"Uh, I'm—kind of a—problem solver. I mean, security, sort of. I work—security." His reply lacked conviction as he stumbled over his words. Maybe he was drunker than I thought.

I laughed—couldn't help myself, but I kept it in check. "Hate to be the one to tell you this," I mimicked, "but after this show of disloyalty, I'm pretty sure you *worked* security for Tristan's father. Past tense." I might feel guilty about that dig when all was said and done.

"*Nah*, Mr. P. and I are good. But I appreciate your concern for my employment welfare."

I disregarded his scored point. "Guess that explains why your name wasn't on the guest list. Since you were there for *work*."

"I dunno, Sadie. It was a big list. Long. You remember every *total* stranger's name on that very lengthy list?"

Dutch might have caught me in my earlier lie. Not so much a lie as an omission, a feigned non-recollection. Of course I'd remembered Ellis Holland. How could I forget? No matter how hard I tried.

As if he read my mind, he continued, "How is ol' Leo these days?" The metal-on-metal clang got louder as Dutch made slow rowing progress toward land.

Opting to neither confirm nor deny his suspicions, I ignored his implication. "My brother's great. Really good. Lives in New York City. Queens, actually. Finished grad school at St. John's. He's a physician's assistant now. Works too hard and too much to make time to meet the man of his dreams, but he's happy." I hoped that last part was true. It had been a while since we talked and who the hell was I to judge him on work/life balance?

"So busy he couldn't make it to his kid sister's wedding? The kid sister he adores more than life—"

I pulled out the flask again and busied my mouth with it.

"It's nice he's keeping the Klein family's medical tradition alive." Dutch softened his tone. "I was mighty sorry to hear about your grandparents' passing."

My heart had barely stitched itself back together over the last year and a half, but I didn't show my pain. I wasn't a big sharer. My grandparents, Drs. Avigdor and Talia Klein were the only parents I've ever known, and I suppose I should count myself lucky to have had them as long as I did. Still, the ache ran deep. Worse, if I allowed myself to dwell on the loss, both of my grandparents and the mother and father I never knew. So, I didn't. I took in a big helping of sea air.

"Yes, well, Mee-maw and Grandaddy raised us right, but it was too soon. I'm grateful they went together. It's the only way they would have had it. One wasn't long for this world without the other. Besides, physics says when the eighteen-wheeler hit them, they never felt a thing. I think it bodes well, to be honest. Our parents went down together in an ocean storm, 'course, I was too young to remember, and our grandparents, in a car wreck. When my time comes, I hope it's like that. With the one I love." Welp, so much for not dwelling. Why would I ever share that? Least of all with Dutch Holland.

More *splash* and *clang* filled the void before Dutch spoke again. "Some might call it a curse, but you always did look at life a little differently." He took two more long, slow strokes before he sputtered, "W—was the one you love supposed to be Tristan?"

"*No.*" My adamant reply came fast. "Never."

"Good." Dutch's reply flew from his lips just as quickly.

"Why good? What makes that good?"

"If he was the one, and you still ran away, you'd probably be sad right now. And I don't want you to be sad. Not over the likes of Tristan Pembroke, anyway."

It had been a long time since Dutch and I'd known one another, and in the night's mayhem, wondering what memories of me he might have carried with him made my brain hurt. But I'd always been a runner. I ran *into* situations with little thought and often ran *away* if things got messy, then criticized every figurative misstep, coming or going. Now, there he sat, all these years later, acting like maybe he did recollect a thing or two, and being sweet about it to boot.

"*Hm.* Like I said, aren't you the gentleman?"

Dutch simply sniffed and kept rowing.

Two

SADIE

present day

As soon as Dutch looped a rope around a dock pylon, I rolled to my feet, yanking my elbow from his grip when he tried to steady me so I could slip on my shoes and grab the mounted ladder to climb up the three rungs to the quay. Plenty of light made him easier to see, and I didn't appreciate the look he gave—whatever it meant to say.

"Fine." He raised his hands in surrender.

With one hand on the salt and rust-covered ladder rail, my other tried to hold up no less than fifty square yards of silk organza. I struggled to make lift-off and grunted in the effort, all while wearing a man's suit coat.

"Hold on." Dutch placed both hands under my ass and gave one stout heave, launching me up onto the pier with an impressive show of strength.

I squealed mid-flight and caught a light pole, spinning into my rescuer when he cleared the top of the ladder. My hands on his chest, I snickered until his serious stare bore into me. That close, in better light, I took in the full sight of him. I swallowed hard and flattened my grin. "You got taller, Ellis." I pressed my lips together, realizing I just blew whatever remained of the earlier "stranger" ploy.

Dutch smirked. "So did you."

"Not really." I lifted my gown to show off my shoes. "I'm in heels." I flexed and pointed. "They're fancy and totally not my usual thing, but I love them. Don't you?"

"Um, yes. Very nice." He nodded with a sweet smile, but not at my shoes. "Beautiful."

"Oh?" I might have blushed as I examined my Manolos again. "And just how into feminine footwear are you?"

His grin faded, and he moved to push past me. "Good God, Sadie," he murmured. "You asked."

I grabbed for his arm, having clearly embarrassed the man. Once upon a time, it was my favorite hobby. "Now, don't be like that. I'm just having a little fun."

Dutch focused on the distant parking lot. "What now?"

"Well, it's late," I stated the obvious—a habit that reared up when I got nervous.

"Whose idea was it to have a midnight wedding?"

"Probably the same person who picked a maritime casino named for a duplicitous Welsh sea witch as the venue. And in case it isn't clear, that person was not me. I'm this way." I pointed toward the dark parking lot and walked in that direction.

The mooring bobbed and weaved, not a great combination with the fancy footwear. Dutch helped me balance more than once. I let him. Even barely off the water, the night air warmed, making my companion's dinner jacket no longer necessary, but I liked the smell of it and didn't want to give up the flask before getting another nip of the fine Scotch.

By the time we reached a gravel path, officially on dry land, Dutch had rolled up the cuffs of his expertly fitted dress shirt. I'd have sworn it was custom. Puzzle pieces sorted in my brain, and my builder nature wondered what they would show me if I completed the picture. Then again, that would likely take time, and time spent with Dutch Holland seemed like more than I could hope for, if not an overwhelming distraction. Nope, time to cut bait.

"You don't have to see to me anymore, you know. I don't need an escort." But as soon as I gave him the brush-off, I regretted it and tried to rewind. "Of course, without return-passage to the *Sapphire Selkie,* I guess you're kind of stuck. This is me." We had zig-zagged through parked cars to the farthest row where a Candy Apple Red 1974 Ford F100 shined like new under a utility pole's bright LED. I reached under the wheel-well, pulled out a magnetic hide-a-key, and unlocked it.

"This is *your* truck?" He couldn't help but admire it. It was a truck, a nice one, and Dutch was a southern boy, as I've mentioned. It's what so many of them did. It's what I did too. Loved all things mechanical so much, I got a Ph.D. Fancy shoes, fancy truck, fancy degree.

I shoved the romance novel I'd left bookmarked on the dash behind the headrest and crawled across the classic bench seat to open the passenger door. "Nice, right?"

"Very," he replied, distractedly fondling the glovebox door.

I might have had a pang of jealousy. "Thanks. It was a gift," I bragged, hoisting an oversized, stuffed-full duffel from the floorboard. It contained most of what I owned, aside from the truck, a storage unit I'd need to empty someday and a one-hundred-year-old house an hour down the road. I lugged out the bag and heaved it in the truck bed, but not before pulling a phone from the side pocket.

"Tristan picked this out for you?"

I *hmphed*. "No, Tristan would have chosen something lame. Something small, sporty and not cool. This beauty was my pick. Fully restored with some minor updates, but—"

"Still, that's a mighty nice gift." He squinted at me. Dutch shouldn't have jumped to conclusions. The gift was *from* me *to* me, but I decided to let the presumptuous oaf think what he wanted for now. I'd pocket that teachable moment for another time.

"I'm a mighty nice girl." My aping came with a saccharine smile as I settled into the driver's seat. I had severely underestimated the fluffy gown-to-truck-cab ratio, but I only needed to get down the road a bit before I could make a stop to change my clothes. Booting up the phone, I set it on its mount.

"Sadie? What's going on? You seem remarkably prepared and even-keeled for an out-of-the-blue, reckless fugitive bride." Dutch had one foot on the running board, his arms draped across the open doorframe and roof as he leaned in from the passenger side. Man, that shirt fit him well.

"Reckless?" I glanced at my phone just to prove I could. "You son-of-a—!" The heel of my hand thumped the steering wheel.

"Whoa, I'm only asking—"

"Not you, Ellis. Tristan." I held up the phone for him to see the single text.

Tris: *I'm sorry, Sade. I really am. Maybe we should reconsider. I think I love you.*

"Why's *he* sorry? What should you reconsider?" Dutch paused before he asked, "And what's that last part mean?"

"Well, let's see. Why is Tristan sorry? When is Tristan Pembroke *not* sorry?"

"Fair point." Dutch shrugged in quick agreement.

"What should I reconsider? How about thinking *that* man would ever *grow* a pair and see the plan through. *His* plan, by the way." I smacked the steering wheel three more times after tossing the phone into the retrofitted cupholder.

"What about the last bit?" He practically whispered.

"Well, I told you I was nice. Apparently, a little *too* nice." I winked.

Dutch winced.

"Oh, Ellis, Tristan wouldn't know love if it walked up and bit him in the ass. The boy is a sweet narcissist, but a narcissist all the same."

"But—he was about to marry you."

"No, he wasn't. See, we had a plan. We weren't even supposed to get on the boat, much less get married—" I gasped again just before another F-bomb dropped, and I thrashed out of the beautiful Fresco jacket and shoved it toward its wide-eyed owner.

"What's happening, Sadie? What ton of bricks just hit?"

"That son-of-a-biscuit-maker was going to marry me. He was gonna stand up in front of hundreds of people he doesn't care about and say things he didn't mean, dragging me along for the ride all because he won't stand up to his mommy and daddy. And he thought I'd do it too."

"Sadie—"

"No, I have to go now, so either get in or get out, but I'm out of here."

"Should you drive right now?"

"Oh, I'm driving. I'm driving twelve miles to Rte. 17 and then another two and a half to a Waffle House where I will change out of this silly dress and eat a plate of hash browns covered, chunked, and diced. So, in or out, Ellis Holland, but either way—you better believe I'm driving."

Without a word, Dutch climbed in, shut his door, and buckled his modified seatbelt. I may have stared a beat too long.

"What? I'm hungry, and like you said, I'm stuck, and though it's been years, memory serves, nothing heads off a hangover like Waffle House."

I cranked the ignition and peeled out of the parking space. Gravel and dust flew as we sped to a windy road, away from the *Sapphire Selkie*, away from my double-crossing ex-fiancé, and away from that near-mistake that might have been a tad nearer than I knew.

The door chime announced my entrance to the Waffle House for the second time. The first time I'd walked in wearing a bespoke gown and crystal-adorned Manolos. Now I wore cut-offs, a Foo Fighters t-shirt, and well-loved cowboy boots. The gown had been folded with care, zipped in a bag, and locked in the shiny truck. Tight curls still topped my head, but that's where I kept them most of the time anyway. I felt like myself again.

"Sorry, darlin'. That seat's taken—oh, is that you, Sadie? I didn't recognize you without your custom finery." Dutch snickered behind his laminated menu.

"*Har-har.* And since I'm so nice, as previously established, I'm going to forego the joke about you being able to spot couture, so—you're welcome." I plopped in the booth across from the man who still wore his fancy wear. Dutch appeared more relaxed, sober, with at least some of the shock of our run-in subsiding. Cautious, maybe, but he still carried a quiet confidence I'd adored when we were kids. But we weren't kids anymore.

"I ordered for you."

"How'd you know—"

"Covered, chunked, and diced—you said—"

"And to drink?" I grimaced at the unappealing plastic tumbler of ice water that sweated on the corner of my paper placemat.

Dutch pulled the elegant mini canteen from his inside jacket pocket, placed it in front of me, and then resumed reading his menu like it was some riveting page-turner. Dubious, I squinted at him over the tip of the flask, enjoying another taste of his good Scotch before I spoke again. "You might be my favorite person, Ellis—in this restaurant." I took another swallow.

"Might be?" He craned his neck to look around the place—no other patrons, only the waitress and short-order cook. They were making out and sharing a cigarette in front of the vent hood while on company time. So, #lifegoals.

"At least someone's having fun tonight." I eyed the kissing couple a little too long, unable to hide my frown.

"Jealous?" Dutch continued his perusal of Waffle House fare.

"No. You?" I sneered.

"Hardly. I'm sitting across from the prettiest girl in the place. No need for jealousy."

"Ellis Holland, are you flirting with me?"

"No, ma'am. Just stating facts. No more, no less. Now, wanna tell me what's going on here? What kind of scheme Tristan Pembroke got you roped into? A scheme that seems to have gone awry—not surprisingly."

I took another belt of booze and appreciated how it swirled its heat through my system. I hadn't eaten since breakfast, and that was more than sixteen hours ago, but I'd enjoyed my share of champagne in the ensuing hours. Getting some food in me soon was paramount. I didn't have much interest in baring my soul to Dutch, so yet another swig filled the quiet before he reached for my hand to slow the liquor flow.

"I'm fine to let you keep drinking, but if you continue, it means I'm driving wherever it is you plan to go next." He kept hold of my hand wrapped around the container of tasty booze. "Choice is yours." He raised a brow but didn't let go.

"You looking to get me drunk, Mr. Holland, or are you trying to get your hands on my sweet ride out there in the parking lot?" I punctuated the double entendre with a hard squint.

The man blushed in the bright lights of the Waffle House. He let go with speed and shook his head, mumbling, "You make it hard to be a gentleman, Sadie."

"I make it *what*?" I rarely let a questionable joke go by untold. I swallowed a laugh when he got redder. "Still quick to get pink in the cheeks, I see."

He fidgeted in his seat, and a moment of remorse hit me for poking fun. With my flask-free hand, I reached to take his with a squeeze. He didn't pull away, and it felt kind of nice until I realized he was less interested in my touch and more entranced by the three-carat princess cut in a platinum setting that decorated my left hand. I let him stare, holding my naturally manicured fingers. They rarely looked so pretty, squared off at the tips of each digit with a coat of sheer, pink polish, unlike my toes. I had those painted blazing red like my truck, but just for me. No one would see my bare feet anytime soon.

Dutch let go of my hand when the waitress appeared at our booth with a kissed-raw mouth and two plates of food. She snapped her gum and smiled. "Getcha anything else? I'm about to go on break." She eyed the fry cook over her shoulder, and her smile grew.

"No. We're fine. Thank you." I clenched my fist, already missing the rugged warmth of Dutch's grip.

"Miss?" Dutch pulled a thick money clip from his pants pocket and peeled off a fifty-dollar bill. "Keep the change. That way, you don't have to concern yourself with us anymore."

The young woman gawked at the money wad Dutch tucked into his coat. "Sure thing, sir." She fanned herself with the crisp bill, pirouetted away, and beelined to her make-out partner, unable to contain her glee.

"Are you sure that was wise?" I dug into the fried potato goodness still sizzling on my melamine plate.

"Taking care of the bill? Yes, she looked like she might get engrossed in—other things, and I'd hate to have to wait around."

"*Pfft.* No, flashing a hunk of money like that."

"Says the woman flashing a hunk of money around on her ring finger. And I'm not worried."

I shoveled in another bite, slipping my left hand into my lap.

"That thing real?"

"What kind of question is that?" Indignant, I wondered why he'd ask such a thing.

"Well, I'm over here picking up clues, connecting some dots, so now it seems a reasonable one. A legitimate one. An *important* one."

"Well, it sure as hell better be." I hoovered my American cheese, tomato, and ham hash brown concoction while Dutch had yet to taste his egg white omelet. Someone didn't understand the Waffle House assignment.

"You mean to tell me, you don't know?" He dug a paper napkin out of a stainless dispenser to place it in his lap while looking at me askance.

Sleepiness came on fast. Booze mixed with carbs combined with an adrenaline crash on top of a very long day, and I needed to close my eyes. Some parts of the plan hadn't been well-thought-out—a plan that had been ditched long before anyone informed me. I foolishly took another good gulp from the flask before meeting Dutch's pointed stare. Digging into my shorts, I freed the keys and set them on the table, but his stare stayed put with an added raised brow.

"I know, and it's real, and I have the paperwork to prove it."

Dutch smiled. "That's my Sadie Jane. Now, where are we headed next?" He took a big bite of his eggs, still grinning.

Too tired to counter his "my Sadie Jane" quip, I pushed aside my empty plate. The truth was, I liked it—even more than I remembered. I stifled a yawn and slid the keyring toward him. "Home, Ellis. It's been a long time, but I'm going home."

Three

ELLIS "DUTCH" HOLLAND

fifteen years ago

"OH, I'LL GET SADIE home, Ms. Toogood." Scrambling out of the diner booth, my seventeen-year-old arms and legs flailed while my mouth did its best to speak to the owner and namesake of Midge's Diner. I never felt gangly or uncoordinated in everyday life, navigating high school halls, drilling precision plays on the football field. But when faced with the intimidating Midge Toogood and fearless Sadie Klein, the awkward stick hit me—doubly.

"Is that right, Dutch? It'd be just this once." Midge's tiny frame forced her to crane her neck to keep my eye. But despite her vantage point, the middle-aged woman with her lavender hair and prickly demeanor stared me down.

"Yes, ma'am. It's the least I could do with Sadie helping me all these weeks with my calculus grade and you giving us a quiet place to study. It's no bother." The hardheaded fool in me thought holding Midge's stare might make me look brave. Bravery seemed like something Sadie might like. Plus, I'd been looking for an opportunity to offer Sadie a ride home after our tutoring sessions. I jumped at my chance.

When more than a few seconds ticked by, Sadie entered the standoff, much to my relief. "*Um*, does anyone care about my thoughts on the matter? Because while I *love* being talked about like I'm not in the room, I do happen to have an opinion."

Our attention focused on the spunky girl with tight curls bound in a high ponytail.

"I'm almost sixteen and perfectly capable of walking home. It's not far, and I've done it a million times."

"It's getting too dark now." Our unison reply sounded as if Ms. Toogood and I had rehearsed it. We hadn't. Motives aside, it was a fair point. In late October, the sun seemed to sink fast, and by the following week, it would be that much worse with the end of daylight-saving time.

"Fine. I'll take the ride," the girl sighed, sharing a glance with Midge I couldn't read. Another example of the complicated ways of girls and the things they *didn't* say. I'd never much cared to try to figure them out—an unwinnable game. Not until Sadie, anyway.

"I guess we'd best be on our way. Thanks, Midge." Sadie grabbed her backpack like she was eager to escape whatever she and Midge weren't saying to one another.

"Straight to the Klein bungalow, young man." Midge's husky voice and steely squint made up for her short stature. Not that I would ever disregard an elder, and certainly not one so close to Sadie. Midge Toogood was like a second grandmother to her—as near and dear as you could get without being actual family. And since Sadie and her older brother Leo lost their parents when they were very small, Midge was just that much more important.

"Yes, ma'am." I dared another attempt at prolonged direct eye contact.

"Mind your speed," she insisted.

"Always, Ms. Toogood. I'm only fast on the football field." A more earnest remark had never been uttered.

Midge cut short her bawdy laugh. "Glad to hear it, Dutch. And maybe a little sad, too."

My cheeks glowed pink, the reaction quick, uncontrollable, and my telltale flaw. The woman snickered, making it worse. Sadie seemed to ignore us, making a mad dash for the exit. Midge's questionable sense of humor was one of the things we teenagers liked most about her. That and her pie, but *not* when her jokes got aimed in our direction. I threw my bag over my shoulder and chased after my math tutor.

"Give my best to your Mee-maw, Sadie."

"Will do, Midge." Sadie waved without looking. The bell dangling overhead chimed as we both pushed open the steel-framed door. Canaan Cove's skies faded to purple from the orange glow at the horizon. I almost mentioned it, but the girl shivered when a chilly breeze hit us. Shoving her arm into a cardigan, she struggled with her overstuffed book bag. She twisted to catch the sweater's second sleeve but lost to the momentum of the heavy load.

"Whoa. Let me help." I grabbed her backpack before it hit the sidewalk.

"I've got it," Sadie squawked in defiance, but I already held the sack straps. "Thank you." She softened with the trace of a shy smile. I returned it with my own.

Once she regained her composure, adjusting her sweater, she allowed me to slide the pack onto her shoulders. The dusky light had me wondering if she looked different, a little prettier, because it was Wednesday. Wednesdays were when she tutored me in Intro to Calculus. Well, Wednesdays *and* Fridays. Not that I needed it. Wednesdays because that was the one day without football practice, and Fridays because that was game night, so I had a couple of free hours between the end of school and kickoff. My made-up math struggle let me seek out "help" during my only spare time, and that help came from a brainy sophomore with an aptitude for arithmetic. I didn't like lying, but what's a guy to do?

We walked in the quiet down Main Street to where I'd parked my truck, neither of us in any hurry. Then we spoke at the same time.

Me: "Chilly, isn't it?"

Her: "So, starting next—"

Both of us: "What?"

I gestured to her to continue.

"Starting next week, Friday, our sessions will need to be shorter. End earlier."

That was a bummer. I didn't reply.

"I have to be home before sundown, and with the clocks changing, it's dark that much sooner."

Sometimes, if you say less and listen more, I've learned that you can apply the newfound information to help your case. I kept my mouth shut, knowing Sadie would likely keep talking. She was definitely a talker.

"Only on Fridays because of Shabbat," she continued to explain. "My grandparents aren't sticklers about a lot of things, but Friday nights are one. We light the candles just before sundown. It's a—a religious thing." It was a rare instance when Sadie let slip a hint of unease.

I stalled on our stroll for a brief moment, then continued walking. "Is—is that why you never come to see me play? Not *me*. I mean *us*. Why you never come? Because games are on Friday nights?" Not a game night went by when I didn't scan the bleachers for her wild curls and hazel eyes. She never showed. Not that I asked her to be there.

The day's light faded, but a streetlamp helped me catch what might have been the start of her playful grin. I braced myself for some of Sadie's signature teasing—ribbing I secretly got a kick out of, even though it made me blush.

"Are you worth watching, Ellis? All that speed on the field you bragged about to Midge back there?"

"I wasn't bragging," I rushed to say. I might have been bragging.

"Oh, I think maybe you were. Sounded like it. You puffed up some, even."

"No, I didn't—"

"Might have strutted a bit, too." She raised her dark brows, and those sly hazel eyes twinkled more brown than green in the nighttime light.

"Is it bragging if it's true?" I asked with unusual swagger I couldn't quite pull off.

A laugh snuck out of her as we reached my truck. I wasn't boastful. I was quiet and *usually* confident and smarter than I let on. And every now and again, my dry sense of humor tumbled out, and Sadie always caught it. But in moments when I feared I'd gone too far or when my confidence fell, I took brief hold of the nape of my neck to rein myself in. Like my blush, it was a clue I'd lost my typical cool head. And no one made my head spin more than Sadie.

"I bet you are a sight to see, Ellis. But yes, my Friday Night Lights are of a different variety. Georgia football might be king, but God is God, so Shabbos wins—at least as far as the Drs. Klein are concerned."

I released my neck grip and nodded, ready to use this newfound information in my favor. "Well, then. I reckon I'll be getting you home before sundown on Fridays then."

"Oh, that's kind of you, but Midge said this is a onetime—"

"I'll be seeing you home from now on. I mean, if you don't mind, it'd be my pleasure." It was as forward as I'd ever attempted to be, and I hurried to open the passenger door, hoping it all came across like casual chivalry.

Sadie paused before climbing into the truck. "Thank you, Ellis." It was another illustration of 'what girls didn't say,' but I wanted to believe it meant it'd be her pleasure too.

I chuckled, satisfied at the apparent win. "You know—everyone calls me Dutch. No one calls me Ellis."

"I've been calling you Ellis. I like calling you Ellis. Do you mind?" She cocked her head with her usual bravery, that courage I tried to emulate. But I thought she held her breath while I pretended to ponder my reply.

"You know? I don't. I don't mind at all, *Sadie Jane*. Buckle up now." I smiled and closed the truck door.

My heart thudded as I jogged around the front of the pickup to hop in behind the wheel. As promised, I made a slow drive of it all the way to her house. And if I could have gone slower, I'd have done it.

Four

SADIE

present day

I THREW OFF THE sheet, the muggy heat threatening to suffocate me, and I wondered why the air conditioner wasn't moving air—or why the ceiling fan didn't spin. And how did I get into this bed in the first place?

Swamp cicadas played the role of the alarm clock, but when I registered the sound, it took a few moments to calibrate to my surroundings. Those mid-morning singers began their tune with a soft buzz, mutating into a pulsed drone with a crescendo. Their sharp hum tapered off, stopped, and restarted in fifteen-second increments. Someday, maybe that familiar noise will be a comfort again.

My cowboy boots stood upright, side by side, next to a bedsheet-draped writing desk and chair. I still wore my cut-offs and t-shirt. Spying my red-painted toes reminded me of the night before and brought me to my feet too fast. I plopped back on the daybed, sucking in humid air, and for a few seconds, the squeaks and creaks of the antique iron frame overtook the bugs' outside racket, but I bolted to the door before the next chorus.

The molded glass doorknob hung loose in its fitting. One of just about a thousand things I imagined needed fixing around the old house. Freed, I hurried out of the front room that once lived its life as a cozy library and skidded into the foyer. Crickets—this time of the metaphorical variety. My duffel sat on the floor, and the zip-up bag holding the costly gown hung on a floor-standing hat rack perched at the front door. I didn't make a sound, and no one else did either. Running from window to window, past more sheet-clad furniture, I searched for the truck—my truck, but it wasn't there.

"Well, shoot. And why is it so hot in here?" I opened the mint green Frigidaire and got my answer. No power. "*Huh*, of course not." No one had lived in the house for more than a year. The fact the utilities were off made sense. As I slammed the refrigerator closed, the back door opened, nearly sending me out of my skin. With a hitched breath, I spun to see Dutch, still in crisp-looking dress clothes, minus his jacket, carrying a large grease-splotched paper sack in his teeth and a cup carrier with four lidded cups. A beautiful sight to see.

I slid my fingers into the back pockets of my cut-offs and eyed my shiny red toes. *Dammit*, Ellis saw my toes, I groused in my head.

He raised the breakfast goods in a two-handed offering and shut the door with his foot. "Hi." He made the one-syllable greeting charming with a touch of shyness, and it carried a slew of memories.

"Morning. Thought you stole my truck." Not really. I stayed put while he walked toward me; the scrumptious aroma of something southern-fried mixed with coffee met me first.

"Thought about it, but no. Just borrowed it. Parked around back. Hungry?"

"I could eat. Thanks for getting me settled last night. I crashed hard."

"Yeah, you did. I'd have gotten you upstairs but—"

"But what?"

He set the cups and bag on the kitchen counter and arranged brown paper-wrapped food items and napkins. "You're not exactly feather light."

I glared as he continued unloading the goodies. "I have the distinct recollection of me asking you not to be an ass, Ellis."

He *hmphed* with eyes to the original shiplap ceiling. "*Asking* me? Is that how you remember it? Funny. I only meant you were dead to the world. That old staircase is unusually narrow, and I thought it safest for all involved that I deposit you on the ground floor. You're perfect, always have been. Now quit being insecure. It doesn't suit you—and eat some breakfast."

The rebound from insult to high praise had my head swimming, and I hoped the coffee would rectify the situation. And when did he learn to say so many words in one breath? "Are those Midge's biscuits? How did you get Midge's biscuits this late in the day? If you don't get to Midge's by eight a.m. there are no biscuits to be had—how did you—"

"Christ, Sadie. Stick a biscuit in your mouth and shush a minute."

I did as I was told. Not because I had to, but because it was the taste of home I hadn't known I'd been missing. "*Hhhhot.*" I bounced the bite around in my mouth, trying to cool it.

"Fresh out of the oven. Careful."

I moaned with pleasure as the buttery flakiness melted in my mouth. Eyes and head rolling back, I sank onto a stool and into bliss as wonderful childhood memories rushed me. I had to smile, but the delight was short-lived. "Don't stare like that. It's impolite."

"Don't groan like that. It's inappropriate." He couldn't hold on to his frown any longer and tried to hide his amusement with his own bite of egg and cheese biscuit.

"Really. How'd you get these? Fresh from the oven, even. Do you live here?" Last I knew, Dutch had left Canaan Cove the winter of his senior year in high school and never returned. He'd left in the dead of night after he rejected my one attempt to see him, thank him, or even to say goodbye. I honored his request to stay away.

"No, I don't, but Midge remembered me. She liked me back in the day."

"No, really."

"I'm a likable guy, Sadie."

"No, *really*." I grimaced as long as I could.

"Eat. We've got work to do."

"Work? What work? And who's this we?"

"Don't know if you noticed, but it's hot. And I can't very well leave you without any power, and it being a Sunday, you aren't going to get your utilities back on today. So, before I go, I'll get out to Cecil's, pick you up a generator and an A/C window unit to help get you through the next day and a half or however long it takes to get power running here."

I coughed a laugh while enjoying another yummy morsel.

"What?"

"Two things."

He raised a brow with a huff.

I ignored it. "You're awfully sweet to want to help."

"Not sweet. It's just the right thing to do." Ever the stoic hardhead.

"Do you *always* do the right thing?" I already knew the answer, but he lied.

"No, Sadie. I do not. What's the second thing?"

"I think it'd be easier to hook up the seventeen-kilowatt standby generator out back. This is hurricane country, and I made sure my grandparents were prepared. It'll manage the central air and the fridge, and more if need be. I'll be fine for the next day and a half, or however long it—"

"Right. Miss Independent. I get it." Dutch snatched up wrappers and used napkins, stowing them in the paper sack.

"Good to see some things never change. Looks like you'll do just fine without your Tristan."

My last bite of biscuit caught in my gullet, and I swigged hot coffee, hoping to urge it down. "He's not *my* Tristan. Never was. So, you'd be wise not to talk about things you don't know."

"Why don't you tell me then?"

"Why don't you mind your business?"

"Seems you made it my business when you coerced me into your runaway treachery."

"Coerced? Treachery? I don't recall you having such a flair for the dramatic, Ellis."

"*Stop* calling me that. No one calls me that."

"I used to call you that. Seemed to me you liked it when I—"

"Enough." His growled shout told me I'd teased more than he had the patience to endure. He quieted. "No one calls me that anymore. No one. Not even you." He crushed the bag of trash. "I should go. I don't even know what I'm doing here." Pushing off the counter, his foot caught on his stool leg with a *clank.* He lurched one way while I grabbed the tipping seat to keep it from capsizing completely.

"Jesus, El—is that an ankle monitor attached to you?" I righted his stool and slipped off of mine, backing away until I hit the Frigidaire.

"What? No." He jostled his pant leg. "No," he repeated.

"There is most definitely something strapped to your ankle, so please don't bother denying it."

"I'm not denying—it's not an ankle monitor, Sadie. Do you really think—is that what you think?"

"Do you really want to crack open the 'what I think' can of worms?"

"It's a gun, Sadie."

"I'm sorry. It's a what?"

"A firearm. A weapon."

"I know what a gun is."

He gave an incredulous look.

"Well, shoot, Ellis. I mean, Dutch." Nope. I did *not* like how that felt in my mouth. "That might be worse."

"Worse?"

"I'm not a fan of guns."

"I seem to recall you being an excellent shot."

"That's different. That's skeet. Long-range targets with long barrels. Hunting gear. Your ankle jewelry is only for one pursuit, and I don't like it, and I definitely don't like it in my house." I kept my back to the refrigerator and my arms crossed, eyes to my toes. Dutch's detailed recollections of me were getting uncomfortable. "Is it loaded?"

"Doesn't do me much good if it isn't."

It felt like a standoff and knowing only one of us packed heat put me at a disadvantage. *Another* disadvantage. I didn't live my life feeling out-flanked, but the last ten hours had me discombobulated. Not that I imagined Dutch would ever brandish the weapon, but it threw me. He had changed. How could he not? Life-altering events tended to live up to their name.

"You can ask, you know. You can ask me anything." His quiet way squeezed my insides, and I knew some of him had remained the same. Dutch always possessed the opposite of my rambunctious loudmouth—the mouth I shot off with zero restraint. I had no skill in treading lightly while the man standing in my kitchen was the most judicious one I knew. Except I didn't know him—hadn't known him in fifteen years, and this latest version came armed with distinct memories of me, a quiet sweetness I'd missed, and a gun.

Too many questions came to mind, but I opted for the one I thought might level the playing field when it landed. "Okay. Weren't you about to *leave*?"

His shoulders dropped with a noticeable exhale. Like he said, I was an excellent shot. Direct hit. A hand gripped the back of his neck. It was almost like he waited for me to take it back, but he knew better.

"I reckon," he whispered.

Rooted in my spot, I knew not to engage in any sort of eye contact. No good would come from that. He'd almost passed me when a muffled, tinny blast of The Village People's *Macho Man* rang out from my duffel bag. Dutch stopped.

"Is that Leo calling? I've been wondering why he wasn't here—even for a fake wedding."

The musical ringtone repeated, but instead of complimenting his reasonable guess, I sighed, "No. It's Tristan."

Neither of us moved as the phone "rang" a third time.

"You gonna answer that? Could be—important."

I exhaled with my mimicked, "I reckon."

"Maybe I'll stick around a bit. Just in case." He only had eyes for the bag at the front door.

"That's not necessary—okay." I had a quick change of heart. "You did warn me, after all."

"Warned you?"

"On the dinghy. That you might stick around." The phone had stopped its noisemaking but let itself be known again with a single ping telling me Tristan left a voicemail. "I wish I had some clothes to offer you. Anything here would belong to Leo, and he has five inches on you. You'd be swimming in them."

"He is a giant of a man," Dutch offered.

"In every good way there is to be. Yes. You two have that in common, I guess." I pushed off the fridge and walked away before he took the opportunity to reply, and I appreciated his choosing to let the praise hang. *Macho Man* played again, and I hurried to grab my luggage and disappeared into last night's sleeping quarters to take the call.

Five

SADIE

present day

"Hey, shit-for-brains. How's it going?" I employed a sugary lilt when I finally answered Tristan's call.

"*Aw* shucks, Sade. You know I love it when you use cute pet names on me. It lets me know how much you really care."

I could imagine him brushing aside his beach blond hair that tended to get in his eyes in a too-cute boyish way. Tristan was the epitome of a too-cute, too-blond, too-tan beach boy.

"Care? You know what I care about? Making a plan and sticking to it. God, what a ridiculous plan it was, too. How did I ever let you talk me into it? I should have known better. Six months of you moving the goal post, making plans, the dress, pushing off the break-up. I knew better than to step foot on that boat last night. Jesus, Tristan. Were you actually going to say, 'I do?' Were you? Because I think maybe you were."

A *shush* of breath came through the phone before Tristan asked, "Would it have been the end of the world, Sade? Really? We're great together. You're funny and smart as hell, and you put up with my bullshit. You're very attractive when you aren't covered in grease, even though you've made it clear sex is off the table, but—like I said, you put up with my bullshit." The words were Tristan's version of sincerity, a rare occurrence, but then—the boob kept talking. "Speaking of, *phew*, a cute blackjack dealer from last night gave me a run for my—"

"Tristan. In what world do you think I want to hear about your sexual exploits on what was almost our wedding night? Or ever, for that matter?"

"*Almost*, being the operative word. I gotta be me, Sade. But if you want to give it another go, I bet I can clean this up with Mommy and Daddy."

"I am not marrying you, Tristan. And not just because you call your parents Mommy and Daddy. I was never going to marry you, and you know it. Now, I more than stuck to my end of the deal. It's your turn."

"Yeah, yeah. I'm gonna need some time. Did you get into the house all right last night?"

"Yes, but what do you mean, time?"

"My mother is dealing with public humiliation right now, Sadie. And my father is tending to that. I'm going to need some time to refocus attention on the travesty of *my* agonizing grief, which will be far more believable given your display last night. Then I'll get you what you're owed. Besides, you have plenty of resources to hold you over—"

"This isn't about money, shithead. It never was—wait. What resources?"

"For starters, look at your left hand."

I didn't look but clenched my fist, feeling the roughness of the diamond band. The ring did not belong to me, but I knew what it was worth. When we'd first hatched the scheme, Tristan tossed me the robin's egg blue box across the bed of a pickup truck. It was the "upside-down" version of the fake-dating trope, a favorite of romance readers and writers, with zero chance of ending in a love match. A near-perfect plan. We were friends. Then again, Tristan had lots of friends, but I surmised many of them were only in it for the over-the-top good time he brought to the party. He was wild but also calculating, and it was easy to get swept up in the amusement of it all. And he did make me laugh.

"It's just for show. And you'll want to think up a better proposal scenario than the Piggly Wiggly parking lot scene we've got going on here. And, uh, even though it's fake, like the rest of this—take good care, okay?"

Not long after, the sheer beauty of the ring had me doing research. Yes, I was mechanically minded, but rocks were my first love, and a college classmate had expertise. Gotta appreciate a strong university alumni network. Not only that, but she also lived four hours away in Atlanta—a safe distance from the prying eyes of coastal Georgia elites. It was well worth the day's drive to wax nostalgic for our Yellow Jacket and Ramblin' Wreck years studying geology. She stuck with the pure science while I went the applied route, adding my other favorite thing: mechanics, earning a master's degree in mechanical engineering, and eventually a Ph.D. in geotechnical engineering. All the sips of subpar chardonnay paid off when, after a good hour of her peering through a jeweler's loupe, she informed me this bauble was no bauble at all. Tristan had chucked a nearly $45,000 rock across a grocery store parking lot, and a Ph.D. in geology-turned-gemologist furnished me with a certified gem appraisal to prove it. Fake my ass.

"It might be worth more than I led you to believe," Tristan confessed.

"You don't say." I met silence. "Then I should return it to you. I'll stick it in an envelope and mail it tomorrow." I flopped onto the daybed and kicked up my feet with a smirk.

"No. Good lord, Sade. Don't *mail* it."

"Well, I'm not too keen on seeing you, but I guess we can meet at the Piggly like old times. Hand it off there."

"I want you to keep it. Keep it, sell it, whatever you like."

"Oh, no. If it's worth something, you should take it back. Your father might—"

"My father doesn't know anything about it and never will. It's yours. Bought in your name, even. I'll send the paperwork."

So much paperwork. Rich people lived for it. I groaned in my head, deciding to be done with the conversation for now. It seemed the Pembroke family wasn't out of my life for good.

"Speaking of your father."

"I wish you wouldn't." Tristan's disdain made me chuckle, but I stopped short when the ceiling fan suddenly spun to life, slowly increasing speed. Caught in the sunlight, the dusty consequence of months-long neglect sparkled as it floated on the new, refreshing breeze. It was like a cue, a prompt for the out-of-sight man's mention.

"You know a man named Dutch Holland?" I asked.

A *crash* and *thud* came through the phone.

"Tristan?" Muffled scratching sounds of movement rustled into my ear. "You there, Tris?"

"Uh, yeah. Tipped back in my chair is all. H-how do you know the name Dutch Holland?"

"Well, not because he was on the wedding guest list."

"Why would he be on the—?"

"Never mind. I might have bumped into him on the boat last night. Said he works for your dad."

Tristan took a loud breath but gave me nothing else.

"Maybe I misunderstood," I nudged for more data.

"No. You heard right. Though I'm pretty sure Mr. Holland is on a leave of absence right now. Are you all right?"

"Me? All right? Aside from your antics, you mean?"

"I'm serious, Sadie."

"I'm fine, Tristan. Don't get weird."

"Do me a favor."

"Sure, I'm feeling particularly generous toward you right now, so your timing is aces."

"Let me know if you see Mr. Holland again. And, no joke, stay away from him."

"And why should I do that?"

"Dutch Holland is a dangerous man. Stay out of his crosshairs." Tristan's usual devil-may-care attitude had evaporated. The man lived a playboy life, emphasis on the *play*, but now he sounded more serious than I had ever heard him. The term "crosshairs" didn't do much for my already burbling queasiness. "Are you hearing me, Sadie?"

"I hear you."

"I'll be in touch."

"You better." I ended the call.

Mesmerized by the shimmering dirt finding its way to the floor, I recognized the new coolness of the central air as well as the buoying dust count. I added "clean air ducts" to my growing list of to-dos. It occurred to me, I should probably go thank the responsible party, no matter Tristan Pembroke's warning.

"Yes, sir. I assure you everything is being handled as if I was there myself. I have the utmost confidence in the men I hired to do the job on that end. I'll stick around to see to things here, on my own. I don't need assistance. Consider it handled... I stake my reputation on it. I believe my record speaks for itself. I've never let you down before, and I don't plan to begin the practice now. But I should say your wavering, your apparent doubt is—well, it's regrettable, but perhaps we can chalk it up to your son's unfortunate evening.

Perhaps your questioning *my* ability to do *my* job is misplaced. Projecting, maybe? Any reservations you may have likely have nothing to do with me at all. Isn't that right, Mr. Pembroke?" With his back to me and a hand in his pocket, Dutch strolled a short path in front of the kitchen window.

I snuck back into the library, careful not to touch the door lest it squeak some alarm, alerting Dutch to my presence. Had it made noise when I opened it? He never moved to acknowledge me. The tone implied an important conversation, but who was the employer and who was the employee appeared less than black and white by the end of what I heard. More confounding? It seemed the leisurely Ellis "Dutch" Holland had lost his accent or exchanged the drawl I knew I shared for something else entirely. Whatever it was, it was not the cadence he had as a teen or the one he'd been using with me these last hours. But which one was real? Which one was the ruse? Rest assured, I planned to find out. I slipped into my boots and out of the diamond ring, placing it back in its box and into the still-draped writing desk drawer.

Tucking my wallet into my back pocket, I exited the front room as if I hadn't a moment earlier. "Thanks for getting the generator started—" meeting wide eyes, and the raised index finger of my guest, I stopped speaking mid-sentence.

"You know how to reach me if you feel the need, Mr. Pembroke, but I don't imagine that will be the case. Will it? My best to the missus." Dutch ended the call with a dazed focus on that finger he still held in the air.

I didn't know what to make of so much in the scene, so I started there. "Everything okay? Something wrong with your finger?"

"Wrong with it? No, apparently, it's magic. Who knew that if I simply pointed it just so, while in your vicinity, you would stop talking? I've never felt so powerful—"

"Oh, you've got jokes now? Shut up."

The man's ability to amuse me proved both irksome and attractive, which only compounded my discombobulation. I fought my grin without much success but figured if I kept moving, Dutch wouldn't notice how much I enjoyed his company, even as I made plans to see him stay awhile. I'd discovered some new puzzle pieces, and I did *love* a good conundrum. Dutch Holland might turn out to be the brain teaser to end all others. "Come on, Ellis. Bring my keys." I tested his boundaries by using his given name again and rushed past him out the kitchen door. My stomach lurched with disappointment when footsteps didn't immediately follow. Knowing Dutch tilted toward cautious, I assumed he was overthinking things on the three-season porch. "Less thinking, more getting your ass in my truck. Let's move." I shouted from the driver's seat with two bangs of my palm on the door panel.

Careful not to turn my head, I spied him, using a side mirror. Hands to his hips, he paused at the top of the porch stairs. A subtle head shake preceded his slow steps to the passenger side window. He reached in to hand me the keys and took a brief gentle hold of my hand in the exchange. Still unsure if I had won, I gave him my winningest smile. When he finally returned it, my stomach lurch was of a different sort. He got in, buckled up, and flipped the sun visor before I could catch another breath, but my smile remained affixed.

We traveled two blocks before he spoke. "Where're we headed?"

"Seems to me we have quite the list of stops to make. Then again, when you have Cecil Ford's Feed 'n' Seed in your town, there's a good bit of one-stop-shopping to be done there."

Cecil's Feed 'n' Seed was a misnomer. Sure, there was feed and seed to purchase but also a lot more. Known for tractor parts, duct tape, and nuts and bolts in every size, I knew we would also find charcoal and cleaning supplies, plus fresh fruits and vegetables, eggs, and a couple of steaks for grilling later in the evening. Summer weekends meant a small farmers' market set up in the back loading dock.

Despite its dirty asbestos tiles and the ingrained scent of fertilizer, we'd also be able to outfit the man who had nothing but the swanky finery on his back. Jeans, shirts, boots, and other sundries were available at the front end of the store—all Dutch would need to wear if I had my way. I white-knuckled the steering wheel when my mind pondered the boxers or brief situation and quickly upped the blower on the truck's A/C.

"I haven't been here for years, except for Grandaddy and Mee-maw's service. But I only stayed the day. Leo closed up the house." I still harbored guilt for leaving all that to my brother. "When were you here last? In Canaan Cove, I mean." I meant to make easy conversation, small talk. No such luck.

"Not since my court date, so nearly fifteen years, I guess. But that was a quick visit, of course."

I met his reply with silence and more white knuckles. It seemed Dutch liked cat and mouse games, and I never quite knew which one of us was which. I did know the roles were constantly in flux, and if I could keep my mouth shut, I'd be in a better position to compete. But as I've mentioned, keeping my mouth shut is not my strong suit.

"I was there. At court."

"I know."

"They weren't letting anyone in that day."

"I know."

"I wish—"

"You wish what, Sadie? You wish I'd let you apologize. You wish I had let you speak up way back when? You wish it had never happened?"

In a moment of cosmic fortitude, I simply nodded.

"No apology necessary. No use in that. And me too. There. We can be done with that conversation now."

"Not by a long shot, Ellis. Not even close. But I'll leave it for now." I didn't want to think about it either, yet I had so many questions I'd never had the opportunity to ask. The details were legally sealed, never spoken about, and clearly, Dutch wished it to stay that way. And given everything he'd endured, how could I force the issue? I scrambled to move on to other topics. "What's kept you busy since?" I kept my eyes on the road, but I sensed he only had eyes for me. The A/C couldn't keep up.

"The abridged version? A sealed no-contest plea led to military school. Military school led to the military. Military life led to private contracting. Private contracting led to Pembroke Industries."

"And?"

"And what?"

"Married? Kids? Pets? Hobbies?"

"No, hope not, not home much, and when I'm not doing goat yoga, I knit."

I knew he meant to lighten the mood, ease the brewed tension with his droll humor, and I gave him the win with a smile.

"That's it. That's all I get? No pictures on your phone? Not gonna share the story about your commanding officer's daughter and how she was the one that got away and that tattoo you undoubtedly regret now?"

"Wow. That's an oddly specific scenario."

"*Pfft.* I've got a million of them," I quipped before realizing how I'd inadvertently admitted to how much thought I'd been spending on Dutch Holland and what he'd been up to over the years—and with whom. A glimmer of what might have been satisfaction sparkled in his eyes, and I squeezed the steering wheel tighter.

"That so? Well, I'm not one to kiss and tell, but getting involved with the boss's kid sounds more like your thing than mine. Thank God for laser tattoo removal, though, huh? It does sting like a son-of-a-gun. Speaking of, how'd your chat with the prodigal son go this morning? Is he licking his wounds?" Dutch expertly rerouted the conversation, but despite my curiosity, I didn't fight the shift in topic and ignored his jab about the boss's kid—for now. I also fought thinking about Dutch's possible tattoos, real, imagined, or removed.

"Oh, he was licking someone—never mind. Tristan's fine. Not too pleased to hear his loss was your gain—"

"Whoa, Sadie. You didn't tell him I—"

"No. Not exactly. Tristan doesn't know you're here—with me. He doesn't know anything about us. But I did mention you. Only that I met a man with your name on the boat last night. He seemed to think you were on a leave of absence from Pembroke Industries." I opted to keep Tristan's warnings to myself.

"Yes. I have about a year and a half of paid leave between sick, holiday, and comp time owed to me. I'm cashing in some of it. Sort of a sudden decision."

"And you decided to start your long overdue vay-cay drunk, in a dark room, all alone at my wedding?"

"Didn't know it was your wedding. Not until it was too late. I considered jumping ship but then—"

"I crashed your pity party and provided an escape?"

"Something like that."

"I saved you?"

"And I didn't even know I needed saving until you came cussing through that door."

"Well, I owed you one. Least I could do. Still doesn't feel like my debt is paid."

He sighed. "Thought we were done with that conversation."

"Pretty sure I said not even close."

Dutch smiled and made the bold move to stretch across the bench seat and squeeze my bare thigh. It might have surprised him more than me with the speed his limb flew back to his side of the truck. But despite the short-lived touch, the heat of his hand lingered on my skin. We both needed some throat-clearing.

"It sure is good to see you like this, Sadie Jane."

"Like how?" I asked through a knotted throat.

"Happy, healthy," he paused. "Not married to Tristan Pembroke. Maybe that third thing more than anything." His talk made me dizzy, and I was relieved to swerve *almost* between bright white painted lines of a last row parking spot at Cecil's. We both lurched with the sudden stop.

"Not that it matters, but Tristan Pembroke with me isn't a scenario you ever need to be concerned about." I pulled the keys from the ignition. Dutch had already unbuckled his seat belt and opened his door.

"Well, he was just the latest on a long list, but—that's one down, I reckon." And just as quickly as Dutch's accent had come, gone, and returned again in my kitchen, he took off into a sea of parked cars at the Feed 'n' Seed, leaving me with that cryptic confession.

Six

SADIE

present day

"Did he just—" My question wasn't directed at anyone other than me, and it didn't quite make it out in its entirety. In the shock-and-awe of Dutch's casual remark, I tried to chase after him but forgot to unbuckle my seat belt, nearly garroting myself in the not-so-graceful move.

My sudden jerk triggered the safety belt's inertial lock, automatically seizing the mechanism like I had been in some sort of collision. And let's be frank, the analogy to a hit-and-run was apt. Who admits to years of speculating about someone else's private life and then flees the scene for the safety of a Feed 'n Seed? The first few violent tugs on the belt only tightened the apparatus, and an unladylike growl of frustration grunted out of me before I found myself in a tangle of the suddenly unconstrained tether. Finally released, the metal tongue of the latch smacked the window as I flailed my way to freedom, kicking open the door. In my scramble, I banged my hip on the steering wheel, tumbling from the raised cab, my boot heel caught on the running board, and I hit the asphalt upright but hard.

A furtive glance around found no one witnessed my clumsy mishap, and I beelined to the store's entrance with a fitful mix of quick and slow limping steps, bypassing the surprising number of parked cars in the lot for Sunday. The smooth blacktop should have been the first hint something was amiss, but it was the festooned sandwich-board touting a "free tasting at the kombucha bar" that threw me. Distracted by the baffling advertisement, I ran headlong into the backside of the sturdy and stock-still frame of Dutch Holland. His speedy turn and firm grasp kept me from landing on my ass.

"What the hell?" I gasped.

"My thoughts exactly." Dutch spun back to face the store, pulling me with him. We gaped at the bright lights, gleaming floors, and fancy signs peddling *heirloom* this, *organic* that, and *farm-raised, free-range, grass-fed, farmhand-hugged* everything. And what was that smell? Lemons, lavender, and vanilla floated on a cool breeze of what had to be amped-up oxygen. Dutch and I inhaled synchronized deep breaths and exhaled the same whispered question.

"Where are we?"

"Welcome to Cecil's Feed 'n' Seed." A perky teen dressed in a tidy green uniform smiled as she offered us a placard with the day's specials and a reusable hemp-woven tote. "If I can be of service, don't hesitate to ask. My name is Tabitha. And be sure to hit up the kombucha bar for the free tasting, and Not Your Mama's Llama is here today with a BOGO on their woolie socks. Your feet will thank you come December."

"A BOGO?" Dutch's gaze bounced from one shiny surface to another.

"Buy one, get one," I explained, pulling the slack-jawed man out of oncoming foot traffic. "Thank you, Tabitha—oh, do you sell charcoal?"

"We sure do," Tabitha chirped. "Straight back just beyond the Honey Hut and then all the way to the left. Clive is the charcoal specialist on duty today. He will see to all your sustainably sourced, all-natural, hardwood lump charcoal needs."

All I could do was nod as I backed toward the Honey Hut, pulling a bewildered Dutch by the arm. We took silent, slow steps through the bulk section. Bulk steel-cut oats, bulk fair-trade coffee, bulk every nut, seed, grain, and legume known to humans.

"Is this—?"

"The one where Canaan Cove is in the Twilight Zone?" I murmured.

"Yeah." He let out more air than sound.

"Must be." We stared at our new and improved surroundings. "Hey, let's see if they have clothes other than socks. Wait. Is that Cecil?" A brawny man we'd known our whole lives spoke to a Feed 'n Seed employee, looking like he hadn't aged a day—like he had actually gotten younger. The Twilight Zone quip hit home, and I couldn't make sense of anything.

Dutch pulled from my grasp. "Junior? Is that you?"

Cecil Ford, Jr., looked up from his clipboard, and his bright eyes got brighter as genuine delight stretched across his face. "Dutch? What in the—Dutch Holland?" The two men thumped chests and then embraced with rowdy back slaps. Eventually separating, they clung to each other's biceps and laughed. "What are you—wearing?" Junior's eyes traveled the length of Dutch still in his impressive dress shirt, tailored suit pants, and fancy leather shoes.

"Yeah." Dutch shrugged. "Got anything in this joint I can switch out for these threads?" The reunion included Dutch's own broad grin, and the beautiful sight made me light-headed.

"Sure do. We can get you outfitted in the finest organic cotton, sustainable denim, and vegan boots these parts have to offer. Everything for the everyman's eco-friendly, fair-trade wardrobe." The twosome walked away with arms draped over each other's shoulders.

"Um, hellooo?" I waved, quickly left behind.

Dutch halted. "Oh, Sadie. Junior? Do you remember Sadie Klein? She was a year behind you, two behind me—"

Junior kept his smile as he ping-ponged from Dutch to me. "Yeah, sure, I remember." They detached from one another, and Junior reached his hand to shake mine. "Good to see you again, Sadie." The scene got awkward with Junior standing between Dutch and me, his gaze bouncing back and forth like he sat front row at Wimbledon.

I tried to remedy the uncomfortable predicament. "It's been a while. You are the spitting image of your dad."

"Actually, I was at your grandparents' funeral—I got to know Avi and Talia well over the years. They helped with my knee rehab. Guiding me from specialist to specialist."

"Oh, sorry. I didn't—yes. That day was a blur." All the earlier smiles vanished with the reminder of my grandparents' death. Their standing room only memorial service had been surprising, but in the whirlwind trip shrouded in grief, I hardly registered a single face that day.

"So, you two are here together, then?" Junior's head-bobbing resumed.

"No," Dutch and I replied in hasty unison, followed by, "Well, yes."

Both men landed their gazes on me.

"It's a long story, but first, let's get this man some new duds and some kombucha." I pushed past them.

"Yes, we're hosting a tasting today," Junior added, in return to sales mode.

"That's what I heard," I called over my shoulder, relieved to be out of the unnerving impasse. The two old friends juddered into motion, following like I knew where I headed.

"Okay. Zoey, is it? What exactly are *vegan* boots?" I held up a pair of fine-looking work boots to another green-uniformed store associate.

"Well, for starters, they're *awesome*." But Zoey, the bubbly young saleswoman, didn't get much further with her pitch as Dutch stunned us into silence when he exited a changing room. He modeled jeans, a gray tee, and an unbuttoned black shirt; the sleeves rolled up to show off his muscular forearms. His head hung while his hands finished cinching his belt, and a flushed Zoey grabbed my shoulder like she needed to steady herself in the glory of it all. And I couldn't help but wonder how dangerous this man truly was and how soon could I find out?

"S'pose this'll do." Dutch barely glimpsed himself in the mirror.

"Oh, yes. You'll do fine, sir. You'll do very fine, indeed." Zoey's grip on my shoulder grew painful. The poor girl hadn't blinked, and I started to fear for her corneas.

I patted her hand but kept my eyes on Dutch, asking, "A couple of pairs, then?"

He glanced at me, then busied himself with a few of the low buttons. "Let's make it an even five. And could you gather up more shirts and tees like this, Zoey? A variety of colors but nothing showy."

Zoey and I both lit up—her likely for the big sale, me to hear Ellis "Dutch" Holland planned to make good on his warning. He intended to stick around, and that pleased me very much.

We loaded my truck bed with more supplies than I ever knew I needed.

"So, Junior's great and says blowing out his knee in a Super Bowl was the best thing to happen to him. Limped away with a well-diversified portfolio before his brains got scrambled. And what he's doing for this community? Well, it's admirable."

The hours were wisely spent, and I knew the house would have cooled considerably by the time we got home. I hadn't intended to be gone so long, eager to get the bungalow in some sort of livable shape. But the Feed 'n' Seed begged to be explored, and when Dutch and I reconvened, he appeared a more relaxed, happier man with quiet ease reminiscent of the teenager I knew so long ago. For a moment, I found pleasure in his altered state. The man of few words nattered on, but it soon occurred to me I had nothing to do with it. Furthermore, I likely had the opposite effect, and his earlier brusqueness had to do with the company he kept—my company.

"And who knew such a difference existed with your domestic oak, hickory, and maple mixes compared to your South American Guayacan, Guayaibi, Mistal, and White Quebracho varieties." He patted two fifty-pound bags laid flat on the tailgate. Charcoal-expert Clive was having a good sales day too. "Guess we're fixin' to find out."

I listened while silently scolding myself for thinking I could have been a warm reminder of days gone by. Of course, I wasn't. And when I feel chastised, even when it's self-admonishment, I tend to get grouchy, then I lash out at the nearest anyone. A vicious cycle. "First, I think you're making up some of those charcoal words, and second, what's the deal with the adaptable accent?"

And just like that, I had a frowning, rigid man slamming the gate of the truck closed while I filled with instant regret and tried to recant. Sort of. "Sure, I understand flattening it out on occasion, for professional purposes. Shoot, I've flattened mine into near-submission over the years, but it's the fluffing it up again, around 'friends,' no less, that I don't get." Yes, I air-quoted. No, I'm not good at the backpedal. "You know, Junior and I have been places, seen things. You don't need to make yourself sound all folksy on our account while you speak like an articulate yank on the phone with your boss. Just wondering who the real Dutch is? Who is it that's sleeping under my roof?"

Dutch shook his head as he set his new duffel full of the casual wardrobe young Zoey had coordinated for him into the truck bed. It was the last of our purchases. "Why don't we get back to the house and get these supplies unloaded. And rest assured, you'll be sleeping alone tonight, Sadie." What his tone lacked in twang, it more than made up for with stoic hurt. Somehow, I stood surprised that my condescending probe had a negative outcome. Shocker.

I kicked the tire like a petulant child while he, the forever grown-up, climbed in the passenger side and waited. For whatever reason, no matter the years that had passed, all the study, the Ph.D., the patents in my name, when standing in front of Dutch Holland, I'd reverted to that snot-nosed, almost-sixteen-year-old.

Temper in check, I drove the speed limit and endured the quiet for a full mile before I roused the nerve to speak. "I apologize. That was rude and unnecessary and had more to do with me than with you. And while it's no excuse, being back here and seeing how much has changed and yet, how so much is still the same, and seeing all that with you—you of all people in that picture too, well—never mind. Today was supposed to be a very different kind of day. A good day, but now you're here—shoot, no—that you're *here* hasn't made it a bad day, not at all. Anyway. I'm sorry. And thank you for your help last night and today—and for fifteen years ago. The least I could do is grill you a steak and give you a place to rest your head."

We rode another block before he spoke, and I'd bet good money he was weighing each word. It took every ounce of patience I possessed, waiting to hear his measured response.

"I remember a time in school, military school, an instructor assigned the task of writing an essay about the person who had been most impactful in our life. The person who, at some point, entered our orbit and changed the trajectory of our story irrevocably. I was seventeen, young and dumb and pissed and scared, and I wrote about you."

A car honked when I idled at a four-way stop too long. I gunned the engine, chirping the tires in the take-off and waving in the rearview, embarrassed I held up traffic. Dutch hadn't resumed telling his tale, and we approached the country lane where I grew up. Surely, he had more to say. And I burned through that last grain of patience.

"How'd you do on the essay? Get a good grade?"

"I did. An A, but the teacher explained the good mark was for the last lines of the essay, the conclusion, because he surmised the rest of the writing was fiction. It wasn't, but that was neither here nor there."

We pulled into the driveway and inched toward the back of the property to park. "And how did you finish it, making the essay worthy of an A?"

"I don't recall verbatim, but something to the effect of—I would never again give anyone the power, allow anyone into my orbit that would control or even alter the trajectory I set for myself.

My journey, my path, the course of my life would be mine and mine alone, come hell or high water."

"Wow." I wasn't sure if I had uttered that aloud.

"I've stuck to that, and that includes not letting anyone hurt my feelings. You have nothing to apologize for. Also, I'm a vegetarian." He exited the vehicle, slung his new duffel over his shoulder, and grabbed two more stuffed hemp totes from the truck bed.

If I hadn't been seated, you could have knocked me to the ground. Still, I found yet another apology rebuffed.

He leaned his head in the open window. "Just kidding, Sadie," he sighed as he sauntered to the back stoop. "I like it medium-rare. Warm red center, one hundred thirty-five degrees, no more, and only salt and pepper to season it. Now grab some bags. I'm not your pack mule." He disappeared onto the three-season porch.

Seven

DUTCH

fifteen years ago

"Let me carry those bags for you, Dr. Klein." I had barely stopped before I cut off the engine and sprang from my truck to offer assistance. Not that hurrying from what little time I had to spend with Sadie ever ranked highly on my to-do list, but opportunities to make a good impression on her grandfather, the man raising her, were rare. Offering to hoist heavy bags for the older man made for a good one.

"Thank you, Dutch. How's that shoulder, though? Can't be risking the star player this late in the season. The town would have my head."

"Shoulder's fine, sir. They're taking it easy on me these days, and I didn't have practice today, so—" I pulled two forty-pound bags of grass seed from the doctor's trunk and followed him to the outbuilding. A glance back caught Sadie sliding out of my truck, and I wondered if she would holler a goodbye and head inside or wait for my return.

"Hey, Grandaddy." Sadie Jane beamed affection for her grandfather.

"Hello, Ahuvati. Mee-maw could use your help with supper," he called over his shoulder. The mix of southern and, I guessed, Hebrew endearments struck me as peculiar, but there was no mistaking Sadie had been lovingly dismissed. Without hesitation, she dutifully obeyed. I had an inkling that I wasn't the only one taking advantage of an opportunity.

Nearly dark, the temperature had dropped enough that thin plumes of our breath floated in the glare of the cinder block building's floodlight.

"We'll stack them over in the far corner."

"Yes, sir." I moved as instructed.

"How's the tutoring going?"

"Well, thank you. Sadie's a good tutor. Limits, derivatives, integrals—"

"Speaking of limits." The doctor had mastered segues. "Sadie's only fifteen."

I paused a beat. "Almost sixteen. Yes, she's told me."

"I'm sure she has."

We shared a quiet chuckle.

"And you're—"

"Seventeen," I interjected. "And not by much. Late August birthday."

"Even so—"

"Sir?"

"Sadie's grandmother and I have raised her and her brother Leo since they were small. Sadie doesn't have any memory of her parents. As her de facto guardians, older ones at that, it falls to us to look after her best interests."

I kept silent, steeled for the imminent bad news.

"At the risk of sounding old-fashioned, we believe—her grandmother and I—we believe Sadie shouldn't date until she's sixteen. Arbitrary? Perhaps. But limits are important."

I waited. That wasn't bad news. That wasn't "stay away from our granddaughter," or worse, "you'll never be good enough for our granddaughter." That was "whoa up until January," and it being November and still football season, waiting until January seemed a burden I could handle. No, that wasn't bad news at all.

"And tutoring?" I had to ask.

"Well, far be it from me to hold a young man back from exploring the fundamentals of infinitesimal calculus."

I nodded. "Dr. Klein?"

"Dutch?"

"At the risk of sounding disrespectful, and I do not mean to. I mean, I have every intention of abiding by your wish, but I think if Sadie ever knew about this conversation, she'd, well, she'd—"

"Blow a gasket like on one of those engines she likes to tinker with?"

"And then some, yes, sir." I wondered if he underestimated how explosive his granddaughter's reaction would be if she learned he had done an end-run around her, managing her social life. Visions of the Hindenburg disaster we'd recently studied in A.P. American History played in my head.

A smile cracked wide across the older man's face. "The fact you recognize that very real possibility relieves me. She's not one to be trifled with."

"No, sir. She wouldn't stand for it." I joined her grandfather in his grinning, and held his gaze as his face grew serious.

"And neither will I," he declared.

I kept his stare and stepped toward him with my hand outstretched. "And neither will I, sir." I meant to assure him.

We shook hands in a shared allegiance.

"What's going on out here?" Sadie bounced through the garage bay opening.

"Supper ready, Sadie?" Dr. Klein released his hearty grip.

"Just about." She squinted at our now parted hands.

"Guess I'll go get washed up then."

"I'll be in a minute. Ellis and I need to go over our next tutoring session schedule. He has a test soon next week—"

"Ah. Yes, it is a complicated, logistical nightmare, I imagine. Your busy schedules." Sadie's grandfather creased his brow. "Good luck, Dutch. Good to see you. Good game Friday. Nurse your shoulder in the meantime."

"I will. Thank you, sir."

Dr. Klein moseyed out into the night. Sadie's silhouette forced my mouth to go dry, and I swallowed hard. Just beyond the throw of the harsh fluorescent light, heeling one cowboy boot into the toe of the other, she made me dumb. January. I had until January to get up the nerve to ask her out.

"Are you going to the fall formal?" she blurted.

"Huh?" No, no, no, no. This was not how this was supposed to go.

"Are you going to the fall formal?" She asked again, slower this time.

My hand went to the nape of my neck with a firm grip. What was I to do now? I couldn't go to the dance with Sadie. I didn't want to go with anyone else. But I also couldn't tell her why our going together wasn't possible. That would betray her grandfather's confidence, plus the whole Hindenburg fallout.

"Ellis?" She waved from across the chilly concrete that got warmer by the second. "I know you're not a big talker, but it's not a tough question. Two choices. Yes or no?"

"Sadie Jane Klein, get your *sass* in here for supper," Leo, Sadie's brazen older brother, bellowed from the back porch. We were in the same class but ran in different circles.

She stomped her foot, and I moved to make a hasty retreat. "Shut. Up. Leo," she shouted, then practically whispered, "Ellis?"

I scooted by her. "Don't want you to be late for supper. Friday after school? Midge's?"

Sadie's wide-eyed look fell to the toe of her boot.

"Calculus test on Monday," I reminded her. "So, I could use the help—"

"Yeah, calculus. Friday."

I walked backward, half-desperate to escape her, half-disappointed I had to go, all kinds of bummed by the hurt cloud that hazed the girl. No, this was not how it was supposed to go. "I'll see you Friday, and I'll get you home. Before sundown."

"Uh, maybe." Her usual confidence conspicuously absent.

"I'll see you Friday, and I'll see you home," I reiterated and hopped in my truck, careful not to peel out of the long driveway like the ass she probably already thought me to be.

Eight

SADIE

present day

DESPITE FEELING LIKE A complete ass, I took our exchange about military school essays and meat temperature preferences as a debatable checkmark in my win column. Spouting off was my obvious *modus operandi*, and Dutch had taken it in stride, moving past our dust-up with ease as if he lived a grudge-free life. I couldn't wait to learn what made the man's gears go and how his easygoing nature held up over the years despite all he had faced.

"I found the grill in the outbuilding this morning when I got the generator fired up and the water turned on. I'll pull it out and get it cleaned up for cooking." Dutch didn't look up from unloading the shopping bags but moved around the kitchen like the place was his. I liked it.

"Just so we're clear, I'll be doing that cooking so you can skip the whole grunt-grunt-grilling-is-man's-work routine. Not that strutting around in your tailored haberdashery the last twenty-four hours gave off the 'I cook' vibe, but—"

"Just so we're clear, huh?" He slid one of the sacks I'd deposited on the counter closer to him and lined up cleaning supplies. His crooked grin said I amused him.

I liked that too.

"I only planned to set up the grill; the meal is all you. But just so we're clear, you don't know the half of what I'm capable of." Dutch took his time opening drawers and cupboards, finding the appropriate place to stow the Feed 'n' Seed haul. "You know what I think you should do? What you need?"

"Oh, *do* tell. Because if you think I enjoy being told what to do more now than I did as a kid, have I got news for you." I played along, enjoying our banter.

"You need a shower."

I waited a beat before tugging the front collar of my t-shirt to sniff myself. Dutch wasn't wrong. I squinched my nose, all but agreeing with him. "I was going to clean the house. Get it in more livable shape." My gaze darted around at all the draped furniture. As a hardworking woman who spent hours in the field, often in the heat and grime of the maritime environment, I was all-too familiar with the stink that could come from it. No reason to be ashamed. Still, Dutch's candor was sharper, more piercing than the kind he dared in his teenage years, and I appreciated the grown-up version.

"Your grandparents lived fastidious lives. There is nothing out of place here but bed sheets and dust. Take a break. You'll feel better. You'll *smell* better." He wriggled his nose, too, with a smile that said he enjoyed the fun torment. "I'm gonna prep the grill." He hung the emptied reusable totes on a hook in the pantry and headed for the back door.

We didn't look at one another, but I caught his reflection in the sink window glass. "Thanks, Ellis."

"You're welcome, Sadie Jane." He headed into the early evening heat.

With my luggage slung over my shoulder, I gaped at the narrow half-turn stairway that led to the bedrooms. One main bedroom with an ensuite belonged to my grandparents, and two more shared a bath my brother Leo and I used for as long as I could remember until I took off to college, never looking back. I couldn't get out of Canaan Cove fast enough, and both Georgia Tech and the University of Georgia offered to pay my full way to do it. And though Athens was a good bit bigger than Podunk Canaan Cove, getting lost in a sea of millions in metro Atlanta felt like a relief. I couldn't wait to become a tiny fish in a huge pond, only noticed by the ones I cared to attract. It wasn't the first time I ran, and it wouldn't be the last, but at the time, I thought it a brave move for a daring young woman. I'm pretty sure I was the only one fooled in that exercise.

I hadn't been up the old staircase in years, and my feet weren't eager to make the climb. But when Dutch came through the back porch door, a wire brush and roll of paper towels in hand, I scooted up the wooden steps, unwilling to let him see me hesitate. Maybe he didn't see.

Science tells us warm air rises, cold air sinks, and while much of my world stood upside down at the moment, the laws of thermodynamics held true. Sometimes it's the little things. The air conditioning had run most of the day, so the second story was habitable, and by sunset, it would be comfortable for sleep. I planned to move into my childhood bedroom. Still, a hint of mustiness hung in the stale air of the long-closed-up space. All three rooms opened onto the hall common area, brightened by cheery sunshine. Dutch had been right—again. The place was in museum-like condition, minus the dust and furniture drapes.

I peeked in each doorway. Mee-maw and Grandaddy's room, full of ghostly-looking furnishings, may have harbored some actual ghosts too. Dutch must have removed the coverings in Leo's old room the night before when he slept up there in sweltering conditions. My brief journey of rediscovery ended in my room, also draped in white, but what I saw wasn't what I had expected—bare walls and empty bookshelves. A large lightweight shroud hung over the corners of the four-poster bed, all the way to the floor, and I dragged it off before I even set down my bag. The duffel's strap slid from my shoulder, landing on the large area rug, the sheet puddled next to it. More dust danced on the beams of sinking sunlight, sparkling to life in a space long since left for dead.

Atop my bed, two boxes labeled *Sadie's Childhood* in Leo's hand sat side-by-side. Two boxes. How much physical space does youthful angst, doubt, and self-loathing take up anyhow? Two boxes- worth, apparently.

I wasn't ready to play *This Is Your Life* home edition yet and tripped over the heap of sheets to move the taped-closed cartons to the floor. The heavy contents of the first rattled and clanked, landing with a muffled crash as it slipped from my grip.

A friendly, "All good up there?" called from downstairs.

"Yeah, all good," I replied, placing the second box with more care, then toed out of my boots and padded to the bathroom for the much-needed shower. Letting the water flow to clear the neglected plumbing, I found folded towels and stacked boxes of my grandmother's favorite beauty bar tucked away in the linen closet. It was as if the place had long awaited my return while doubting I ever would.

At the stairs' halfway landing turn, the cooler air from downstairs hit me, and my damp curls chilled my neck. The slight shiver ended at the bottom of the well-worn steps, interrupted by the sight of the unveiled living room, looking no different from years ago. Dutch had been busy. Movement spied through a back window drew me to hide behind crisp blue and white floor-length draperies to watch my hardworking guest in his outside chore.

Dutch took a long draw on a beer before taking off the top layer of shirt. He'd sweated through the gray tee but kept it on as he retrieved the second bag of charcoal. He slung it over his shoulder like it was nothing and headed to the storage building on the backend of the property. Back to the grill and another swig of ale, he rearranged a couple of lumps of charred hardwood and closed the lid.

I didn't hear it, but it seemed his phone chirped to life. But while he pulled the phone from his back pocket to see the screen, he didn't answer. A head shake was all the caller got, and the phone slid back into Dutch's new jeans. Maybe he was taking this vacation thing seriously.

When his gaze spotted mine through the gauzy sheers, I didn't bother hiding. I waved, then brushed aside my tightening curls, adjusted my relaxed sundress, and searched out my own beer. In a wordless toast, I lifted my bottle toward him, watching from a perch on the back porch.

"Canaan Cove microbrew," he called across the yard. "Who knew, right?"

"Who knew?" I replied. "Thanks for the tidy-up." I gestured over my shoulder.

He didn't respond but walked my way, and the early evening heat seemed to jump a few degrees. I rotated ninety degrees and pressed to the door jamb to give him room to enter.

"If you have matches, I'll get it lit." Stopping unbearably close, Dutch used his dampened shirttail to rid one hand of charcoal dust. "And if you don't mind my saying, you make a shower look very appealing. Think I could—"

"Yes. Yes, of course. Help yourself to anything you find in the bathroom up there. Make yourself at home."

"Won't be doin' that. As I said, I'll be leaving. Junior and I are gonna catch up, and he's nearby, so he'll get me to the Motor Lodge."

"Really?" My disappointment seeped out of those two syllables.

"Seems more appropriate than my staying here."

"Appropriate? Yes, of course. I forgot that coming back to Canaan Cove also meant traveling through a portal to some arcane puritanical time and space. Now I remember why I left." That wasn't true. Not entirely.

"Aw, come on. This town wasn't that bad. Couldn't have been, or you wouldn't have come home."

Looming over me in the shared doorway, his quiet appraisal roused a shyness I hadn't experienced in years. My sweaty palm pressed packing wrinkles from my linen dress, but another uptick in the temperature compelled me to slug the rest of my drink and toss the bottle in an empty recycling bin. Twisting back, I flinched as Dutch's hand came toward my face. He tucked a curl behind my ear, and my breath caught in my throat.

"Your hair is shorter." He'd gone wide-eyed, probably surprised by his forward act, and his hand dropped to his side.

"Yours too. It does that. Hair. It grows, gets cut, grows some more. Fifteen years is a long time. Things change."

"Some don't," came his hasty reply. He pushed through the door to the kitchen, leaving it open for me to follow. "Matches in the pantry, you think?"

"Drawer by the Frigidaire." I pointed, taking solace in not being the only one feeling on edge. "It's early—for supper, I mean."

"Junior's coming to get me, and I don't want to feel rushed, so..."

"Right. I'll get on it then."

Dutch moved toward the backdoor as I walked to the fridge, and the wide-open country kitchen suddenly shrank. A jerky, hands-up, shuffled dance around ensued, both of us avoiding the other's touch, with mumbled *excuse mes,* high-pitched *oopsie-daisies,* and zero eye contact. Tension crackled, and I couldn't remember feeling a flood of anxiety like it since I was a kid. Back when the unassuming football star caught my eye and then stole my heart.

"Coals should be ready in thirty minutes." Dutch had returned from the patio and jutted a thumb over his shoulder while I sliced fresh-picked Georgia cucumbers for a salad.

"Dinner in an hour, then. Stay out of my way until it's ready." I didn't know why I said that last bit—why I pushed him away when I wanted him to stay near me. "Shoo, now." I flicked fingers toward the stairs, hoping that took out some sting, but my guest didn't indicate one way or the other. He headed to the wooden steps while I forbade myself from sneaking a peek.

Alternative grunge played low, and my head and bare feet rocked out while I set placemats on the stainless caster-wheeled island where we would sit on stools to eat. Somehow, the dining room felt too formal, too intimate for the current situation.

The man could follow directions; I'll give him that. An hour later, to the minute, Dutch appeared, showered and dressed in another button-down and jeans combination. He dropped his bag at the foot of the stairs, and I chided myself for the mealtime site decision. No, a casual supper in the kitchen would be best.

"Not in any hurry, but can I help?" No sooner had he asked, when the timer on my phone chimed.

Determined to appear nonchalant and willing to accept assistance, I offered him a plate and grill tongs. "Perfect timing. You can pull the meat in ninety seconds. It'll need to rest for a few minutes."

"Down to a science, huh?"

"Cooking *is* science, and you know I love science." Time ticked by as we stared. "Sixty seconds." My head jerked to the back door.

"Yes, ma'am." He hop-skipped to the task with a brisk salute.

We sat across from one another wordlessly, dining on the organic, sustainably farmed, and ethically beneficial bountiful, but simple feast set between us. But the clank of silverware and Nirvana were finally interrupted when I decided there were too many unasked questions looming, and I thought their time had come. I plowed ahead.

"So, what are you doing for Pembroke Industries?" I kept my tone light, my eyes on my meal.

"Nothing. I'm on vacation, remember?" Dutch's quick reply sounded more like a stall tactic, but I let it slide while I continued to dig for intel.

"And when you're not on vacation? You said something about security, I think. What's your typical nine to five, Monday to Friday?"

"*Ha*. It'd be nice if I could work such banker's hours." More hedging. Interesting. But I had no plans to let up on him.

"Yes, well, Pembroke has lots of irons in lots of fires. Lots to keep *secure*, I'd imagine." My look held a mix of innocence and flirtation while I made eye contact now, determined to score some points in what seemed a burgeoning battle of wits.

"I'm in asset protection." His focus shifted to the bloody steak on his plate.

"Ass hat what?" Why couldn't I let the cheap joke slide?

His shoulders shook with a grinning exhale.

"Sorry. Asset protection?"

"Corporate lingo for a glorified security guard—like I said." The answer came freely, but then his broad shoulders dropped. He bowed his head like he'd confessed some secret or maybe felt shame. Considering the gun I'd seen strapped to his ankle earlier and just about everything else about the man, the vision in front of me couldn't have been further from some night watchman. Unease oozed from his side of the stainless island, and I wondered if he worried I'd think being a security guard was beneath him.

I tried to alleviate his concern. "Makes sense. I knew they planned to have security at the wedding. It surprised me. Didn't know Intercoastal Waterway pirates were a thing, but what do I know?"

"My job is less about protecting the people who hire me and more about safeguarding their interests. Pirates are one thing, but I find it's the *privateers* you need to watch out for. The commissioned enemy is harder to fight because they come armed with paperwork."

"Sheesh. Rich people and their paperwork." Thinking about my patent woes, I pushed my plate aside despite the food still on it. I shook off my work worries. Dutch's intelligent response inspired more questions and further obscured the riddle I tried to solve. "Gotta read the fine print. All of it."

"Yes. You do." That assertion felt serious and aimed at me, but I veered the conversation. Dutch moved salad around his plate with his fork.

"Don't you want to ask how Tristan and I got togeth—met?"

He sat back on his stool and wiped his mouth with the cloth napkin he'd pulled from his lap. "Well, I admit I did a little Googling and saw you were some big university researcher type."

"You *Googled* me?"

"I did. This morning. Before you woke up."

"First time?"

"Looking you up, you mean?" His voice tightened.

"Yeah. It's just I've typed your name into a search engine or two over the years, but you have zero digital footprint. Wild, sort of. Like nothing at all." I fidgeted with my napkin, wondering why I'd admit to cyber-stalking.

"Yes."

"Yes, what?"

"For the first time. I—I never—" Dutch shook his head. Pained eyes met mine. "I never let myself do that before today. I couldn't. And I'm not very interesting, so nothing to see here. Certainly nothing internet-worthy. Obviously." He shrugged off the awkward moment with a deep inhale and moved on like we hadn't both owned up to fleeting thoughts of one another over the years. Again. "But you? No wonder. You were always so smart. Lots about you on the internet. Anyway, I figure Pembroke Industries funded some project you were involved in, as they do, and somehow your work got co-opted by the conglomerate, putting you and Tristan in the same boardroom at some point. He fell head over feet for your geotechnical engineering brain while you swooned for his—well, I don't know what you saw in him, actually." He picked up his knife to cut another bite of his filet.

I stared a moment, struck by how much thought Dutch had spent on the idea of Tristan and me this morning. The number of words he'd strung together added up to a lot—a lot for Dutch, to be sure.

"*Huh*. Nope. Not even close. Tinder, actually." I jerked in my seat when Dutch dropped both utensils with a loud *clank* on the china but then pushed my teasing further. "But I'm totally stealing your version of events. Makes me sound *way* better than some opportune late-night swipe right." A glance allowed me a quick peek at the deepened color in Dutch's cheeks.

My dining companion shoved his unfinished dinner aside. On his feet, he took quick strides toward the refrigerator. "Another beer?" he grumbled.

I bit back a smile, enjoying his ruffled reaction. "No, thanks." Both our bottles were half-full. Dutch kept his head in the icebox longer than necessary and emerged with another Canaan Cove pale ale.

"I'm kidding, Ellis," I admitted. "It was almost exactly as you said—except no one fell or swooned for anyone's anything. And I have said as much. Repeatedly. Tristan and I are friends. And we have never been anything more." I fidgeted, peeling the label off my bottle. "Pembroke has sole use of a couple of my patents, and yes, they provided some funding along the way—so, legally, they are entitled to part ownership. My first Pembroke marriage of convenience. That one's gonna stick 'cause—"

"Paperwork?" he interjected.

I sighed. "Yeah." I stalled, uncertain how much to share. "I've got another patent-pending, and it doesn't have anything to do with—well, Tristan was supposed to help me get it back. Make it mine, all mine."

"Why? What did Tristan get out of it? Never mind." He set down the newly opened bottle with enough force that foam surged and dribbled over its lip.

I didn't appreciate the implication. "Tristan got to continue living in the manner to which he has become accustomed."

"What the hell does that mean? No, don't tell me. I shouldn't—I don't want to know."

"My God, Ellis. I know it's been a while, and we don't know each other well, but I'll be damned if I'm gonna sit here and be judged by you. Like you've never done a dumb thing for a good reason."

"Knock it off, Sadie. That water is so far under the bridge. We were kids, and it all worked out. No harm, no foul. But it is a little disappointing to see fifteen years on, and you're still acting without thinking. Bulldozing your way in some act of righteousness with no regard for the consequences."

"Whoa. The marriage was *never* gonna happen. Did it get out of hand? Yes. Did I wait until the last minute to—jump ship? Also, yes. But I was never going to marry him. I never would have said, 'I do.' Not for anything. Not even for something that's rightfully mine."

"I don't know, Sadie. Money can be an awfully potent lure."

"Money? This isn't about—money? My parents left me money, my grandparents left me money, and I have—do you know what I do? What I've done? Money? I have more money than I—forget it. It isn't about money, not on my end, anyway." I grabbed my plate, scraping my dinner into the sink, then gripped the sink apron, staring out the kitchen window. Dutch carried his own plate and stood at my side.

"I'm sorry. In my work, I'm surrounded by people corrupted by—I apologize." His softened face reflected in the wavy glass, but he kept mum.

Still, I needed to explain and defend my position. "I don't know how much you know about the Pembrokes. Tristan is a trust fund kid. But on his thirtieth birthday, Trust Fund 2.0 kicks in. But because Tristan is an only child or because his parents are dominating assholes or big on 'family values,' or just because they're weird, it comes with a caveat. And that stipulation was news to Tristan."

"More fine print?"

I snorted with a nod. "Yeah, fine print. And the blond beach boy missed it until a year ago. Turns out he needs to be married to level up in the *Who Wants to Be a Billionaire* game. But when he does, it'll mean a bigger bank account and more Pembroke Industries business control. Long story short, Tristan gets my pending patent freed from Pembroke Industries, so I can get it to do some good, and he—"

"He gets to marry you? Good God, Sadie." Dutch practically tossed his plate onto the counter, then gripped the back of his neck as he spun away from me. "Do you have any idea what they could do to you? Once you are legally bound to that family? You think they own you now? Just wait. You will never be free—"

"For the last time, I was never going to marry him. I was supposed to break his heart. Devastate him. Call off the engagement and leave him so decimated, destroy him so close to his thirtieth birthday, his parents would acquiesce and sign over the fund anyway. They would try to mend their precious son's wounded soul with a billion-dollar salve. If they buy his performance and give up the cash, Tristan will be just fine."

"And you?"

"*Not* me. The people of Chile, Western Africa, Pakistan, California, even—they get water. They get a solution to a drought problem."

A short laugh barked out of him.

"You're laughing? Why are you laughing?"

"Hell, if I know, because it sure isn't funny," he sighed. "When are you going to learn?"

"Shut up."

"No. Seriously. When are you gonna realize you can't stand up to the big bad guys all by yourself to defend the proverbial weakling? It's naïve and only lands you in trouble."

Just what the scene called for—another reprimand and my already defensive ego split wide open. If I had been a violent person, I'd have punched him right then. I'd done it before, made him bleed. Ellis Holland was testing my restraint, and it nearly failed. "Get out."

"Sadie."

"Get. Out. And don't come back, and if you believe that, if you truly have lost your sense of right and wrong, then you best be rethinking that lie you've been telling yourself for the last fifteen years."

"What lie?"

"That lie where you say we were just kids, and it all worked out. No harm, no foul. Because that's a giant load of horse sh—"

The strident trill of the century-old doorbell jolted us out of our argument—an argument that got more heated than seemed appropriate for two people who hadn't known each other for the last decade and a half. I pushed by him on the way to the front hall, but he grabbed my arm and held it too tight. Tristan's warning that Dutch Holland was a dangerous man echoed, and my gaze bounced from the door to his grip of my arm to his steely glare. I stifled a panicked noise, but a whimper of fear snuck out of me. His next look was one of shock. He let go of my arm, and I clutched it in the release.

"I'm sorry, Sadie. I didn't mean—" The doorbell rang again.

"That'd be your ride." I hurried to greet Junior, and his buoyant cheeriness met me when I flung open the door, but it quickly dissolved despite my effort to return it with my own plastered grin. "Junior. Good to see you again."

He stepped across the threshold with a shrunken smile and darting eyes.

"He's all yours. Take him. No backsies." I hoped it sounded like a joke.

"Junior, could you—give us a minute?" Dutch placed his hands to his hips and had trouble meeting anyone's eye.

Junior didn't say a word but waved in a way that said, no problem, and then reversed his stride to stand back onto the front porch.

"Not necessary, Junior. Elli—*Dutch* and I are done here."

"Sadie," Dutch implored in a whisper.

"Goodbye, Ellis." I stood back with a firm grasp of the tarnished door handle, thankful for the support. No one moved for what felt like a long moment. When Dutch retrieved his duffel, I breathed some relief, looking everywhere but at him. He stopped beside me.

Junior gave no help when he backed farther away. "I'll be at my car," he murmured before stumbling down the steps to the stone walkway below us. I'm not sure what I hated more—Junior leaving or the mix of emotion that thudded through me when I found myself alone again with Dutch. Sweat prickled the back of my neck, and I wished I had pinned up my hair like usual.

Tossing his bag over his shoulder, Dutch cleared his throat but didn't speak. Instead, he took a tender hold of my free hand. I wrenched away from his touch with more force than I meant. We both flinched in the wake of the rejection.

"I would never hurt you, Sadie. Tell me you know that." It was a gentle plea, but a plea nonetheless. I didn't offer him relief. "Good God, if you know anything—"

I couldn't bring myself to tell him I understood he didn't mean me any harm, even though I knew it was true. I couldn't bring myself to say anything at all. Struck dumb twice in as many days, and each time compliments of Ellis Holland.

He pulled a business card from his back pocket and offered it to me. "If you need anything—ever. Don't hesitate." Another long moment ticked by, but I took it when he pushed the card to my palm. Mustering some bravery, I lifted my chin to meet his eyes, but before they reached the hollow of his throat, he pressed his lips to the top of my head. He kissed me goodbye like I was his little sister, which officially became the thing I hated most of all.

Nine

SADIE

present day

MUSICAL IRONY KEPT UP a strong game when I trudged into the kitchen to the angsty wail of Pearl Jam. The stiff card in my hand begged me to look at it. No flimsy, generic, lightweight bond. The canvas texture spoke of high-quality while the black background with platinum embossed print said sophisticated, mysterious even. At least to my romance reader brain. A mysterious and sophisticated hero was my frisky fiction jam. But the card held little information: his name, written as merely Dutch Holland, and a telephone number, including the country code. More questions. But apparently, his work included contacts outside U.S. borders, and he'd completely relinquished his given name. My mind flashed to images that skewed more James Bond than Paul Blart, mall cop, but I tossed those pictures and the card aside, happy to have a kitchen to scrub clean.

No sooner had I folded the dish towel than my phone played a song from a different era. A piano plunked out the intro of *New York, New York*, and I jumped at the noise with a mix of glee and regret. The Kander and Ebb tune meant my big brother was calling. I adored Leo, but I'd dodged his recent calls, reluctant to tell him about Tristan's and my scheme and feeling guilty for lying by omission during prior catch-up talks. We both lived busy lives, but at some point, he'd given up trying to track me down, leaving me "it" in our ongoing game of phone tag. I'd been "it" for quite a while.

"Leo, I was just thinking about you."

"Aw. Stop it, Shorty. No, you weren't, so don't even try," my brother shot back.

It may have been an exaggeration, but I *had* thought of him—and not only the two times Dutch brought him up—once the night before and again this morning. Relieved we had finally connected, I plopped onto a familiar sofa, upholstered in a risky white.

My grandparents hadn't decorated with their reckless, often grease-covered granddaughter in mind, but why would they? My brother and I were unplanned additions to their daily lives, and they had earned their *nice things*. Raising two children in the twilight of their years disrupted enough, I imagined. But it didn't get in the way of a beautiful home. Drs. Avi and Talia Klein were extraordinary guardians, encouraging with high expectations they gave us room to meet. They loved unconditionally, if not with overt affection. But where I ignored the cloud of sadness that hung around the Klein bungalow, the ever-present fog of loss, Leo fought it with song and dance, self-deprecating humor, and his own brand of flair. He was the bouncy Tigger to my more Rabbit and Owl-like ways—a planner and over-explainer of things. Despite our personality differences, our mutual admiration was fierce. I stretched my long legs, resting my bare feet on a glass-top coffee table with unusual care, eager to reconnect with my only sibling.

"No real—"

"Lies!" he roared as a joke, and we giggled. It was funny because it was true. "But enough about you. You are never going to believe who called me. Nope, don't even try, because in a million years you will never, ever—"

"Ellis Holland?"

"Well, fine, Sadie. You are always the wet blanket to my fiery fun and games."

"Always," I sighed. That was true too, but it was the role I had to play because long ago, Leo won center stage as the life of the party. He even sang like an angel. I didn't mind.

"Well, imagine my surprise."

Too impatient to sit through his long, drawn-out tale, my questions bombarded the man on the other end of the line. "When? What did he say? How did he sound? What did *you* say?"

"Simmer down, Shorty," Leo paused, and I could hear his brain gears at work. "Maybe you ought to tell me your version of events first."

"My version? Version of—? I don't know what—"

"Sadie Jane Klein, do not even try to shrug this off. And that I have to hear it from Dutch Holland first? Dutch Holland? Sadie." Leo's apt *tsk* cut me to the quick.

I flopped to my side and curled up in a ball to tell my big brother *my* version of the scheme I had hatched with Tristan Pembroke and seen through to its watery end the night before. On the second retelling, the wisdom of the plan didn't shine any brighter than when I told Dutch about it. With the added shenanigans of the *Sapphire Selkie* escape and my walking into a Waffle House in high fashion, the saga took on a lampoon-ish quality, and even I couldn't help but roll my eyes. Hindsight is such an annoying waste.

"I swear to Cher, you are the dumbest genius I know. Tell me you at least got the patent?"

I answered with silence.

Leo grumbled my name again. "But you're not *married* to this Tristan guy, right?"

"No, I'm not married," I huffed. "Like I could ever get married without you at my side." More guilt swarmed me when I realized his hurt feelings.

After too much silence, my usually mouthy brother stammered, "Well, I—I just—I just don't know, Sadie. Of all the things—I mean, how could you? Have you no respect for yourself? The Klein family name? *My* fabulous and well-earned reputation? Come on. The *Sapphire Selkie?*"

I exhaled into a laugh, realizing his mock-reprimand. God, I'd missed him. "Now, will you tell me about your conversation with El—Dutch?" The sun had set, and the four-poster bed in my old room called to me. I pocketed the tossed-away business card and shuffled up the stairs, hoping Leo and I would continue to talk.

"Conversation? Oh, honey, I don't answer calls from unknown numbers. He left a message. I never spoke to him."

"*Leo.*"

"I always could get you to spill your guts," he gloated with laughter. "Remember that time with the lawnmower?"

"Remember? *Pfft.* I could rebuild that ancient push mower in my sleep," I groaned at the memory of my mechanical tendency emerging early.

"Grandaddy warned you not to take it apart again. Who knew me adding one *itty-bitty* extra piece to the pile would be such a problem?"

"It was a machine, Leo. Not a piece of Ikea furniture. It could have blown up for all my eight-year-old self knew. When I couldn't figure out where that extra screw went, I had to come clean. He made me take apart that beast and put it back together every day for two weeks that summer."

"While I got off mower-duty," Leo cackled some more. "Best two weeks of my young life. And then we got the John Deere rider. Sweet baby Jesus, I hated mowing the lawn." He exhaled. "Anyway,

Dutch only said who he was and that I should call you. 'Check-in,' I believe, was his word. He was concerned and apologetic for sticking his nose in. He was calm and cordial, but obviously, it was a bit unnerving. I called you immediately. I wonder how he got my number." We both pondered that question. "So, you and Dutch Holland are in Canaan Cove... together... again. I thought I felt some cosmic shift. Like the earth tilted hinky on its axis. Now I know why."

"What are you talking about?" I lay on my childhood bed as heat rose up my body at the thought of Dutch, not unlike many nights of my teen years. Of course, I knew more now than I did then, which only made things warmer—much warmer.

"Oh, good. Glad to know your school-girl crush was just that."

"What crush? What are you—I didn't—" I didn't sound at all convincing. "Yeah, I liked him," I confessed.

"What wasn't there to like? Those light brown curls, his greenish-blue eyes, that rock-hard—"

"All right, Leo. That'll do."

"Forehead, I was going to say forehead. The boy was as hardheaded as they come."

"Tell me about it. Still is. But Ellis is not a boy anymore. Nothing *boyish* about him at all." I fanned myself.

"Just goy-ish, right?" Leo snickered at his joke, and I couldn't help but join him.

"Pretty sure this lapsed-Jew's ham-eating mouth doesn't care."

He gasped, "Sadie, now you took it too far. I'm your brother, for goodness' sake. Behave."

"I'm pretty sure you're the one responsible for my wayward ways."

"Um, no. That would be Midge Toogood's doing, thank you very much."

My giggling got the best of me; tears leaked down my temples. We spent another hour playing catch-up, vowing not to let so much time pass before our next call.

The tinny jangle jolted me awake. It drew me from that early-onset deep sleep, and I didn't recognize the noise or my surroundings until the metallic clang erupted again. The doorbell? My phone, yanked from its charger, showed it was nearly midnight.

"Seriously?" I groped the bedside table where I had dropped Dutch's swanky business card, knocking my latest kissing book to the floor. After a vigorous eye rub, I focused on the numbers, thumbing them on the phone screen and hitting the call icon. The doorbell screeched again, officially using up the last of its vintage charm. I scrambled out of my sheets, waiting for Dutch to answer on his end.

"Yeah, hello?" he growled.

"Don't yeah, hello me. Why are you ringing my doorbell? At midnight?"

"Huh? Who is—Sadie?"

"You're the only one in town who knows I'm—never mind. I'm coming down."

The bell rang again as I shoved my arm through the sleeve of a short robe I'd hung on a door hook.

"*Ellis*, I said I'm coming—"

"Sadie. That's not me. I'm not—*Don't* answer that door." Dutch's sudden shout said he was wide awake now, and I skidded to a stop at the top of the stairs.

"If it's not you, who'd—"

"Stay upstairs. Don't turn on any lights." His volume rose and fell with his obvious movement wherever he was. "And don't hang up the phone."

"Mm, 'kay—not the boss of me, and if someone is ringing my bell in the middle of the night, it must be an emergency. Someone might need help." Despite my bravado, I took slow, quiet steps to the stair landing, peeking around the corner to look for movement on the front porch. Nothing. "Gosh, it's dark out here," I whispered the obvious detail, creeping down the last of the steps. The banister creaked when I leaned into it, startling me. More scuffling sounded through the phone, but Dutch had nothing to say until I sucked in a gulp of air.

"Sadie?" He said my name through what sounded like a clenched jaw. His agitation frightened me, but at the same time, gave me something to prove.

My nerve waffled the closer I got to the sheer curtained glass front door, and I stopped short, swallowing hard when I detected motion. "Someone's here, Ellis." Another bell ring obscured another pointless statement. Of course, someone was there. "Well, whoever it is, they're persistent and if they meant me harm, I think they'd be a bit stealthier, don't you?" I kept my voice low as I reached for the knob. Who was I trying to convince?

"Do not answer that—"

"Tristan!" I hissed when I flung open the door.

Dutch's resounding "Shit" entered my ear as Tristan opened his arms and bared his toothpaste grin.

"There she is. I was starting to think I had the wrong shack." Tristan charged toward me for a quick, harmless but noisy kiss on my cheek. My palm to his chest sent him back a few steps. "Don't tell me you were in bed already? And if you were, please say you weren't alone."

I rolled my eyes. "It's midnight, dingus."

"At home, Club 51 is just getting interesting at midnight." He added his trademark hair flip with his devilish leer.

"Yeah, well, this isn't home. Not your home. And there's not a big clubbing scene here in Canaan Cove." I wondered if that was true after the Feed 'n' Seed stunner earlier in the day. My mental note to explore downtown quickly went by the wayside when I remembered Dutch listening on the line. "Give me a sec, Tris." I returned the phone to my ear. "Sorry to have bothered you. Everything's fine here. False alarm."

"Sadie. I'm not sure Tristan should be trust—"

"Bye." I ended the call, slipped the phone into my robe pocket, and leaned in the doorway, arms crossed.

"Who ya talkin' to at this late hour? Should I be jealous?" Keeping up with Tristan's couldn't-care-less to green-eyed-envy routine could cause whiplash. Best to ignore it.

"Town sheriff," I lied with ease. "I've got 'em on speed dial, so *next* time you should text first or call, and definitely *not* just show up in the middle of the night. That's how people get shot out here in the boonies."

"See, now all I heard is there will be a *next* time, and we haven't even had *this* time yet. So, score one for me." Tristan had an agile eyebrow, and he employed it in an annoyingly charming way. At first glance, it wasn't difficult to see why women fell for him. The money, the swagger, the sweet talk, *the money*. That said, having known him quite some time, it baffled me how no one had pushed him off a tall building yet. Still, he wasn't just a pretty face. He had more going on upstairs than it appeared, but I could never be sure if the young Mr. Pembroke would use his powers for good or not. I surmised it depended on which way the wind blew.

"Why are you here?" I relaxed, my adrenaline rush dissipating.

"Aren't you going to welcome me in?"

"Nope." I stood my ground. "I know the vampire rules. Can't come in unless I invite you."

Tristan yelped. "Ha! See, Sade? That alone makes me want to try to love you. You make me laugh."

"*Try* to love me? Yeah, that's not how it works. Again, why are you here?"

"Don't know if you heard or not, but I got jilted at the altar." He wiped non-existent tears. "I'm supposed to be totally bummed about it, but I can't stand having to walk around pretending to be all glum while people stare, wondering if I'm okay, worrying about my broken heart. Being 'sad' all the time is *exhausting*." He air-quoted his feelings. "So, I had to get out of town. That, or I've come to win you back. Take your pick."

"It's only been twenty-four hours. And this heartbreak routine was your brainchild. Don't suppose you've made any headway on *my* win in this deal?"

"Uh, it's only been twenty-four hours." He wasn't wrong to throw that back in my face, but I could have done without the snide tone. "I'll get your patent freed. I will. Somehow," he said the second part with unusual sincerity, and we stood in the dark, our mutual silence accompanied by the hammering call of late-mating carpenter frogs.

I was *this* close to ushering Tristan inside, but a car I'd seen in the driveway earlier that evening reappeared. It made a slow approach under the faraway streetlight and turned onto the property again, sparing me from my foolish hospitality. "Oh, no," I murmured.

"Another late-night caller? Now I *am* getting jealous." Tristan puffed up in a way I had seen him do in a boardroom and on a squash court. Everything was about the win, not the prize, but the victory itself. He loved a fight and never sidestepped. I feared Dutch might oblige him. The night air got thicker, and I wished I could take off the bathrobe sticking to me. Things grew more curious when the massive figure exiting the car parked behind Tristan's wasn't Dutch Holland.

"Sadie? Sadie Jane Klein? Is that you?" Junior, sleepy-eyed and dressed in gym shorts and a faded UGA t-shirt, strolled up the stone path. "I thought I saw movement on the porch. Didn't realize you were back in town." All that was an obvious lie, considering he knew damn well I was here, and it was far too dark to see anything on my porch from the distant road. "All good here?" He looked at me, then Tristan.

"Junior?" I reached inside to flip the switch to the front porch light, and we all winced at the sudden brightness. Squinting harder, I craned my neck to see if anyone else joined him, but he appeared to be alone.

"Welcome back to the Cove." As he climbed the steps, his smile told me to play along, so I greeted him with a friendly kiss on his cheek. "How long's it been?"

"Dunno. Four years, four hours? Hard to say. Time flies."

Junior agreed, and a twinkle in his eye said I amused him. Then he faced Tristan with an outstretched hand. "Hi, I'm—"

"Sorry. How rude of me, Junior. This is Tristan Pembroke. Tristan, this is Cecil—"

"Good lord, you're Cecil Ford." Tristan stiffened and his wide eyes shot to me. "This is Cecil Ford. Cecil—UGA *Go Dawgs*, College Football Hall of Fame, Atlanta Falcon, blown-out knee in the Super Bowl—Ford." Tristan gaped while gripping Junior's limb in a rabid two-handed shake.

"Cecil Ford was my dad. Please, call me Junior." Junior pried himself loose like he'd touched something sticky.

"Junior and I went to high school together. Did I not mention that?"

Now, with eyes only for the ex-football player, Tristan replied, "No. No, you definitely did not."

Seeing Mr. Personality Plus gobsmacked in the presence of a sports idol made this late-night visit worth the trouble. Tristan's more child-like qualities, at times, were some of his most endearing. But amusement aside, I needed to end the awkward meet-and-greet.

"Nice of you to check on me, Junior, but Tristan was just leaving."

"I was?"

"You were."

"Come on, Sade. You're just going to push me out in the dark of night so far from home?"

"You were never in, and you showed up in the dark of night."

Junior watched our back-and-forth, then interjected. "The Motor Lodge is about a mile down the road. And I happen to know they've got vacancies. It's nicer than it sounds. I'd be happy to show you the way."

While I appreciated Junior's help in getting Tristan off my porch, the idea of Dutch and Tristan staying at the same motel felt like a mistake. Then again, none of that had to do with me. With one last pleading look, Tristan exhaled. Begging in front of his football hero wouldn't do. He accepted his defeat.

"That's mighty neighborly, Junior. Thank you." Tristan nodded his loss. "Breakfast in the morning, Sade?"

"Sure. I'll meet you. Midge's Diner on Main Street." My mouth watered at the thought. Positively Pavlovian. "The biscuits are heaven—"

"Oh, it's Midge's *Café* now," Junior corrected with a grin.

"Huh." I hoped I wasn't drooling and moved on to the more important issue at hand. "Uh, speaking of—neighborly. Don't suppose you'd know if any other—*visitors* might be popping by?" I hoped Junior would read the subtext.

"Oh, I'd bet on it," he answered with almost gleeful enthusiasm. "And soon too. You know how fast word spreads in these parts." Junior stepped off the porch.

"Boy, do I," I exhaled, wondering just how soon I could count on another late-night caller.

"Good seeing you, Sadie. Tristan, why don't you follow me. It's not far," Junior reiterated. Whether on the football field, in the aisles of the outsized Feed n' Seed, or the front stoop of my childhood home, Cecil Ford, Jr. displayed a persuasive leadership that even alpha-dog Tristan Pembroke couldn't defy. With a mini-shrug, Tristan skipped down the stairs after the burly frame disappearing into the night.

"I'll woo you back tomorrow morning, Sadie. With biscuits, apparently," Tristan called over his shoulder.

"Don't hold your breath, but I look forward to breakfast." I waved at a moth overhead, not the only poor creature drawn to bright light. Tristan pointed like an awe-struck goof at his new friend Junior. I snickered with a head shake, slipping back inside the dark house to flip off the switch on the incandescent bug magnet. The old brass bolt lock clunked when I turned the knob, and the nature noise faded. Cool A/C air brought relief, but coupled with an eerie calm, a shiver ran through me.

"Hi." It was his usual quiet greeting.

"Jesus, Ellis." I clutched at my robe collar.

"You trust him, don't you?"

"How the hell did you—"

The banister groaned when Dutch pulled himself from his squat on the stairs. "I texted Junior, then ran here. Came in the back door."

"So, *not* a vampire then."

"Not a what?"

"Never mind, and I'm pretty sure I locked the back door."

"Yeah, I'm pretty sure you need better locks. Are you sure your arrangement with Tristan isn't more than business?"

"I am, not that it's any of yours." I walked past him to find the kitchen light and stay out of arm's reach.

"I'm not sure you fully appreciate the extent Pembroke Industries will go to keep proprietary information in-house and money-making assets in line."

I pulled two beers from the fridge and offered him one. "I don't mean to sound elitist, but you have quite the vocabulary for a security guard, and Tristan is a person, not a corporation."

"I don't trust him."

"Then trust me."

He stared a beat before taking a swig of pale ale. "I don't trust anyone, Sadie Jane."

I nodded, not surprised but saddened by his confession. "You ever think what life might be like if that night never happened?"

"God, why are you so hung up on that night? Wouldn't you rather forget it?"

"It's the last time I saw you. It changed everything. For you, in particular. For me. The whole town."

"And look at us now." He raised his bottle like a glib toast.

"I'm looking at you now." I set my drink on the island and stepped toward him, hoping my breath kept steady. "I'm looking at you, wondering, why are you here?" I took another step and placed my hand on his chest. "Why did you run here? Why are you standing in my kitchen in the middle of the night after pushing me away, avoiding me for years?"

Dutch's Adam's apple twitched when my hand slid down his torso, and I moved closer, taking a gentle hold of him at his hips. He smelled earthy, with a hint of my grandmother's beauty bar. More than the summer heat radiated between us. My forehead met his breastbone, and I was thankful not to see his eyes while I rallied the courage for the next bit. The scientist in me knew conducting an experiment meant having a hypothesis, and I wished mine not to be true.

"Why, Ellis? What brought you here? What's keeping you here? Because if it's me, if I'm the reason, I'd like to talk about that." I squeezed his sides and took a deep inhale, gliding my nose up his body until my chin met his shoulder. "We should definitely explore the possibilities." My cheek brushed against his as my lips made it to his ear. The roughness of his days-old beard grazed my skin, and his breath hitched when my hands inched up his midsection, appreciating every ridged muscle. "But—"

"But what?"

"But—if this has anything to do with my patent, you better get the *hell* out of my house." I pushed him, and he staggered backward while I spun and grabbed my beer for a gulp. When his arm reached around me, I froze, but he simply set down his bottle. Without a word, he walked to the front hall, unbolted the door, and left.

I'd never been more disappointed to prove a theory correct, but I guess I got my answer.

Ten

DUTCH

fifteen years ago

"Is that your final answer?" Sadie reached across the Formica table and tapped her pencil eraser on my notepaper. "Wanna phone a friend?"

"Huh?" Something distracted me. I couldn't put my finger on it, but something had changed. Her hair, maybe? Was she wearing perfume? No, Sadie acted indifferent, more aloof. It seemed as if the weeks we'd been getting to know one another had been wiped out, and we were nothing but student and tutor again.

"I asked if that was your answer. Look, if you're envisioning running plays, mentally preparing for the big game tonight, we can call it quits. You're gonna do great on the test Monday. As a matter of fact, it seems you've got a pretty good handle on the class. You probably don't need me anymore."

Even with the earlier November sunset, we had another whole hour before I needed to take her home, but she piled up her schoolwork like she meant to leave. "And it being early, you don't need to drive me. Plenty of daylight, and it's kind of warm. I'll be fine."

And there it was. I was getting the brush-off. Sadie was right. I did have a handle on the class, and I would ace the test on Monday. I didn't need her to tutor me. But this had never been about calculus. "I'm not sure that's true, Sadie Jane."

She winced when I said her name but ducked her head to load up her backpack. "Sure, it is. I bet it's sixty degrees out there."

"Not the weather. The part about me needing you." My grip found my neck.

"No, I think you've moved beyond the need for a math tutor. You're welcome." She teased me, but the tone sounded wrong, strained.

"I didn't mean—" I mumbled.

"Then what did you mean?"

"Nothing." I closed my binder and slipped it into my bag, wondering how everything had gone so wrong, so fast.

"Whatever. Oh, and about that thing—at my house. It occurred to me that maybe you thought my asking you about the fall formal might have seemed like I was asking you—well, I wasn't asking. That would be ridiculous, obviously. I was just making conversation so—" Neither of us had broached the subject after that uncomfortable encounter in her grandfather's garage until now.

"So, you're not going?" I knew we couldn't go together, but I thought we'd see each other. We could drink punch. Talk slopes and tangents. Maybe even dance.

"I'm going. Of course, I'm going. Why wouldn't I go?" She didn't look at me—too busy rearranging textbooks and binders.

"Right, sure." I sipped my water, relieved to know we'd both be there.

"Got a date and everything."

"Huh?" I coughed. "Who?" My voice hadn't cracked in over a year, but it chose that moment to remind me of the good ol' days.

"Why? Don't you believe me? Is it so hard to imagine someone would ask out the nerd-girl?" She stood, shoving her arms into the sleeves of an oversized plaid flannel.

"No."

"No, you don't believe me?"

"No, it's not hard to imagine that someone would ask you out. I bet lots of guys would like to ask you out. I bet *lots* of guys will be disappointed to find someone beat them to it. They'll be kicking themselves for the missed opportunity." I pulled the strap of my messenger bag over my head and slid out of the booth.

It seemed Sadie had lost all her fight. Her hands found her hips, and she stared for a long moment before saying, "Yeah? Well, lots of guys are idiots."

A sigh caught in my throat. "Yeah," I found my nerve and chanced looking her in the eyes, "we are."

"Everything all right out here?" Midge pushed through the swinging kitchen door, drying her hands on her apron. "You need a ride, Sadie?"

"No, I'll be seeing Sadie home, Ms. Toogood," I answered.

"You sure? I'm done here if you need to get to the game."

"Plenty of time, and we're ahead of schedule," I assured her. "Thanks, though."

"Hello. I'm standing right here." Sadie flailed her arms and beelined to the door. "Sheesh." A cat stretched out of its nap on a window ledge near the door, yawning with a squeaky meow, and Sadie stopped to pet it. "You see me, don't you, Shady? Yes, you do. You see me," she cooed, and the cat purred.

I saw her too. The sinking sun highlighted her curls and face. The fading daylight let those hazel eyes show off the green in them. Ironic, since I was the one fighting envy. And losing. Worst. Fall formal. Ever.

Sadie talked the whole way to her house. Everything she saw provoked some thought to be shared. Her mind worked like gears and fast. One thing led to another. Seemingly unrelated topics were cobbled together, and all the parts moved in tandem, a whole other creation you didn't see coming. She was smart and so funny, with genuine interests.

"But do you get nervous during games? Remembering all those plays? Always having to know where everyone is and who has the ball?"

"Actually, I like playing because it's the only time I *stop* thinking. I guess we probably shouldn't go telling Coach that, but no, with all that noise, everything goes quiet in here." I tapped my forehead. "But I'll be glad when the season's over. More time for other things. Less attention paid to me. It's kind of exhausting." I'd never told anyone that truth before. Any of it.

"I get that. The attention thing. But it's a shame I never got to see you play."

"Now that might have made me nervous." That unplanned confession popped out. *Fumble.* Sadie was kind enough to let it slide, and I fidgeted in the driver's seat as we pulled into her long driveway. Her brother Leo was practicing his jump shot at the far end and waved at our arrival. Sadie's and my alone time officially ended, but with a sweet smile, and I felt lucky to have seen it, even though it wasn't for me. She adored her brother, and anyone could see they were close. Their tragic past contributed to it, but for a younger sister, Sadie had steadfast loyalty and a fierce protective instinct for her big brother. One didn't have to spend much time with her to learn that. On occasion, it made me want a sibling. Her feisty bravery might have been what first caught my eye, but her devotion was one of the things I liked most about her. But let's be real—that list was long, and she kept adding to it.

Leo Klein exhibited a different sort of bravery. He was who he was: funny, gregarious, and some might say flamboyant. But Leo wasn't a big brother in name only, at least not anymore. Since May, he'd gone from standing two inches shorter than me to two inches taller, and I had grown some also. The taller Leo got, the more his personality swelled, too. He grew into his own, despite his environment. I'll say it again. *Brave.*

I climbed from my truck, and Sadie did too.

"Hey, Leo!" she called as he jogged our way.

"Hey, Shorty," he quipped, eyes on her while he chucked a stout chest pass at me. "Mee-maw's waiting on you."

"No, she's not. I'm early."

"What can I say? She was asking for you." He turned to me. "Nice catch. Wanna shoot some hoops? I'm thinking of going out for the team now that I'm—" He extended an arm overhead in a showy pose.

"Tall?" I finished his sentence.

"Yeah."

"He's more than tall," Sadie bragged. "He can run all day, and his eye-hand coordination is nothing short of precision. And his jump?"

"Just call me twinkle-toes," Leo chirped.

"Hey, no one is doing that," she insisted, employing her defensive impulse to save Leo from himself this time. Not that he needed it. Not in my company, anyway. "And Ellis can't stay. Friday's game night."

"I've got time. Like you said, we're early." I threw the ball back to Leo, eager for another opportunity to make a good impression on someone else important to Sadie.

"Yes, Mee-maw?" Leo called out in response to *absolutely* nothing. "Sure thing. Sadie's on her way." He jerked his head toward the house, and Sadie went like going inside had been her idea.

"Good game tonight, Ellis. Go, Grizzlies!" She skipped up the porch stairs and inside. Even though she was gone, I stared like maybe she'd come back.

"Hey." Leo lobbed the ball at me, hitting me squarely in the stomach. "That's my kid sister."

"Huh?" I grunted, barely catching the pass, then tried a casual dribble.

"Never mind." He stole the ball. "First one to ten wins." The ball sailed through the air and into the hoop—nothing but net. He bounced the rebound to me. "Tutoring, huh?"

"Yep," I missed my shot. "Intro to Calculus."

Leo caught the ball and made another basket. "How's that going?"

"I thought it was going okay, but I think I got fired—or she quit." My next throw hit the rim and considered going in but then wobbled out.

Leo snagged the rebound again and held it. "Yeah?"

"And I've got a test Monday, but yeah, seems so." I shrugged.

"Yeah." He took an easy lay-up.

"You knew?"

"She might have mentioned something." We kept up our basketball back-and-forth. Leo never missed a shot.

"Ah. I guess there's some guy. Maybe tutoring me is a problem." That thought had just occurred to me, and it seemed like the knowledgeable Leo might have some insider information if some sulky sophomore had a problem with his dance date teaching calculus to the senior quarterback. Then again, that kind of attitude wasn't something Sadie Klein would ever cave to. Not ever. Still, it couldn't hurt to pry a bit.

"A guy?"

"Yeah, we didn't go into it. Didn't want to pry. Her fall formal date?"

Leo stutter-stepped and the basketball rolled off his fingertips for an awkward air ball. He chased the Spalding down. "Her *date*?"

Leo's obvious surprise brought me hope. "You didn't know?"

"No. I didn't." He looked toward the house, then to the horizon. It was nearly sundown.

"Oh, I thought maybe you would." I kept an even tone despite my growing relief. I *knew* big brother Leo would know, and suddenly I didn't feel so bad. Nah, I wasn't out of the game yet. "I should be going." I took one more shot. Nothing but net. "And *you* should definitely go out for the basketball team."

"Yeah? You know where we live, right?" Leo rolled his eyes. "They abide us in the drama club, chorus, the art studio. Yearbook, maybe. Not sure they're ready for people like me in athletics."

I scoffed, reaching my truck. "Aw. Come on, Leo. I think you're wrong. Jews play sports." I'll admit I appreciated Leo's raucous laugh. Of course, I recognized his real point, but I needed him to know I didn't care—about any of it. I was an ally, no matter what, but I hoped he'd be one too.

"Hold up, Dutch." Leo cleared his throat. "Hey, Shorty!" he yelled.

We heard her before we saw her. "Seriously, Leo? You've been taller than me for like *two* minutes. Are you really trying to make that nickname stick—oh, hi, Ellis. I thought you'd left." She had taken her hair down and tucked a curl behind her ear now. Dizziness hit me, but I held the open driver's side door for support.

"What's up?" she asked Leo.

"Dutch and I were talking, and he mentioned he has a test. When's that test, Dutch?"

I managed to sputter the word, "Monday."

"Monday, right. So, we thought you should meet up again for tutoring after that test to see how he does. When would that be, again?" He raised his brows at me.

"Wednesday," I squeezed out.

"Yes, Wednesday. At Midge's, right?"

I nodded.

"Sure. I can do that." She spun on her heel, hurrying back to the porch. "It's time, Leo. Bye, Ellis."

"Bye, Sadie Jane." I got my bearings.

Leo smirked and murmured out the side of his mouth, "You're welcome."

"Thanks, Leo. Math is—tricky." We shared a knowing grin.

"Yeah, she is. See you around." Leo bounced the ball twice and headed in for the start of what Sadie had called Shabbos. I took off for another kind of Friday night ritual, relieved to know I still had a math tutor. Not only that, but I also guessed my math tutor didn't have a real date for the fall formal. *Score.*

Eleven

SADIE

present day

By morning, I had systematically outlined every possible scenario that *could* have occurred the night before. A few of the more enjoyable fantasies ran on a loop. A good romance novel is perfect for fanning those fantasy flames. Still, in the end, I decided, except for one less likely version where my house caught fire (speaking of flames), the real-life incident represented the *worst* case. My stomach hurt, but not so much that I needed to cancel breakfast at Midge's Diner, even if it was a café now—and even if it meant more time spent with Tristan.

The truth was, I needed to stay on top of Tristan, in a metaphorical sense, if I had any hope of getting free from Pembroke Industries. Dutch's words rattled around in my brain, and they didn't help with the brewing nausea. *I'm not sure you fully appreciate the extent Pembroke Industries will go to keep proprietary information in-house and money-making assets in line.* The fact I had no hope of cutting ties to the corporation regarding my past work was something I had made peace with long ago. But if I could extricate this latest development, a project Pembroke had no real interest in anyway, it secured me the freedom to go elsewhere, or better yet, out on my own—shake my moneymaker for a new audience, as it were. But there was the rub. While money was of little—okay, *less* interest to me—it proved to be the end-all, be-all for Pembroke Industries. This meant they might not only care about that proprietary information in the rearview but also any future ingenuity my puzzle-loving mind happened upon. With my desalination innovation in my back pocket, walking away from my past accomplishments became an easier proposition, not only for the do-gooder in me. Sometimes money could be made in altruism, but I was willing to bet the ability to sleep easily would be worth any price paid.

"You look awful," Tristan spoke out the side of his mouth, barely looking over the top of his menu at an exhausted me, slipping into a chair across from him at Midge's Café.

I looked at my calico sundress, scuffed cowboy boots in full view under the ruffled hem that stopped at my knee. "If this is your idea of *wooing* me—well, you might want to look up the word. I'm guessing it doesn't mean what you think it means. Coffee, please." I flagged down a silver-haired server hurrying through the busy dining room that, in my youth, had been packed with Naugahyde booths and Formica tables with a backlit slotted menu. Now, tables were whitewashed wood with charming, mismatched chairs, and specials scrolled on chalkboards included menu fare like "organic avocado toast" and "sriracha and herb free-range frittata."

"A coffee? What kind, sweetie?"

"Kind?"

"Americano, a pour-over, cold brew, flat white—"

"Let's get her a redeye," Tristan cut in to save me in my sleepless haze. "I think she needs it but leave her some room, and she'd prefer two percent. Oh, and do you have the chunky brown kind of sugar? She doesn't use much, but that's what she likes. And I'll take another."

"Sure thing, doll." She winked at Tristan, nudging my shoulder. "He's a keeper."

I opened my mouth to correct her, but she sped away, leaving me to squint at the blond pretty boy sitting opposite me.

"See? I can woo." He brushed his hair aside, and his Colgate grin distracted me. I found my left hand in his right. "Where's the ring?"

"Dammit, I forgot it." I pulled from his grasp. "I'm sorry. I didn't get much sleep—"

"I'm not asking for it. I just thought maybe you'd—"

"Wear it? You thought I'd be wearing it because I'd had a change of heart and decided I do want to marry you. Because why not? You're a great get, after all, and a weirdo nerd-girl in her thirties should be happy to settle for a loveless marriage, especially when it comes with so many commas and zeros. Relieved even. Grateful my future could be less bleak, not so lonely, absent the otherwise inevitable cat hair. Why not concede marital bliss for—what? Tolerable companionship? Right? Why should I—hell, why *would* I strive for genuine happiness when *meh* is offering itself up so freely?" I grabbed my napkin, letting the silverware fall out of it, crashing onto the tabletop.

"Whoa." A wide-eyed Tristan glanced around to see if anyone had noticed my rant, then leaned in with a serious face. "That's a joke, right, Sade? You're—you're not in your *thirties,* are you?"

I glared, but when the telltale sting of unusual tears prickled behind my eyes, my gaze shot to my lap. I wasn't sad. I was tired and angry and maybe—a little sad, but I'd be damned if I let Tristan Pembroke take any credit, or worse, *glory* in seeing me in a weakened position.

"Oh, no. No, no, no, no, Sade. Please don't cry. I was kidding. It was a *joke.* Why are you—Please don't." He scrambled to free his silverware, offering me his napkin as a substitute for a chivalrous handkerchief he didn't have on his person.

"Shut up, Tristan. I'm not crying—"

"Sadie Jane Klein." My name bellowed across the café in a husky octave you wouldn't expect from the petite woman responsible for it. I bolted out of my chair as a tiny, apron-clad frame rushed me.

"Midge," I sighed in her fierce embrace. A casual hug wasn't something I typically tolerated—from anyone. But Midge knew that and clung to me, anyway. And there was nothing typical about Midge Toogood. "How are you?"

Midge Toogood was the proprietor of Midge's Café née Diner and my late grandmother's best friend. With her lavender-tinted beauty parlor hair and hot-pink lipstick, she didn't look her nearly seventy-eight years. Funnily enough, the pink and purple combination had been her hallmark look for as long as I could remember.

"Well, I'll be. It's like old home days. You walk in here today, and yesterday I saw—"

"Ellis?" I pulled away with a cautionary squeeze to her absent biceps and gave a subtle head shake, hoping she wouldn't say the names Dutch or Holland in front of Tristan.

She cocked her head and *hmphed*, "But who cares about that ne'er-do-well."

I replied with a woeful smile—relieved she had a keen sense of telepathy but sad to hear her say anything contrary about the unnamed man, even when she hadn't meant it. I moved on with the unavoidable introductions.

Already on his feet, Tristan appeared abnormally pleased to make a new acquaintance, particularly in such a backwoods coastal town. He wrapped his arm around me and mugged like there was a camera nearby, calling himself my "beau" after kissing Midge's hand with too much flair. "I've been telling my girl here she needed to bring me to her hometown."

"Not your girl," I growled.

"And Cannon Cave is—"

"Canaan Cove," I corrected.

"Canaan Cove is just simply a delight. Charming, actually. Something out of a storybook. And the Motor Lodge? Well—"

"Sadie's *beau* is staying at the Motor Lodge?" Midge frowned while her head bobbed to me, then Tristan, and back again.

Tristan squeezed me tighter. "Sadie's nothing if not old-fashioned. One of the things I like best about her."

"*Like* best?" The old woman didn't hide her skepticism.

"Stop talking now, Tristan."

"Right. Oh, look, coffee. Thank heavens." He returned to his chair.

"Enjoy your breakfast." She reached up to hug me again, but more to speak in my ear. "We need to catch up. And soon. Let's make it this evening. Say, five o'clock?" It wasn't a question. Midge meant business.

"Yes, ma'am. Five o'clock." I kissed her cheek, and she left me to my redeye, two percent, and chunky brown sugar.

I wouldn't say all was right with the world, but the buttery biscuits and strong coffee made huge improvements, giving me the *oomph* to move ahead with my plans for a permanent return to Canaan Cove. While in good shape, the dust-bunnies and some peeling paint aside, my grandparent's house needed some updates. I had the time, the funds, and the do-it-yourself skills for the job. It would be a good time-filler while I waited for Tristan to see to his end of our deal. But first, I needed to get him out of the storybook Canaan Cove and on to his fictional grief so Mommy and Daddy would release his fortune and then my patent.

"Don't send me back there, Sade," Tristan groaned. "Not yet anyway. Show me around this enchanting town. I'll pay anything for the nickel-tour."

The bright sunshine and my full belly did beg me for a stroll, and I admit I was curious to see what other changes had been made alongside Midge's diner-turned-café and Cecil's upgraded Feed 'n' Seed on the edge of town. And though I would never admit it aloud, sometimes the frivolous antics of Tristan Pembroke were just the right antidote to a bad mood.

Picturesque shops with quality garb, touting considerable price tags, dotted Main Street. Hand-painted signs advertised it was "always wine o'clock at sea" and "my other electric car is a golf cart." The sayings were varied and a bit clunky, but nestled around cashmere throws, fresh-scented candles, and nautical figurines. The merchandise pointed to a decidedly different clientele than the one I had left behind more than a decade ago.

One of my favorite spots that hadn't changed, save a fresh coat of paint, was Canaan Cove Cones, an old-timey ice cream parlor. The black and white penny-tile and milk glass pendants remained, and I wished I'd forgone that third biscuit so I could stomach a scoop of rocky road. I'd definitely be revisiting another day.

When we'd explored both sides of the four-block downtown district, we ended back at my truck just before the meter expired. About to say goodbye to Tristan, I could have sworn I saw a stranger, two parking spaces away, snapping a picture of us standing closer than seemed necessary. The man jerked in a quick turn, nearly colliding with a cast iron light pole in his getaway.

"What was that?" I peered over Tristan's shoulder.

"What was what?"

"That guy. He just took our picture."

Tristan didn't bother to look. "I don't think so."

"I'm pretty sure."

"Don't be silly. Why would someone—I mean, look at this place. It's a picture-postcard—totally photo-worthy. Don't be paranoid."

"Which is it, Tristan? Am I silly or paranoid?"

"Could we not fight, please? This has been nice. Fun. *Easy.* Not a bad way to live a life, incidentally. You might keep that in mind. Future reference. In the meantime, here." He pulled an envelope from the inside of his on-brand seersucker jacket.

"What's this?"

"Paperwork."

My heart skipped a beat, thinking the natty dresser had been holding out on me all morning. Had my fellow schemer already procured the rights to my pet project?

"For the ring. I told you it's yours. This proves it, plus there's an appraisal and an insurance policy. It's the least I could do. And I'm sorry if I put you in a spot the other night." He flashed a smile that would melt the panties off a more gullible woman, but something new tinged it. Disappointment? Defeat? Tristan's usual spark had dimmed.

"Which night?" I joked...sort of.

He huffed. "Yeah. I've been a jerk. Sorry."

"Yeah." I likely mirrored Tristan's letdown, but I didn't want to argue.

His chest broadened, and just like that, his inner light brightened. "I'll see you 'round, Sade."

"Not if I see you first, *Tris.*" And for the second time in less than twenty-four hours, a hunky man, who was not my brother, kissed the top of my head as if he were.

The truck A/C felt good in the heat of the day, but I had barely gotten any real relief when I turned into my driveway I found myself greeted by the sullen charm of Dutch Holland. He rose from his perch on the front porch steps with a timid wave and a short-lived grin. I drove by to park around the back, propelled by demon butterflies colliding with what remained of my morning's biscuit binge.

Twelve

SADIE

present day

DUTCH PACED ON THE walkway when I opened the front door. I'd taken my sweet time coming from the backend of the house, unsure how the next part would go. His brief one-handed grip on the back of his neck gave away his faked, calm demeanor.

"Smart," I said, leaning in the doorway.

"What's that?"

"Keeping your B and E to the nighttime hours. More likely to get caught in the daylight."

He exhaled a chuckle and eyed his shifting vegan boots on the flagstone. "I shouldn't have done that. Come into your house without an invitation. I apologize. It was completely out of line, but I—"

"Apology accepted." Why his apology surprised me, I couldn't say, but I knew he deserved one too. "I shouldn't have made any judgments or assumptions—one way or the other—about your reasons for being here. It's your hometown and—"

"No need," he cut in with a firm nod that indicated we were past it now. Another rejected apology.

"Is that why you came?" I asked with an intent interest in my fingers.

"To make apologies? No."

"Oh. To get one then?" I raised an inquisitive brow. "Because you never give me the chance to—"

"Definitely not." His brow furrowed with his gruff denial.

"Then, why?"

He fidgeted again, and I couldn't tell if he was searching for an answer or wondering if he should share the one he already had.

"Not sure I should say now."

"Well, now you gotta tell me."

He paused again, eyes skyward. "I heard—I heard you cried—at Midge's, and crying's not something I've ever known you to do. I mean, I've never seen you—"

"*God.* This town." Not much exasperated me more than Canaan Cove's gossip mill. It spun fast, flinging hearsay far and wide, often with baffling and unfortunate accuracy. Other times it got it entirely wrong.

"Did you? Did Tristan make you cry?" Dutch asked the questions to the ground, and his earnest concern annoyed me *and* stoked those inner butterflies again.

"Two things, Ellis."

He may have bit back a dig, but I relaxed when he found his way to look at me.

"One. I didn't cry. And Two. Tristan never has and never *will* have that kind of—influence over me."

Dutch simply gave another solid nod, looking a bit chastened but also relieved.

"Three things, actually." I crossed both my arms and legs, focusing on the upturned toe of my boot, eager to end the confrontation. "It was mighty kind of you to come to check on me." My next moment was one of inner-panic, afraid that last statement sounded like a dismissal. I stammered a quick follow-up. "Iced tea?"

"That—that'd be nice." His shoulders dropped, and he grinned after his rush to reply.

"I should tell you, I don't make it sweet. Sacrilege for a southerner, right?"

A broader smile moved toward me. "Works fine. I don't take it sweet."

"Well, then." Our eyes locked.

"Well, then," he echoed, and for a moment, I wasn't sure we were talking about iced tea at all.

"Grab a rocker. I'll bring it out all proper-like." I motioned to the pair of weathered rocking chairs that had seen better days and added another to-do item on my fast-growing list. Dutch's snicker drew me from my mental catalog of chores. "What?"

"Nothing. Just Sadie Klein and proper-like don't quite—I mean, you're not—"

"I'm not what?" My hackles were up again, and I didn't hide them.

He sighed. "Not everything has to be a fight, you know. A personal affront? You don't have to live life on the defensive." He spoke in his quiet way with more tenderness than I knew what to do with, so I escaped to the safety of inside to fetch the tea. Of course, my time indoors prepping the glasses and situating them with the cut-glass pitcher on a tray gave me plenty of time to formulate my comeback. And while my hands may have been full, I returned, taking a verbal swing.

"Seems I can't ever get it right with you, Ellis. I'm either too much on offense or too much on defense, but in case you were wondering, I'm not too terribly concerned about what people think about the way I live my life." I'd set the tray on a small table that matched the chairs and kept my eyes on my pouring task.

Dutch stood on the porch stairs, wiggling the wrought-iron railing loose in its masonry base. "This could use some shoring up," he offered before rejoining me on the porch; he took a seat. "And it's not too bad here in the shade, but an outdoor ceiling fan might make a nice breeze and keep the bugs at bay." It seemed my guest didn't have any more to contribute on the subject of my lifestyle choices and had moved on to my fixer-upper's maintenance issues.

"It's on the list." I sat with my own glass and rocked back, enjoying a long swig of iced tea.

"Which?"

"Both, actually."

"You got a list, huh?"

"Getting longer by the minute."

"What else?"

"On my list?"

Dutch simply nodded with another sip.

"Cleaning air ducts, tightening doorknobs, changing the locks." I gave him a pointed look. "I plan to get a structural engineer out here, a friend of mine, to see what I'm dealing with before I begin major renovations."

"Major renovations? Before you sell it, you mean?"

"Sell it? Nope. I'm gonna live here. Make it my own. And with Savannah north and Atlanta farther west, I can find plenty of traffic if I start to miss it. Airplanes too. Of course, it's a digital world. I can work from just about anywhere with an ethernet cable, and I hear the fiber-optics in little ol' Canaan Cove are the latest and greatest. Who said you can't go home again?"

"Thomas Wolfe," came his matter-of-fact reply.

"*Huh*. Could have sworn it was Bon Jovi." I said it straight-faced, happy to have a drink to hide behind, but I couldn't help stealing a peek at the man displaying literary aptitude I hadn't expected. Security guard, my ass. "Anyway, utilities are all back on, so it's time to get to work. I mean, not right this minute, but—something to keep me busy while I see what happens next."

"A project."

"Yes, a big project to keep me occupied. Idle hands, you know. How about you?"

Dutch didn't hurry to answer. I'd like to think he considered the notion of idle hands, either his or mine, better yet both, but I knew a pipedream when I conjured one. Yep, a ceiling fan would be nice, maybe two. The creaking rockers weren't enough to fill the void, so I plowed ahead with precarious questions.

"Where'd your folks end up? Are they—"

"Mom and Dad are still around. They moved to the Georgia mountains to be near me as I finished my—school. Found a place on the water. A lake, but water. It wasn't far from the academy, so they could visit. When they decided to settle in, they built a place. It's the county seat, so Mom turned to civil law work. Dad taught at a university, played golf. He's retired now. It's quiet. Dad still plays golf. Mom keeps her license up-to-date, does some pro bono work, loves her garden." He showed no sign of regret or remorse about his family uprooting to be near their only child while he served a short but unjust sentence.

"You see them then?"

"Not often enough, but I'll be headed there while I'm—" Dutch stalled.

"On vacation? Vay-cay-shun. This really is a new concept for you, isn't it?"

His head bobbled. "Yeah. I could use a tutorial."

I got thirsty again.

"Guess you'll be keeping busy with your list and big project. No time for a how-to on time-outs? An R&R refresher?" What little ice remained in his glass clinked when he drained the rest of his tea.

"Well, I've got all the time there is, just like everyone else. Work hard, play hard, I say. But if I'm going to make Canaan Cove home again, I should do some exploring. Seems a few things have changed, but I could take a closer look. And I know where I'd like to start if you have some interest."

"Oh, I'm interested." He stood, making his way to the stairs.

"I didn't say where yet."

"Don't s'pose it much matters. Name the time and place."

I bit back my grin as I glided to a casual lean against a porch pillar. "I'm meeting up with Midge this evening, so after? Say eight o'clock, Canaan Cove Cones?"

"Rocky road?"

"You know my favorite flavor?"

"And your favorite color, your ATM PIN, that one C you got in college." His tone said all of that was true, but with his back to me, I couldn't be sure. One C could have been a lucky guess. Who knew the History of Modern Dance would be such a challenging course? "Eight o'clock. It's a date."

"It's a *tutoring* session with ice cream." I stiffened when he spun one-eighty, hands in his pockets.

"Oh, good. Because I haven't been on a date in a very long time. I'll need a primer on that, too."

"A good-looking guy like you. Hard to imagine your social calendar isn't full."

He lifted his chin, showing a smile and pink cheeks. "My social calendar is dusty and definitely not full. I've been career-focused lately."

I had my reasons for backing out of the energy business—a lot of digging for very little reward, being one of them. Getting Dutch to share felt a lot like that. I decided to let this round go to him and ended my probe with a polite nod. I'd delve deeper another time.

"Thanks for the iced tea."

"Thanks for stopping by." I gave a half-hearted wave, watching him turn and walk down my driveway to the road and, I presumed, the mile hike back to the Motor Lodge.

Thirteen

SADIE

present day

Midge's Diner had always been a breakfast and lunch spot, but now that it was a café, she served light dinner fare too during peak season, except on Mondays. A tarnished bell *ting-a-linged* overhead when I entered, and a gray and black tiger-striped cat greeted me with a squeaky meow.

"Shady? How in the world are you still alive?" I bent, offering him my fingers to sniff, and his motor revved as he head-butted my boot shaft. He enjoyed a gentle head-scratch while I took in the updates of the restaurant that had been a mainstay of my youth.

"Slim?" a gravelly voice beckoned.

I popped up from my squat. "Midge."

Midge clutched her apron bib. "Cheese and crackers, Sadie. You're like to kill a woman jumping out at her like that."

"Sorry." I shrugged. "And hush. Like anything could kill you. Or your cat, apparently. Shady was old thirteen years ago. What are you feeding him, and can I have some?"

"That's not Shady. Shady died eleven—no, twelve years ago." She picked up her pet. "This is Slim Shady."

I snorted. "Really?"

"No, Sadie. I just don't want anyone to know I own the world's oldest domestic shorthair. What with all the notoriety that would cause. Guinness World Records, TMZ, *Oprah*, probably—the hassle would interfere with my pickle ball." Her sarcasm came with an exasperated headshake.

"Glad to hear you still got some vim with your vinegar, and I meant the name. Slim Shady?"

"Well, he is. Just like Shady, but skinnier. And Skinny Shady is a mouthful. Isn't that right, Slim?" They purred in each other's ears, and I felt it best to end the cat conversation there. The moniker was, evidently, a happy accident.

I explored the new-to-me dining room with the attention I hadn't given it earlier in the day. Everything was charmingly rustic, with shiplap walls decorated with works for sale by local artists: photographs, watercolors, and small oil on canvas. A sprawling chalkboard hung at the far-end, advertising the daily and decidedly gourmand menu.

"What can I get you?"

"Gee, I don't know. Looks awfully fancy."

"Your turn to *hush*. It's not fancy. It's organic and fresh and not deep-fried—except for the parmesan truffle fries, which frankly are the yummiest thing we offer."

"You still make your egg salad?"

"Uh-huh. And I suppose you'll be wanting that on toasted seedless rye?"

My mouth watered like it did at the mention of her biscuits. I nodded. "Ooh, and some of those fries, but hold the truffle oil. It's wasted on my pedestrian palate."

"I happen to know your so-called pedestrian palate has lived in big cities all over the world, so cut the crap."

"I'm a simple girl, Midge." I sighed with a shrug.

"Sit down. You are predictable. I already made your meal. Let me grab the plate." She waved over her shoulder with her loving gruffness on the way to the kitchen.

Midge and I played catch-up over a leisurely dinner. Keeping the upper hand, I peppered her with questions, steering the conversation away from the pitfalls that could have proved troublesome. Time flew. I sat back in my shabby chic ladder-back chair, rubbing a sated belly with a fleeting thought of whether Canaan Cove had a gym I could join. My waistline might demand a membership. But I quickly moved on to other things when a lull threatened to wreck a pleasant evening. Too much room, and Midge would begin hounding me with questions I'd rather not answer.

"You know of a good handyman around?"

If anyone wondered about the origin of my less-than-lady-like sense of humor, it wouldn't take more than a minute or two with Midge Toogood to connect the dots.

"How handsy are you looking for him to be?"

"Har-har. Could be a woman—and don't make that joke. It's beneath you."

Midge took a millisecond to pout. "To be honest, so much revitalization going on around here, it's hard to find available labor. Quality labor. And college kids are headed back to school. Let me ask around."

"No worries. I've got a structural engineer coming by to make me a punch list. I can probably handle it all. I've got skills." I raised my shoulder while folding and refolding my napkin. "What else have I got to do?"

"That sounds like my cue to ask what the heck are you doing here, kiddo? And who's the Dapper Dan from earlier today, and what kind of coincidence is it that Dutch Holland appears on the scene all broody and handsome at the same time?"

Dammit. Snared at the two-hour mark. "People can be both broody and handsome at the same time. They're not mutually exclusive traits."

"Not what I meant, and you know it. Now spill."

I had learned from sharing the Tristan Pembroke scheme with Dutch and my brother Leo how questionable the plan sounded when said aloud. I kept that part to myself. As far as Midge knew, I was in-between projects at the moment—a true statement—and Tristan was someone with whom I worked—also true—and he had, on occasion, implied he'd like our relationship to—evolve. Vague, but also technically true.

"But I have no interest in pursuing any sort of romantic relationship with Tristan."

"Certainly not with Dutch in pinching distance," Midge added, like it was obvious and commonly known.

"*No.* Wait, what?"

Midge stood, collecting my empty plate. "Still, huh?"

"Still—?"

"Fifteen years on, and you still can't admit you're hung up on that boy?"

"*Pfft.*"

"You mean to tell me you *aren't* hung up on that boy?" For an old woman, she could roll her eyes with the agility of a tween.

"I mean to tell you he's not a boy anymore."

"Whew." The old woman wilted in her seat. "Tell me about it."

"Right?" We both pondered Dutch Holland's "maturity" for a long, silent, almost reverent moment.

"Come on. I wash and you dry while you tell me all about the latest in geotechnical engineering. We'll save the love life scrutiny for a porch rocker and moonshine night."

"*Ha.* Right. Like I'd fall for that—again. Fool me once. You keep your demon liquor to yourself, granny grunt. I'll BYO, thank you very much."

Midge howled as she scurried to the kitchen with me close at her heels.

A half-full dishpan waited to get washed, the remnants of a few late lunches. We worked at a snail's pace, not wanting the finished task to end our time together. Neither of us would admit it, but we needed an activity, a physical distraction, to keep our conversation flowing. I loved my time with Midge, but it couldn't help but remind me of my grandmother and the time I'd never have with her again. It wasn't difficult to imagine Midge felt the same, and it made the whole interaction bittersweet.

She had rinsed the last plate and stacked it on the few I had left to dry. The pause signaled a turn to a quiet sincerity neither of us would ever claim as a regular personality trait. "It's mighty fine—your moving back into the bungalow. They'd be happy about that."

The growing lump in my throat kept me from speaking and slowed my drying hands, too.

"I sure do miss her. Every damn day. But seeing you standing here in my kitchen, well, you could be her fifty years ago. Tall and pretty and tough as—"

The brass bell chimed at the café's front door, and not a moment too soon.

"Ah, *hell.* I forgot to lock up. I swear. Who needs avocado toast at eight o'clock on a Monday night? Excuse me, sweetheart." She squeezed my wrist, reminding me I had dishes to dry, and hurried through the kitchen and out to the dining room to shoo away the would-be customer.

Tears were not my thing and certainly not twice in one day. I lifted my chin with a deep inhale, sliding the dish towel through my loose grip a few times before finishing my chore. The clatter of the last plate disguised the start of Midge's faraway cackle. Draping the towel on the edge of the stainless sink, I wiped my hands down the front of my borrowed apron and went to see what—or who amused my old friend.

By the time I pushed through the swinging door, Midge wasn't the only one in stitches. Dutch, nearly doubled over with hushed laughter, had the old woman clinging to his brawny forearm, howling a bit louder when she saw me. Despite my misgivings about whatever I had interrupted, the rowdy scene made me smile, more so when the duo struggled to rein in their hysterics. Dutch straightened up first, clearing his throat and knuckling away a tear at the corner of one eye.

"Hi, Sadie Jane," he greeted me, still settling himself, barely making eye contact. "You look nice this evening."

I looked down at the damp smock while tucking a wayward curl behind my ear. The humid kitchen had encouraged my already unruly hair to go wilder still. "It's a stinky wet apron, Ellis. And my hair is—"

Midge exploded with more laughter she'd tried to hold back. "See? Told you." She poked his arm.

Dutch had the good sense, to flatten his grin, but it didn't appear anyone planned to let me in on the joke. I untied the strings at my waist, pulled the neck strap over my head, and tossed the work-garb into a laundry bag of other soiled linens. Head held high, I joined them near the front door.

"What brings you here tonight, Dutch?"

"Thought Sadie and I had a date. At eight." He eyed the fancy-looking watch clasped to his wrist.

Midge made a throaty noise of approval.

"A tutoring session," I reminded him, enjoying his pink cheeks.

"Right. Tutoring." His hands found the back pockets of his jeans when he glanced at Midge.

"Tutoring? Like the old days? Still trying to get a handle on calculus, Dutch?" she snickered. "I always thought you were so brave to go to a student two years younger for help in advanced math. Sure, Sadie was a prodigy and all but still—mighty courageous of you."

His blush darkened a shade, but his eyes locked on mine. "Sadie was the smartest person I knew, so, I was no dummy. Plus, she had first-rate stealth skills for sneaking free pie from you, Midge."

I might have reddened when he confessed my crime, but I couldn't pull my gaze from his to see Midge's reaction to hearing about the repeated petty larceny.

"Is that so?" Midge groused as she stepped between us to reach the door. "It's kinda cute how you two schemers thought you were getting away with something when you weren't really fooling anyone."

An alarm went off in my head.

"Well, the kitchen's closed. You'll have to get your sweet treats elsewhere tonight." The bell jingled as she gestured to the sidewalk in a not-so-subtle goodbye.

"Ice cream," Dutch murmured.

"What's that?" she asked.

"We're getting ice cream. Rocky road," he spoke louder, and we both jerked back to Earth after our quiet trip down memory lane.

"Sounds messy," she mumbled.

I squinted at the woman like she spoke a foreign language. "Messy?"

"What with the melting in all this heat." She wagged her finger from me to him.

I stiffened at her insinuation; my mouth hung open a beat or two. "Good night, Midge." I hurried out into the muggy night air, hoping Dutch didn't recognize the woman's teasing. It was something like déjà vu.

"Dutch. Always a pleasure. Oh, and Sadie, I'll get you the number for the handsy-man."

"*Handy*man," I corrected with a glare.

"That's what I said." Midge swiped a hand at me. "G'night, y'all," Midge sing-songed and closed the door with a loud clunk of the bolt lock.

Dutch and I stood still in the glow of the café's lantern sconce but flinched when a hidden Midge flipped the switch, leaving us in the dark quiet of the small coastal town that rolled up its sidewalks early on a Monday, no matter the season.

Fourteen

SADIE

present day

I BLAMED THE OVERSTUFFED sandwich and parmesan fries for the tension in my gut, but I knew the real cause. Midge's insinuations needed to get out of my head, and the nervous schoolgirl in me needed to get out of my way.

"Ready for that rocky road?" Dutch blurted.

My eyes adjusted to the late twilight, noticing his own stilted, deer-in-headlights look. That helped. I didn't want to be the only one walking on fifteen-year-old eggshells.

"Absolutely." We took the first steps in the two-block walk to Canaan Cove Cones. "Oh. So at this point, you could—hold my hand."

Dutch came to a hard stop and opened his mouth to speak but didn't.

"*Pfft.* I mean, if this were a *date*. Which it's not. It's a tutoring session, so we can—skip that part. But for future reference, if you're on a date, you could, at a moment like this—hold my—*her* hand." I chided myself for the lack of finesse and took a deep breath, leaving my student in my wake.

I slowed, hearing the shuffle of hurried feet behind me. "Sadie?" He reached my side, and we fell into an easier gait. "I think maybe I should confess something."

My stomach tightened again. A confession didn't sound like something I wanted to hear. A confession sounded serious.

Confessions made for a hostile date environment, even if it was just a practice run. No, a confession didn't sound good at all.

"What's that?" My breezy tone belied everything happening in my insides.

"Well, it might not sit too well with you. The way you're so forthright, upfront about things."

"Obnoxiously frank?" Blood throbbed in my ears; fists clenched at my sides. Our pace slowed further.

"Candid, I'd say."

"Get on with it, Ellis."

"Right. So—" he stalled again.

I waited while Dutch fumbled for the words.

"So, back in high school—"

I relaxed a fraction. "High school?"

"Yeah, back then, I—well, I didn't need a calculus tutor."

I stifled a laugh, sounding like a rooting animal.

"No, really. I didn't. I—"

"I know, Ellis."

"What do you mean, you know?"

"I *know*. I knew then."

"You did?"

"When on the first day, at my feeble attempt to explain the Fundamental Theorem of Calculus, you asked, '*Oh, so not only does it establish a relationship between integration and differentiation, but it also guarantees that any integrable function has an antiderivative?*' I pretty much figured you had a better-than-average grasp on *Intro to Calculus*. But *gosh*, you were cute." I choked back another laugh. "Anything else you wanna get off your chest?" To save the man some pride, I kept my eyes forward.

"No, I don't s'pose so."

And just as I recognized the relief in his voice, I found my hand in his. Our fingers laced, and he offered a gentle squeeze while my inner sixteen-year-old swallowed hard with a giddy grin.

The short-lived handholding ended when we reached the ice cream parlor, and Dutch rushed to open the door for me. A less charming, electronic chime sounded as we entered the bright white lights of the vacant shop. Bistro tables sat empty, and no one tended the gleaming glass freezer case or occupied the soda fountain stools at the stainless service counter. I scurried to the ice cream dipping cabinet to study the options in case rocky road wasn't among them.

"Good evening, folks. Name's Jeremiah. What can I do ya for?" Despite the jaunty vernacular, the bowtie, and vintage soda jerk hat, the man entering from the back room wasn't a man at all. As a matter of fact, given a chance, I'd bet good money he wasn't old enough to be bar mitzvahed yet. Of course, that couldn't be true, but young people looked younger every day.

"One scoop, rocky road, on a sugar cone for me, please."

"Good choice. And for you, sir?"

"Mint chocolate chip. One scoop. In a bowl." Dutch nodded, reaching for his wallet. "It's not green, is it? The mint ice cream? Didn't used to be."

"No, sir. Made with genuine mint extract and no artificial coloring." Jeremiah dug in to make my cone. "So, you folks are locals, then?"

I answered yes at the same time Dutch replied no. The confusion halted the scooping, and the youngster waited for an explanation.

"We lived here a while ago," I clarified.

"A long while," Dutch added. I didn't understand the addendum, but the ice cream scooper seemed satisfied.

I pulled out my phone and the cash I'd tucked in its case. "You don't have to buy my ice cream. I've got my own." I fumbled to free my dollar bills to prove it but got distracted by the notice of a voicemail on the screen. Leo had called.

"Buying your ice cream seems like pretty basic date etiquette. No?"

I didn't respond.

"Everything all right over there?" Dutch took the cone Jeremiah held out and handed it to me.

"Yes, sorry. Voicemail." I took my dessert.

Dutch's jaw clenched for a microsecond. "You need to check it? If it's work-related, I don't mind if you need to—"

"Nope. It's just Leo. Besides, checking voicemails, texts, or emails on a date is bad form. Like *really* bad form. FYI."

"Now, I think I should be taking notes." He joked while paying the bill. When he picked up his cardboard-bowled scoop, he caught me gaping at my phone.

With a sheepish headshake, I tucked it back in my dress pocket. "It's just two calls from him in two days, that's—"

"Your favorite number. Twice." He held up two fingers. "You should eat that before it melts." Chocolate dribbled down the golden-brown cone.

"Aw, you just want to watch." My wink was accompanied by the falsetto yip of poor pubescent Jeremiah. Both "men" blushed, but my lingering lick was for Dutch's eyes only. He didn't stick around to encourage my teasing. No, he bolted, leaving me chuckling with the soulless *ding-dong* of the battery-operated door chime.

Dutch didn't get far and recovered quickly from my inappropriate, albeit predictable, innuendo-filled antics, but with his bowl and spoon, holding hands was a disappointing no-go. We ambled the last two blocks of the downtown district, enjoying another walk down memory lane.

So much had changed. Some business owners like Midge had adjusted with the shifting tide, and it appeared all for the better. Storefronts that sat empty years ago now contained niche retail from artisanal soaps to herb-infused oils and fancy vinegar to custom-dyed wool yarn. A wine bar, a tea shop, and a bakery added a foodie flair to the district Hollywood would love to emulate, or given how recent the transformation, maybe it was the other way around.

Our conversation flowed easily while keeping to the shallow end of things. And with every place closed for the night, the reconnaissance consisted of nothing but window peeping. We strolled to the Main Street quay. Just as the town's thoroughfare lacked many parked cars, very few boats were tethered this late in the year. Another hint we neared the end of the tourist season. If it weren't for a prickly undercurrent, it might have been my best first date ever—if it were a date, which it wasn't, of course.

"Have you missed this?" My eyes focused on the sea, but his silence brought me to his stare. "The seaside, I mean."

"Oh, uh, no. Not the ocean. It's big. I can always find it if I need it."

"You travel a lot? Where's—home?"

"I travel so much I don't really have a home," he said it like the thought had only just occurred to him, and it made me laugh. "Sounds awful, doesn't it?"

"No, well, yes, but it also sounds very familiar. I have moved around enough that I have never even signed a lease, much less bought a home. I own the bungalow—Leo and I do, but aside from that, I made it to my thirties and have never been more than a subletter. Isn't that sad?"

"Over the years, I have amassed more hotel loyalty points and frequent flyer miles than I could ever hope to use in two lifetimes." His small grin was one of resignation.

I gasped and laughed again, "You gotta use the points, Ellis. What are you doing here?"

"I'm—I'm eating ice cream. With you. And there's no place I'd rather be." He tossed his emptied cup and spoon in an aesthetically pleasing trash-and-recycling receptacle that matched the downtown's streetscape. Then we were face to face, all smiles gone. I wondered if he could hear my heartbeat.

"Do you recall that little strip of beach a couple blocks from the bungalow? A dinky dirt parking lot leads to a pathway through the dunes."

"I remember it." A fleeting grin danced across his face.

"I bet you do," I *tsked* with a gentle shove, an excuse to touch him, but it also got us walking again. We strolled back down Main Street to where our evening began.

"No, I mean only by reputation. Though I'll admit, I *imagined* visiting it a time or two."

"Yeah?" I asked.

"Never did, though." He took my hand again.

"No?"

"You?"

"Sure."

"Really?" His tone pitched a bit higher. I heard true displeasure in it, and something in me couldn't bear to let him stew.

I gave him a playful poke and rested my head against his shoulder as we wandered. "Only during daylight. And only alone. It's a good thinking spot. I'd sometimes go to talk to my mom. Silly, since I never knew her, but kids do silly things, I guess." I'd never shared that with anyone, and doing it now scared me a little.

"That's not silly. That's—"

"Anyway," I straightened quickly. "I hope it's still there. I'll be adding a visit to my to-do list."

Dutch was kind enough to let the topic go, slipping into another memory lane side street. We talked and sighed and laughed some more, recalling a simpler time. But when we reached my truck, our comfortable conversation ebbed as quickly as it had come and gone and come again all evening.

"Give you a lift to the Motor Lodge?" I didn't want the evening to end, but Dutch's reply would help me gauge where we stood. "You're still without a car, aren't you? The shared upside of big-city *and* small-town living—have feet, will travel."

"True, but Junior is giving me a lift early tomorrow back to the *Sapphire Selkie* dock. I've got a ride waiting there for me. My car's been there since—"

"Oh." My remark sounded like a muffled, gut-punched grunt. The unfortunate update knocked the wind out of me, and my hand on the driver's side mirror steadied me in the aftermath of the newsflash. Dutch's vacation was over—our time was up, and *apparently* I wasn't okay with that.

"I'd feel better seeing you home. And it seems like more Dating101 protocol, too, doesn't it? And I kinda like that walk from your house to the Motor Lodge. A mile-long stroll with nothing but the summer night noise. Wouldn't mind taking it one last time."

"Taking what?" I only half-listened.

"The walk—to the Motor Lodge—from your place."

"Okay." Distracted, I tried to imagine a scenario that would convince Dutch to change his plan to leave Canaan Cove so soon, and while I'd been known to spout off, I recognized the need for a well-thought-out argument when a situation called for one. *This* was one. And I had a very short drive to my country lane to formulate it. "Hop in."

Dutch reached for the driver's door handle.

"Forget about it, Ellis. You're not driving my truck."

"No, of course not. I was only opening the door for you. Showing off more dating skills."

"Right. Sorry. Nice work," I quipped, hoping to draw back my snappishness, but the damage was done.

Strain weighed heavy on the quiet ride. I couldn't find what my last words to the man should be—what I *needed* them to be. I worried there was no way I would ever get it right. Turning into the long drive, the nighttime light hid the bungalow's exterior wear and tear. But charm glowed from the inside, every window lit. I didn't like to walk into a dark house. The property brimmed with potential, only needing love and a bit of elbow grease.

I parked around back, recognizing failure when I caught my reflection in the rearview. The timer ran out. I lost. We sat in the dark for a beat before I took Dutch's hand for a goodbye squeeze, but a zap shot through me—a current I couldn't believe only traveled one way jolted up my limb and into my chest. The sensation forced me out of the truck. I needed air, and I *wanted* Dutch Holland.

When I reached his side of the Ford, he too had sprung from his seat, waiting with the familiar one-handed grip of his neck. The dauntless teen liberated herself from the tentative one. Or maybe the grown-up finally found her way to the front. "I could joke about dating tutorials or make an indecent proposal because we probably won't ever see each other again. Though I don't know if I could actually—well—or maybe I just *do* something instead of saying something—because I'm *always* saying something—and because a part of me feels like you're still the stoic football guy and I'm the starry-eyed nerd-girl, but we're not, we're adults." The word salad tumbled out of me fast and breathy.

Dutch, with his back to the closed passenger door, straightened. Despite the dark, I read the confusion as it crossed his face. "I'm sorry, what are you—?"

I stepped closer, toe-to-toe with the man. Heat radiated. "I think you should kiss me. I mean, I want you to, and I think you want to too, so—you should." I would have done about anything for a dose of oxygen at that moment, but the only thing I wanted more was Dutch's lips on mine.

"Sadie Jane," he whispered my name, the name he used way back when and all the years in between fell away, but then he kept talking. "Sadie, I'm not sure that's a good idea. We've had an unusual few days after a *long* split following a difficult incident, and our Pembroke connection is—*complicated* and could be—"

"Anyone ever told you that you talk too much?" It was a criticism I'd endured my whole life but certainly not one he'd suffered.

"Uh, talk? No. Never. *Thinking* too much, on the other hand—"

I pounced with force. Hungry and awkward. Our mouths crashed into one another with a combination of lament, regret, and want that had brewed for years. Sure, the powerful teenaged angst fueled by hormones was no longer at issue, but fifteen years of experiences, *grown-up* experiences, brought a different fervor to this first kiss we should have enjoyed all those years ago but never did. I clutched his face from tiptoes, my body pushing his into the truck. His lips softened after my initial ambush, and I took advantage with a gentle tongue. A low, gratifying moan escaped him at the tender touch. He tasted like mint chocolate chip, like home, like everything I'd ever wanted.

I gasped when he pulled from my mouth, spinning us both, so I landed pressed to the truck with the weight of him leveled against me. His forehead rested on mine; our breathing labored in the quick tussle. I fought not to grab him, and he kept his hands on the truck frame, boxing me in.

"You're doing it again," he murmured, his lips an inch from mine.

"What's that?" I rasped.

"Making it hard to be a gentleman."

It was a good answer. "Do you hear that?" I asked.

Dutch stiffened. On sudden high alert, he scanned the darkness over the vehicle roof. "No. I don't hear anything."

"Exactly." With a playful tug at his shirt, I whispered, "No one is asking you to be," then I captured his mouth again to be clear. It was the kiss to ruin me for all other kisses, better than I had ever imagined—and I had imagined it more times than my ego would allow me to admit, but just as it felt like we were firing on all cylinders, I pulled back on the throttle. "Wait. Is—is there someone else? I mean, it doesn't feel like there's someone else, and I sorta asked earlier today, tried to ask, anyway, but if there is someone else, then—well, we have to stop because I'm not, I don't do that. I wouldn't do that. Never. That's not me, so if—"

"Someone else?" He kept close and cupped my cheek. "No. No, there's not someone else. There's never been—there's no one else."

"Oh, good. That's good. There's no one else on this end, either." I fiddled with the buttons on his shirt, catching my breath. "Not that there haven't been. There's been plenty. I mean, not a *lot*, you know—just the usual amount, I guess."

Dutch shook his head, grimacing. "Yeah, I wasn't asking—"

"Ah, right," I huffed, realizing my error. I lifted a sheepish grin and offered a gentle kiss as a sort of apology. He accepted it with knee-buckling tenderness, and I melted into him and the thick night air.

"Sadie Jane Klein." The words hissed from the shadows behind Dutch, who, in something like gallantry, whipped around keeping between me and the perceived threat—a threat, in younger days, I had neutralized with a rougher than necessary noogie or a vicious wedgie too many times to count.

The back porch light came to life, and my brother Leo loomed, arms crossed, *tsking* like a giant, disapproving, and—if I had my way—soon-to-be-dead man.

Fifteen

SADIE

present day

"WELL, WELL, WELL. *WHAT* do we have here?" Leo's obvious amusement did little to quell my murderous impulses. If someone unfamiliar with Leopold Klein ventured upon this tension-filled scene, they might have cowered. The six-foot, seven-inch frame hovering even taller on the steps, ironically haloed by the porch light's glow, might have scared a stranger. No, Leo was no guardian angel that night. More like a tortuous devil incarnate.

I pushed past a dazed Dutch, who kept an unnecessary protective stance, while I reared up, bent on tackling the party crasher. "What the hell are you doing here?"

Leo descended the short stairs. "Well, I had such a good time catching up with my kid sister yesterday and happen to have some comp-time due me, and my friend forced her frequent flyer miles on me, so I threw a bag together, hopped a plane, hoping to surprise you with a little visit, but then I show up here to find nothing but the house lit up like you own stock in Coastal Electric, which, come to think of it, you probably do. But when I called your mobile, it went straight to voicemail. So, I've been pacing the floors since, wondering why you only have beer and unsweet tea to drink in your house. *Unsweet tea*, Shorty?"

No one spoke in the night noise until Leo exploded again. "*Surpriiise!*" His outburst included celebratory jazz hands, and I couldn't help but squeal and bounce, launching into his arms, all homicidal intentions gone. My big brother was home.

"That's more like it." He held tight and spun us around while we squealed some more.

"I can't believe you're here." My feet found the ground, but my head buzzed with joy.

"I can't believe you're—" His wide eyes and head jerked toward Dutch standing behind me.

Almost afraid to peek, I offered my own saucer-sized eyes, biting my bottom lip. I spun one-eighty. "Ellis," the name gushed out of me. "Ellis, it's Leo." Stating the obvious was my flustered tell.

Dutch steadied himself. "I see. Hey, Leo. Good to see you." He trotted forward with an outstretched hand.

"Is it?" Leo smirked with his hearty handshake.

Dutch exhaled with an uneasy grin.

I sucked in a mini gasp, embarrassed, and shoved my giant brother, barely moving him.

"I hear you recently helped our firecracker here out of a mess of her own making."

Dutch demurred. "Right time, right place. She'd have done fine on her own."

"No question," Leo agreed. "She's a force."

"Yes, she is."

"And *she's* standing right here and *loves* being talked about like she's not." I hurried to resolve the awkward scene. "Let's go inside, boys. Get out of this heat."

Leo and I moved toward the house, but I turned to see a stock-still Dutch.

"I'm gonna head on out. Let you two catch up. I know a third wheel when I see one."

"*No!*" Team Klein chorused, one with more enthusiasm than the other. I elbowed Leo in his ribs.

"Yeah. I've got an early morning with Junior and—"

"Shoot," I murmured, grabbing Leo's arm. In the frenzy—the kiss and my unexpected visitor—I'd forgotten Dutch would be headed out of town in the morning. Out of my life. Again.

My brother read my mind. "Well, I'm going inside. New York's got summer heat, but this is a whole other breed of cat. How soon we forget." He employed a dramatic brow swipe. "Dutch." Leo gave an earnest nod before scaling the steps with a grace that contradicted his frame.

I sent him telepathic thanks, then focused on the handsome man standing in my backyard. "You gotta go?"

His chin dipped. "It's best I do."

"It is? It's best? Because I disagree."

"Sadie—"

"No, really, Ellis. I don't typically subscribe to fate or luck or destiny, but it sure does seem like providence that you and I have—reentered each other's orbits—to borrow your military school poetry. And that it happened at such an opportune moment is kind of wild. And not to be presumptuous—except you know I am, it sort of feels like there's something here, something that has maybe *always* been here and that kiss—well, it didn't suck."

A flicker in his eyes said Dutch agreed. He moved to speak, but I kept talking. "Now, far be it from me to get in the way of your work life. I know work. I *love* work. *Work* has been my life, and it sounds like it has been yours, too. So, if you have work you have to do, I understand. I get it, but if you don't—if you have the PTO and the wherewithal to take it, I think you should. I *mean*, I wish you would, and I wish you'd do it here. Screw Thomas Wolfe."

Dutch grinned his appreciation of my literary callback but gave a subtle headshake I didn't like, so I kept spewing my categorically *not* well-thought-out argument.

"And I apologize for springing that kiss on you. Okay, that's a lie, but I know it was forward and fast, but I can totally dial that back. I mean, I used to be a fracking engineer, *literally*, so I can figure out how to put the toothpaste back in a tube, right? I'm up for that challenge. I like a good chal—"

"Sadie Jane?" he interjected.

"Yeah?"

"At some point, you are going to have to let me talk."

"Am I? Right. Of course. Now?"

"Now seems like a good time."

I gestured for him to go on, sure if I spoke again, I'd only embarrass myself further.

"Two things," he teased, his sweetness making it hard to breathe, which only got worse when he continued—but not in the good way. "I think there's been a misunderstanding."

"A misunderstanding?" The question flew from my lips, but I clamped them closed just as quickly. An f-bomb went off in my head as my humiliation mushroomed. Had I gotten it all wrong? Every heated, heart-pounding, electric moment since the *Sapphire Selkie* had been one-sided?

"Yes, and that's on me. My mistake."

"Yeah, it was," I grumbled.

He squinted at me with a cocked head.

"Nothing. Go on. Misunderstanding?" I crossed my arms, waiting to hear how delusional I'd been.

"Evidently, I wasn't clear earlier."

"When earlier?"

"This evening. On Main Street, when I said I—"

"You know what?" I knocked the heel of one of my boots into the toe of the other. "We don't have to do this. You don't have to explain. I get it. Well, no, I don't get it, but—"

"Sadie, you're talking again."

"Right. Go on." I squeezed my arms tighter across my chest.

"Tomorrow? When Junior gives me a ride to the *Sapphire Selkie* dock? I'm getting in my car, and I'm coming back here."

"Here?" I peeped half an octave too high.

"To Canaan Cove, yes."

"You are?"

He nodded.

"Wait. So, you weren't stuck at all. You weren't stranded? On my wedding night?"

He hung his head. "I prefer to think of it as *not* your wedding night. And in my defense, I'd been drinking, so I shouldn't have been driving, but no, not exactly marooned."

"Huh. And tomorrow you're going, but you're definitely coming back?"

"It's been my plan for a while now. And not just because of that kiss, which definitely—didn't suck. To borrow *your* poetry."

The Earth's tilt wobbled.

"So, I'll see you again?"

"I'd like that."

"And I just said all that stuff when I didn't really need to."

"S'pose not, but I'm glad you did. I reckon when it comes to you and me, if there are things to be said, you'll likely be the one saying them."

I laughed. As usual, it was funny because it was true.

Dutch took slow steps closer, but I kept my arms wrapped around me, feeling exposed and uncharacteristically tight-lipped. "But right now, I'm going to say good night so you can have some time with Leo. You two—are a thing to see. Don't waste the opportunity." He kissed my cheek, then backed away to make a well-mannered exit.

"But you'll be back?" Awed by the exchange, my floaty brain needed confirmation.

"I will."

"Wait. You said two things. What's the second?"

He slipped his hands in his pockets, making a slow retreat farther into the dark. "You sure are pretty when you get riled."

Sweat tickled as a bead rolled down my breastbone, and the flattery made me that much dizzier.

"Yeah? Well, Ellis, you rile me."

His gaze moved to his feet. If there'd been better light, I know I'd have enjoyed his pink cheeks. "The feeling's mutual." He barely looked up before he spun in the grass to start that mile-long hike to the Motor Lodge.

I swayed in the impact of the moment. "Whoa," I called after him, "A kiss on the cheek? That's it?"

Dutch kept walking but called over his shoulder. "Thought we were putting that toothpaste back in the tube, Dr. Engineer. Good night, Sadie Jane."

"Good night." Ear-to ear, I lingered to gaze upon that fitted, eco-friendly denim as it sauntered into the darkness before I skipped to the porch stairs taking them two at a time, eager for an evening with the other best man I knew. And he happened to be my brother and my dearest friend.

Sixteen

SADIE

present day

"Leo." I pushed through the porch door, half-expecting to find him snooping on my goodbye to Dutch, but he wasn't there. I called to him again before the clatter and *thunk* of dry goods led me to the butler's pantry beyond the kitchen, and said my brother's name a third time before it occurred to me we had a problem.

"*Uh-oh.* What's wrong?" I leaned in the extra-wide door frame; my arms crossed again. This time my posture stemmed from annoyance, not insecurity. I waited.

"Wrong? What's wrong, Shorty? Besides the utter lack of acceptable beverages in this house. I swear there is at least one bottle of peach brandy tucked away in some hidey-hole here. Grandaddy always kept a little somethin'-somethin' nearby."

"Check the spandrel."

"Are you making up words, Shorty?"

"The spandrel." I scurried to the hidden cabinet under the stairs. The secret door clicked open. "Ta-dah! Peach brandy. Manischewitz. Rot-gut tequila—weird, and—wait a minute—an unopened Glenlivet, eighteen even."

"Is that good?" Leo gaped with fascination, like we had happened upon the lost Ark of the Covenant.

"Well, I prefer the oaky taste of Glenfiddich, but yeah, it's too good for you. Take the brandy." I shoved the bottle at him and hid the decent single malt for another day. Leo served a short pour, neat in a jelly jar, without an offer to me—the indicator that our "problem" had nothing to do with beverage selection and everything to do with whatever my well-meaning sibling had decided to stew about.

"Thanks, no, I'll just have a beer since I know you aren't a fan." I used my friendliest tone, sensing a firestorm brewing. Until that tempest touched ground, I'd keep the chit-chat light and incessant. "So, good flight? Nice that they have JFK non-stop to SAV now. How long can you stay? Did you get a rental? I didn't see it. Guess you parked out back for the surprise."

Leo ignored all of it. "Sadie. What are you doing?"

"It's called conversation, Leo. One person says stuff, the other person says other stuff. Words. Back-and-forth. How long have you been up in that big, bad Yankee city?"

"What are you doing with him?" All humor dissipated from the room. "What were you doing sandwiched between a truck and Dutch Holland?"

"Not much, but I was getting there." I took a big swig with a grin.

"Sadie."

"Last I checked, I'm an adult, and while I appreciate your mother hen routine, I assure you it isn't necessary. And to think there was a time when I was the one nosing in on your social life."

"Yeah? When was that?"

"Never mind," I hurried to say. No good would come from revisiting that past mistake. It was a lesson learned quickly, and I never interfered again.

Leo didn't pursue it. "It's not like you've given me a whole lot to work with, sister mine. But given this opportunity, you best believe I'll be nosing."

"What's that supposed to mean?" I turned my back on him with a sudden need to fluff sofa pillows.

"It means you cut a man loose before you ever get 'em reeled ashore."

"*Pfft.* That's not—"

"Professor Scott?"

"We worked on the same campus. Plus, he was short." I continued to beat the couch cushions.

"Cameron, the investment banker?"

"Always wore a suit, like *always*. Look at me. Is there anything about me that says Armani?"

"Chef Perry?"

"*Sous* chef Perry, and I gained fifteen pounds dating him."

"Oh, and the bartender—Kevin?"

"*Devin*," I corrected with a sigh. "Now he was nice, but not too nice, if you know what I mean."

Leo's pitying head shake irritated me in a way only my brother could manage. "What is it about smart women with horrible taste in men?"

"I have no idea what or who you're talking about, but you can take that broad brush of yours and stick it where the sun don't—"

"Sadie. Dutch was *this* close to going to jail."

Anger lit fire with a quick spark, and I realized the looming storm would rain down from me if we didn't veer from the current topic.

"He was a *kid*, and he went to military school a very long time ago."

"Probably doesn't feel so long ago for the *kid* he put in the hospital that night. The man who no doubt still walks with a limp. That's what happens when a baseball bat shatters a femur. I know that sort of thing now."

I blanched, remembering the thud, the crack, the grunt on impact. But then I had to remind myself, like I had so many times before, I wasn't even there. "Last I heard, the records were sealed, so unless you have some evidence, something other than Canaan Cove chinwag, I suggest you not jump to any conclusions because those who *do* know aren't talking, and it seemed all parties privy to it were amenable to the case outcome. And doesn't your faith have something to say about forgiveness? Most of them do."

"It's *our* faith."

"It's your faith, Leo. And until yesterday, we haven't spoken in weeks, and I've missed you, and I don't want to fight, not about booze, not about Dutch Holland, and certainly not about religion. Okay?"

"It's our heritage, Sadie. Our upbringing."

I groaned, exasperated by my brother's Pollyanna attitude. "Our heritage? We were the super nerd-girl and the queer raised by old Jews on the outskirts of town, Leo. In the rural south. And that's only because our parents died. Parents I have no memory of, and yours can't be much. Who knows what our *heritage*, as you say, would have looked like if life had gone a different way? If we'd been raised in Connecticut like our parents planned. If this had been a place that we *visited* instead of where we grew up. Yeah, our upbringing would have looked a bit different. A hell of a lot different. And it's only because Mee-maw and Grandaddy were doctors, *good* doctors, that this community abided us, but we were outsiders. Sure, we did fine. You and I, we had each other, but it's no shock the two of us bolted out of here at our first chance. I'm glad you find solace in your faith but don't cherry-pick and don't think you know Dutch Holland because you don't."

The tick-tock of the mantel clock made impressive noise in our quiet before Leo spoke again. "And you do?"

"And I do what?"

"You *know* Dutch Holland?"

"I know he's a good man. I know he does right, even when right's not easy. I know he thinks highly of you, which only makes me think more highly of him. And as of about twenty minutes ago, I know he kisses like a—"

"And I'm out. Nope. Nope, nope, nope, nope. Lalalalalala." With fingers firmly in his ears, eyes squeezed closed, my brother stopped listening, begging for it to be done. And suddenly, I had a new weapon to deploy—a relief because wedgies were definitely out of the question these days.

I grinned at his silliness, hoping we had bridged the divide. Our time was short and spending it at odds didn't sit well with me. "Okay, okay. Tell me about work, tell me about New York, tell me about your generous friend."

"She's a hot mess, and moved to Boston…" And we hunkered down on the ill-advised white sofa with our beer and peach brandy for a late-night slumber party that would include very little sleep.

It was after midnight when Leo hopped to the kitchen. "Let's play cards." He poured another jelly jar of peach brandy, then lifted the bottle in an offer to me.

"No thanks and no."

"Aw, come on. Gin-rummy. Like the old days. A dime a point. I'm feeling lucky." Leo knew exactly which drawer to find a deck of cards and a notepad filled with score tallies from years of games played.

"No thanks." I poured my own glass of water.

"Why not? You scared? Jokers and aces wild."

"That's why. You cheat."

"Shorty, you wound me." Leo collapsed on the sofa with high drama.

"You can't just go pretend a card is something other than what it is. It's not fair. You play with fifty-two cards, and each card has its stated value. Anything other than that is wrong. You know it, I know it, *everyone* knows it. Just like shuffling the deck less than seven times is wrong."

As I said it, Leo attempted a shuffle and sent cards flying.

"Oh, give me those. I'll do it." I gathered the strewn cards and began a round of fast, even shuffles, aligning the deck with two sharp taps on the glass-top coffee table between each riffle.

"Wow, you're really good at that," his tone mocked me as he leaned back with another sip.

I chose to take the compliment, no matter how he meant it. "Thanks. I play a lot of Solitaire." I continued shuffling until I reached the optimum number seven.

"Oh, Shorty," he grimaced, "that's not something you should be bragging about—and I figured. *Whew.* You need a—companion. One that doesn't require batteries." He started a booming laugh, but I cut it off with a face full of pillow.

"And no one *needs* a—*companion*, Leopold," I huffed with another pillow slam atop his head. "But they sure are nice to have around every once in a while." I grinned.

"How 'bout it," he piped in agreement and dealt the cards.

The next morning, Leo and I sat at the kitchen island, eating breakfast while I sulked because I failed to convince him to go to Midge's for biscuits. My phone rang. The name "Structural Engineer Sam" appeared on the screen.

"Ooh. This is important, Leo. Sorry."

Another alum chum from my School of Engineering days was clawing her way into the independent consulting biz, hanging out her own shingle to launch a structural engineering firm. At a time of building restoration, infrastructure renewal, and new development, her work could fill a growing hole. It was a good wager, but also a tough business, highly competitive, and male-dominated, three things I understood all too well as a female engineer in a different specialty. When I learned that she had taken the plunge into starting her own company, throwing her some business was a no-brainer no matter how small the job. As an independent contractor between projects, I knew the *what's next* feeling intimately.

I answered, "Sam. Good morning. We still on for tomorrow?"

"Hey, Sadie. Yeah, that's why I'm calling. Hate to abuse our friendship like this, and you know I appreciate the work, and I have every intention of coming to check out your house, but I'm hoping you won't mind pushing it back a week, maybe two."

"Oh, sure. Everything okay?"

"Everything might be great, actually. I got the call that might make all the difference. That one heavy-hitter, that if it pans out, could mean a lot more business, from them and others like them."

"That's fantastic. Glad to hear it. Anyone I might know of?"

"Uh, yeah. I think they've written a check or two to you, too. They're everywhere. Pembroke Industries."

"Wow. Small world."

"Probably not. They've got a Midwest project happening, and I'm not sure how they got my name, but those are my old stomping grounds, and I'm happy to travel."

"Yes, of course. Get back to me when you know more. Don't worry about my little bungalow. It's peanuts."

"No. And I'm your inspector. We'll examine it all. Foundation to attic rafters. Electrical. Plumbing and gas. With old houses, you never know. But thanks for understanding. And we need to catch up on other stuff. I'd love to hear what you're doing these days."

"Sure thing, Sam. Good luck." I ended the call with a frown.

"Who's Sam?" Leo tilted in with a leer.

"An old grad school pal. A structural engineer just starting out with a new business. Thought I might help out by offering a little inspection job."

"Hmmm. Sounds smart, ambitious, broad-shouldered with the *structural* thing, and without childhood baggage. I like the sound of this Sam."

"Well, not sure where you picked up those last two bits, and I don't know about Sam's childhood anything, but *her* shoulders are actually quite slim. So, congratulations on joining the patriarchy and perpetuating gender stereotypes, and if you can't say anything nice about Dutch, don't say anything at all."

Leo pursed his lips, showing a smidgeon of shame for jumping to conclusions. "Sorry about that, but the fact I said 'childhood baggage,' and you knew who I meant, says everything I need to on that subject."

"Excellent, then it won't come up again. Now, I have one full day with you; what are we going to do?"

Leo rubbed his temples, then took another gulp of coffee. "We're gonna start by pouring the rest of that peach brandy down the drain. Stat."

When our grandparents passed away a year and a half ago, Leo and I both changed in the wake of it, and unfortunately, it hadn't brought us closer. There was no rift, no relationship fallout, nothing like that. It was a matter of geography and new life choices. We lived farther apart, and we got busy. Poor excuses in this day and age, to be sure.

Leo decided to go to grad school to further his medical career, and that new path sent him to New York. I realized I needed to make a change, too. Doubling down to finish a Pembroke project, I looked for an exit strategy and a way to put my aptitude to better use. Nothing like an unexpected tragedy to serve as a wake-up call.

In those earliest days, before either of us had caught our breath, much less considered our career changes, Leo returned to Canaan Cove, leaving an unsatisfying life he'd barely gotten started in Charleston. I swooped in and out of town in a single day, unable to endure the minutiae of everything sudden death entailed. Things that could be handled remotely by phone and email, I tackled with speed and skill. Closing the estate was simple. Leo managed the more personal details. He quickly arranged a service before I arrived and closed up the house neither of us could bring ourselves to sell after I left.

We were both surprised to find Mee-maw and Grandaddy wished to be cremated, not typical for Jews. But their request made more sense when we learned they wanted us to scatter them in the Atlantic, laid to rest where their son and daughter-in-law drifted for eternity, though certainly not by choice. Our grandparents' ideas about an afterlife were ambiguous at best. Leo thought perhaps they were hedging their bets. I thought a return to the sea, where life began, was poetic. The debate showed a rare moment of a jaded Leo and a more quixotic Sadie, a clear role reversal. Our altered character traits must have been shock-induced, but the personality shifts were short-lived for the most part.

All this to say, Leo had seen the changes in our hometown on that last extended stay. So while I was still grappling with the Canaan Cove makeover, Leo had come to terms with it. Frankly, he didn't seem to care much at all.

"It's good, though, right? You're not changing your mind, are you? Because if you want to sell, now might be a good time."

"Sell? No, I don't want to sell. I want to stay. I want to make it mine and give you your half, of course."

"Why?"

"Because it's fair, and New York City is an expensive place to live."

"No, why do you want to stay here? Here, of all places? And I'm doing fine, thank you."

"It's quiet here. I need some quiet. It's a big chunk of land, a charming house in good shape, near the water. No one will bother me here, and I can work, travel, go, do, see, then come back here to quiet. And you can come to visit—often." My own version of returning to the sea.

Leo squinted, disbelieving.

"I know it's counter-intuitive. The opposite of everything I thought I wanted. But I've been all over the world, running from one short stay to another, seeing extraordinary things both amazing and horrible, but never really slowing down, always moving to avoid sprouting roots, I guess. Or I fear I'm missing something. Maybe hoping to find where I belonged. Turns out, I'm not sure I *belong* anywhere. So, the full-circle thing seems apropos. I've run home instead of away. I think it might be time to stay."

"You'll be alone, Sadie."

"You're alone."

"No, I'm not. I couldn't find solitude if I wanted to, and I don't. I live in constant noise, and I love it. I sing. I help make people better. I enjoy art everywhere. I am unapologetically me, and I don't have a single blade of grass to mow. It's heaven."

"They'd be so stinking proud of you."

"They'd be so happy you were moving in here."

"That's what Midge said. And did you see her place?"

"I did, but we should go by before I leave."

"Dinner tonight." A wincing smile hid my dismay at Leo's departure.

"Is there something I should know about this Tristan fellow?"

"*Ugh*. For the umpteenth time, it's business, nothing more. And everyone needs to mind their Ps and Qs." I snatched breakfast dishes and hurried to the sink.

"Who's everyone?"

I gave a pointed stare.

"Ah. The plot thickens. Kinda wish I could see the dynamic of this soap opera. All three of you in a room."

"Well, me in a room with Tristan and Dutch would be a very bad idea. Worlds would collide that I'd rather keep separate." I brushed past Leo's quizzical look. "It's complicated. And you in a room with Tristan? I'm pretty sure that much personality in a confined space would threaten more than a few laws of physics. Life as we know it might combust."

"I gotta be me, Shorty. I gotta be me." Leo echoing Tristan's own mantra proved my point. For the sake of humankind, I hoped I could keep all three men out of each other's pathways forever. Lucky for me, avoidance was one of my well-honed superpowers.

Seventeen

DUTCH

fifteen years ago

SADIE JANE HAD AVOIDED me for a week. The closer we got to the school dance, the less I saw her until the final blow, when she canceled our last tutoring session. So, unlike most Friday nights, my mind didn't go quiet when I stepped on the field. Thoughts of Sadie interrupted my usually brainless gameplay, and it showed. Sure, we still won, but it wasn't pretty, and I was tired—tired of football, tired of the wall that had gone up between Sadie and me, tired of a lot of things. And the last place I wanted to be was in a crammed-full, smelly gym getting jostled by my amped-up classmates. My head throbbed with the spinning lights and the driving beat of some Fall Out Boy song. The mix of Axe body spray and polyurethane hung like an invisible heavy cloud.

No matter which direction I veered, someone shouted my name and grabbed my sore shoulder. Apparently, I was still the man of the hour despite the close call of the game the night before, and too many fans wanted to talk to me about that late-game hit that rang my bell pretty good. I loosened my necktie and downed some sickeningly sweet punch.

I only wanted to talk to Sadie, and the dance was where she said she'd be. So, pushing my headache and growing nausea aside, I was there too. Stubbornness drove me, determined to get things back to normal—whatever normal looked like—but second thoughts came on strong, along with another wave of queasiness.

I stumbled when a couple of rambunctious headbangers in the already overcrowded space mistook the gymnasium for some kind of concert mosh pit. Giant hands grabbed me from behind and saved me from a fall, keeping me upright in the rowdy commotion.

"Whoa. Simmer down, kids. Oh, hey, Dutch." Leo, having grown another inch in the last week, squeezed my aching limb.

I winced. "Hey, Leo." I pushed past the pain, realizing my best chance at finding Sadie loomed large in front of me.

Leo spoke again, but the racket and strobes overwhelmed my senses.

"It's loud." I leaned toward him.

"You all right?"

I nodded, wondering how to ask about the giant's kid sister.

"Seen Sadie?" The giant saved me the trouble.

"No. She's here?" Shouting while faking indifference was an odd combination.

"She is."

"And—her date?" I braced for the truth.

Leo shrugged. "A red-head I'm pretty sure isn't exactly her type."

More nausea.

Leo frowned. "Sadie's here with a girlfriend, Dutch. Sadie doesn't have a date. Never did. And—she looks amazing."

I had no doubt but stayed rooted to my spot, trying to look like I didn't care, but I don't think Leo bought it.

"So—you should go find her. Like *now*." His eyes widened, and those hands that caught me a moment earlier rotated me one-eighty, then shoved.

Leo warned something about being a gentleman, but a glimpse of curls across the jam-packed room made everything stop. Sadie sipped a drink and talked to a red-headed girl I didn't know.

When another body barreled into me, I lost my cool and elbowed the oblivious assailant harder than I should have, sending him to the floor.

Frightened eyes looked up from a cowering squat; the young kid knew who hit him and flinched like he thought there'd be more punishment to come. Why? No reason other than the stereotype of high school football players. Far more fable than fact. I'd never been that guy, so why someone would think it stumped me. "Uh, sorry, Dutch. Didn't mean to—"

I offered him a hand up and a forced smile, surprised by my uncharacteristically bearish action—like I'd fallen for my own hype. I patted his shoulder in apology, aware people noticed the altercation. "No problem," I shouted, not wanting to get stuck in any kind of back-and-forth that risked me losing track of Sadie, still several yards and dozens of dancing teens away from me.

"Great game last night. Hard hit that last play." Exactly the kind of rehash I didn't want to encourage.

"Thanks." I lifted my chin and sidestepped to squeeze through the crowd. My head-pounding resumed when I spied Sadie as she walked away. Her curls grazed her bare shoulders, and a dark dress that met the back of her knee sparkled in the swirling party light. Yelling out her name was another unusual move, but it's what I did. "Sadie Jane."

She stiffened straight before spinning to face me. The timid smile and wave that followed felt similar to that late fourth-quarter hit, but it was a personal foul I'd endure anytime, anywhere. I stepped toward her as she head-gestured to a mat Velcroed to the wall. We found a spot out of the way of the busy entrance and the hall corridor's bright lights.

"Hi."

"Hey, Ellis." She waved again.

"You look really pretty tonight."

She cupped her ear. "I can't hear you," she shouted.

"Your dress," I pointed at her. "It's—I like—it works," I stammered.

"It *works*?" She looked down her front, then squinted at me.

I nodded. *Words, Dutch. Use words.* "You're beau—

"*Duuutch*!" An arm hooked around my neck, and someone's knuckles bore into my already aching skull.

Stars of pain exploded behind my eyelids, and my recently swallowed party punch revisited my mouth.

"Who saw my boy QB-one splayed out on the field last night? Times like that, I'm glad I'm number two, man." Junior Ford, one of my best friends, was a year behind me and apparently glad for it that night. Next year he'd be the man of the hour, and we figured we'd meet up again when we both played for UGA. *Go Dawgs!*

I pushed him off with a rough shove, then hurried to restrain my quickening temper.

Junior eyed Sadie in a way that made me clench my fist. When he twisted back to me, something he read on my face sent him on his way. "Go, Grizzlies!" Junior roared, flexing like a bodybuilder as he walked toward the dance floor.

I made a mental note to apologize to him come Monday.

"Are you okay, Ellis?" Sadie took hold of my wrist, and I wondered if she noticed my racing pulse.

"Yeah. It's just so loud in here."

"How hard did you get hit last night?" Genuine concern crinkled her eyes.

"Not very."

"Are you—sure?"

"I think I'd know."

"Yeah, well, my grandparents are doctors—"

"So that makes *you* a medical professional?" I barked.

She stepped to me when, I'd guess, most would shrink away. My ratcheting anger didn't deter her, even as it confused me. "*No.* But I hear things, and I thought *I* was the irritable one." She tightened her grip.

"I'm sorry. Sorry, Sadie. Really." Of all the people to lash out at, she should have been the last.

Neither of us moved.

"Hey, you know I'm wearing this dress—not my usual get-up—and you sure do look handsome in that coat and tie, and we're at a dance, so maybe you should—ask me. To dance, I mean. If you want. Spoiler alert. I'll say yes."

Leave it to Sadie to find the words when I couldn't.

"Sadie Jane, would you like to—"

"I love this song." She pulled me toward the crowded dance floor before I finished asking.

The next moments were a mix of fast and slow, colorful spinning lights, a loud but slow song, and too many bodies, but the only one that mattered was the one pressed to mine. Her arms clung around my neck, like other girls had done before, like other couples around the gym did now. Sadie looked up with a tentative grin, but it was all wrong. I'd seen my parents dance at the golf club, in our kitchen, on the patio by our pool. They were weird like that—or *great* like that—I hadn't decided which, but it was different from how everyone else in the gym did it.

I stepped back, and a question flickered across her face. Those hazel eyes darkened. Placing her hand on my sore shoulder, I took her other in mine while I settled my other palm on the small of her back, gently pulling her close. She softened, except for the squeeze of my hand. We exhaled at once as she nestled her head to my chest like it always belonged there and swayed until the end of the song. It was the best three minutes of my life.

"Ellis?" Her warm breath directly in my ear gave me a moment's freedom from the pulsing headache. "Would you take me home?"

I nodded; our cheeks pressed so we could hear one another. "I need to tell—ask—tell Leo."

She silently agreed but kept close for another beat before the dance floor erupted with another moshing number. We parted, her heat gone, but we still held hands, searching for her brother. I'm not a religious guy, but I gave thanks for Leo's stature. He was easy to spot.

Sadie tapped him on his shoulder.

"Shorty," he shouted, stooping to pick her up but stopped when he saw our linked hands. "Oh my," he gasped.

"Ellis is going to—"

"Hey, Leo. Mind if I take Sadie home? She says she's ready to go, and I could get out of this noise. You okay with that?"

The siblings shared a telepathic moment I couldn't decode.

"Yeah, sure. Helps me out, actually. Some guys from basketball tryouts this week invited me to hang. Thought I might go, so—"

"Wait. You're going where?" Sadie's face flashed alarm, and she tried to pull from my grip, but I held tighter.

Leo scowled.

I tugged Sadie's arm. "That's great. Leo. See? Told you."

"Told him what, Ellis? What did you tell him? Leo?" Sadie's gaze bounced between her brother and me.

"Goodnight, Shorty. Straight home, you hear." He waggled his finger, then guarded his mouth like he told a secret. "Then again, what do I know about straight?" He winked and snickered at himself.

"Leo!" Sadie's turn to gasp, but hers disapproved of Leo's humor.

"Goodnight, Leo. Thanks. For everything." I shook his hand and led his sister through the raucous mob that bounced in time to the bass-thumping music. Sadie never let go as we inched our way to the edge of the dance floor, then out of the gym. Even in the glaring fluorescents of the hall, students mingled. Giggling, talking, dancing, teenagers clogged the corridor in front of glass display cases, congratulating students with trophies, ribbons, and medals for all sorts of sports. My name among them.

"I'm gonna stop in the bathroom. Too much punch. Meet you in a few minutes?" She spoke too loudly in my ear as we stood in a sea of people that flowed in both directions, the girls' restroom on one end of the hall, the boys' version on the other.

"Sure. I'm gonna head this way." I pointed behind me, thinking I'd kill for some ibuprofen. "I'll meet you right here." We walked away from one another but kept touching until our fingers could no longer reach. Sadie disappeared into the masses. I blinked hard and struggled down toward the bathroom, passing shout-outs and offered high-fives.

"Dutch!" Junior Ford bellowed for me again, but kept his hands to himself this time. He followed closely as I continued to push my way to the restroom. "How's it going? Having fun? Sort of surprised to see you here. Not your typical scene, dude."

"Yeah. Hey, got any Motrin, by chance?"

"Motrin? What do I look like, your sister?" Junior punched my arm. So much for hands-off.

"I don't have a sister," I snarled. "Sorry, man. My head's just killing me." We staggered into the restroom. More ear-splitting voices reverberated off the floor to ceiling blue and white tiles.

"Yo. Listen up. Anyone got Tylenol? Aspirin? My boy's got a headache. Anything? Anyone?"

A faceless voice piped up. "I've got a—"

"Not you, Walsh. We've got one more game to get to State. Your shit could get Dutch booted from the team." Guys laughed, but no one had anything else to offer.

I did my business and washed my hands. "I'm headed out. See you Monday. Take it easy, and uh, sorry about earlier."

"No worries, man. Wasn't trying to run interference. Block your play." He raised a brow and smirked like he thought he was clever. "You with—" he didn't say Sadie's name. "Because she's kinda—"

"Night, Junior." I walked away, uninterested in his opinion. Either way, it wouldn't sit right—not with my headache.

"Oh, so it's like *that,* then?"

My fists balled as I spun, and Junior flinched. "*Night,* Junior."

He raised his hands in surrender, and I exited.

I didn't know what time it was, but I guessed the dance must be winding down. The hallway teemed with even more raucous classmates. Traveling the packed hall to meet Sadie would take more time than I had to spare, and I was pissed that I let Junior and my stupid headache get in my way.

Several yards ahead, Sadie clambered from the girls' restroom, wild-eyed and flushed with what looked like dread. She barely searched for me, and I couldn't catch her eye before she plowed through the crowd, away from where I stood. I'd made it halfway down the hall but got stalled at the bottleneck of students leaving the gym. Music blared out the door, and my fellow Grizzlies whooped and sang, burying my shouted calls to Sadie.

Sadie broke through and ran.

More people, more noise, more shoulders bumped mine. Panic hit me. I peeled out of my dinner jacket and further loosened my tie while I scrambled at a snail's pace, tangled in too many bodies, desperate to get free. The redhead I'd seen earlier appeared. Lunging, I grabbed the girl's arm too hard. "Where's Sadie?"

"Ow," she howled. "What's your prob—" Startled eyes met mine, but I had no time for apologies. "Oh my God. Hi, Dutch." Her attitude softened on a dime. "Good game last night—"

"Where's Sadie?" I shouted again. "She's your friend, right? Where'd she go?"

"I don't know. She left. She was upset."

"Upset?"

"Something about needing to find Leo and the baseball field, I think. Some girls were talking, and that new kid has a problem with him, I guess. Leo, I mean. Wanted to teach him a lesson or some—"

"The baseball field?"

"I think that's what she said. She kinda freaked. Like totally raging."

I pushed by the ginger, finally finding room to move, and darted down a vacant hall with a dead-end fire door that opened to the outdoor sports complex, close to the tennis courts and baseball diamond. Ignoring the signs that said, "for emergencies only," I slammed the metal push-bar, calling for Sadie before I even crossed the threshold. I shouted her name again in a flat-out sprint. Where was she? And where was Leo?

Eighteen

SADIE

present day

AND JUST LIKE THAT, Leo was gone. Busy life in New York forced him home. I understood it, and I also felt confident I hid any heartache he left behind when we said our goodbyes. On the other hand, our impromptu get-together provided the boost I needed to move ahead, make my new life in our old house, and it reassured me to see him the happiest I'd ever known him to be. He'd found his home and encouraged me to dig in and find my own.

"Text, email, Facetime! And behave! Love you, Shorty," Leo shouted as he coasted down the long driveway, waving his enormous arm out of the compact rental car window.

I clung to a front porch railing until he disappeared in the blur of afternoon heat. Sandy dust swirls dared the skies to pour. We could use a break in the weather, and it seemed about time for a storm to make landfall. But staring down peak hurricane season, I would keep quiet from asking the rain-gods for any favors.

When the peeling handrail moved in my grip, an image of Dutch jiggling the wrought iron rushed me with a sinking feeling. I thought I'd have heard from him by now. I hadn't. Two days and nothing. And with my brotherly distraction gone, I had plenty of time to ponder the reasons why. Or I could shore up the balustrade, and that was merely the beginning of my list.

I ran errands all over town the rest of the day, collecting the supplies I needed to tackle the growing to-dos for my fixer-upper. Anything major was now on hold until Structural Engineer Sam could be sure I'd be renovating on a sturdy foundation, with safe and sound utilities coming to and inside the house. But more minor projects like scraping and painting porch furniture offered safe bets to start dipping my toe into the joys of first-time homeownership.

Every place I went, people greeted me by name—usually all three of them, so any notion that I had slipped back to town unnoticed evaporated. News spread with indiscriminate speed and random direction, including people I had never known. If I hadn't subscribed to the idea of southern hospitality and small-town goodwill, the generous invitations to "give a holler" if I needed anything might have been construed as creepy. One unfamiliar man offered to follow me home to help unload my purchases, seeing as I was "all alone on that big ol' property." I declined. No, that wasn't creepy at all.

When I laid my head on my pillow that night, my thoughts drifted from the sweaty realities of property improvements to sweaty fantasies I'll keep to myself. The fact I hadn't heard from Dutch proved unsatisfying on all fronts. Any proverbial toothpaste had dried to a hardened clump of cracked mess, and the metaphor lost what little appeal it had in the first place.

By nine o'clock the next morning, I had two ceiling fans installed, circulating hot air about the front porch while I moved on to the aforementioned scraping of chipped paint off outdoor furniture. By noon, I had soaked through my overalls and was ready to spray a bright red lacquer that would make my porch rockers *pop*. I ended the workday anchoring in a coordinating swing bed on one end of the house-wide veranda. The comfy addition hanging from the bead board ceiling was another fantasy, and I was giddy to have at least one of my dreams come true.

Every inch from my hair to my feet hurt from the strenuous day, but when the last link of the last hanging chain clipped into place, I leaned on the still-wobbly wrought-iron railing to admire my hard work. Sure, I might never lift my arms over my head again, but a few well-placed Sunbrella pillows and Canaan Cove was starting to look a lot like home sweet home.

After a much-needed shower, I padded downstairs for an even *more*-needed beer, where the rumbled vibration of an otherwise silenced text greeted me. It might have been the most beautiful message I'd ever read.

Ellis: *Dinner?*

While I may not indulge in it often, I'm a fan of brevity.

Sadie: *Too tired to cook.*

Ellis: *I'm buying.*

Sadie: *Too tired to go out.*

Ellis: *I'm delivering.*

Sadie: *When?*

Ellis: *Now.*

I nearly choked on my beer and peeked around the corner to see movement through the sheer curtain that covered the glass front door.

Ellis: *Porch looks great, btw.*

I crept to the foyer, pulling the gauzy drape a few inches to look outside. Dutch eyed his phone until he saw me and lifted an overstuffed bag as an offering. My stomach craved food too much for me to play indignant at Dutch's radio silence since earlier in the week, so I threw open the door, eager for all the rugged stoic had to give.

I didn't speak. Dutch didn't move.

"Hi." Text or talk, Dutch didn't waste syllables.

I couldn't hold out long. "Hi, yourself. Thought maybe you lost my number." Okay, I mustered some indignation.

"Nah. Just wanted to give you and Leo your time."

"Leo left yesterday."

"I know."

"You know?"

"It's a small town, Sadie."

"So, are you having second thoughts or just playing hard to get?" I finally got the semblance of a smile out of him.

He looked around like the answer was plain. "I'm standing on your front porch, bringing you dinner, so I'd say neither of those things is true, but maybe it'd be nice if we took a step back and continued to get to know one another again."

Something like relief washed over me. Truthfully, I wouldn't have done the pouncing I did that Monday night had I known we'd see each other again. Fast—that kind of fast wasn't my thing. And Dutch—when he spoke—was a fountain of all the right things to say.

"I think dinner is a great place to start." I gave credit for my floaty feeling to the day's hard work in the heat and the influence of half a beer on an empty stomach. "Besides, that looks like food for more than one. What'd you bring?" I ushered him in.

He barely hesitated before he entered and beelined to the kitchen. "It's from a place called Soul Food."

"Mmmm. Like fried chicken, collard greens?"

"Uh, no. Like dak galbi and—"

"Banchan?" I yelped and grabbed at the bag.

"You like Korean barbecue?"

"I like it better in Seoul, but yeah, I love—*Seoul* Food? Ha. Clever." I inhaled the garlic and tang of pickled vegetables, then hurried around the kitchen island for plates.

Dutch stayed put. "You've been to Seoul?"

"I did what was supposed to be a month-long exchange program at Hanyang University, then extended my stay when I finagled a student visa. That's how I started my Ph.D. program.

Help yourself to the fridge." I busied myself arranging place settings, happy the meal came with chopsticks.

Dutch didn't move. "In Seoul or Ansan?"

The question stopped me mid-napkin-folding. "You know South Korea?"

"I do."

I shuddered off the surprise and fetched the beer Dutch hadn't. He hadn't budged from his spot, cemented in place, ignoring the bottle I set in front of him.

"Didn't realize Pembroke Industries had been in Korea long. What kind of stuff did they have you—security guarding—over there?"

"It was before my Pembroke days. And the DMZ."

The hiss of an opening bottle coincided with my mini gasp, but I didn't say anything. It was my first real glimpse of those lost years, and I wanted more, needed him to want to share. But something about his disconcerting stare had me wondering the wisdom in that plan.

"When?" he asked. Tension thrummed around him.

"When what?"

"When were you there? In Seoul?"

"Oh, it's been six, maybe seven years ago now."

His eyes opened wider. "Which? Six—or seven?"

"Closer to seven, I guess." I dared to ask, "How about you?"

"I came back stateside almost exactly seven years ago." Dutch's gaze stayed locked on me.

I didn't understand his manner, his shell-shocked look, but I worried we had happened upon another bleak memory, an unhappy time. So I tried to keep the conversation light. "Ah, had enough, huh? It was some culture shock. But I met some of the loveliest people."

"No. I mean, yes, but no. I did my eight years—my service obligation. That was my last official station. Considered staying in, actually, but then I—I put in my papers and got an interview with a private contractor when I—" His hand found his neck, but he finally let a grin crawl across his face, tinged with something like doubt. Like whatever thought crossed his mind couldn't be true.

"When you what?" I squinted at his bewildered state while returning the slow smile that lit up his eyes.

"Well, I know it sounds nuts but, it was when—the day—the day I thought I saw you."

"In Seoul?" A strangled laugh forced its way from my throat. "That couldn't be."

"No, of course not. I knew it couldn't be either. Because—how?" He shrugged. "Still, it was a warm, sunny afternoon, and she wore a red sundress. Long, but not to the ground. Hair up, but dark brown curls like yours." He told the tale slowly, like it was a scene he'd witnessed over and over in his mind, a favorite movie clip or video snippet he kept tucked away but revisited throughout the years. A moment he'd played on repeat. "It was very quick, *too* quick, a few seconds maybe, and I was half a block away. There was a crowd, and she ran to them, smiling, something clutched in each of her hands, toward a car, no, a line of identical cars outside—"

"Myeongdong Cathedral." My interjection was more air than sound as I recalled the beautiful July day when a friend and a fellow researcher married in the huge Gothic cathedral with an elaborate Catholic ceremony and the most spectacular reception I'd ever attended.

I've been to a variety of weddings over the years. Participated in different ways for many friends. Some in churches, some in hotels, a few more intimate backyard ceremonies, but each of them had a commonality apart from the bridal couple's obvious intention. No matter my role, be it bridesmaid, a witness, even the officiant once—thanks to the internet and the Universal Life Church—every time, without fail, Dutch Holland sprang to mind. The thought was fleeting. I never dwelled on it for long. But it always included me wondering *what if,* with a prick of sadness I pushed aside, knowing there was no answer to the question.

"They were flowers."

"Flowers?"

"Little nosegays of daisies. One of the other bridesmaids left hers behind. I ran to get them before we left for the reception. It *was* me. You *really* did see me." We both shook our heads in disbelief.

"It's why I came home. Why I didn't re-up."

I swallowed hard, gripping the cool stainless-steel counter. "Seven years?"

Both our smiles faded, and I wondered if the regret for so much time lost washed over him like it did me.

"Seven years." His focus pulled from me to his beer as he took a deep inhale. "*Geonbae.*" He lifted his bottle and waited for me to grab hold of mine to toast with him.

"Geonbae," I replied. "And the world gets smaller and smaller. Let's eat."

Stuffed with marinated meat, varied vegetables, and cold noodles, I begged my unexpected guest to leave the dinner mess, but he would hear none of it. When I returned from a search for over-the-counter painkillers, Dutch gazed into the backyard. The sun had set, but a purple sky allowed a dim view of a three-bay outbuilding and the handful of acres beyond it.

I had arrived too late in the season for the small peach crop the property produced. We'd only grown it for personal use, but I remembered early summers when we ate peaches morning, noon, and night, canning all we could before pests had their way with the vulnerable fruit. Midge's peach moonshine was legendary.

Dutch in my kitchen, with fading twilight as the backdrop, was a sight I could get used to, but twinges of nerves mixed with an aching need to make up for lost time. That combination made the long-ago torment of teen impatience fresh again. The banister's squeak betrayed me, and I smiled when he caught me staring.

"Find something to help combat the pain?" The dimming light behind him made his face difficult to read.

"Yep," and some ibuprofen too, but I swallowed the suggestive quip. *See? Sometimes, it's almost like I'm a real grown-up.* I took it as further proof of how adult I could be, no matter the giddiness tickling its way through me at the moment. "Wanna check out the source of my muscle woes?" I motioned to the front porch.

"Sure." The prospect of changing venues seemed to relieve both of us, but that respite soon fell apart.

"Oh. Those won't be dry yet." I pulled Dutch to me before he sat on what would have been still-tacky red paint. "Twenty-four hours at least and in this humidity, who knows?" We stood too close, prompting a head versus—*not*-my-head battle. My head won when I released him and stepped from his reach.

I glanced at the new oversized porch swing, then back at Dutch. The house faced east, so our view was a dark sky that I hoped hid my nervousness. "A new spin on the 'there's only one bed' trope, huh?"

He tilted his head but didn't ask.

"Never mind." Explaining an adored romance plot device to a man who apparently read Thomas Wolfe didn't seem like the best idea. I gestured to the large cushioned swing. "And before you ask if it'll hold us, I'd like to remind you what I do for a living. My fancy degree."

"Ah, yes, Dr. Klein."

"That's right," I smiled, rarely hearing the well-earned title. "You go first."

Dutch gave a double-take before "inspecting" my work with sturdy tugs on all four suspended chains.

I cleared my throat in mock-irritation.

"I'm just admiring your craftsmanship."

"In the dark?"

To be honest, I didn't know which made me more anxious: whether the swing would hold us or what might happen once it did. Dutch eased himself onto the thick, framed mattress, relaxing into a gentle glide. A collective breath exhaled. I stepped closer, prepared to sit too but lost my nerve.

"Something to drink? Another beer? Iced tea? Unsweet, of course." I spun to head inside when Dutch's fingers caught a hold of mine.

"I don't need a drink." His next tug was on my arm, and he didn't let go. Inching toward one end of the swing, he invited me to sit beside him. I accepted, curling up in the deep seat close to him, our fingers still entwined. After a few swings back-and-forth, he whispered, "Would you look at that. I didn't doubt it would hold for a second." He tightened his grip.

A short giggle peeped out of me as I held his hand in both of mine. Burgeoning night noise and the quiet scrape of chain played the soundtrack to the sweet scene, and I nestled down, resting my head on Dutch's shoulder. I could have rocked to and fro on my fantasy porch swing with my dreamy high school crush forever. Or at least until, "*Ow!*" I yanked my hand free and slapped a sting on my bare thigh. "Motherf—"

"Mosquito?"

I'd straightened and noticed the sweltering heat between our bodies and the ample cushions. The new ceiling fans failed me twice. "I'd forgotten how vicious they are here." I hesitated before finding my way back to our relaxed pose, afraid I'd broken the spell. My mouth went dry in the ruined moment. "In a month, this spot will be perfect."

"I don't know," Dutch murmured. "Seems pretty great right now."

I lifted my chin to find his mouth an inch from mine.

"Sadie Jane?"

"Don't second-guess, Ellis." This time, I waited for him to close the distance. And he did, in a slow, tender kiss that barely got started.

"*God dammit!*" My open palm smacked my thigh again, then another to my calf. "It's some kind of conspiracy." I swatted my arm, then my neck, as I flew to my feet.

Dutch chuckled while I danced around, hoping to keep the bloodsuckers from landing on me.

"They love me."

"I see that. Quite the burden you bear."

"Coupled with the thigh-biting jokes I'm swallowing over here, yeah—it's torture." I was rewarded with a full laugh as he got to his feet. "The jokes really write themselves. *Ouch!*" Another slap echoed. "Can we—" I motioned to inside and scampered to the door. Dutch agreed as he followed.

The Frigidaire offered the only light when I reached for the last two Canaan Cove ales. I kicked it closed, a bottle in each fist, and spun into Dutch's waiting hands. He placed the drinks on the counter before cradling my face. Another inch away, and the man stalled—again.

"For God's sake, kiss me already."

He needed no more encouragement, and I found myself backed into that old appliance, wholly unprepared for the rousing combination of hard and soft that assailed my mouth, stole my air. I clung to his collar to stay upright and keep him near, then held tighter when he lifted me off my tiptoes, nearly tossing me onto the stainless island.

Breathless, I filled my lungs in the brief separation, desperate to feel his lips on mine again. My legs squeezed his hips when his teeth nipped my lip. Ankles locked around him; I leaned back onto my palms, stealing another brief breath. "This is—" I attacked his mouth again, but he withdrew.

"A bad idea?" He pressed his forehead to mine with the rasped question.

"I was gonna say, 'fun.'" My eyes, adjusting to the dark, focused on his.

He pulled away, but I held firm, bringing my lips to his ear to whisper, "Tell me you want this, Ellis. Tell me you want me."

His grip on me tightened even as I sensed him hesitate. A struggle between desire and reluctance waged. Everything about him said this was meant to be, fifteen years in the making to boot, and yet something slowed him.

"Please don't start overthinking now, big guy." The plea gave away every bit of desperation I couldn't help but let slip from me as I nuzzled his neck.

"Well, if you keep talking, I'll stop overthinking."

"Huh. So—now you *like* the talking, hmm?" I teased, then gasped when an even firmer hold of my hips and a forceful tug slid me to the edge of the counter and into him.

"I always liked the talking." He growled that confession directly into my ear before he nibbled it and trailed my throat.

I sighed, "That might just be the sexiest thing anyone has ever—oops." My body jerked with surprise.

His hungry mouth had traveled along my collarbone, lingering not long enough, reaching my shoulder.

I twitched again. "Ellis, I'm—I'm on vibrate."

He paused on his way back to my neck. "Me—too?" It sounded more like a question.

"Ha. No, I'm *vibrating.* My phone. In my back pocket." I stifled a laugh as he shrank from me.

"Oh, I thought maybe it was—something people say when—never mind."

I bit back more laughter, imagining the pink cheeks our surroundings didn't allow me to see while I dug for my phone. It was a bit how I imagined a seventeen-year-old might be—clueless with the lingo, but eager to please. The screen lit, showing Tristan's name, but I dismissed the text and flung it aside.

"Important?" Whatever progress we'd made was withering.

"Not more important than this." I yanked at his shirt. "And I think you were right about—here." I pointed to the magic spot in the dip of my clavicle.

The phone signaled again. "Ignore it," I exhaled. "I'll turn it off." I fumbled for it, but the longer pulse of a phone call buzzed in my hand. A glimpse at Dutch's face in the screen glow showed a reaction I couldn't decipher. "Two seconds," I whispered, then answered, airy and rushed. "Not a good time, Tris. Call back tomorrow." I wrapped my legs around Dutch, locking my ankles again.

"Whoa. No hi? No hello? No, how's it hanging?" a relentless Tristan asked.

"Hi. Hello. Don't wanna know, but I could guess. Seriously. Call back tomorrow."

"Wait, Sade. Last time you said to text first, to call before showing up. So, I did. I texted. I called."

"Wow, that's real progress, Tristan. Who's a good boy?" I teased. "Now, do it again tomorrow, and I'll give you a treat."

Dutch wrenched his neck with a disapproving squint at my end of the conversation. I waved it off with a faux frown.

"But I texted. I called—"

"*Tomorrow*, Tristan."

"Where are you, anyway?"

"In Canaan Cove. At the bungalow, *my* house." I liked the way that sounded, but I didn't love Tristan's prying.

"Great. Because I'm on your front porch." The shrill warble of the old doorbell cut through the night, and I shoved Dutch away, scrambling off the island to my feet.

F-bombs away.

Nineteen

SADIE

present day

Tristan pounded the door.

Dutch moved like *he* planned to answer it.

"Where are you going?" I hissed, hooking his arm. "Tristan can't see you."

"Oh, he can see me." Dutch seemed more than eager for that altercation as he re-tucked the shirt I'd had a hand in rumpling.

"Sade, open up. We gotta talk." Tristan's fun-loving tone faded from his muffled shouts.

I clung tighter to Dutch. "Wait, Ellis. Please let me handle this. I'll hear him out and get rid of him."

He pulled away, determined. "My way's faster."

"Well, I like where your head's at, but—"

"I don't like this habit of him showing up on your doorstep in the middle of the night." We kept to a whisper.

"It's barely ten o'clock, but this jealous thing is *totally* doing it for me."

"Sade, come *oooon,*" Tristan whined through the door. "It's important."

"Jealous? Of Tristan? That's not what this is."

Unfortunately, I believed him. "Stay here. Out of sight." I sprang for a peck on his cheek, then darted to deal with the persistent disruptor. I didn't get far before making a quick about-face, grabbing Dutch with eager roaming hands and another hungry kiss. He responded in kind, and we both emitted breathy groans when I had to tear away to see to yet another pest on my porch.

Flushed and winded, I adjusted my tank top and yanked open the door but barred Tristan's entry.

"There's my girl. Why's it so dark?" He leaned in to kiss my cheek, but I dodged it with cat-like reflexes.

"It's nighttime, you half-wit, and I'm not your girl," I said that last bit half over my shoulder for anyone listening inside. "Now, what's so important?"

"You okay? You sound all—" Tristan craned to look inside the unlit house. I stepped out and closed the door behind me. Even in the dark, I could see him exercise that eyebrow. "Still not getting invited in, I see."

"Nope." My hard-hit plosive *P* emphasized my thoughts on the matter.

He nodded, resigned, then side-stepped toward the rockers.

"Can't sit there," I blurted. "Paint's wet."

In a jerking swivel, he faced the swing bed.

"Just installed that today. Not sure I'd trust it." I shrugged and pointed to the steps, intent on keeping the fantasy swing for worthier company. "Cop a squat and tell me what's up before the mosquitoes carry me away." I slapped my thigh with a fleeting thought of West Nile.

The uninvited visitor sighed, grasping the rickety railing to take a seat on the porch stairs. "You should have someone fix this." He jiggled the wrought iron.

"I can fix it myself, thank you. Don't get off-track. Why are you here?"

"Yeah. Um. We've got a problem."

"A problem?"

"Could be more than a problem. What's more than a problem? Bigger, I mean. What's bigger than a problem?"

"A *big* problem?" I offered, my stomach tightening.

"Yeah. We've got a *big* problem."

"Go on."

"Turns out, Pembroke Industries isn't too jazzed about releasing your patent. P.I.'s not happy at all."

"Okay. Someone is going to have to explain to me why people keep anthropomorphizing Pembroke Industries. It's just a company."

"It's a corporation, a huge international one, and I'm gonna need you to dial back the big word technical talk. I'm not an engineer."

I pressed my palms into my temples, squeezing until I saw stars. "Go from the beginning," I groused.

"Well, it started off wrong from the get-go. Daddy Dearest wasn't surprised when I, off-handedly mind you, mentioned you were interested in gaining full rights to the saltwater patent. Like, he wasn't surprised at all."

"Meaning?"

"He said it wasn't an issue, that it was already being taken care of. At first, I was surprised, happy, until I realized 'taken care of' meant you were *never* going to see those rights apart from Pembroke."

"Okay. If we can't do it the friendly way, I guess I'll get a lawyer, and we'll come at it from a different direction." I smacked my shoulder and winced as I stood, feeling the day's labor in every muscle.

"Yeah. P.I. doesn't work like that. Not when it comes to things that will affect the bottom line."

I begrudgingly sat again. "Explain."

"Daddy employs teams of people who handle these types of matters. It's a big business. *Energy* is big business. And little people aren't allowed to get in the way of that."

"Jesus, Tristan. That sounds like a not-so-vague threat."

His silence did little to help the boa constrictor in my insides, but his subsequent explanation made it all worse.

"Usually, these things get taken care of simply. A letter gets sent. Scary legal jargon gets thrown around and whoever is raising the issue backs down. That's typical." He paused, wringing his hands. "On occasion, another team takes over, and a sit-down happens. A face-to-face. Some added, um, *pressure* is applied. Ninety-nine-point nine percent of the time, that's the end of it. They're *very* good at what they do."

"Tristan." A bolt of cold hit me, and the screeching tree frogs upped their shrill tune.

Tristan's silhouette fidgeted in the nighttime light. His head shook.

"So, I have to sit down with these people? These corporate bullies? Will you be there?"

More head shaking.

"*Tristan.*"

"We're beyond that already."

"Beyond that? How?"

"Sometimes, rarely—I'm pretty sure—*rarely*, a heavy-hitter gets brought in. When that happens—well, let's just say not a lot of questions get asked."

"Questions?"

"And sometimes—" he stalled.

"Sometimes?"

"Sometimes, stuff happens. Accidents? Maybe. I don't know. It might all be a bunch of hooey. Myth. A story gets told over and over, and then all of a sudden, it's true."

"Wow. Okay. Forget it." I groaned to my feet. "Go back to *Daddy* and tell him to keep the patent. I don't want it. Tell him—"

"Sadie. That's the thing. It wasn't my asking that got this boulder rolling. This has been in the works for a while now. I didn't blow the whistle. He already knew."

"And your father went straight to the nuclear option? Didn't even want to start with the legal letters or a threatening meet and greet? To what do I owe the—"

"*No.* That's the next twist. That mythical fixer? The last resort? He volunteered. He came to us."

"Okay, I'm out. Done. Time to call off Keyser Söze."

"Whoa. Solid reference there, Sade. *Nice.* Dark, but—*solid.*"

I'd have enjoyed Tristan's compliment of my late-twentieth-century pop-culture silliness but the alarms going off in my head distracted me.

A pondering silence followed before he continued. "I might have gone more Dread Pirate Roberts. Similar ploy, just not so—grim. Plus, Kevin Spacey or Cary Elwes? Who would you rather have come after you, right? I mean, that's not even a contest—"

"*Tristan,* call him off."

"Don't you think I would if I could? But the dominos are falling, Sadie. The train has left the station."

"One more doomsday metaphor out of you and—*come on.* It's a freaking phone call."

"Gee, now why didn't I think of that? Oh, I know. Because it's *not.* Our notorious 'problem solver' is off the grid. MIA."

My stomach lurched, and my skin prickled when something in Tristan's last dramatically air-quoted words coerced my brain into speedy calculations it didn't want to make.

"Have you seen anything? Noticed anyone strange around?"

"Yes. The guy taking pictures when you were here last. But *nooo,* you were all—*don't be silly, Sade. Stop being paranoid.*" I smacked Tristan upside his head this time.

He rubbed it. "Anything else?"

"No. I mean, everyone here knows me—or seems to. Strangers even. That's kinda weird, but also pretty on-brand for Canaan Cove." The creepy stranger's offer to help get my supplies home the day before niggled the back of my mind. I never wanted to be right about some weirdo's overture of unsolicited assistance like I did now. I couldn't help but glance at my front door.

"You sure?"

I slowed my pacing with a mental run-through of the other parts of my week. It had been a whirl. "Who would I be looking for?" But I already knew the answer.

"Well, you mentioned the guy on the boat."

And there it was. "Yeah." I stopped in my tracks.

"Would you recognize him if you saw him again?" He stood and held me at the shoulders.

"Dutch Holland?" I swallowed hard and jerked out of Tristan's grip. "Why would I see him again?"

"He's the guy. The fixer. Dutch Holland *is* Keyser Söze."

"*Whoa.* Dread Pirate Roberts," I spat, quick to make the distinction.

"Whatever." Tristan shrugged. "He's *him*, and he's coming for you."

Twenty

SADIE

present day

Tristan's genuine concern served up another curveball, making me realize the gravity of my predicament, but I felt numb—and mildly guilty. The news of Dutch's real occupation hit harder than I cared to admit. He hadn't lied. In retrospect, he'd been fairly upfront about his job *safeguarding his employer's interests.* I had simply paid little attention; overlooked the evidence staring me in the face. A few strolls down memory lane and some toe-curling kisses, and I'd ignored the fancy clothes, the corporate vernacular, the high-end mysterious business card, *ahem*—the gun. But it didn't take long for me to recalibrate. I knew he'd have an explanation. Now, I had to get rid of Tristan, so I could go inside and get it.

"Are you going to the Motor Lodge?" I asked, not that Tristan's answer mattered. I couldn't let him in my house.

"No. I'll be home before midnight. I've got to go to work tomorrow."

"Work? Like at an office? Suit and tie? Ferragamos?"

"Exactly. Except—at a country club, in Under Armour, and Nike Airs, but yeah."

"With cocktails?"

"Oh, for sure. Always."

I yelped a short laugh at our moment of fun as Tristan tried to bring some lightness to our dark before a blanket of worry snuffed it out. Quiet settled in again as we stood in a faint breeze that carried a whiff of paint.

"You're my priority, so you know. I'm gonna track him down." His sincerity would have been a breath of fresh air if I hadn't been so preoccupied. If I hadn't known what I knew.

"Who?"

"Dutch Holland. We'll get this squared away."

"I'm not concerned," I lied, but not for reasons Tristan would think. "But thank you."

"You're braver than I am."

"I think the adjective you're looking for is *naïve*. Good night, Tristan." I slipped through the barely opened doorway like the cat I didn't own might escape. Well—I didn't own a cat *yet*. *Sigh*. Resting my head on the sheered glass, I turned the bolt latch. The slide and *clunk* echoed loudly in the stillness of the house. Too still.

"Ellis?" The first summons came as a whisper, but the clock offered the only reply. I called again. This time, the banister squeak mocked me when I considered looking upstairs for my missing guest. Instead, I flipped the kitchen light switch, half-worried I'd find Dutch lurking in a darkened corner, half-worried I wouldn't. The latter won.

I surveyed the scene. Two beer bottles sat on the kitchen counter, my phone on the island, nothing else out of place until I spied the backdoor. That deadbolt was locked, but it shouldn't have been. A bad habit or not, I kept it unlatched throughout the day, only locking it just before going to bed. Not only had Dutch snuck out the three-season porch, but he also took care to jimmy the lock—or un-jimmy it as it were, leaving me in the safety of a secured home. Like he wasn't the danger to me. Like he wasn't the potential threat. Son-of-a—no, Mrs. Holland was a delight. Her son, on the other hand—no matter how much faith I had in him—her son had some explaining to do.

Do you know what else needed to be locked? The spandrel. That's where an unopened bottle of decent Scotch hid. Except not anymore. Now it sat opened, tucked between my itching mosquito-bitten thighs, while I slurped leftover cold noodles from my fingers, hoping I didn't make a mess of the sofa.

I'd set midnight as the arbitrary deadline for the mind-blowing kisser with questionable motives to make contact, to explain his position, make his excuses, and with any luck, grovel for forgiveness. When that hour came and went, I gave him a short extension: however long it took me to empty the cold noodle carton balanced on my lap while I sipped one more serving of single malt. That time, too, had passed.

I had half a mind to call Leo, but I knew his take on the situation, and it assuredly wouldn't meld with mine. A bit tipsy, I wobbled to stand with a takeout carton, Scotch bottle, and a lowball glass in hand, cussing Dutch and my sore everything—not for the first time. After tidying my mess, I eyed my phone, thumb hovering to make a different call—that quarter-after-one-and-I'm-a-little-drunk call, but I was saved by a text.

Ellis: *I'm sorry, Sadie Jane.*

I slipped the phone in my pocket and trudged upstairs, my sore limbs and fuzzy brain eager for the oblivion sleep would bring.

For the next couple of days, I took out my aggression on my to-do list. Floors gleamed, windows sparkled, and beating giant area rugs became my new favorite thing—and they took a beating. Trips to the grocery store and the Feed 'n Seed kept me on high alert as I scrutinized anyone who appeared to scrutinize me. I rolled my eyes at my own paranoia, then found another rug to thrash.

By the end of day three, with no word from Dutch, I got ballsy in a way I didn't know why I hadn't earlier. Sure, a meeker woman might have replied to that spineless "I'm sorry" text. A slightly braver one would probably go so far as to call the gutless man who had slipped out the backdoor in the night. Me? I went in for the face-to-face confrontation. I sped my freshly hand-washed and waxed vintage truck the mile ride to the Motor Lodge, barged into the motel lobby, and up to the reception desk demanding to know Dutch Holland's room number.

"Sadie Jane Klein. I heard you were back in town. I *heard* you were planning to stay, too. If that don't beat all. And I'm so glad to know you are taking up care of your Grandaddy's place. It's a beautiful property. Hate for it to fall into disrepair. Listen to me go on and on. How are you?" The petite, short-haired brunette standing pixie-like behind the desk wasn't someone I recognized. Well, maybe a bit familiar around the eyes but—

She squealed, "Ah, you probably don't remember me. It's Addie. Addie Watson. Well, Addie Watson-Dodson now, but isn't that a mouthful? Plus, he left me, well, I left him after he stepped out on me with a flight attendant and *maybe* our dental hygienist. But all that is kinda new so—"

That seemed like a lot to learn about a person in three and half seconds, and I didn't know what social norms said the correct response should be in this particular instance. Surely, Miss Manners had covered this, but with all the Stochastic processes, Newton's laws, and the litany of geologic principles I'd crammed into my brain, some more practical stuff got lost along the way.

"Oh, I had a terrible perm back then and wore braces all of high school. Totally worth it, though." She displayed a giant smile of perfectly straight teeth. I appreciated she didn't leave me hanging with the over share. "And I was the school mascot for three years." Then she roared, hooking her hands like clawed paws.

"Grizzly Gus," I gasped, relieved to have something to add to our little reunion.

"Yes! Aw, you do remember me."

I did not.

"Of course, we aren't the Canaan Cove Grizzlies anymore." She leaned onto the high counter, getting way too comfortable for what I needed to be a very short chat.

"Oh?" Why did I encourage her?

"Nooo," Addie grew serious. "It was a big ta-doo. Locational appropriation."

"*Cultural* appropriation?" I asked.

"No, *locational*."

"I'm not sure that's a thing, Addie."

"It is." Sincerity oozed from her. "We had a whole town meeting about it. Turns out this area is not a natural habitat for grizzlies. Even Black bears stick to the mountains, some in the center of the state and way south at the western part of the Florida-Georgia line, but not here on the coast. It'd be a rarity for sure, and if a *grizzly* showed up in this neck of the woods, well, it'd be because she was *very* lost, and people just didn't think that was right." It was like the word "right" somehow contained two syllables. Long ones. "The citizens of Canaan Cove are super sensitive about stuff like that now."

"Oh." Naturally, my curiosity got the better of me. "So, what are we now?"

Her eyes widened, and she spoke in slow awe, "Canaan Cove Riptide."

I had no response to that.

"Like Miami Heat, Orlando Magic. Utah Jazz." She employed Fosse-like hand gestures that rivaled Leo's theatrics.

I squinted.

"Those are professional teams," Addie clarified.

"Uh-huh, I've heard of them." I fought not to smile at her earnestness. "Canaan Cove Riptide?"

"Yes, because we sneak up on you and Take. You. Down." More mascot-like gestures punctuated her cheered explanation. "Plus, we have the whole ocean thing."

"Clever. Like nautical ninjas."

"*No.*" You'd have thought I slapped her. "*That* would be *cultural* appropriation, Sadie."

"Right. Sorry." I apologized, chastened. "So, what's that costume look like?"

Addie frowned. "No mascot anymore." With a wistful gaze at nothing in particular, she sighed, "End of an era. But you should see us do the wave." Her arms rose over her head and down again, and we gave the moment the quiet deference it deserved before she startled me with the abrupt change of subject. "Did you say, Dutch Holland?"

It was like I'd forgotten my reason for being there. "Yes." I caught up to Addie's sharp veer in the conversation. "What room is he staying in?"

"Well, I'm not allowed to give out that kind of information. I think it's the law even. I can't just throw around guest room numbers. It could be dangerous, and we need to protect the privacy of our patrons. You never know who might be coming in off the street or what their intentions are. You just never know these days. Sad really. Not that we've ever had an incident here, mind you. But that's because we follow the rules—the law."

"Of course. I understand, Addie." Disappointed I might lose the element of surprise, I forged ahead. "Could you call him then? Just to say that he has a visitor in the lobby. Maybe not mention my name—if that's not against the rules."

"*That* I could do. That is most definitely not against the rules. But that does leave us with one teeny-tiny problem."

"What's that?"

"He's not here."

"Huh?"

"Dutch Holland isn't here. Not anymore."

"What do you mean?"

"He checked out late at night. Two, no, three days ago. Weird because he paid in advance, in cash. We owe him money, but he's gone."

I backed away from the check-in desk, stunned by how stunned I was to learn Dutch had left town. Of course, he left. Why would he stay? Son-of-a—no, I refused to bring Mrs. Holland into it.

"Anything else I can do for you, Sadie?"

"Uh, no. Thank you, Addie."

"Well, give a holler if you think of something."

"Will do. The place looks great, by the way." I motioned at the remarkably high-end renovation and finishings despite the circa 1960 structure.

"Why, thank you." She beamed pride, and her straight teeth showed through a broad grin.

I offered a weak wave and pushed through the glass door. Autopilot kicked in, and before I knew it, I'd parked on Main Street, a few doors down from Midge's Café. The low glow of sunset highlighted street signs and ricocheted off shiny surfaces, but I was glad to see the downtown quiet. The late-summer lull had arrived when visitors all headed home, and locals weren't ready to venture out yet.

The brass bell chimed, and Slim Shady meowed, while Midge backed out of the kitchen carrying a small tray of glasses. "Closed at eight, sorry," Midge said before turning to see me. "Ah, I see." Her look was of the all-knowing variety.

"What do you see?" My brow furrowed.

"I see moonshine time has arrived. Let me grab my backroom stash. I'll follow you home."

I didn't even try to fight her.

Twenty-One

SADIE

present day

"Red. I like it."

I knew Midge approved of the bright crimson lacquer because if she hadn't, she'd have said as much. It was one of the things I liked most about the spry septuagenarian. Rejoining her on the porch rockers, I brought two glasses and poured a generous splash of her infamous peach moonshine in each.

"Cheers." She lifted her jelly jar to me.

"L'chaim," I countered, as I knew my grandmother would have.

We drank.

"Oh *my*, Midge. I need to cut this with something." From my watering eyes down, everything burned.

"You need to hitch up your dang ovaries and drink like I taught you."

"When I was sixteen?"

"Start 'em young. Learn 'em right."

"Yes, ma'am," I mumbled and rocked, enjoying the ceiling fan while I waited for the boozy heat to subside. I'd barely sip any more of the harsh liquor, but it provided the diversion Midge and I needed to make small talk, catch up on our week. She waited until near-dark before she got to the meat of it. I had to believe it was strategic.

"So, what'd the boy do?"

"The boy?" I scoffed. "The *boy* took off."

"Why?"

"Dunno."

"Why?" Her question included more weight the second time.

"I'm really not sure." I didn't aim for obtuse, and my small taste of moonshine wasn't responsible, but I couldn't do the math.

"*Why*?" Midge had a way of getting it out of you. A one-syllable way, but a way, nonetheless.

"Two possibilities." I took another ill-advised nip and coughed with my consideration. "Either because he got caught doing something wrong, or he went to go make something right. But I don't suppose it much matters. He's gone."

"Ah hell, Sadie." She slammed her glass on the table between us and rocked to standing. "It *does* matter, and you know which it is. So, you can either sit back and wait or woman-up and figure out what to do, a way to help, how to fix it. You've never been one to wait around for someone else's solution. You're a problem solver, always have been. Don't go changing just because you're chicken." She tucked the bottle of hooch under her arm.

"Chicken?" I jeered while the phrases "fix it" and "problem solver" struck a bit too close to home.

"Bok, bok-bok." She cackled at her noisemaking and sauntered to the steps. "You should fix this too while you're at it," she exhaled, jiggling the railing. "Place looks good, though. Who needs a handyman when you've got the likes of Dutch Holland around to vex you enough to spit nails? Keep up the good work. Don't be a stranger." Midge climbed up into the wood-paneled Jeep Wagoneer she'd driven my whole life.

I glanced at her glass. Even in the dark, I could see she'd hardly drunk any of her liquor either. A means to an end. It didn't take much to loosen lips, and Midge had no desire to fog my brain. I knew why Dutch had left. Maybe not every detail, but I knew.

Now it was just a matter of figuring out where he'd gone. Son of a—

I smiled and hurried inside to pack a bag and get some sleep. I had a drive to make, and I'd leave at first light.

I didn't have to dig too deep into the state's geographic information system to get an address. It was public record. The map app told me I'd make the trip in five and a half hours if I drove the speed limit and didn't stop. But a fitful night prompted a later-than-planned start. It would be early afternoon before I arrived.

The landscape morphed from lush maritime to urban density to rural mountains. My views ran the gamut without leaving the state. And when I reached the hilly northern region, I enjoyed a ten-degree temperature drop and less humidity. If I hadn't entertained second thoughts about my rash road trip, it might have been a bit like heaven.

The route wound its way, twisting with significant ups and downs. Cottage-sized homes sat near the unmarked road with an enormous tree canopy stretched overhead like a leafy green tunnel. The shade spread thicker as the houses appeared less often the closer I got to the lake. Inlets jutted in and out like at home, cutting coves and creeks into the land, but these were the freshwater variety.

Street signs were few, so I relied on the curt voice coming from my phone for directions, and with every zig and zag, I lost confidence in her navigational abilities. When she informed me that I had arrived at my destination, bloomless mountain laurel and rhododendron masked any structure that might have been perched on the water's edge in the oak forest, but a dirt driveway cut through the twelve-foot wall of shrubbery.

I idled on the shallow shoulder made of equal parts sand, gravel, and asphalt until the unmistakable rumble of an open-air Jeep rolled up behind me. A postal worker rotated inside. The scrape and clank of a metal mailbox opening and closing sounded over the Jeep's *putt-putting* four-cylinders. Nerves bounced in me, feeling "caught," loitering in the middle of nowhere, but I thought I'd look more suspicious if I gunned my engine and took off. So, I waited.

The delivery driver pulled alongside me, and a young blond with a low ponytail appeared very near in her red, white, and blue, right-hand drive Wrangler. "Nice truck," she exclaimed over the engine noise.

"Thanks." I offered a polite smile.

"You lost? Easy to get turned around out here. But if you're looking for someone in particular, chances are I can be of assistance."

"I think I'm where I'm supposed to be. Thank you, though."

"All right then, but if you're wondering if there's a house down that way, there is. A nice one. Folks call it *Holland House* if that helps."

Apologies were due to the woman inside my phone.

"It does." I nodded and thanked the mail carrier a third time. She bounced and rumbled along the vacant road to the next bend and disappeared while I hitched up my big-girl pants, shifted into reverse to turn, and coast down the unfinished drive to Holland House.

The snap, crackle, and pop of a dirt road made a stealthy approach impossible. Add to that the likelihood visitors were a rarity out there, and I wasn't surprised to see movement on the front porch before I shut off the engine.

The postal worker had sandbagged in her description of *Holland House*. Nice was an understatement. It had the strong horizontal lines and wood and stone of a prairie-style home coupled with the southern hospitality of a welcoming porch that wrapped the structure from front to back.

"Sadie Jane Klein," Dutch's mother called out, louder than necessary, as she folded her arms and leaned on a massive river rock pillar. An amused smile accompanied the greeting.

I took off my sunglasses and squinted up at the beautiful woman as I closed my truck door. "Mrs. Holland. Hello. It's been a minute," I joked.

"That it has." She had a genteel inflection, proper and welcoming with a hint of "bless your heart," a phrase that often meant the opposite. "I hadn't heard your name in fifteen years," she paused for effect. "Well, there was that one time, but—I learned my lesson." It didn't appear to be a fond memory, so I thought better than to ask her to elaborate. "Then, three days ago, my son shows up out of nowhere, and suddenly I'm hearing your name a lot."

Clearly, the reunion wouldn't include warm hugs. I didn't mind. I wasn't a hugger. "I'm not sure if that's a good or bad thing."

"Yeah, no. Me either." A slow Cheshire grin stretched across her face, and Elspeth Holland's blunt way came back to me. She was a formidable attorney straight out of central casting, and part of me appreciated it. "Wish I could say I'm surprised to see you, but I'm not."

"That right? Guess I'm sorry to hear I've gotten predictable."

"Ha. I don't know about that. I'm starting to think this is more a case of 'better late than never.'"

I didn't know how best to respond to her quip, so I bit my tongue to keep from doing it, anyway.

"Well, you're in time for a late lunch—"

I registered the first half of that statement, but the thudding of fast feet approached, and Dutch skidded around the portico corner, coming to a quick stop; that hand gripped his neck like it was the thing to slow him. No one spoke, nothing but the chirp of a midday bird call to be heard.

"Hi," Dutch finally said.

"Hello, Ellis." It took all the air I had.

"Oh, boy," Mrs. Holland muttered. "I hate being right all the time."

I felt her gaze on me, but I only had eyes for Dutch.

"Maybe I should set up the guest room. Should I, son?"

Dutch barely nodded.

"Yeah, no. I'll do that. Good to have options, right? Okay. Lunch whenever you want it. I'll just—" She pushed off from the pillar, pointing to the massive wood and glass front door, then she was gone.

"What are you doing here, Sadie Jane?"

Dutch saying my name like that said he was glad to see me, whether he wanted to be or not. I was okay with that.

"Seem to recall you saying that when it came to you and me, if there were things to be said, I'd be the one doing the talking. And I have things to say, and you're here so, I came to say them. To you. Here."

"How'd you know—"

"I'm smart, Ellis," I grinned. "I mean, I'm no rocket scientist, but I probably could have been."

He smiled too but shook his head. "I have no doubt. But for someone so smart—"

"I can't believe I'm going to say this, but you should stop talking now. I've had a long drive. It's hot out here though cooler than home, but I could use some freshening up, and your mom has lunch. So, I'm going to say this next part, so you don't have any doubts about where I stand, and then we will take some time to get used to one another in this new space before we talk about what happens next. That okay with you?" The engineer in me appreciated having a plan of action.

Dutch nodded.

"I am not afraid of you, Ellis. I know you wouldn't hurt me. And I should have let you know that the night I sent you off with Junior. I'm sorry."

He opened his mouth, probably to protest my apology.

"Nope, not done yet. That was unnecessary, cruel, even. I also know what kind of man you are, and no folklore will change that. Not a myth I heard from Tristan Pembroke or a fiction that got told fifteen years ago. I don't care how many times a story makes the rounds; it doesn't make it true. I allowed one lie to get between us, and I'll be damned if I let another do it again."

"It wasn't your lie," he interjected.

"Wasn't it? I let it get told."

"Please keep your voice down." It was more of a plea than a demand, but I didn't like it, didn't understand it. I bristled, wondering if I had misread the situation in my impulsive rush to get there, running in without enough data, allowing implicit bias to color my view. Number one no-no for a research scientist. I knew better; I should have anyway.

"You know, you could be right. This might be a bad idea. Maybe too much time has gone by. Maybe we are more strangers than anything. I don't know what I was—"

"You graduated top of your class at Canaan Cove High, except you finished a semester early and didn't take any of the accolades. And you were due all the accolades. Completed your first degree—geology—early too at Georgia Tech, probably because you wanted to get lost in a big city rather than be seen in a small one. You were awarded your first patent while still an undergrad. You stayed in that big city to get your master's in mechanical engineering but ended up sticking around for a doctorate when South Korea called. The youngest woman ever to—"

"Well, will you look at who found my Wikipedia page?" For a woman looking to rekindle a connection, I had a snarky way of showing it.

He shifted his feet and slipped his hands into his back pockets. The smirk of the hardheaded teenager I once knew flickered across his face as he exhaled a short, silent chuckle. His gaze scanned over my head from his higher vantage point, but I couldn't pull mine from his chiseled jawline and the slight silver of his old scar.

"Rocky road is your favorite ice cream flavor, though a chocolate shake will do in a pinch but only if it's made with vanilla ice cream. Your favorite color is red. Not too orange, not too pink. Red. You prefer Foo Fighters over Nirvana, but Pearl Jam most of all, and you love a sad country song that tells a good story, but you'd rather no one know that, or about the romance novels you like to read. Your feet are oddly ticklish even when you're asleep, and when you get so anxious you don't know what to say, you keep talking anyway and say the most blatantly obvious thing like it's news. It *never* is. You think you're a cat person, and there's nothing wrong with that, but you're not. You're a straight-up dog person, but we can argue that another day. You adore your brother more than anything, I think, and not to make it weird, but if anyone looked at me like you look at him, I'd be a happy man, and if that person was you, good God, I'd be the luckiest. We are not strangers and this wasn't a bad idea. It's complicated, but you've had a long drive and, by the looks of it, little sleep, so come inside, get washed up, and eat some lunch. Then, we'll talk."

Oh my, I needed to sit down. And a stiff drink. "Can you?"

"Can I what?"

"Talk. Because I always figured you had a strict word count cap—that you rationed them, and after that little display, I figure you're used up until Christmas. Thanksgiving at least."

He gestured to the front door, back to fighting a grin, and I hopped a step to move.

"Got a bag?"

"Yeah, it's—"

"Better grab it. Still not your pack mule."

I slid my duffel across the bench seat and closed up the truck again. "Hey. Off-topic. Does the Dread Pirate Roberts mean anything to you?"

"Should it?"

I flailed a hand. "Nope. Forget it."

He took the bag handle from my grip, slung it over his shoulder despite his draft animal denial, and made off to the front door. "As you wish."

"Hey—" I hurried after him.

Twenty-Two

SADIE

present day

I STRETCHED MY FACE like a funhouse mirror after splashing cold water on it. Dutch wasn't wrong. I looked almost as tired as I felt. God, he called it like he saw it. Points for honesty—I guess. Wild curls sprang from a typical messy bun, but the dark circles under my eyes were the real giveaway. I'd been working hard, physical labor, but nighttime hadn't been restorative. Once my body stopped going, my brain took over, and I'd tossed and turned a few miles—if that's possible.

Yeah, I needed a nap.

The bed in the daylight basement guest room Mrs. Holland "put together" in no time lured me until I caught the lake view through the back windows. The gorgeous scenery gave me new life and enough *oomph* to find my way upstairs to the main floor where I'd entered. A cheerful voice guided me.

Mr. Holland nuzzled his wife's neck as she worked at the kitchen sink. "...I'm telling you, El, Big Bertha and I were on fire today. I couldn't hit 'em any straighter if I tried. Right down the fairway." Someone had played a good round of golf.

"Hang onto that feeling, Davis, because we've got company, and it's not—"

"Hello, Mr. Holland." I topped the stairs into a large open-concept space that included a wall of windows and doors to a porch that circled the entire home. Dutch paced outside with a phone to his ear.

Davis Holland swiveled slowly, and his exuberant face fell. Frosty reception notwithstanding, the man had aged well too. If nothing else, those Hollands had good genes. He opened his mouth to speak, but his wife intervened with deliberate sweetness.

"Look, Davis, it's Sadie Klein. From Canaan Cove."

His mumbled expletive cleared up any question I had about the man's grim look.

Uh-oh.

"Dutch is on the deck, Sadie. He's had that phone glued to his hand since he got here. Work-related. It's always work-related. Davis, why don't you get washed up for lunch?"

"She's staying for lunch?" He asked like I wasn't in the room, but his eyes were zeroed in on me.

"Yes, and then some. Be polite." His wife half-whispered the last bit.

I'm not one to look for rescue from most things, but I needed Dutch to get off the phone and save me, if only from myself.

"The guest room is lovely, Mrs. Holland. Thank you for having me."

"The *guest* room?" Mr. Holland's brows shot up along with his volume.

"Davis." She grabbed her husband's arm. "Sadie, why don't you—" She gestured to the glass door to the veranda.

"Yes, of course." I couldn't move fast enough and slipped out the back, wishing for a breath of cool air. Instead, I met unfortunate summer heat and climbing humidity.

"...understand them? I made them. Now reel them in and call me when it's done." Dutch's accent was wholly absent again, like some Yankee doppelgänger stood in front of me.

I reminded myself who he was and cleared my throat. He tried to smile as he slipped his phone into his pocket but worry etched his face.

"Your dad's not too happy to see me."

"Yeah, me either." He looked past me into the house.

"Excuse me?"

"Oh, no. Me. Not you. He's not too happy to see me. He's, well, I'm—I'm glad to see you."

"Real convincing, Ellis." I wanted to touch him—more than touch him. It would have relieved the angst coursing through my veins or at least given me a moment's distraction. But the wall of glass behind me somehow made touching him impossible.

"Settled in? It's a big place, but it really is comfortable. Quiet. And this view."

"Why isn't he happy to see you?"

If Dutch thought I'd prefer to talk home décor and the panorama rather than family dynamics, then he didn't know me at all.

"Don't worry about it. We've just never found our way—"

"Because of—"

"Don't worry about it," he repeated, taking my hand.

In a surprise twist, I pulled from him, realizing my part in the family drama. How had I imagined I'd be welcomed here? The truth was, I hadn't imagined. I hadn't thought it through—another reckless move without considering the consequences.

"I should go."

"You should stay."

"No, this is six kinds of wrong. Seven, maybe. And I can be home by dark."

"I want you to stay. I—*need* you to stay." A hint of concern colored his plea. More of my worry reared up, but he tried to divert from it. "Thought we had things to talk about."

"We can talk on the phone."

"I don't want to talk on the phone."

"That's not what your mom says."

"My mom?"

"She said you've been on the phone for days."

"Work. And I don't want to talk to *you* on the phone." He lifted my chin. "Wow, you're—tired."

I snorted. "No, no. Enough of the sweet talk. Are you trying to seduce me?"

"If I was seducing you, you'd know it."

"Is that right?"

His hand moved to my cheek, and he held my gaze until I couldn't bear it. I closed my eyes and leaned into his palm, breathing in his scent. No, he didn't need to speak to entice me, tempt me to stay. A look, a touch, the smell of his skin, and I was a goner.

"Let's get you something to eat." His thumb brushed my cheekbone, bringing me back to Earth. It was a one-two punch. A soliciting stare *and* the offer of food? Who needed words?

Mr. Holland had gone, leaving Mrs. Holland to make vague excuses and polite apologies, promising he would be back for a late supper—in better humor. Glances between her and Dutch told me little, other than an already existing strain had only gotten worse with my arrival, even though they both denied it. I picked at a sandwich and a serving of pasta salad while trying to keep my eyes open. It was a losing battle.

"Thank you for this, Mrs. Holland. For everything."

"It's probably time you called me Elspeth. Or El. And you're welcome. I mean that." She offered a reassuring nod. "Why don't you two go for a walk? Show Sadie the dock, the garden. It's a beautiful day but rain's coming."

"I don't know. I think Sadie might rather go to bed."

"Huh?" Heat rose up my neck.

"She hasn't slept much this week," Dutch explained.

"She's not the only one. Insomnia seems to be going around. Maybe you two can help each other out with that." Elspeth's matter-of-fact tone and polite smile didn't jibe with what I thought she implied.

"I'm sorry. What was that?" I couldn't have heard her right.

Elspeth rose to clear away the lunch plates. "Maybe together you can work out whatever it is that's been keeping you up nights. Put your heads together and thrash it out?"

"Thrash?" I looked at Dutch, but he'd been focused on his phone, so he likely hadn't been listening.

"Did I say thrash? I meant hash. *Hash* it out. Or whatever. Sometimes it's best to just tackle it. And with both of you looking for a solution—well, two's always better than one, I find."

"Two is Sadie's favorite number," Dutch piped up out-of-the-blue. *Had* he been listening?

I needed to rein in the conversation before it went any further, and I, you know—*died*. "A walk sounds great but maybe after I take a quick power nap. Twenty minutes. Tops."

"Yeah, no. It's difficult to really go at it—a problem—when you're tired. Rest up some. Good idea."

I pushed back in my chair, trying not to bolt from the dining room.

Dutch reached for my arm. "You okay?

I flinched; afraid his touch would make me burst into flames. "Yep, I'm fine. A nap will do me good." And maybe a cold shower. "Give me thirty minutes?" I slunk back to the stairs and gave a sheepish wave. But before I spun to descend the steps, I swear Elspeth Holland winked at me.

Twenty-Three

SADIE

present day

THUNDER WOKE ME. I couldn't remember the last time I'd heard rain, and the sound of the approaching storm soothed me until I looked at my phone. It read seven o'clock, and for a moment, I wasn't sure if that was a.m. or p.m. Whichever it was, my twenty-minute power nap had been an epic failure. Wiping sleep from my eyes, I stumbled into the hall and nearly ran into Dutch as he rounded the corner at the bottom of the stairs.

"Hey, I was just coming for you."

"Okay, you and your mom have a *debatable* way of—never mind," I guessed Mrs. Holland's litigation tap-dance skills and whatever Dutch did for a living, benefitted them both with, shall we say, *complex* speech. Their double entendres were just the sort of thing that made the romance miscommunication trope spiral out of control. I found the confusion less fun in real life.

His sheepish grin said he knew exactly what he was doing. "Supper?"

With my hands in my hair, I looked at the room I'd bolted from without taking a moment to "fix" myself. "I should—"

"You should join my parents and me for a meal. We'll watch the storm roll in across the lake. It's a sight to see."

"I imagine I am too." I patted my curls, one hand on my jutted hip, with a cheeky grin like a vintage pin-up calendar girl.

"You have no idea." He returned the look with a shy smile and a head shake. It knocked the wind out of me.

We dined at a beautifully set table, casual but with quality everything. The simplicity made it elegant, but in a way that didn't feel like anyone tried to put on airs. At the same time, it felt crowded. Mr. and Mrs. Holland, Dutch, and I would have made for a lovely gathering in some parallel universe, but with the addition of the two-ton elephant in the room, something got lost.

Our conversation came in stops and starts, blurted questions, and too-short replies, with Elspeth and me doing most of the heavy lifting. Thank goodness for the delicious food and weather entertainment flickering in the distance, moving toward the water and us. Late in the meal Dutch reached for his phone, vibrating with an incoming call. My stressed brain made the inappropriate leap to a recent memory of me on my kitchen island, a buzzing phone, and Dutch between my legs. A shaky hand reached for my water goblet to quench my suddenly dry mouth.

"No phones at the dinner table, young man. Lunch is one thing, but at dinner, I'm afraid I'll have to insist." Elspeth meant it, and I stifled an unfortunate laugh, narrowly avoiding a spit-take.

"It's work," Dutch replied.

"They'll leave a message."

"No, they won't. It's a rule."

"It's a bad rule," she scoffed.

"It's *my* rule."

"Well, it's an inefficient one, and *my* rule is no phones at the dinner table." Her scolding tone tightened, and a well-timed clap of thunder punctuated her commandment. Any humor I'd found vanished.

"Not sure we should be getting in the way of Dutch's business. Wouldn't want him risking his livelihood, his future." Mr. Holland joined the deteriorating conversation. "He's done enough of that."

Ouch.

I jumped in for the save. "Pembroke Industries does a lot of good for a lot of people, and my understanding is Ellis has proven himself indispensable. The sheer number of phone calls when he's on vacation, no less, is a good indicator of that."

"Sadie," Dutch took my hand, but I didn't know if he meant to shut me up or thank me.

"Do you work for Pembroke?" Davis Holland asked.

"I have done work with Pembroke, yes."

The gentleman wiped his mouth and tossed the linen napkin on the table with an exasperated head shake. "The sudden chaos makes more sense now. You were trouble then, and you've brought trouble again."

"Dad," Dutch barked. Elspeth and I both jerked in our chairs.

"No, Ellis." I released his hand and placed mine in my lap. "It's okay."

"It's not." He stared a warning at his father.

"It is. And it's been fifteen years and several hours now, and I owe you all a long-overdue apology. And your father has every right to say what he needs to say. I'm a big girl. I can handle it." I steeled myself for what I had coming.

"Do you know the story about the fox and the train?" Mr. Holland didn't wait for a response. "A young fox is playing around the train tracks one day. Sure, he's been warned, but a cub's gonna do what a cub's gonna do. Right? When a train whistle blows, the fox hops to get out of the way of the oncoming locomotive but finds the tip of his tail has gotten wedged between the steel rail and a fish plate. That's the part where—doesn't matter. You get the point."

"No, I don't think we do, Davis," Elspeth interjected.

"The train is moving fast, closer and closer, but the young fox can't get free," Mr. Holland continued. "Yes, he knows one quick, strong yank will get him loose, but he won't do it. It might hurt, tearing off a piece of himself, even if it means saving his life, but instead, the idiot gets clobbered by the barreling steam engine."

I stared at the man, unsure of the meaning of it all, but I still believed he was due his time.

"I see you're wondering about the moral of the story."

By the looks, we all were, but Mr. Holland had slowed. I wasn't sure he didn't think he might have gone too far, but he was in deep now. Some trains can't get stopped in time.

"Obviously, I should have shared this little parable with my son some fifteen years ago. Parental failure, I'll admit, but I had thought I'd raised him better. The moral is—don't lose your head over a little piece of tail."

"Davis," Elspeth gasped.

"Dad," Dutch shouted, pushing to his feet, rounding my chair to step between his father and me. The table screeched, and a water glass spilled.

Everyone stared, some pale, some red-cheeked, none of us breathing.

I barred Dutch with my arm and swallowed hard before I spoke. "I regret that night, Mr. Holland. Not a day goes by when I don't wish it had gone another way, but I will also be forever grateful for what Ellis did."

Mr. Holland's fist hit the table, and more silverware clanked in response. "Grateful?" He had an infuriated sneer. "Really, Sadie? I can *almost* forgive a sixteen-year-old girl for misconstruing the consequences of amped-up hormonal teenaged boys. But fifteen years on, and you're still willing to brush it off as boys will be boys. As an adult, you can still look back and think a fight, actual violence to win the affections of a girl is—"

"Absolutely not. *I think* that—wait. What did you say?" My heart thudded.

"Surely, as a grown woman, you can see the stupidity in that. I'd think you'd even be a bit appalled at that kind of caveman mentality, at least in retrospect. I'm certain your grandmother would have expected more of you. Had Dutch been defending you from some sort of physical attack, maybe. But you weren't even there."

"I—I wasn't there? Fight over a girl—me? I don't understand. I think there's been—Ellis? Oh my God." I sucked in air, and my fingers caught in my hair. "They don't know. You didn't tell them? Your own parents? All this time?"

"Tell us what?" Elspeth finally spoke.

"Sadie. Don't."

The room spun, and I pushed away Dutch's arm, ignoring his words. "Mr. and Mrs. Holland, you need to know what happened. You need to know the truth."

"Sadie Jane, *stop*. Please."

Twenty-Four

DUTCH

fifteen years ago

"Sadie Jane, *stop*," I shouted, but it was too late. A clear sky allowed the glow of the waxing gibbous to glint off the aluminum bat as it swung through the air. The cracking thud on impact reverberated in my already throbbing head. A tall figure went down hard, his head bouncing off the ground, and I vomited in a knee-high hedge. Fruity drink burned my throat and nose as I tore over the evergreen shrub, desperate to reach her as Sadie pulled back for another swing.

I grabbed the bat in time, yanking it from her grip, only to have her spin and plant a right hook in the corner of my mouth. A metallic taste mixed with my caustically sweet puke, and stars sparkled in my periphery.

"Sadie Jane," I groaned. I had never taken a punch before. Not in the face, not without a helmet to protect me, and certainly not by a girl. I was pretty sure that last part didn't much matter. A swift fist to the jaw, no matter who delivered it, sucked. I rallied to the seriousness of the situation. Tossing the bat aside, I drew Sadie to me. "Are you all right? Did he touch you? Hurt you?"

She wrenched from me with a growl. "Hurt *me*? No, he didn't hurt me."

I reached for her again, unable to see in the dark if she really was okay. The back of the school's campus depended on field lighting, and none of it was lit. The moon glow faded in and out, or my vision did.

A moan rumbled out of the belly-down body. His head bobbled, then rested face-first on the ground again.

"He's unconscious. Did you hit him in the head?" I stumbled toward him for a closer look, hoping it was the shadows that made his contorted leg look so misshapen. Not likely.

"No, his ass, I think, because he's an *ass*." She shouted the barb in an exaggerated lean.

"What's going on? Where's Leo?" I asked.

"Oh no. Leo. I have to—oh my God, Ellis. You're bleeding. Your mouth, it's—I'm sorry. My ring must have cut you. I just—this asshole was going to hurt Leo. Has some problem with him playing basketball. Teach him a lesson, he said. Girls in the restroom were talking about it, and I saw red. I panicked—couldn't get out here fast enough."

More nausea swirled. "He didn't touch you? This creep didn't—"

"No. I can handle myself, Ellis."

"And the bat? He had a baseball bat?"

"No, I brought the bat. I came out the side door by the equipment room. It was unlocked. I grabbed it."

"Good God, Sadie Jane." I grabbed at my neck. "You brought a weapon to—"

"*No*, I brought a baseball bat to defend my brother."

"Your brother's not here." My shout hurt everything, forcing me to quiet. "You beat some guy with a baseball bat you brought to the scene. And if he didn't do anything to you, that's assault. Pre-meditated assault, I think. That's bad. That's worse than bad." Too many scared-straight lectures and what-if sermons delivered by my lawyer-mom informed me of the terrible situation that grew worse by the minute. "You have to get outta here. This guy needs a doctor, and you need to go." I spat blood and bile.

"He was going to hurt Leo. Just because Leo's—"

"Go, Sadie. Go find Leo and have him take you home. And you were never here. Do you hear me? You were *never* here. You know nothing about this. Now, go."

"I'll get help. I'll get someone to—"

"You can't. What part of *you aren't here* don't you understand?"

She pulled up the hem of her dress, pushed past me, and fell to her knees, crawling.

"What are you doing?"

"He had a phone. One of those Blackberry things. Douchy, rich kid. *Pfft.* Like everyone needs to be carrying around a phone. It's got to be here—"

I snatched her arm and hauled her to her feet. "Get the hell outta here, Sadie. Please."

"He was gonna hurt Leo. I had to stop him. Leo's all—he's all I've got. I had to—"

Later, I'd remember that remark. *He's all I've got.* How did Sadie not see she had me? "You were never here. Now, go."

"But you. You're bleeding, and I hurt you." She touched my face. Gentle fingers wiped at the blood, and I thought she was going to kiss me. There. At that moment, my mouth rancid with blood and puke while some chump whimpered at our feet? No, not happening. Not like that.

I shoved her and spun, yelling, "Find Leo and go home and not a word about this. Run, Sadie Jane."

She didn't say another word.

Twenty-Five

SADIE

present day

DUTCH NEVER SAID A word. For fifteen years, he kept the truth to himself. For fifteen years, his parents believed a lie, thought their son had committed a stupid act of aggression, and wrecked his life as a result. Senseless violence because of a teenage pissing match over a girl, no less. I hoped they found some solace in the truth. But not long after I'd spewed the facts—what I knew of them—I wordlessly excused myself to let the Holland family talk. I certainly didn't feel any more welcomed, not by Mr. Holland anyway. I was still the wrecker of worlds in his mind, and rightfully so. And now Dutch was no doubt angry because I refused to let the lie continue.

The house sprawled large enough, or they whispered, keeping me out of earshot of the exchange. After the storm blew through, a gentle rain lingered. Showered and in my PJs, the hushed rhythm of the falling water lulled me back to much-needed sleep.

I shot to sitting in pitch dark from another hard nap, confused as to my whereabouts, both time and place. It was the middle of the night, and the once-relaxing hush of rain slacked off to a louder persistent drip, thumping like an accelerated heartbeat, the ominous tick of a time bomb.

After beating a pillow into submission and repeated failed attempts to suffocate myself with it, I scrambled out of bed, frustrated, wired, and in search of trouble.

His door groaned open after I rapped on it with a tentative knuckle. I detected a jerk of movement in the dark and was relieved to hear a whispered, "Sadie?"

"Ellis?"

"You shouldn't be in here."

"I know." I crept in and inched the door closed behind me.

"You should go."

"I know. I agree with you." I kept my back pressed to the door. "But—suppose I play devil's advocate. For just a minute."

"Sadie." Dutch lay on his back, and my adjusting eyesight saw him press the heels of his hands to his eyes, emitting his own groan.

"Hear me out. Two things."

"Sweet Jesus," he murmured.

"One. I don't want to go. And two," I paused because I was less sure about the second thing. "And two, you don't really want me to go either. Wait. Three things," I rushed to continue so he couldn't deny number two. "I have questions."

"Yeah. I imagine you do. Let me get dressed."

"You're not dressed?" A note of panic sprang from me. Excitement. Nerves. *Whatever.*

"I'm not wearing a shirt."

"Oh. Well, I could take off mine, and then we'd be square." *What was I doing?*

"Sadie. My parents are upstairs."

I exhaled. "I'm joking." I wasn't. Okay, maybe a little. Maybe not. "Not for nothing, but we're in our thirties, and I'm pretty sure Elspeth gave me the thumbs up earlier."

"She did? No. No, I don't want to know anything about that."

"Of course that was before the truth bomb, so—"

"She's okay. Relieved, I think. They both are, in a way." He slid to sitting and fumbled for something on the bedside table.

His limbs stretched overhead as he pulled on a t-shirt, and I squeezed the doorknob at the small of my back to keep from doing something inappropriate. The phone lit his face when he glanced at the time, then placed it aside. We remained in the dark, and it was likely best. "Questions?"

"Hm?"

"You have questions?" He rested against the headboard in the center of the bed, and I wished I had the nerve to climb in with him.

"You mind?" I gestured to an armchair in the corner. Midge's chicken sounds played in my head.

"Sure. Of course."

I wanted to believe disappointment laced his reply, but I slunk to the chair and wrapped myself in a blanket before curling up in the seat too far from the warmth on the other side of the room.

"So, you are actually some kind of fixer?" I knew to focus on the gravity of the moment.

Dutch didn't say anything.

"And I was your first?"

"My first?"

"Your first 'fix.'"

"I got better at it. But yeah, I guess you could say that."

"How'd you get him to keep quiet? To keep our secret? What did you do?"

"You don't want to know."

"I do," I insisted.

"No, you don't." His grim refusal startled me, but then anger bubbled up, confused why he continued to keep me in the dark.

I rolled out of the chair and stood at the end of the bed.

"What are you doing?" He straightened in his spot.

I didn't know what I was doing. I simply stared into the dark. For years I'd wondered what happened in those hours, days, weeks after that night and the one person with all the answers sat in front of me unwilling to talk because *not* talking was his default mode. I folded the blanket and draped it on the chair, moving slowly in the hopes my brain could catch up, and my mouth would say the right thing before I had to leave because staying felt like begging, and I was never going to do that. Not for this. Not even for him.

"I don't want to hurt you," he whispered.

"Yeah, well, we've reached the part where I'd rather feel hurt than nothing at all. I've been feeling a whole lot of *nothing* these years. Nothing until you stumbled back into my life. And now I might feel too much, and I don't think I'm built for it. Lack of infrastructure. But if I'm going back to that numb existence, back to the nothingness, then I'd rather just be on my way. No sense in prolonging the inevitable. So, if you can't meet me halfway, if you don't *want* me, if you won't *talk* to me, then let me go. Keep my fucking patent and your secrets but let me go."

So much for not begging. Dutch was on me before I reached the door. I spun to face him, ready to push or pull; I wasn't sure which, but our mouths collided as my back hit the wall. My hands groped, his arms held tight, and our mouths explored, all desperate to get closer. All frantic for more.

"No, we're not doing this." His rasped words contradicted what every inch of his body said.

"Feels like—we are," I panted between more probing kisses. "I mean, I'm saying yes. This is consent. I hear it's the new sexy." I pulled at his t-shirt, but he stopped me, gripping my wrists hard against the plaster, his mouth devouring mine again.

He pulled his mouth from mine, slowing the frenzy. Kisses grazed my cheek until his lips met my ear. "We're not. Not like this."

"Like this?"

"Angry, hurt."

"I don't like secrets, Ellis."

"My job is secrets. That's non-negotiable."

"We're negotiating? Because I have concerns."

"Concerns?"

"Two things."

His unexpected chuckle hummed into my mouth, and I lost time enjoying the sensations of it all—his muffled laugh, his mountain smell, his firm lips, and soft tongue.

"Sadie Jane." He beckoned me like a hushed prayer. "You stopped talking. You still with me?"

"Oh, I'm with you. Just a bit taken aback by how good you are at this. How good this feels, how right. You definitely out-perform the fantasies, and there have been a few. You're the book that's better than the movie."

"The book's always better than the movie." Dutch released his grip, letting his hands slid down my limbs. A tender kiss met my lips, and he snaked his arms around my waist to hold me. "How did we get here? After all this time? I've been all over the world, you've been all over the world, and now here we are in my parents' basement, of all places, trying not to tear each other's clothes off."

"Speak for yourself, mister." I toyed with the drawstring of his pajama pants. "And it's a really nice basement. Now tell me a secret."

He paused before saying, "I know who the Dread Pirate Roberts is."

"I *knew* it—" Another deep kiss ended that exclamation in a throaty moan.

In need of air, we separated long enough for an inhale and him to say, "Your turn. A secret." Featherlight lips brushed my nose, my temple, my forehead, but definitely not like his sister.

"I don't have any, Ellis. You can ask me, and I'll tell you anything. You're the one with the soul to bare, so you go again.

A real secret this time." I gripped his chin to look him dead on but closed my eyes when he placed another soft kiss on my mouth. Sweet, chaste, but sexy as hell.

"Look at me." His nose brushed mine, but I didn't raise my gaze to meet his. Instead, I lifted my chin further to reach his lips, to interrupt his talking before things went too far, before secrets, *real* secrets, got shared. Careful what you ask for. He stopped me. His gentle hand met my cheek, his thumb grazing the kiss-swollen curve of my cupid's bow. "Look at me," he repeated, like he had never craved anything more. I couldn't refuse him. But when our eyes met, he drew in a short breath before he spoke again. "I've been in love with you for half my life, Sadie Jane."

A quiet gasp escaped me as I clutched at his shirttail to hold me there, afraid I'd run, that my baser instincts would send me fleeing. But no, I was exactly where I wanted to be, hearing what I'd always wanted him to say.

He continued. "For half my life, I've put my head down, worked hard, and loved you. Military service kept me moving and made an excellent excuse to avoid my parents or not to commit to—anyone. And when this persona emerged, the fixer with a reputation, somewhere along the way, I disappeared, but I didn't care. I've never regretted a thing except not letting you see me that day at the hospital, but I don't even regret that anymore because now I'm here and you're here and—"

I pulled his face to mine, wrapped my arms around his neck, and stopped the talking. No more needed to be said now. Later, yes, but not now. His more eager hands found my skin, sliding under my cotton pajama top. A button popped loose, maybe two, and I nodded encouragement with a whispered, "yes," as I nudged him backward, tugging off his t-shirt.

The world fell away. All the time we'd lost, the wondering if we'd been blinded by misperceptions of our youth or the unsatisfied desire we couldn't really comprehend as kids—none of that mattered. Despite the years gone by, we'd found one another again. He sank to the mattress edge, and I stood between his thighs, my fingers making slow work of the remaining buttons as his hands skimmed up the backs of my thighs. Tickled, I smiled at his expectant eyes before bending for another taste of his lips before the last mother-of-pearl disc almost slipped free of its loop.

"Dutch?" That uttered name and the knock that accompanied it were the last things in the world I wanted to hear. Or so I thought. His forehead met my nearly bared breastbone.

"Son?" Elspeth repeated. "Is Sadie with you? It's—I'm sorry, but it's an emergency. Midge Toogood—"

That last button provided my only modesty when I flung open the door, not caring. "What's wrong with Midge? What's happened?"

"Oh, boy." The typically even-keeled Elspeth tried to keep up the facade and her eyes off my mostly exposed chest. "Yeah, no. Uh, she called. Midge called. Looking for you. Thought I might know where you were. I guess because—" Her gaze shifted to Dutch scrambling in the dark behind me. "Well, you didn't answer your phone. And she didn't have Dutch's number. Ours hasn't changed—"

Dutch stood at my back, pulling on his shirt, but I pushed past Elspeth in the doorway. "My phone. It's in the other room."

Mother and son followed me.

"Mom, what is it?"

"It's your house, Sadie. It's—it's on fire."

Twenty-Six

SADIE

present day

THANKFULLY, MIDGE ANSWERED ON the first ring and told me everything she knew while I flew around the guest room, repacking my bag one-handed. Dutch typed on his phone, briefly leaving the room to make his own man-of-mystery calls. Elspeth paced. The next surprise came in the form of Davis Holland, appearing with four cups of piping-hot coffee.

Volunteer fire crews were on the scene in Canaan Cove and with them, the saving grace of the torrential storm that had blown east, dousing the coast. Maybe the house had been struck by lightning. On the outskirts of town, it was sheer luck someone drove by in the middle of the night and noticed the blaze.

A good Samaritan made an anonymous 9-1-1 call that might have saved some damage. The fire still burned, so no word on a cause or any assessment of the harm done, but everyone was relieved I wasn't home and no one was hurt.

"I'm on my way, Midge. It's five and—maybe six hours, depending on traffic. Who knows? But I'm on the way." I ended the call.

"*We're* on the way," Dutch hurried to say, sidestepping the mini crowd to return to his bedroom across the hall.

"Not necessary," I shouted, grabbing a sundress from the bag I'd just repacked and hurried to the ensuite.

"Sadie, let him go with you," Elspeth implored through the bathroom door in little more than a whisper. "He can help. He'll want to help."

My head swirled as I thrashed into fresh clothes and splashed cold water on my face, remembering not long ago I had joked to myself about this very thing—my house catching fire. Not so funny now.

My chest tightened along with the telltale tingle in my feet. An imaginary itch telling me it was time to flee. I needed out of the small space, out of the house. Dressed, Dutch held both our bags when I exited. Elspeth offered me a coffee mug, but I declined. Davis stood in the background, silent but looking no less alarmed.

"You're not coming, Ellis." I avoided his eyes, shoving my sleepwear into a pocket of my duffel hanging at his side.

"The hell I'm not."

"No. You're staying here with your family. You're on vacation, remember?" I hated my tone, knew what it meant, knew what I was about to do. I ignored Dutch's parents but found enough nerve to meet his gaze despite the looming cowardly act. "I have to go. And I need to go alone."

He dropped the bags. "Do you? You *have* to? Really? After—" He gave the slightest head tilt toward his bedroom.

"What is—"

"Shh, Davis," Elspeth hissed at her husband.

"But I don't—"

"*Hush.*"

The twosome's back-and-forth played like white noise with all my attention on the hurt-filled eyes and strangled voice of the man inches from me.

"Why?"

"Why what?"

"Why are you running?"

"I'm not. I'm—"

"You are. You're running. From me. But why? Did things get a little too real in there? Too honest? Scary?"

"My house is on fire, Ellis." I lunged for my bag, ready to bolt, but he kicked it out of reach. Stating the obvious gave me away. Again.

He cocked his head, then nodded. "Yes, Sadie Jane, I heard, and you're upset. I get that. Now let's get in the truck, and we'll do this later."

"Please, Ellis. It's not—just let me—"

"No, I won't. Time's wasting. Let's go." He collected our bags. "Plenty of time to have this fight down the road."

"I'm not fighting."

"Even better, then. Truck. Now."

"*Fine.*" I shoved past him, disappointed at myself for allowing my old habit to take hold, angry at him for calling me on it. Ripping my duffel out of his grip I lashed out even more. "I'll take that. Not my pack mule. Remember? And don't even think you're driving." I called back before bounding up the stairs. "Thanks for everything, Mr. and Mrs. Holland. We should do this again soon. Oh, don't worry, Mr. Holland. Not *too* soon." Yeah, I'd have to apologize for that snark someday.

I tapped the steering wheel, waiting in the dark for Dutch to say quick goodbyes to his parents. Elspeth got a kiss on the cheek and a warm embrace. Davis offered a hearty handshake that morphed into a back-thumping hug. Some things had healed in the last several hours. The Hollands had mended some hurt. A decade-and-a-half-old wrong had been made right, or started to, anyway, and I couldn't help but be glad for it.

Dutch tossed his bag in the truck bed, then waited at my open driver's side window.

"What are you staring at?"

"Did you forget something?" If he referred to the last half-hour in his bedroom, that wasn't something I'd likely ever forget. No, that memory was seared to me, every second of it. He dangled my truck keys just out of reach. "Guessing you'll be wanting these."

I huffed, "Well, it sure beats the hell out of pushing." I lurched to grab the keyring, but he caught my wrist instead. I let him hold it, then I let him kiss my fingers. "Get in the damn truck, Ellis." Despite my eagerness to get on the road, I made a careful turn and slowly creeped down the dirt driveway. The glow of red taillights bathed Davis and Elspeth in the rearview, arms wrapped around one another. Davis kissed his wife's temple. A pang of jealousy hit me, followed by guilt, and I reached for Dutch's hand. The squeeze he offered would help power me through the rest of the day.

We drove in darkness. The sun wouldn't rise for hours, and my map app suggested a different way, bypassing high-traffic areas. The rural route provided little streetlight, and my adrenaline-abused body started to crash in the quiet nighttime.

I stole glances at my passenger. Dutch sat still, hands folded in his lap, eyes fixed on the road. His disciplined posture was rigid, but it didn't surprise me.

"What's going on over there?" I stifled a yawn, and he joined in while making a show of looking at his watch.

"Twenty-seven minutes, Sadie. I'm stunned."

"Stunned?"

"You kept quiet for twenty-seven minutes. And while we haven't seen much of one another in the last fifteen years, I venture a guess that might be some kind of record for you. Twenty-seven minutes. And you were awake the whole time. I assume with you driving and all."

"Wow, look who's all Chatty Cathy now. And if you have any hopes of seeing any *more* of me any time soon, you might wanna check yourself, big guy."

He grunted, showing the first signs of fidgeting in his seat. I had a feeling any light would have highlighted his pink cheeks. I enjoyed knowing I could still do that. Keeping my hands to myself proved a challenge, though.

Silence resumed. A minute passed, and I reached for the radio. He beat me to it but didn't click the power button.

"We should talk." He rested our joined hands on the bench seat between us. I let it happen. "Back at the house—" He stalled.

"Is this about what we did or what we said?" I liked talking points. An agenda. Knowing exactly what items were up for discussion in a conversation. Again, engineer.

"I s'pose both," he offered.

"All right. Well, if you would like to take anything back, retract, rephrase some—or all of it. Blame it on the rain. The sooner, the better, I think." There's nothing like being trapped in a moving vehicle while your heart, gut, and ego are about to get shredded. If I had only reached the radio knob faster. He let go of my hand, and my sinking feeling went from bad to worse. When his other hand reached for his neck, I guessed it was more dire than I'd initially thought.

"There is nothing I want to take back. Nothing I said, nothing I did. You?"

Relief should have been instant, but shame coiled in me. I'd tried to run. I knew it before it happened, and he saw it too. And then he called me out on it.

"No," I lied and unconvincingly.

"Not even the part where you opened the door to my mom with your top mostly undone? Because that was—"

"What your parents must think of me."

"Don't. Don't feel bad about one of the best moments of my life. Not the door part. The button part."

I smiled. "Best moment, huh?"

"Top two—hey, your favorite number."

"What's the other? The high-ranking event in your life?"

"Our dance."

"My goodness. Ellis Holland, for a notorious fixer, you are one hell of a cinnamon roll."

"*Dutch* Holland is the fixer, and I don't know what that other thing means."

"It means you're the sweetest of heroes." I patted his hand, happy to have an excuse to touch him again.

"Is that a bad thing? Because if it helps, I wasn't thinking of being particularly sweet an hour ago in my bedroom."

Prickly heat rose up my sundress. "For the record, my skittish routine back there? It wasn't about you—or us. It was about me having a problem, a problem that has *nothing* to do with you, a problem I don't want to burden you with, and me being enough—smart enough, strong enough, capable enough to take care of it on my own. I'm sorry if you—"

"I don't want your apology," he interjected. "I want you to let me in. Let me help."

"Why won't you let me apologize?" I blurted. Once it came out, I tumbled headlong. "Why won't you let me say I'm sorry—about anything? Why can't you hear my apology and then forgive me for trying to bolt, because I feel awful that you think it had anything to do with you."

His reply took too long. Bile rose in my throat.

"Ellis—"

"God, Sadie," he swore.

I jerked the steering wheel in the shock of it, swerving on the dark two-lane road.

"Because what if it does have to do with me? What if your problem is *because* of me?"

"How could that be? How could you possibly be responsible?"

"I don't know, but you don't understand the business. The moving parts, the six-degrees, firewalls, plausible deniability. I can only swear to part of it. The fire *wasn't* me. But if it was Pembroke—if it was *someone*, rest assured I will find whoever is responsible, and I'll—handle it."

Okay, maybe more alpha than cinnamon roll.

"And while we're noting things for the record, if you don't know that I would forgive you *anything*, that there is *nothing* in this world you could ever do or say to change how I feel about you—well, Sadie, then you haven't been listening." He retreated as far to his side of the truck cab as he could move, arms folded, head resting against the window. "I'm going to close my eyes. Wake me if you get sleepy. Daylight will bring answers."

We were definitely done talking now.

Twenty-Seven

SADIE

present day

No one has ever accused me of being delicate or docile, nor do I appreciate being labeled—in any way. So, when Dutch teased me with his "praise" for my ability to keep mum for a full twenty-seven minutes, my obstinate gene reared its impetuous self, and I didn't utter another word until we hit Canaan Cove's county line. Nothing new. My standard operating procedure means if someone implies that I'm one thing, sure as shooting, I will go to great lengths to prove that I am quite another. Don't pigeonhole me. It's the principle of the thing. No, it's not one of my most endearing qualities. That said, my speaking sacrifice let Dutch get some rest while allowing his words to stew, filling me with more guilt that felt nothing short of stereotypical. And I couldn't help but envy a man that could sleep anywhere, anyhow, no matter the swirling circumstance.

Skies brightened as we slowed, coming toward town. Dutch stirred, easing into consciousness. Still, neither of us spoke.

The weight of the day swelled the closer we drove to that idyllic country lane, and the sick feeling in my gut grew. Viral fear. I dreaded what we'd see in two short turns and a few hundred yards. My foot let off the gas. A stoplight provided a brief delay, and I'd never been happier to see one. But when the light switched to green, we sat. No traffic. No noise. Only a dark pink sky and the old adage, "Red sky at morning, sailors take warning."

Dutch took my hand. "It's going to be okay, Sadie Jane. We'll see to it. I promise."

My foot remained on the brake, my mouth shut, but this was no willful act of defiance. The opposite, in fact.

"It's the one on the right." He squeezed my fingers with an encouraging nod.

"Huh?" My first sound in hours and an elegant one at that.

"The pedal. The one on the right. You press it. With your foot."

The start of a laugh exhaled out of me, and we moved through the intersection. That laugh was short-lived. After one more turn and another half-block until our destination, the smell reached us first, followed by the residual smoke, steam, and fluttering ash like gray snow I'd never in my life seen fall from this particular piece of southern sky. One firetruck remained on the scene with a skeleton crew of Canaan Cove's volunteer firefighters. Two hose operators continued to spray as a precaution, but most others had peeled down to suspenders and undershirts, presumably milling about in search of lasting danger.

An f-bomb whispered from my lips as I rolled up behind a police cruiser parked in my long driveway. Hunching over the steering wheel, I took in the scene until—"Oh my God. How the hell?"

I freed myself from the seatbelt and tore out of the truck. "Leo?" I shouted and ran for my brother, who stood on the front lawn staring at what was left of our family home. He spun and caught me in his giant wingspan, but when he let loose, I clung tighter. Maybe sometimes I am a hugger.

"Why are you—how did you get here?" I craned my neck to see his face, unwilling to let go.

"Dutch sent—" Leo looked beyond me without finishing his thought. He shook his head. "Doesn't matter. I'm here. Pulled up ten minutes ago, fifteen maybe."

I spun to face Dutch, who had followed me from the truck. "You did this? You got Leo?"

He shrugged. "I made some calls. Junior helped—"

I rushed him, planting a short, hard kiss on his mouth, and pressed my forehead to his. "Thank you, Ellis. It's exactly what I—thank you." In a beat, I hurried back to Leo, hooked his arm, and asked, "Now, what do we know?"

In the Hollywood version, the prime time must-see Dick Wolf TV firefighting-medical-police procedural, we'd have had a full accounting of the hows, whys, and wherefores, and be well on our way to the solutions part of the episode. Real life had more questions than answers, a shit-ton of red-tape wrapped paperwork, and the acrid, dank smell of char and fast-growing mold. This much the engineer in me knew for sure: the house was a total loss.

Dutch remained onsite but appeared to be operating a parallel investigation to the one Leo and I participated in with the police, a fire investigator, and our insurance agent with her own expert who had descended on the scene. If Dutch's phone wasn't to his ear, he was in someone else's—asking questions. I heard him press for details but in a mild manner, careful not to raise any red flags. Midge arrived with her Wagoneer full of sandwiches, coffee, and sweet tea to feed the troops. Junior returned after opening his store with the standing offer of extra Feed 'n Seed hands to help move debris and rescue possessions as soon as the authorities cleared the structure safe for civilians. Small-town living at its finest.

Late-day access to the ground floor proved to be sensory overload for me. Barely through the front door, I became the proverbial deer in headlights—frozen in the sweltering heat of the day, the freshly extinguished fire, and a fury that burned from my insides out for all we didn't know about the fire's cause.

"Let's get out of here. Get you to the Motor Lodge. I called ahead—" Dutch hovered close-by, offering help in his sweet, quiet way, but I couldn't cave to it.

I stepped away, bristling for space as my independent streak flared. "I'm not done here. I need—"

"Give us a minute, will you, Dutch?" Leo intervened. "Sometimes, only a big brotherly size fourteen will do. Hate for you to get any on you in the fallout."

It was the first sign of levity and leave it to Leo to bring it. Dutch backed up to give the siblings our privacy.

"Do I have to throw you over my shoulder and toss you in the back of your truck? Because I can, I have, and I'll do it again, Shorty."

"No." It sounded like pouting, but I was tired.

"Good. You should also knock off the push-me, pull-you routine with the fine fella over there. Kissing him one minute and rebuffing him another isn't a good look. And he's moved some mountains for you today and shows no signs of stopping."

"It's complicated." I avoided my brother's eye.

"I see that, but you should apologize."

"You're right. I should, but it's not like he'll let me."

"Let you? Like you'd ever ask permission." He hooked his arm around my shoulders to drag me out of the blackened foyer to the front yard. Dutch waited in the soggy grass, frenetic fingers typing on his phone. He stopped when my brother and I approached.

"I'm ready to go now, Ellis. Thank you for making arrangements, and I'm sorry I snapped at you back—"

"No need to apologize."

I shot Leo my "I told you so" look as he coughed.

"Dutch. Don't make me muzzle you. I once reigned supreme in a Queens ER when the power went out on a full moon Saturday Halloween while Mars *and* Mercury were in retrograde, so let there be no doubt—I can take you. Now let the woman apologize." Leo spun toward the driveway, leaving Dutch and me wide-eyed, stifling tight-lipped grins. Leopold Klein had spoken.

The three of us crammed into my truck in silence to make the short ride to the Motor Lodge. I didn't even balk when Leo shoved me into the center of the bench seat, wordlessly telling me he'd be driving. I found solace sandwiched between the two best men I knew, even if only for a mile—a calm that fooled me into thinking the worst had passed.

Sweaty exhaustion dripped from all three of us as we trudged through the door of the Motor Lodge lobby. Addie Watson-Dodson's delighted squeal was a mite more than I thought I could bear.

"It's a big day this late in the season for the Motor Lodge," Addie chirped. "Of course, I am truly sorry for the circumstances, and you will definitely get the friends and family discount, but the good news is we have plenty of space for y'all—"

The short handle of my duffel I insisted on carrying caught on the arm of a chair. It was the mere two-second distraction I blamed for failing to circumvent what came next.

All hell broke loose.

"Sade!" A briefly cheerful Tristan called from across the small lobby, but that pep evaporated when Dutch entered behind me. "*You.* Get the hell away from her—" Tristan barreled toward Dutch.

Dutch dropped his bag and reared back, ready to deliver a defensive blow I doubted that Tristan would survive.

"El—Tristan—*Dutch,* don't hit him." My bag strap jerked me to a halt when I tried to angle in between the two men, but it was too late. Tristan staggered back from the mercifully diluted punch, landing on a lobby loveseat. Addie gasped, and Leo dragged me out of the way of any melee that might ensue.

"Stay down, Tristan," Dutch warned, but he only had eyes for me. A questioning look like he couldn't believe I had sprung to Tristan's defense, *or* that I had done it invoking the name Dutch instead of Ellis. Disappointment lingered on his face, and maybe hurt.

"Now, I don't know you, but as a man of medicine, it is my professional opinion that you should heed that advice," Leo quipped to the fallen Tristan, keeping a firm hold of my elbow.

"Tristan, it's okay." I hurried to Dutch's defense now. "Dutch isn't—he wouldn't—"

Tristan's anger morphed to confusion seeing me with Dutch and obviously not under duress. "Did you—did you do this? The fire? Is that your handiwork because there's no way my father would have sanctioned it—"

"Jesus, Tristan. You're going to want to stop talking before I have to make you stop talking. Something I assure you your father would *absolutely* sanction. We'll speak privately. As for Sadie, she is a grown woman capable of choosing who she spends time with, so we'll be leaving those decisions up to her. Now, get settled in your room, put some ice on that jaw, and await further instructions from me. And if you hear from your father, be sure to tell him I'm expecting his call." Dutch flexed his fingers, scooped up his bag, and greeted our host with a more benevolent tone. "Addie, good to see you again. I believe you're holding three rooms for the Kleins and me."

A wide-eyed and wordless Addie laid three enveloped card keys in a neat line on the check-in desk and pushed them toward a coolly calm Dutch. With her elbow as support, her chin sank into her palm, and I thought I saw heart emojis thumping in her pupils. I didn't like it.

Leo tugged me even closer to whisper in my ear, "Soooo, are we gonna talk about Dutch's sudden loss of southern lilt, or are we gonna pretend like he didn't just *Eliza Doolittle* himself right here in front of everybody?"

"See? I told you it was *complicated*."

Twenty-Eight

SADIE

present day

IT COULD HAVE BEEN the best shower of my life, but the weight of the day destroyed any chance I would enjoy the sparkling Motor Lodge ensuite. Soot and ash hung in my curls and my nose, smoke clung to my sundress, and visions of my now-scorched childhood home burned in my brain. The structure was in ruins, and the proof swirled a dingy escape down the bath drain.

My hair wrapped in a fluffy towel and body clad in a cushy robe to match, I splayed out on the king bed, eager for any distraction as the wreckage continued to bombard my senses. A stomach rumble reminded me I hadn't made it by the sandwich stash in Midge's Wagoneer. I hadn't eaten since the wrecked dinner at the oh-so-welcoming *Holland House*. It didn't take long before my thoughts snuck their way back to the lake house basement—Dutch's hands on my skin, his lips exploring mine, his words in my ear... a knock at the door. I groaned, sliding up onto my elbows. I couldn't even reminisce without interruption.

Another tap at the motel room door forced me to the peephole. Leo. I opened it a crack, hoping to find him alone and maybe with a cheeseburger.

"Oh, good. You're awake." He pushed through the door, empty-handed, without an invitation. Not that I would have turned him away. "How about this place, huh, Shorty? The color palette, the detail, the yummy soaps and such."

"I'm pretty sure you're not supposed to eat them." My stomach growled again, but Leo kept talking.

"Addie Watson-Dotson has a real gift. This place is fabulous."

"Uh-huh."

"You okay?"

"Uh-huh."

"You look kinda—sweet baby Jesus." He spun three-hundred-sixty degrees, "Is someone in here with you?" His wild eyes shot to the bathroom door.

"Shut up, Leo. No, I'm very much alone here. Thank you. Just me and my thoughts."

"Great. How about we devour the minibar and discuss the broody high school crush versus the bouncy beach blond? And when I say bouncy—I mean, *boy* did he *bounce* off that sofa when Dutch—*ka-pow, right in the*—Now, you know I don't condone violence—oh hey, and what was that about this being Dutch's handiwork? What'd the *himbo* mean by that? And I have not forgotten about the mystery of the glum one's forgotten twang."

"Oh my. Someone's had too much sweet tea. I'm gonna need you to slow down. And *himbo*? Come on," I scoffed, wondering if Leo had taken up my reading habits.

"Tristan is pretty. Too pretty. I can see why you don't want to have to compete with that. I mean, I love you, but you'd lose on the daily. So, we're definitely Team Dutch, right? Because if we're not, I'm gonna need a moment to, you know—what's the engineer word?"

"Recalibrate?"

"Exactly."

"Leo. Our house burned down."

"*Your* house burned down. Yes, but you weren't in it when it happened. And if you had been, it would have been the death of me, so, time to *live*. The rest is just stuff, and I come with news.

Good and bad. Which do you want first?" Leo dodging the grim reality was just that—evasion. When the adrenaline wore off along with the sugar and caffeine of the sweet tea, he might liquify into a giant emotional puddle, and I hoped he'd let me be there if he fell apart.

I shored up the tie belt of my borrowed bathrobe. "Bad news first. Always." I closed my eyes, waiting for the blow, but a playful, rhythmic rap at the door brought the next interruption. Leo, without a fisheye peek, yanked the door wide.

"Sade." With a makeshift ice pack pressed to his face, Tristan winced with his welcoming smile that faded as his eyes traveled the full height of my brother. "Who are *you*? You're *ginormous*."

Before Leo reconsidered his thoughts on violence and Tristan suffered his second punch of the day, I clutched my bathrobe collar with one hand and stepped between the two men.

"Tristan, this is my brother Leo. He lives in—"

"New York. Yeah. I remember. I do pay *some* attention." Tristan tossed the baggie of ice on the bureau, wiped his hand down his linen trousers, and offered it to Leo. "She talks about you a lot." The two shared a hearty shake.

"How's that chin?" No matter the one in need, Leo was a born caretaker. He nudged Tristan's jaw, examining for damage. "The way you ran *right* into the clenched fist of the notorious Dutch Holland. He's been known to do some damage."

"Leo," I hissed with a mini shove.

"Ah, so you've heard about our legendary fixer—wait, Dutch *hit* me, I didn't run into—"

"I'm sorry, legendary *what*, now?" my brother interjected, with a speedy twist to me. His furrowed brow demanded an answer, but another quiet thump at the door provided a stay of explanation.

I ignored the security eye this time, tearing open the door without considering the consequences. Dutch wobbled, balancing an armload of paper sacks and a six-pack of Canaan Cove ale. "Hi." His gaze stuttered at my chest, where my robe gaped, bordering on inappropriate, then over my shoulder at the Statler and Waldorf impression carrying on behind me. I adjusted the terrycloth and inwardly welcomed myself to the ninth circle of hell while ushering Dutch into the suddenly very crowded motel room.

"Look, guys, Dutch brought beer," I chirped.

"Ew," the duo replied in stereo, followed by a helpful Leo steering a rubbernecking Tristan to the other side of the room. "Let's float like a butterfly to the minibar, Rocky."

I rolled my eyes at Leo's jumbled metaphor joke with another gesture for Dutch to enter. "More for us, I guess."

Dutch hesitated but offered what he'd brought. "Burgers, fries, and the small bag on top has a pint of rocky road. You should stick that in the mini-fridge." He didn't cross the room's threshold.

"Why does it look like you're not staying? You're coming in, right?" Of all the men I wanted in my motel room...

"I've got work to do, and you look—cared for." He eyed the two other visitors who explored the well-stocked hospitality offerings.

Exhaustion, hunger, and a traumatic day were the excuses for my candor. "Feels like I haven't seen you since dawn. From a distance, I guess, but not—well, I'd like to—see you, spend some time with—be with—wow, that sounded needy—"

"*Good*," he exclaimed. "No, it sounded *good*, I mean. I'll come in. For a bit."

"Great, because I have all this beer." Heat rose out of that bathrobe. I glanced over my shoulder. "Come make nice with those two. It's important to me—plus Leo's got news, good and bad, apparently. I'd like you to be here."

"Absolutely. Now get this ice cream put away before it's soup."

"Ellis?"

"*Hm?*"

"Thank you." I grabbed the bag that held the ice cream instead of grabbing Dutch, but if I'd had my way and no audience, melting ice cream would have been the least of my concerns.

"So, why's he here, Sade?" Tristan asked from as far away from Dutch as he could get.

Dutch opened his mouth to speak, but I stepped in to answer. "Because, Tristan, El—*Dutch* and I knew each other a very long time ago, and when we happened upon each other on the Selkie, he was kind enough to help. This is his hometown too. We're both from here. And we're—friends." I did my best not to grimace at my own words while Dutch stood motionless, eyes focused on the plush carpet. His jaw clenched, and I thought he held his breath.

"You didn't tell me that. On the phone, you implied you had never met him before—"

"You're right. I did not admit to knowing Dutch. I apologize. Your depiction of him was not what I think him to be—not the man I *know* he is, so rather than debate it with you, I moved on from the subject. I didn't mean to be deceitful, and I'm sorry if I've hurt your feelings. I hope you can forgive me."

"Yeah, of course." Not for nothing, but that's how you accept an apology. But now Tristan was quiet and unusually compliant.

"And why are you here, Tristan?" It was the first time Dutch spoke to the room. "How did you even know to come here? Hard to imagine news of a little house fire in Canaan Cove made it all the way to your tony neighborhood so quickly."

"That's none of your business, and you best remember just who works for who here."

"Whom," Leo cut in. "Who works for *whom*. Let's try to keep this civilized, boys. Grammatically correct, at least."

I elbowed Leo, but asked, "I'd like to know, Tristan. It is curious."

Tristan sighed. "If you must know, I was concerned about you and your safety." He cleared his throat and shot a stern glare at Dutch. "I hired a private investigator to keep an eye on you. He was the one who called in the fire. Happy?"

"But I wasn't even in town. I left early yesterday morning."

"Well, yes. I learned that after the fact. And I never claimed I hired a *good* private investigator."

Leo intervened. "Not that anyone asked, but *I'm* here because I'm the only one looking out for my sister and her best interests."

"That's not true," Dutch and Tristan quickly insisted in unison.

"*Hmm*. Interesting," Leo replied with a smug frown, looking askance from one defiant man to the other on opposite sides of the room. The sudden quiet and steely stares made me squirm.

"I'm starving. Let's eat. Carpet picnic? And Leo, fill us in on what you know. Good news. Bad news. Bad news first."

Leo played host while Tristan and Dutch gave each other wide berths. I popped the tops of two beers and handed one to Dutch with a private smile. Taking a spot on the floor, I leaned against the end of the bed frame. The bad news? It would be days, maybe longer, before a thorough inspection could be done to determine the blaze's cause. The good news? We were well-insured.

"How'd your initial inspection go? The one your engineer-friend did?" Dutch sat next to me, an arm's length between us. Too far.

"Sam, you mean? Structural engineer Sam?" Leo offered.

Dutch looked at me, then Leo. "I guess," he shrugged. "She didn't mention his name."

"*Her* name," Tristan piped up, a mouth full of cheeseburger. "*Sham's* a girl."

I cocked my head. "She's a *woman*," I corrected Tristan, "and she didn't do it, the inspection. We postponed it. Something came up at the last minute."

Dutch's head slumped back on the mattress. "No, Sadie. Tell me you didn't cancel because of me—because I left—"

"*No*. I didn't cancel. *Sam* did. She got a—" The burger in my belly turned to stone. My mouth went dry while I watched Tristan shove the last bite of his burger past his lips. Then all eyes were on Tristan.

"Whaaa?" He barely chewed and swallowed with a visible gulp. "Why's everyone looking at me?"

"Why are we looking at him?" Leo murmured out the side of his mouth.

"Sadie?" Dutch stretched to touch my shoulder.

"She—Sam got another opportunity. A make-or-break kind of thing out in Illinois, I think. She's from there. Could be a real game-changer for her and her start-up."

"I don't understand, Shorty. Why've you gone pale?"

"The—opportunity—the last-minute offer? It was with Pembroke Industries."

Everyone stared while Tristan *hmphed,* brushing crumbs off his Tommy Bahama shirt. His sweeping motion slowed when he registered everyone's renewed, watchful eye. "What? *Whoa.* Wait a minute. You think I had something to do with that? How would I? You're sitting next to *him*, and *I'm* the one in the hot seat? You're accusing *me*? Jeez, Sade, why aren't you asking *him*?"

"Because I'm asking *you*. How'd you know Sam was a woman?"

"Wow. Just—*wow*." Tristan got to his feet.

"Answer the question, Tristan." Dutch stood, too.

"Okay, simmer down, boys." My brother rose to referee.

"She asked a simple question, Tristan." Dutch gestured to me. "All one-syllable words. Answer her."

"Sade must have mentioned it at some point. Gee, Dutch, what's it to you?" Tristan took on his squash court swagger, and I should have sensed the danger, but I was too intent on remembering if that was true. "*Huh*, I don't know. Maybe she talks in her sleep sometimes." He barely had time to wink.

It happened very fast. Leo didn't move quickly enough, and my squawking "*Ellis, don't*" had no effect. Tristan found himself sprawled across another motel loveseat, dazed, this time, blood trickling from his nose. Dutch massaged his hand, eager for his would-be opponent to stand again. Tristan didn't.

Leo surveyed the scene, hands on his hips. "*Huh. Very interesting,*" he quipped again before moving in for another first-aid check on the once-again wounded Tristan. "Tristan? You okay? Say something."

Tristan groaned, "Uh, who the *hell* is Ellis?"

When Dutch answered his motel room door, I handed him some ice wrapped in a washcloth to soothe his hand. "You need to stop hitting people."

"I'm not hitting *people*. I'm hitting Tristan." He tossed aside the ice. "And my fists have found far-harder targets." Exasperation more than anger wafted off him as he trudged away and sat at the computer workstation he'd set up on a small table and chair combination in the corner of his room.

"He was joking, you know. Tristan was joking."

"Was he? No one laughed, so I couldn't be sure. Plus, he intended to provoke me, and far be it from me to disappoint the heir apparent." Dutch tightened his jaw and flexed his fingers, keeping his eyes focused on the laptop rather than me.

"Oh, so that was about the two of you. Nothing to do with me. And here I was all flattered."

"I didn't hear you shutting down his insinuation. And I'm not a jealous man, Sadie, but I have a tendency to bristle when a woman is disrespected. You've met my mother, right?"

"Are we really fighting about this, because I'm pretty sure I've made it clear my relationship with Tristan is business and friendship, nothing more. Not that I have to explain or justify anything to you, but if there's something you'd like to ask, the floor's yours. Ask away, and I'll tell you. Like I said last night, I'll keep no secrets from you."

He didn't ask, and I wasn't sure he could say the same. But I wasn't here to argue, so I tried to navigate the choppy water.

"Now, I wonder if I *do* talk in my sleep. Stands to reason since I talk too much when I'm awake. Why wouldn't that trend continue when my head hits the pillow? Then again, maybe my voice is so tired by then it takes a break. *Hm.*" My fatigue coupled with the second pale ale and my candor had risen off the charts and into potentially risky territory. "Guess there's one way to find out."

Dutch didn't take the bait of my shameless suggestion. Disappointing.

"Well, either way, Tristan wouldn't know." I moped, taking in the window view, followed by an angsty back-and-forth. The man of few words lived up to his tacit reputation. "All right. I'll ask the questions then. If this isn't you, then how is it Pembroke? Aren't you Pembroke's last resort?"

"I'm lots of people's last resort."

I squinted at the stoic fixer. "Is that meant to sound scary? Because it sounds kinda scary. But I've already told you that you don't scare me." That wasn't entirely true, but my fear didn't stem from Pembroke Industries or Dutch Holland's fixing ways. My fear had more to do with my heart than my life or limbs.

Dutch sat back in his chair, and I recognized the look that said he was about to use some of his well-guarded words. "You want to know why I'm good at what I do? Aside from some—luck, I'd guess you'd call it."

"Tell me."

"I keep quiet. I talk less and listen more. Everyone wants something. And everyone has an Achilles heel. It's about desire and weakness and leveraging the two. There's always a deal to be made, and in the end, the perception might not be the reality. Then again, you'd be surprised how flexible 'reality' can be." He could have air quoted. "Sure, sacrifices get made, but no one walks away empty-handed. As long as everyone walks away with their mouths shut."

"And your reputation? For being dangerous, I mean."

"You said it yourself, Sadie Jane. A story gets told often enough, the 'facts' get jumbled, changed, and then there's more than one incident, true or not, and all of a sudden, I'm responsible for all sorts of backroom mayhem, unsolved accidents, missing persons. If only those people ever existed in the first place. For the record, they didn't. But everyone knows someone's cousin's brother-in-law who worked with a guy that had a friend who met somebody who saw it all happen. From a distance, of course."

I sat at the table opposite him, absorbing this new data, looking for signs of pride or remorse. I found neither. But now I realized the origin story of the infamous Dutch Holland. The blame lay with me. I was the radioactive spider. I reached across his temporary desk, wanting to touch him, be nearer to him, but he kept his distance. "Why are you telling me this?"

He shook his head with a sort of sigh. "I said no secrets; I meant no secrets."

"None?"

He evaded. "Also, I'm thinking Dutch Holland might be retiring soon."

"Oh?"

"This one anyway."

"What does that mean—oh my gosh. You *are* the Dread Pirate Roberts."

Sadness laced his forced chuckle. "Maybe so. Competition is always gunning for the top spot. Or what if Pembroke sent someone else? Didn't trust I'd get the job done. I don't know why—but it's possible. Someone might be stepping up to take my title, but he—or she—tends more toward fact than fiction if this fire thing is someone's attempt at a fix. It's a choice. The lazy one, in my view, but what are you gonna do? I'm in no position to argue ethics."

"Seems to me you might have a leg to stand on."

"Oh, Sadie, don't mistake my gray hat for a white one."

It surprised me how little I cared. "You guys got a union? Fixers United? Problem Solvers of America? Super-Secret Federation of Kick-Ass Name Takers? Okay, I hope it's not that last one, because that's a mouthful." That earned me a quiet laugh, but it was short-lived. I finally asked, "What are you going to do?"

"Are you asking for my help?"

"I'm not sure I can afford you."

"Are you asking for my help?" he repeated, taking it all far more seriously than I wanted him to.

"Take it out in trade, maybe?" I smirked.

"Don't joke. It's not funny."

"What's your plan?"

As it was, Dutch had already begun work on finding solutions to what he saw as two separate problems, one personal, one business. He'd conscripted his mother. Elspeth Holland was an attorney. Most recently a civil litigator, and while patent law wasn't her specialty, she knew things, knew people, knew how to pull apart a contract. If freeing my patent was possible, he was confident his mother would find the way to do it.

"She has the pertinent files, and she's combing through them," he explained.

"How did you get a hold of those? I couldn't, Tristan couldn't."

"Tristan *didn't*. There's a difference, and we've discussed what I do for a living, right? I deal in information."

Part two meant finding the truth behind the bungalow fire. Dutch knew an official investigation would take time, and he would apply pressure to shorten that schedule, but meanwhile, he had his own rocks to turn over, cages to rattle. He promised to find answers.

Fatigue, waylaid by the earlier commotion, crept back, settling behind my eyes with weight and pressure. They begged to close, but a jolt of energy sparked through me when Dutch's hand touched mine.

"You should go to bed."

My eyes flickered to the one beside him, and he read my mind.

"Not that bed." His quick rejection included letting go of my hand. A sizable gut punch, to be sure.

Determined not to show my impatience, I stood, resolutely sliding my chair under the table, then stared at the man using his computer to avoid my eyes again. Seconds ticked by before I moved toward the door, but it was a false start.

"Ellis?"

"*Hm?*"

"Look at me," I demanded in an almost-whisper.

He did.

"I'm standing here—and I'm starting to feel a little foolish."

"Don't."

"Don't do what? Stand here, or feel foolish?"

He rushed to his feet but kept to his side of the room; the telltale neck grip betrayed his frustration. "Let me fix this, Sadie Jane. Let me do what I do, and then we can—"

"Sometimes, we don't want things *fixed*. Sometimes we just want to be heard."

"None of this means anything if you aren't safe, and I'm not certain you are. Whether you want to believe it or not, there are people in big business that play dirty. Dangerously dirty. And Pembroke is not immune. I'm proof-positive of that. And I've waited fifteen years for you and established myself as a go-to in my nefarious field. I'm not about to risk any of that by getting sidetracked."

"Losing your head over a little piece of tail?"

That zinger hit him, and he buckled some from the blow. "You know that's not true, Sadie."

"Well, while you're over there fixing, talking less, and listening more—hear this. There are only so many times you can send a woman away before her pride refuses to allow her to come around again."

"I'll worry about that when I know you're out of jeopardy. When I know there isn't a Dutch Holland 2.0 out there looking to make you disappear."

"Are you seriously telling me to go?" The prick of tears stung my tired eyes, and I spun to the door, already knowing the answer.

Twenty-Nine

DUTCH

fifteen years ago

"You want me to tell her to go?" My mother sat on the edge of my hospital bed, stroking my arm like some kitten. Staff had drawn the blinds to block the morning light that made my head throb harder. It did nothing to mask my mother's red, puffy eyes. Those hurt my head and my heart even more.

"Yes, ma'am. Please."

"Dutch. Sadie's been here since dawn. She looks like she's been crying."

Sadie crying? I wondered what that looked like. I thought I knew her every expression, every smile, look of surprise, each thoughtful gaze, no matter the situation. Her tears had never occurred to me. Closing my eyes, I tried to imagine, but couldn't see them. Was it my scrambled brain or simply because crying was something the bold and unshakable Sadie Klein would never do? Not ever.

It was a calculated risk. Despite my aching everything, I'd run the analysis. Seeing Sadie safe from blame for the night's disaster was priority one. I'd deal with the fallout of pushing her away once I knew she was out of trouble. Besides, if she stayed angry at me, she'd be more likely to let me take responsibility.

Even so, as long as the other kid kept to the story—a story of his own making—it would be our word against Sadie's if she tried to take on any of the burden.

"Are you sure, Dutch? I don't know when you might be able to see her again." Mom squeezed my arm now, a grip a kitten wouldn't have enjoyed.

Those were the only words that made me pause, but I shook them off, much to my beaten-up brain's dismay. How could I never see Sadie again? That couldn't be. That's not how life worked. I convinced myself it would be all right in the end.

"Tell her to go."

She hesitated, still with the tight grasp of my forearm, before tilting to kiss my temple.

"Mom, where's Dad?"

"He's meeting with a lawyer. Everyone thought it best I stay out of it. For propriety's sake. Oh, and Dr. Klein will be in to see you soon."

"Does it have to be Dr. Klein?" Sweat tingled on my upper lip, and nausea swirled at the thought of facing Sadie's grandfather.

"She insisted."

"She?" I assumed wrong. I shouldn't have. Lesson learned.

"She'll be in soon."

I barely nodded.

When my mother and Dr. Klein returned, Sadie's grandmother took immediate control of the scene.

"I understand Dutch is only seventeen, but I'll be blunt. I think our conversation will be more fruitful one-on-one, but only if everyone agrees." Her tone scared me, like maybe Sadie had confided in her grandmother, the one thing I implored her not to do. I feared Dr. Klein could blow-up my less-than-sturdy plan.

"Yes, thank you, Dr. Klein. Mom, could you give us a minute? I could use some Jell-O. Any kind but green."

My mother's pleading look settled on Dr. Klein.

"I'll take good care, Elspeth." A gentle reminder we were all friends here, neighbors, anyway.

"Thank you, Talia," my mother whispered.

Dr. Klein led my mom to the door, a kind but definitive dismissal.

The penlight seared into my brain when the doctor shined it into my carefully pried open eyes, one at a time.

"Well, you have a pretty bad concussion, Dutch. Did that happen in the fight?"

"What fight?"

She cocked her head. "The one between you and the other boy?"

Shit, Dutch. Get it together. "Right. No. I didn't hit my head in the fight. My head didn't get hit, I mean."

"Except in the mouth. You received two sutures when you came into the emergency room." She pointed. "They couldn't get it to stop bleeding. You don't recall?"

My face was still numb—more than my face, but the tip of my tongue grazed the corner of my mouth, and I felt the prickly end of a stitch.

"So, the football game, then? I heard you took a hard hit."

"Yes, ma'am—ma'am?"

"Yes?"

"How is he, the other kid?"

"His leg is broken. Seriously broken. He's had surgery. He's awake. The prognosis is good. He'll likely limp and be a good predictor of rain." Her flip reply surprised me, but then I thought of her granddaughter and her dearest friend Midge Toogood, and it seemed kind of right. She was a tough lady who had gone through the unthinkable pain of losing her son and daughter-in-law. While the community accepted and even appreciated her and her husband, they weren't exactly adored like some other people might be. Canaan Cove had its backward elements, but that kind of thinking wasn't tolerated in my home.

Relief washed over me when I heard he'd be okay. But the truth remained. Sadie had attacked him with a weapon she had the forethought to bring with her when she confronted him.

Dr. Klein pulled me to the present.

"Why don't you tell me your version of events."

"Why? Did you speak to him? Didn't he say what happened?"

"He did, but now I'd like your version." Dr. Klein's attitude made even more sense now. If the guy told his story, she'd know her grandchild's part in it and understandably be a whole lot less sympathetic to the new kid's situation. Unfortunately, there hadn't been much time for well-thought-out corroboration. If he'd already talked, I needed to keep my mouth shut until I knew exactly what he'd said. How the hell was this ever going to work?

"No versions, Dr. Klein. What he said is what happened." Another calculated risk, but I was under the impression he had more to lose than I did. He had more to hide, in his mind anyway, and if you looked at it from that point of view, I was doing him a favor. In the end, he begged *me* to go along. I agreed, reluctantly, but time was of the essence, and as long as Sadie was blameless—and never learned the details—I would learn to live with it.

"Are you sure—"

"Could I speak to him? Not long. I'd just like to apologize. But privately, if that's possible. Do you s'pose you could help me with that? A private meeting?"

"I could, yes. If he agrees."

"Oh, he'll agree." I recognized my upper hand in the situation and opted to play it. "Tell him I said it was important."

"I guess I could—" A knock at the door interrupted her.

My mother's red, puffy eyes the size of quarters zeroed in on me. "Excuse us, Doctor, but Davis is here, with our attorney." She swallowed hard. "And a police officer. He has questions."

I reached for Dr. Klein's hand and whispered, "Where's Sadie?"

"Sadie? She went home. She said that's what you wanted."

I nodded.

"Are you up for speaking with the officer and your attorney?"

I nodded again.

"Would you like me to stay? I'll stay." She didn't wait for a reply.

Introductions were made around the room. Small-town living came with its courtesies.

"My patient is not well, having suffered an unattended concussion for more than twenty-four hours. Not only does that have a bearing on any kind of complaint that might be lodged against him, but I insist on being present, with his parents' approval, of course, to ensure his serious condition isn't exacerbated."

No one disagreed, and Dr. Klein's participation likely saved my butt.

Thirty

SADIE

present day

I GOT MY BUTT out of bed for breakfast—one of my top five favorite meals. It came as part of the package at the Motor Lodge, and my heavy feet and tired eyes weren't going to keep me from it. But nearing the lobby, cheery conversation halted me mere yards from fruit pastry and dark roast. Leo and Tristan sat at one of a few bistro tables in a sunny spot against the slant window wall of the mid-century motel. I considered making an about-face to hide in my room.

"Shorty." Leo caught me. "Shorty, I have *got* to figure out a way to get this sweet tea to Queens. Is it the water? The tea leaves? The pounds of sugar? Lord, help me." His accent had multiplied more than Dutch's had faded, and I wondered about his New York City culture-shocked re-entry.

"Nectar of the Gods, I say," Tristan proclaimed his fondness too.

"Dunno. Don't drink it." I poured coffee and joined the new besties. The abundance of the two personalities I'd feared would be too much pulsed in the motel dining alcove. Fortunately, the duo didn't clash. Then again, it probably wouldn't take long for them to join forces and turn their collective over-the-top attention on me.

"How is it we're kin with your non-sweet tea and beer drinking ways? It does not compute." My brother patted an empty chair to encourage me to sit.

"One reason our marriage would work so well." Tristan kidded in his never-ending way. "We'd never fight over the beverage supply. His-and-hers and never the twain shall meet."

I flew from my seat, thighs crashing into the table. Silverware and water glasses *clinked* and spilled. "My God, Tristan. The ring. The ring was in the house."

"There was a ring?" Leo grabbed napkins to commence clean-up.

"Oh, there was a ring. You betcha." Tristan boasted, sitting back in his seat. "Calm yourself, Sade. That's what insurance is for."

"But the paperwork, all of it—"

"If only records were kept...oh wait. They were! Sweet Sadie, don't worry about it." Tristan had zero cares for the jewelry.

"Did someone say ring? And marriage? Is someone getting married?" Addie scurried in from the front lobby desk, flushed and too excited. More personality to squeeze into the small space. "Gosh, I sure do love a wedding."

"Then *you,* Miss Addie, are officially invited," Tristan announced with a hair flip just for the poor gullible hostess.

"Shut up, Tristan." I couldn't handle him this early in the day.

"Oh. So, Addie's not invited?" He winked at me.

"You're so funny, Sadie. I remember that from high school." Then Addie gasped. "You should do it here."

"Do what here?" I asked as three sets of eyes landed on me, wide and wild, but all for different reasons.

"Get married, of course. I have a little garden spot by the pool. There's a gazebo. Have you seen it? Oh, it will be *darling,*" Addie squealed.

"*Darling,*" Tristan repeated.

"Did you hear that, Shorty? It'll be *darling.*"

I rolled my eyes at my brother, mouthing, "I. Hate. You."

Addie squeaked again and clapped her hands. "Leave it to me—"

"Addie, no," I interjected.

"If it's about the ring, Sade, I'll get you another one."

"Stop it, Tristan."

"Oooh, *two* rings. Your favorite number, sis." Leo snickered. Losing interest in the silliness, he returned to reading his morning news on his phone.

"Everybody, knock it off," I shouted as Dutch sauntered toward us through the lobby from the parking lot. He'd been up and out early, clean-shaven and everything.

"What seems to be the problem?" Rarely one to overreact, Dutch stood calmly beside Addie, hands to his hips, surveying the chaos.

Leo shot to attention, dropping his phone. "*Oh darn*, and me without any popcorn." My brother grinned, eager to be entertained, even at my expense. Sibling love.

"It's all very exciting, Dutch. We're planning a wedding. By the pool. I'm thinking mid-October." Addie looked to the ceiling, a mental Pinterest board well on its way to fruition.

"Addie—"

"Oh, I know, Sadie, short timeline, but I can do it. Don't you doubt me." She ignored my pleas. "Someone—*the bride*," Addie stage-whispered those two words to Dutch, employing ardent finger-pointing at me, "is having a case of cold tootsies. She'll be fine."

I feared the absurd conversation would provoke Tristan's third punched face in two days, but a stoic Dutch didn't move, didn't blink, didn't say a word. Stony silence hung heavily.

"Interesting," Leo murmured, sending me telepathic encouragement to do something, say something, to end the burgeoning tension. I returned the mental message, asking for him to run interference so I could speak to Dutch with some privacy.

"Good morning, Ellis. Coffee? Where've you been off to so early today?" A kind greeting hadn't been my plan for the morning, considering our argument the night before, but I like to think I'm flexible and fast on my feet. I ushered him to the self-serve coffee bar, away from the crowd.

"Your house. Hoped I might—" he shrugged. "How are you? Did you sleep? You feel better?"

"I'm all right. But that talk—the wedding talk—"

He frowned. "No need to explain."

"I know, but it's not—we're not—Tristan and I aren't—"

"I know." Dutch prepared two mugs of coffee while I stumbled over words.

"You know, huh?" I huffed with not quite a smile.

"I know I'd kill him before that ever happened, so yeah—I know." He grinned too.

"Is that a Dutch Holland threat?" I lifted the cup he slid toward me.

"Not a threat." He sipped, ready to move on to a new topic. "I have to leave."

And our morning banter came to a halt. I didn't reply.

"Just for the day. I got a thing I need to run down, and Leo has to be home tonight—"

"He does?"

"He has to get back to work. He knows who to call when he's ready to go." Apparently, Dutch had a handle on everyone's itinerary while I had my head up my—

"Does your thing have to do with my thing?" I asked, unsure if that broke some unspoken tenet. The "fixer" game seemed to have rules, Fight Club rules, and learning a whole network of fixers existed in the shadows, jockeying for status in some hierarchy of questionable endeavors made me wary of boundaries I couldn't see.

"*Your* thing is my only thing, and the sooner I—"

"Yeah." I placed my hand atop his resting on the coffee bar countertop, glancing at the trio still seated in the morning sunshine. Leo held forth with stories of New York City medical emergencies. They laughed and gasped and carried on over the dregs of their breakfast. "Look, last night was—"

"Yeah." As usual, he cut short my impending apology.

"And I sure would like to kiss you," I whispered.

Dutch set down his coffee, a slight tremor to his hand—the first sign he wasn't in total control. "I sure would like to be kissed by you. But I'm not sure Mrs. Watson-Dodson over there would handle that too well. It'd be awfully confusing for her—as your newly-hired wedding planner, and I'm afraid her head might explode."

"Right. I'll refrain then. For Addie's sake."

He nodded. "For Addie's sake." He slid his hand out from under mine with deliberate slowness. "I'm gonna go now. Try to enjoy your day with Leo. Last one for a bit."

The reminder was exactly what I needed to focus on my day. I nodded as the tips of his fingers pulled from the tips of mine, and he stepped away.

"Ah, screw it," he mumbled with a swift turn. His lips brushed my cheek, but just as quickly he headed to the lobby and out the door. He sped off in what looked like Junior Ford's car.

I only allowed myself a moment of dizzy giddiness before zeroing in on the things I needed to in the remaining hours I had with Leo. Gracefully clearing the distractions would be the first order of business. I thanked Addie for her hospitality and congratulated her again on the fine establishment. I then implored her not to call a single caterer, florist, or her beachy-themed music dee-jay cousin Mark the Shark.

Next—assuming how unlikely Tristan would be to help, I certainly didn't need him underfoot. I encouraged him to go on his way. But dammit, if he didn't prove me wrong. He knew exactly the insurance people to talk to and the questions to ask. He got us in touch with an attorney who made sure any on-the-fly decisions about the house could be handled solely by me, despite Leo being an equal property owner. In essence, it came down to paperwork, and Tristan's running point proved a lucky break for the Kleins, and truth be told, we needed one.

Tristan also offered to see Leo to the pre-arranged private airstrip and plane so the physician's assistant could get back to work. The playboy showed no signs of seeking any quid pro quo. Maybe it was about keeping up with Dutch, but I had no plans to dip my toe into that quagmire. Leo's travel itinerary was Leo's business, and I didn't want him to leave, anyway.

"You two go do what you need to do," Tristan dismissed us. "If nothing else, I am perfectly capable of entertaining myself—or finding someone to amuse me. When Leo is ready to go, I'll see him gone and then head home to see if I can change Daddy's mind about patents and trust funds. I've been known to charm the panties off—well, I can be quite persuasive—and I'm not convinced Daddy Dearest can resist my sway." Yeah, after a day of genuine aid and comfort, Tristan had to go make it gross, but maybe there was hope for him yet.

After all the "paperwork," Leo and I held each other close, staring at the wreckage from a spot on our long driveway.

"Don't cry, Leo. You said it yourself. It's just stuff." The inevitable breakdown had occurred, but he stood stronger than I had imagined. I guessed he'd seen and done things in Queens I couldn't begin to imagine and those experiences toughened him in all the right ways. Even so, I squeezed him tight.

"These are tears of joy, Shorty. Believe me." He kissed the top of my head.

I knew part of him believed that, but I also knew he held a sentimental attachment to things in a way I never did—never admitted, anyway. It was our childhood home—a house that became our sanctuary in the wake of a catastrophe I had no memory of, and our family never truly recovered from. It was the one thing left to cling to in the unexpected deaths of our grandparents—in some ways, a more profound loss. And while I didn't know how to protect him from this kind of assault, I did what I could to help him find some peace.

"And now I can rebuild. It'll be the same, but better with all the latest in green engineering tech, masked in southern country charm, and more bathrooms."

"And bedrooms," he added.

"Nope, bedrooms only encourage visitors to overstay their welcome."

"No. Bedrooms are for the basketball team of curly-headed nieces and nephews I see in my future. And you with such quality options for the sire."

"Well, that was an impressive transition I didn't see coming," I elbowed him. "And you shut your mouth, Leopold Klein, and don't ever—"

"The lady doth protest too much, methinks. Interesting." Leo *tsked*, holding me closer.

"Options?" I scoffed. "I don't have options."

"You're right, Shorty. That much is plain. Plain as the look on *both* of your faces," he sighed. "I saw it all those years ago, and I see it now, but how'd we get here?"

The words echoed Dutch's, and a flicker of possibility I hadn't ever considered pinged into focus. A domestic life I never wanted or wished for played in my mind. A fairy tale where I could have it all—if I wanted.

"Oh, my goodness, *gurl*, you are *thinking* about it."

"*Pfft*. No, I'm not."

"Except you are. You just floated away, lost in some jaw-dropping, high-powered-career, sexually-satisfying-marriage, domestic-breeding-goddess fantasy. The trifecta! The real-life HEA to end all other HEAs."

"Shut up, Leo. Fantasy is right. Which means fiction, not real. And don't pigeonhole me." *And get out of my head.*

"Having it all is the opposite of pigeonholing, and if anyone could engineer a way, you, my dear, are the one to do it." He pressed a finger to my lips. "Uh, uh, uh. Don't sass me. Just sit with it. Stew in that desire you didn't even know you had, and in the meantime, before I have to head north, let's go get you some sundries—deodorant, shampoo, *much* better conditioner." He examined a clump of my curls with a frown, "and—"

"Toothpaste. Lots and lots of toothpaste," I sighed, not really enjoying my own tired joke.

Thirty-One

SADIE

present day

How many unnecessary trips from my motel room to my truck could I make in an evening? A shocking number. Once Leo and Tristan left and Addie's night manager took over front desk duties, I found myself at loose ends. Logic said I should simply call Dutch with a friendly check-in to see if he had an estimated time of arrival, or if his plans had changed, or whether he had any opinions about a miniature basketball team of curly-haired—*whatever*.

Of course, the grownup in me wanted to know if his day trip gleaned any new answers to our questions. By the fourth unwarranted scouting mission in search of Junior Ford's car, I had changed out of the new organic cotton sundress I'd bought and into old cutoffs and my favorite *It Doesn't Get Eddie Vedder Than This* t-shirt and headed back to the parking lot with a purpose. I measured air pressure and pumped the tires with a portable compressor, checked the oil, added coolant, and got myself sufficiently greasy, elbow-deep under my truck hood—one of my preferred places to be.

As music played low out of the truck's cab, I relaxed into the tinkering routine and didn't notice the sinking sun or hear Dutch's approach. His quiet cough alerted me—a subtle prod not meant to startle. It didn't. Not really, but my heart rate spiked, regardless.

I grabbed a towel to wipe my hands and the sweat from my brow before getting my boots flat on the pavement. The smile that greeted me showed bigger than I'd anticipated, and frankly, a thing that beautiful should come with a warning label.

"Hi," Dutch offered his typically shy greeting, but that big grin had a whole other vibe.

"Hello, Ellis. Good day? Because it *looks* like you had a good day."

"It was. It was a real good day. And it just got better. Uh, you got a bit of smudge there." He pointed to my face.

I wiped my cheek with the back of my hand. "Yeah, it's hard to find a mascara that will hold up in this heat."

"I think it's motor grease, not—"

"Oh, yeah. Now that you say it, that sounds more likely." My laugh cut short when he moved closer.

He took the towel from me and found a clean spot to rub away the black smear under my eye. The act, an obvious ploy, quickly morphed into a tender, knee-buckling kiss, prompting all kinds of fantasies. But he pulled away too soon.

"Is that okay?" He wiped my cheek again.

"*Pfft.* Yeah, Addie's gone for the day, so we're good. Hey, what's that on your shirt?"

He wrenched his neck, looking at his own smudge of sorts near the shoulder of his button-down. The truck hood's shadow shrouded a yellowish-green stain, but up-close, the crusty spot was more obvious. A different kind of grin flickered all the way up to his eyes, like a pleasant memory sparked, but he didn't dwell on it.

"You wouldn't believe me if I told you." Until he stepped away, I hadn't registered his comforting weight pressed to me, and I missed it immediately. But before I could ask him to elaborate on his day, he took another step back and pulled his shirttail free from his jeans. "Did Leo get off okay?"

"He did. Tristan took care of it."

Dutch's head wobbled with something like approval.

"And Tristan?"

"Gone too," I stammered, mesmerized by Dutch unfastening the bottom button of the untucked shirt.

"Even better." He walked toward the motel. "How about dinner? Have you eaten yet? Tell you what. I'm gonna go shower off this day. Meet at my room? Thirty minutes?" He spun to see me slam closed the hood of my Ford and lock up my gear. "That work?"

"Ellis, you had me at dinner," I quipped, jogging to catch up and then pass him in a beeline to my own shower. "Twenty minutes," I sped up the plan, twirling on the heel of one boot in a way totally unbecoming of a thirty-something Ph.D. I couldn't give a damn.

I arrived scrubbed free of grease and wearing the new simple cotton dress again. When Dutch answered his motel room door, I held out the leftover beer he'd brought the other evening. He ushered me in, comfortably dressed in gray sweatpants and a t-shirt, his hair still damp. Gray sweatpants?! #IYKYK

"Wow, you look—"

"Shucks, this old thing?" I curtsied. "Kidding, it's new, seeing as most of my clothes burned in the fire."

"Sadie." His smiling eyes turned sad.

"Stop. It's just stuff." I traipsed across the room, placing my armload on the table still covered in Dutch's computer and other electronic gear. "Could have been worse." That notion spurred me to action. Enough time had been wasted, opportunities lost, and who was I to tempt fate. I rushed him, fisting his t-shirt, pulling his mouth to mine. For all my hard-charging, I appreciated his strong arms holding me close as the warmth of his lips, the stroke of his tongue, made me crumble in the sensation of it all.

"Sadie Jane," he sighed my name into my mouth.

"Yes," I exhaled my reply. It was encouragement, permission, whatever Dutch wanted; however, he wanted it, as long as it was now.

"Sadie." He drew from my lips, grazing my cheek, nuzzling my ear. "Sadie, why so fast?"

"Why so slow?" I tried to pick up the tempo.

Cradling my face, he placed one of those chaste kisses on my mouth, the kind that had the opposite effect. Whatever you call the antithesis of chastity, that's what it provoked.

"Because I've played this scene a million times over the years, and well, I want it to be right, good.

"It is a*stounding* how a man of so few words finds the exact right ones to say, but I think maybe *good* is overrated." I found it hard to breathe.

"Uh, no," Dutch chuckled, "I don't think that's true."

"No, no, of course not, but I'm a little Dutch-drunk, so you should probably ignore me."

"Don't think that's true either." He craned his neck with a side-eye look, still in my arms.

Composing myself, I pulled away, tugging him toward the bed. "Why don't you use some more of those words and tell me how this scene is supposed to go."

His cheeks grew pink as they often did, and I couldn't have wanted him any more than I did at that moment. I sat and slid back to rest my head on a bed pillow, dragging him with me.

"Actually, since the other night, I've been dreaming about—buttons." On one knee, he hovered over me, looking down the length of my dress. A line of small red buttons ran from the sweetheart neckline to the hem at my shins.

"Jackpot," I rasped as he undid the first in the long line. "But you know, these could be considered more *decorative* than functional. I mean, they are functional, as you can see, but the mechanics are such that we can bypass them altogether. To save time, effort, the economy of resources."

"*Hm*, well, a smart woman told me once we had all the time there was so—" He slid another button undone.

"Smart, huh?"

"The smartest," he nodded, and I thanked the universe when my struggle for a deep inhale helped two buttons pop free at once.

"Ellis?" I whispered, hoping not to divert him from his task.

"*Hm*?" His fingers may have stopped, but the desire in his eyes didn't.

"This—this could take a while."

"Good God, Sadie Jane, I sure hope so."

A plundering kiss smothered my reply. Whatever it would have been. Words failed me—vacated my head entirely, leaving me with nothing but the swirl of emotion, a feeling I recognized but couldn't pinpoint. I'd experienced it before. The buzz in my brain, butterflies in my stomach, a tightness in my chest. A barrage of sensory overload hit me from the past.

An overcrowded gymnasium, loud with music, dark with the slow spin of star-like glows. Dutch Holland held one of my hands and pressed the small of my back with his other. The look on his face wasn't new. I'd seen it many times before, across a booth at Midge's, in the cab of his truck, passing him in the hall at school. It was how he always looked at me, but now I knew what it meant. Resting my head on his chest, I breathed in his smell. Happy. I was happy, and I thought it might have been for the very first time.

I stiffened, skidding back to the present, remembering how short-lived that happiness turned out to be. Recalling what followed. Happiness was a harbinger of bad things in my world. Happiness brought misery. Happiness was to be avoided, and lest we forget, avoidance was my superpower.

"Sadie?" Dutch's roaming hands and attentive mouth eased. He'd been distracted from his button mission but now slowed further, stroking my cheek, insisting I look him in the eye. "Where'd you go? You were here, then you weren't."

I shook my head and pulled at his cheeks to get back on track.

"No," he inched from me, "don't clam up on me now."

"Are you telling me no, Ellis?" I forced a grin and tugged at his face again, but he resisted.

"No, I'm asking you to talk to me. What happened?"

I pushed into the mattress with my heels and hands, scooching back to sit against the padded headboard. The only light crept in through half-opened window drapes, a distant but cold white light from a utility pole illuminating the motel property and my truck, the only vehicle in the parking lot. Dutch rolled to sitting on the edge of the bed and clicked on the wall sconce reading lamp. Missing his weight, his touch, I stroked his back, hungry for his return but unable to ask for it.

"Maybe I got a bit ahead of myself. Sorry." Knees under me, I held him from behind, winding around him to kiss that scar at the corner of his mouth.

He kissed my fingers and twisted to face me. "No apologies. We've got all the time there is, remember?"

I knew it was true, but I also knew how much time we'd lost and how it was never guaranteed. Storms happened at sea. Semi-trucks ran red lights. Assholes hated what they didn't understand.

"Thank you. I just need a breath. It's been a wild few weeks. Heavy on major happenings, light on sleep. And I still can't believe you're here and I'm here and how good it feels. Right, but surreal, yet meant to be, but also kind of overwhelming and scary. Not that you scare me—well you do, but not in the way you'd think. Not in the you'd-hurt-me kind of way, but—"

I don't want to hurt you. That's what Dutch said in his parents' basement.

"Glad to see you're talking again," he grinned, nudging my chin.

I cocked my head and gnawed my bottom lip before asking, "Why don't you tell me about your day? Your 'real good day.'" I smiled even as his brow furrowed and he stood. That wasn't good.

"You hungry? I got you here on the promise of dinner. Don't wanna be that guy." His hand gripped his neck. "Pizza, maybe? Or we could go out? Are you still crazy for black olives and mushrooms? I won't pick them off anymore." Dutch flipped through a binder of laminated menus and tourist brochures.

"Whoa. What was that?"

"*Hm?*"

"Ellis, that was evasion if I ever saw it. What are you not telling me? You said no secrets. What did you do?"

It wasn't the first time I'd asked him that question. *"How'd you get him to keep quiet? To keep our secret? What did you do?"*

Thirty-Two

DUTCH

fifteen years ago

"WHAT ARE YOU GOING to do?" the kid groaned, still face down.

"Welcome back, dickwad?" I rummaged around, looking for the rumored Blackberry.

"What are you doing?"

"I need to get you help, but I don't think I should move you. I'm looking for your phone."

"Wait," he half-shouted, then grunted an animal-like wail. "My *leg*. Jesus Christ, she broke my leg."

"No. No, she did not. *She* was never here. Now stop moving."

"Right. Look, you can't tell anyone about this. It'll ruin me. Please. I'm begging you."

"Well, not sure this is something we can keep a lid on. And ruin *you*? How do you figure? Besides, asshole behavior has consequences. Damn, it's dark out here." Multitasking proved a challenge but hearing the injured party was open—willing, even—to consider a modified version of events played in my favor, Sadie's favor. I needed a plan and fast.

"I'm not an asshole," the kid grumbled.

"Wow, you and I have a very different take on assholery then."

"Seriously, you can't tell anyone."

"That you got beat up by a girl? Yeah, I can see how that might wound your rep—whatever that is, but just so we're clear, the *reason* she did it is why you're an asshole."

"No, I—"

"And Leo Klein is one of the nicest, funniest, greatest guys I know, and just because—"

"I *know* he is," he shouted. "I know."

"What?"

He groaned again, and I couldn't imagine the pain. He had to be in shock. I'd taken some hard hits but never suffered more than a broken finger. The thought of his agony reminded me of my own. My pounding head, the cut at my mouth that still bled, the bile-burn in my nose and throat.

"I like Leo."

"Then why the hell would you—"

"I didn't. I didn't do anything."

"But Sadie heard you were—"

"She *heard*? Yeah, well, I say lots of things. Guys say lots of things. Locker room talk."

He wasn't wrong. Stupid stuff got tossed around in a locker room far too often. It was gross and uncomfortable most times, and I wondered if that kind of boys-will-be-boys behavior would ever be held to account. Maybe that day was today.

"Why would you—"

"I like him. I wouldn't," he screamed. "I would *never* hurt Leo. I like him, I like him the way you obviously like your Sadie Jane."

"Don't call her that."

He cried quietly into the dirt while my already swirling brain spiraled further. My stomach lurched again. Everything about this was a disaster. No one was going to win, but maybe no one had to lose either.

"What's your name?"

"Does it matter?"

"I'm guessing it's gonna come up. Just tell me."

"Holden. I'm new this year."

"Holden, huh?" I paced, sucking in cool air, trying to focus, and hoping I wouldn't throw-up again. My foot smacked something, and it skittered across the ground. "Ah, your phone."

"Wait, Dutch, please. I'll do anything, say anything." Holden's desperation seemed to eclipse his physical pain. "She was never here, but I put the moves on your girl, called her something bad. You were defending her. No one would blame you. Come on, you're freaking Dutch Holland. And Sadie is off the hook, and I'm—"

"And you're still an asshole, except you're not an asshole—"

"I'd rather be an asshole than—what I am."

"No. Stop. That's bullshit. It's the twenty-first century, Holden. We're better than this. People are better than this. I get it. It's scary, but hiding doesn't help. Not you, not anyone."

"You *get* it? Shut up. You haven't got a clue. You have no idea what it's like to be like me."

"You're right. But we can figure this out."

"Are you listening to me?" he roared, fear gushing out of him. "You want to help? Just agree and promise no one will ever know. If you can't do it for me, do it for Sadie."

"And what about Sadie? You might not know this about her, but this will destroy her. If she knew what was really going on here, she'd—she'd—Jesus, Holden." I knew she would wake up tomorrow, devastated by what she'd done. But finding out the kid was never a threat? That she hurt someone as scared as Holden must be, someone looking for a connection with someone like him? That would be one revelation too many. She'd never forgive herself. But I could protect her. Protect her from all of it and I'd make sure I did.

"She never has to know, Dutch. I swear on my life, she'll never know." Holden might have been new to town, but the sharp kid recognized exactly how to convince me.

I bent over, hurling another puddle of sweet and acrid vomit before dialing 9-1-1.

Two days later, after visiting hours ended, Dr. Klein made good on arranging a secret meeting. She pushed my wheelchair into a dark, private hospital room identical to mine. The hall light provided all we needed to see a figure lying flat, a leg suspended at a slight angle.

"You awake?" I whispered as Dr. Klein locked the wheels of the chair I didn't need. She insisted I not wander on foot while I recovered from the concussion, which still included a wicked headache and awful nausea that felt like it would never end. I appreciated the dim room after the bright fluorescent-lit hallway.

"Yeah," Holden answered.

"I'll leave you boys for a few minutes, but a few minutes is all you get. You both need rest." Dr. Klein exited, leaving the door ajar to allow us the low light to see.

"How are you feeling?" I asked.

"Great. Pain meds rock. You?"

"I wouldn't know. I'm not getting the good stuff. Concussion, so—"

"I heard. Lucky you. I'm told that might make a person act weird. Easy to anger. Do things they wouldn't normally. Could help us."

"I'm not looking for help. I just want to be sure you want to do this. *Keep* doing this, because—"

"It's what I want. I've already told the authorities. We fought over a girl. I was the aggressor. I lost. I'm not pressing charges. We're clear. *Sadie's* clear. Life goes on."

Hearing Sadie's name hurt. I missed her. But more than anything, I needed her safe. Safe from the legal ramifications and safe from knowing how wrong she had been about the whole situation. "I just think you should—"

"Jesus Christ, Dutch. Just let it be. Get the hell out of my room, stay away from me, just let me live my life. And don't hurt Sadie with the truth. Honesty might make you feel better, but it will only cause the rest of us pain."

"Holden, please."

"Get out, Dutch. Go."

Holden couldn't be reasoned with. I couldn't find the words to convince him to do it another way, so I left. Dr. Klein wheeled me to my room in stony silence just in time for me to vomit again in a small plastic bowl she kept at the ready.

The next morning, to everyone's shock, I was arrested for aggravated assault.

While the "victim" quietly declined to press charges, a town prosecutor felt compelled to make an example of me. It may have had to do with his failing record going against my mother, the defense attorney, but no one could prove such a thing. Holden kept to his part of our "deal." But it had occurred on school property, during a school-sanctioned event, using Canaan Cove Athletic Association equipment. A judge saw to wielding a punishment she felt was commensurate with the crime, considering my doctor's strongly-worded affidavit that I suffered a "diminished capacity" in the wake of a traumatic brain injury.

My record and the details of the proceedings were sealed. My privilege, which included a sizable donation made by my parents, found me at a high-priced military school in the North Georgia mountains for my remaining semester of high school rather than a state-run juvenile detention center. The UGA football scholarship and academic acceptance were revoked, and my reputation, despite how well-regarded I had been before that night, took its own beating. Rumors flew, people swapped stories, baseless judgments were made, and with no one launching a defense or even answering questions, the Holland family left Canaan Cove.

Thirty-Three

SADIE

present day

"Sadie, please answer me. Please let me in. There's more I need to tell you." Dutch's fist or foot or head thumped the bathroom door. I couldn't be sure which with *my* head in the toilet. The news of what transpired all those years ago, the truth I hadn't known, the lie I'd lived with, was more than my system could bear. And it wasn't even the right lie. And what more could there be?

I had assaulted another human being. That in itself had been a devastating weight I'd carried since that night. Allowing Dutch to carry the public burden only added to the anchor. Now I learned my victim was a frightened, vulnerable kid who actually cared for my brother and sought out camaraderie, a connection with someone like himself, but I never even let him talk. I stampeded onto the scene, mind made up, bat swinging. What more needed to be said? Nothing would ever make any of it right.

I flushed, rinsed my mouth, and splashed cold water on my face before I exited the bathroom. Dutch stood too close and nearly fell into me when I flung open the door. I didn't bother to apologize. He wouldn't accept it, anyway.

"For the record, I'm not crying. My eyes water when I puke, so that's what this is." I circled my face with my own index finger, angry for looking weak.

"Are you okay?" His sweetness made my stomach worse, and I flinched from his touch.

In science, the weakest link theory isn't a complicated one, yet it outlines any system's potential complete and irrevocable demise. The quality of any construction is limited by the frailest component. While the destruction may not be immediate, the feeblest of parts will degrade the unit as a whole, dragging it down until often there is a catastrophic failure. Things fall apart. Human behavior has its equivalent. Think of a drowning victim trying to take down her rescuer. This sinking stone went for the stranglehold.

"Okay? No, I'm not okay. I just found out the worst thing I ever did in my whole life was exponentially worse than I thought. So much worse, and you kept it from me. You kept *you* from me, *and* you kept the truth from me. My life has been nothing but a miserable, lonely lie. Because of you."

"Sadie."

I thrashed harder. "And *you*. You made that poor kid—"

"Wait a minute. No, I didn't. He—"

"Everyone wants something. And everyone has an Achilles heel. It's about desire and weakness and leveraging the two. Those are your words, Ellis. You made a career out of manipulating people, and you started with him. You leveraged his weakness. A fear you and I will never comprehend. A fear people like Leo carry all the time." Another wave of nausea hit me. "Oh, my God. Leo. Leo can never know. Leo can *never* learn about this, about me. He would never forgive—" I swallowed more bile.

Often, under the added strain of a diminishing system, even the strongest component will start to fail, lose sight of its objective in an effort to resist the weak link's initial breakdown, only to precipitate a total collapse. Romance readers call it the Black Moment. And here I was living my own version wrapped in nerdy science metaphors. Poetic.

Dutch played his part to a devastating tee. "First of all, Leo is fearless, and he loves you, and you know it. And I made a career out of getting people what they wanted. And let's not pretend my clients are sweet little old ladies. They're powerful, wealthy, greedy people who don't mind getting a little screwed as long as someone else is getting screwed too. God, Sadie. This high-and-mighty routine loses some luster when you're the one trying to weasel out of a contract with Pembroke you *willingly* signed, while at the same time trying to dupe them into giving their idiot son a billion dollars. I'm not going to apologize for being better at my job than your boyfriend is." His neck grip had never been so white-knuckled.

"Really, Ellis. Again, with the boyfriend bullshit? Tristan is a friend, and he tried to help. And it was never anything more."

"Did he, though? Did he help? Seems to me he can't help but talk too much, particularly when it comes to—never mind."

A bolt of cold struck me, one of many in the last minutes. "Why were you on that boat?"

"I don't—"

"The *Sapphire Selkie*? Why?"

"Let's not do this." He walked away from me.

"Why?"

"I was a guest."

"Lying now? You've moved on from mere omission to flat-out lies? To me? What else has been a lie, Ellis?" Somewhere in me, I regretted the allegation as soon as I asked, but I couldn't restrain myself.

"Don't. Don't do that. Don't accuse me of lying about the only truth I've ever known. You don't get to do that."

I'd lost my reins. They slipped from my grasp, and the out-of-control scene careened further. If I could only keep quiet.

"Seems to me what you've known to be true is that I'm high-and-mighty, duplicitous, naïve to defend—what was it? The proverbial weakling? Well, I never thought I'd have had to defend him from you." No such luck on keeping quiet.

"God, Sadie, you're wrong. If you'd let me explain—And your verbal recall is incredibly selective. *That's* what you choose to remember? Out of everything I've said—that's—? Why? *Why* are you doing this? You're pushing me away, determined to go it alone."

"I'm better alone."

"How the hell would you know? When did you ever try it any other way?" he shouted, his cracks beginning to show. I was breaking him. It wasn't my intention. He was collateral damage, but I couldn't slow the onslaught, couldn't regain my grip.

Alone was what I deserved. Now more than ever. He seethed, shaking his head, every limb rigid, every tendon stretched. Red bloomed across his clenched jaw.

"Why were you on the boat, Ellis?" I asked again instead of addressing his questions.

"There was more than a wedding pleasure cruise going on there. A guest list of business associates, a boat out in international waters, at odd hours? Just as I said, I was there on business, like most everyone else. Your scheme had been rumored. Not the trust fund part. Your patent. Someone squealed and I'm sure it wasn't you. And I didn't know it was your patent. Names are not important in my line of work. Forgetting them as soon as you hear them is good; not knowing them at all is best. I swear I didn't know until I saw the wedding program. I had no idea you worked with Pembroke. You think your wedding guest list was long? Try the Pembroke Industries personnel log. And I had no clue you were marrying Tristan."

"When will it get through your thick skull? I wasn't going to marry—"

"Yeah, well, it sure as hell looked like you were. So, when I realized, I got drunk and hid in an empty cabin, contemplating the two-mile swim to shore. Only to have you come cussing through that door and into my life again. Then I went back to Pembroke to say I'd handle the fix. I'd handle you."

Too much information. My circuits overloaded, but still, I pushed.

"Well, one more question, and then I'll be *out* of your life again."

"No. Unacceptable. I will stand here and listen. I can *hear* you without trying to *fix* it. That's what I'm doing. No excuses for any of it. And you can ask me anything, but don't run from me. I won't let you—"

"Won't *let* me?" And just like some self-fulfilling prophecy, my inability to allow anyone to tell me what I can and cannot do kicked in. I did *not* ask any more questions, but I sure as shit did run.

No, I didn't run far. Didn't have far *to* run. Back to my motel room with the *do not disturb* sign hung and deadbolt thrown, I stood in the middle of the dark room. A scream caught in my throat, and it wouldn't let go. I thought I'd suffocate, like I truly was drowning. But an eventual gasp reset my breathing. Another breath followed, then another and another. When I grew certain my lungs would work, continue to move air in and out of me, I staggered to the bed, crawled into the covers to contemplate what came next.

Sleep came in fits and starts. My body ached, and I couldn't help but go from system to system, joint by joint, examining the mechanical breakdown stress wreaked—the chemical corrosion destroying my insides like industrial pollution, nuclear fallout. Guilt lets flow the worst kind of toxin, a poison that threatens to destroy an environment—a machine—from the inside out unless a remedy can be found. I needed a reversal of sorts, an antidote, and I knew far too well the necessity for atonement. It was only just September, but Yom Kippur would arrive early for this lapsed Jew.

Two middle-of-the-night texts set a late-morning meeting, and I hoped the attendees would show, and on time. Meanwhile, I stood under a long, hot and then cold shower, drank too much pod coffee, and ate an entire $36 jar of macadamia nuts from the minibar. I don't like macadamia nuts.

When a timid knock sounded at my door, more of that poison churned as I peeked through the security eye, then pressed my forehead to the cool metal, wishing this could be a very different kind of get-together. I stalled so long in opening the door, another louder rap vibrated my resting skull.

With a slow twist of the bolt and release of the safety latch, I inhaled all I could before allowing Dutch into my room. None of it included eye contact.

"Hi." Dutch offered his usual greeting in his usual way—concise, quiet, but I couldn't help but notice a tinge of awe in that single syllable. Seeing him provoked the same in me, but none of that mattered anymore.

"Good morning." I ushered him in, fixated on his vegan boots. He'd definitely gotten his money's worth out of that purchase. "Have a seat. Sorry, I drank all the coffee. And uh, ate all the macadamia nuts."

"You don't like macadamia nuts." The confusion on his face likely had little to do with my snack habits.

I shrugged.

He didn't sit but rather stepped to me, opening his mouth to speak when another, bolder, rhythmic knock intervened. That's when I caught Dutch's eye while simultaneously opening the door to welcome the third member of our summit. Dutch's crestfallen look at the sight of Tristan Pembroke would have broken my heart if it hadn't already been decimated hours earlier.

"Am I late? Traffic. Plus, I brought danish. The raspberry one is for you, my girl," he cooed, handing me a white paper sack. "The prune is yours, Dutch. Thought it might be the cure to that resting-grump-face you're always touting."

"Thanks, Tris. I'm full-up on macadamia nuts right now but—"

"Aww, I *love* me some macadamias." Yeah, somehow that tracked.

I handed Dutch the bag of pastries, certain he had no interest. His quizzical look grew stony as the reason for the morning face-to-face might have cemented in his savvy brain and his subtle but adamant head shake said he was well on his way to a tactical plan to stop whatever I had brought them there to share.

"Please, have a seat." I'd feel more in charge if I could relay my message to two sitting figures—taking a power position from the high ground.

Tristan spun to make himself comfortable in one of the pair of armchairs. But realizing Dutch had no intention of relinquishing any *Art of War* type of advantage, you'd have thought the blond playboy had been stung by a bee the way he sprang from the seat to remain standing with the grownups.

"Fine." I leaned against the hip-high bureau, presenting a casual in-charge demeanor when, truthfully, I trembled inside, unsure how it all would go. "First, thanks for coming. Both of you."

Dutch mimicked my stance, resting against a table on the other side of the room—arms and legs crossed, both of us closed off to the rest of the world.

"Sure, Sade, and whatever this is, whatever you want to do, or need *me* to do, I'm game, all in—"

"Tristan, let her talk," Dutch grumbled.

"I'm just trying to be supportive, Dutch. Letting Sadie know I hear her."

"How the hell can you *hear* her if you are talking?"

"I'm encouraging her."

"You're interrupting her."

"You're *both* talking about me like I'm not in the room," I squawked, my in-control guise slipping. "Can you just let me get this out? And to be clear, this is not a planning session. This is an announcement. Not something I'm looking to debate—with either of you." That message was meant for one more than the other, and Dutch knew it. A preemptive neck pull said as much.

"So, this boils down to basically three things."

Tristan stifled an amused snort and good-naturedly nudged Dutch's arm. "See, it's funny because she usually says '*two* things'—" The goofball flattened his grin. "Never mind. Go on, Sade."

"I'm going back to Pembroke Industries. Tail between my legs. This is a win for everyone. You, Ell—Dutch, because you can take credit for 'fixing' a contractor's errant ways by being the one responsible for me coming back into the fold. The myth continues. Add 'house fire' to the fiction that gets spewed about you if you like. Take the credit before someone else does. Compelling stuff.

"Me, because I can go about doing what I do best with the backing of a major energy player, doing some good in the world, if only incrementally. Some good is better than none. And you, Tristan, because essentially you *are* Pembroke Industries and, well, I'm a moneymaker, so—money. No little guy will negatively affect the bottom line."

No one said anything, and the quiet made my head hurt, so I continued.

"I know it's not ideal. A win some, lose some proposition, but I've realized I overreached, and going back is penance for stepping out of line, thinking I was fighting the righteous fight when that wasn't true at all. I took a big swing without really knowing who and what my target was, and not for the first time. Lesson learned.

"And Tristan, I'm sorry we weren't successful on your end. I apologize for that, but I cannot marry you. I considered it last night. I did." I chanced a look at Dutch, and my heart found a way to crumble just a bit more. "But I'm—I'm not in love with you, and while there might have been a time when I could have faked it, I can't now. I couldn't if I tried. I will apologize to your parents, and I will make an effort to plead your case, get you what you wanted, but I can't—"

"Okay, and what about him?" A suddenly serious and indignant Tristan I had never seen before jerked a thumb in Dutch's directions. "The notorious fixer gets to save the day? Reins in the cash cow that almost got away? Ingratiates himself even further with Daddy Dearest? Makes an even bigger, better, scarier name for himself in the world of backroom corporate deal-making—while on vacation, no less? What the hell did *he* lose?"

I squinted at the playboy's out-of-character and grownup vernacular, coupled with an astute understanding I never would have given him credit for until this moment.

Dutch pushed off the table to stand. "I lost plenty," he murmured before he flung open the heavy door and strode out of the room, letting it slam shut behind him.

Thirty-Four

SADIE

present day

I SLID OUT OF my truck, smoothing the midi-skirt I wouldn't have bought except for this meeting. My usual choice of a short and shapeless sundress or cut-offs and well-worn rock 'n roll tee didn't seem appropriate for a *mea culpa* at my ex-fake-fiancé's parents' massive Georgian Revival, an hour's drive up the road, on the swankiest block in town. It could have been a lovely home, but every nook and cranny was crammed with gilded this, brocade that, and back-breaking-sized ornate furniture, lots of it. It was no Holland House.

It had been almost two days. Forty-eight busy, heart-wrenching hours, and I used everything in my arsenal to formulate a plan, including reaching out for legal advice. Desperate times called for...

A lively Tristan bounded out the front door and jogged to greet me with a kissed cheek that seemed less for show than other times. Then again, I couldn't be sure Mommy and Daddy weren't lurking behind the heavy jacquard draperies I'd long surmised lived their first life in a brothel.

"How are you?" His tone had lost some of its chirp, and I pulled my head out of my ass long enough to realize I wasn't the only one changed by all that had happened.

"I'm okay. You?"

He shrugged. "Resigned?"

I forced a small smile and nodded. "I hear ya."

"No, I'm asking. Are you resigned to doing this? Both the business and the personal? Because it could be a good life, a good—"

"No, Tristan. I can't, and you don't want me to."

"Yeah. Now that I know what love looks like on you. Don't think I'd enjoy *not* seeing it pointed in my direction." Yet another observation that startled me. I hadn't considered how perceptive he'd been all this time. His ability to notice what I hadn't found the courage to verbalize or even admit to myself stunned me.

"I know that he's your brother, but you adore him. That's clear. I'd like that one day."

"*Leo*. Yes, of course. My brother." A different kind of love. Still, hints of Tristan's inner adult began to show.

"Is *he* single?"

"Tristan," I shoved him harder than I should have.

He stumbled with a laugh, skidding on the pea-gravel driveway. "I jest, Sade."

"Don't be an ass, *Tris*. Just when I think you've reformed yourself, let out the good guy deep down I know you are, you go open that mouth again."

His usual facade fell, the main stage showman veneer gone, if only for a moment. "Don't go ruining my reputation. It's all I have." He added his boy-band hair flip, but the bravado wasn't there.

I nudged his chin. "Not true. You gotta whole lot of potential, Tristan Meriwether Pembroke."

"My lord. How did you find out my middle name?" His eyes went to the sky, but his boyish grin returned at the same time a pang of sadness zapped my insides.

"I know a guy who deals in information. There was paperwork." I shrugged and took the crook of his arm. With a deep inhale, we headed into the garish lion's den.

The ten-minute wait seemed like an eternity, and I grew more anxious with every tick of the grandfather clock that loomed behind me. Tristan and I sat side-by-side on a gargantuan sofa I had sunk into a few times over the last several months. None of those experiences had been especially enjoyable, but this one might prove to be the worst. I kept my eyes forward, focused on five Turandot swagged windows, imagining a line of dancing girls, identically dressed, high kicking in fishnets. Mr. and Mrs. Pembroke's arrival provided an odd relief.

"Mommy and Daddy—"

Those words brought the cosmic sign I needed to affirm I had made the right choice. I patted Tristan's hand, determined to do things my way.

"Mr. and Mrs. Pembroke. Thank you for agreeing to meet with Tristan and me today. My visit is twofold. Both business and personal."

Tristan squeezed my hand, leaning toward me to whisper. "You don't have to do the second part, Sade. Just worry about the job."

I gently bumped him with my shoulder, not wanting my momentum to slow. "On the Pembroke Industry side of things," I continued, "I'd like to apologize for any misunderstanding there might have been regarding my work. After a confrontation or two with an associate of yours—a Dutch Holland," I nearly choked on the name, "I realize where my best interests lie. And now that my house has burned to the ground—in an entirely unrelated incident, I'm sure—this is not the time for me to be fighting a contractual agreement I have no hope of beating. And to be sure, I don't wish any more trouble from the likes of Mr. Holland." I may have been pushing the Dutch angle a bit hard but preserving the notorious fixer's dastardly reputation seemed the least I could do.

Mr. and Mrs. Pembroke stared at each other from their matching armchairs that looked straight out of the Seven Kingdoms of Westeros. In an unanticipated twist, Mrs. Pembroke was the first to speak.

"You actually *met*—Dutch Holland?" Her pause was telling. Fear? Appreciation? Both?

"Yes, ma'am. More than once. On the *Selkie*. In my hometown. My front porch..."

"He's—well, he's—" She fidgeted in her chair, and I recognized our shared appreciation, even if the men in the room read it differently. A mutual admiration society fist bump seemed the obvious response, but instead, I saved her from expounding further.

"Yes, yes he is."

"I'm afraid, Ms. Klein—"

"*Dr.* Klein," I corrected.

Mr. Pembroke paused. "Yes, of course. *Doctor* Klein, while I'm certain Mr. Holland won't darken your doorstep again, I have little say over the matter now. Not that I had much to begin with, but Dutch Holland ended his employment arrangement with me yesterday. All arrangements, I'm told. Called in every contract he'd entered into. Word on the street is he's—retired."

"Retired?" Tristan and I asked in unison.

He'd done it. Dutch had gotten out of the fixing game. But where had he gone? The notion he'd never "darken my doorstep" sounded true and squeezed the remains of my crushed heart.

"So it would seem. Cost me a good deal. His contract with me was ironclad. Important to read the fine print. He was quick to point that out. What can get buried in paperwork—well, Dutch Holland isn't someone I want to insult. The man will get his pay. He also said that if you came here accusing him of a house fire, you'd be wrong. He insists he had nothing to do with it. Now you're here insisting the same. Curious. But I'd distance myself from the man, too, if I were in your shoes. Trust I will, too."

"Water under the bridge," I interjected. I stole the metaphor from Dutch, but I needed to stop thinking about him and our distance. "On to the more personal reason for my visit..." I reached into my brand-new vegan messenger bag and pulled out a blackened, once-robin's-egg-blue box and set it on the coffee table at my knees.

"Sade," Tristan murmured.

"Tristan, I need to be upfront with your parents." I gave a steely glare for his eyes only before I continued. "Mr. and Mrs. Pembroke, I cannot marry your son. I do not love him, well, I'm not *in* love with him, so it wouldn't work. Not in the long-term. I apologize for any harm or embarrassment this may have caused, and while I know Tristan is—heartbroken now, it will save us all from more heartache down the road."

Mrs. Pembroke snorted like a slightly intoxicated sorority girl, and I wondered how often she got mistaken for Tristan's sister. And now I couldn't be sure she wasn't a bit tipsy. Not like *"Oops, I had one too many chardonnays at the tennis club luncheon,"* but more of a *"Dear God, how is this my life day in and day out"* kind of way. I tried to muster some pity for her but failed.

"You realize he's worth a billion dollars," she scoffed. Nope, no sympathy at all.

"Actually, my understanding is he *isn't* worth a billion dollars, not until he's married, right? But I have no doubt he'll be worth far more than that when the right partner comes along." I grinned at my former fake fiancé, then gave his arm a reassuring squeeze. "Anyway, the ring survived the fire, but I couldn't possibly keep it, despite Tristan's generous offer." I slid the crispy, peeling box toward Tristan before standing.

Next, I pulled a manila envelope from my bag. "Here is a new agreement for your people to peruse and then for you to sign. My attorney assures me it is clear, simple, and almost entirely in your favor."

"Wait. What kind of agreement?" Tristan staggered to his feet, stumbling around massive furniture to read over his father's shoulder.

Mr. Pembroke removed the two-page document and scanned it. In essence, the contract dictated that I would continue to be paid my share of the patent royalties that had long-since been part of Pembroke Industries. The corporation had no say in that regard. It was the law. In addition, I would walk away from the desalination patent pending for two full years. If Pembroke didn't use it in that time, all rights reverted to me, no strings attached. They could not sell it. If they did develop a use for it, I'd somehow make peace with the loss—a far simpler scheme than Tristan's shenanigans. There were no guarantees, and the plan included a timetable that slowed me some. I also knew if I didn't gain full rights, I would chalk it up as a debt paid. Restitution. But I would never again seek out funding without better *fine print* to protect me, and never, ever from Pembroke Industries.

"Sade? I thought you were going to stay—"

"I know, Tristan. But this is best. Besides, there's atonement, and then there's self-flagellation. I'll find other ways to compensate for my misdeeds."

"Well, Ms. Klein—"

"Doctor Klein," Tristan spoke up this time.

"Excuse me, son?"

"It's *Doctor* Klein, Daddy. She's said so already. So, you should address her as such. She's earned it—the title and your respect. She's also too polite to correct you a second time, but if nothing else, she's my friend, so I'm afraid I'm going to have to insist."

Turns out, Tristan Pembroke *could* woo, but it was too late for us—too late for wooing. But I'd never been happier to have his friendship. I nodded to him in gratitude.

"Yes, well, I'll need my legal team to look over this, Dr. Klein." The senior Pembroke kept his eyes focused on the document.

"It's barely a thousand words. I don't imagine it will take very long to figure how much of a win this is for you. You have two years to make something out of my work. I will not interfere. Other than that and my residuals, all business relations between Pembroke Industries and me are done. You can pay your very high-priced lawyers to fight me or pay me practically nothing to quietly go away. The choice is yours." I considered a parting handshake, but no one appeared interested. A quick exit seemed the shrewdest move.

"And who is Elspeth Weston?" Mr. Pembroke had reached the end of the document. "I thought I knew all the lawyers in this town, but I don't know her."

I skidded to a stop, then concentrated on smoothing wrinkles from my skirt. Casual. "Elspeth? Elspeth is *my* attorney. She's not around here, but still, she's the person all other communication should go through from here on out. She looks forward to hearing from you. And soon." I bolted for the door.

Thirty-Five

SADIE

present day

I TOOK A SLOW drive back to Canaan Cove, relieved to be done with that business. Besides a final round of that dreaded paperwork, my Pembroke Industries relationship would consist of little more than regular checks direct-deposited into an investment account. I had Dutch's mother to thank for that, and I'd be sure to put the money to good use.

I flopped onto my motel bed to text Leo. Not my preferred way to communicate, but he liked to make a game of it. The winner used the fewest words. Yeah, not my forte. Then again, neither was losing.

Sadie: *Talk?*
Leo: *Can't.*
Sadie: *Grrr (sound, not a word, doesn't count)*
Leo: **shrug* (action, not a word, doesn't count)*
Sadie: *...*
Leo: *You ok?*

I wasn't okay. I carried a horrible secret that compounded another one I'd tethered myself to for years. But while fifteen years ago I'd fooled myself into accepting the earlier unmentionable incident was justified, now I knew that wasn't true—not that I ever believed I'd been vindicated. I couldn't deny the reality of what I'd done, and now I knew how wrong I'd been about the young kid I did it to. But I also refused to saddle my brother with the new—or old—news. All of it would only hurt him, and I'd find no relief in it either. Suddenly, texting instead of talking was like clemency.

Sadie: ...
Leo: Curly-headed baby-making?
Sadie: Bye
Leo: Wait!
Sadie: ...
Leo: ...
Sadie: I'm Pembroke-free.
Leo: Yay!
Sadie: ...
Leo: ...
Sadie: I love him. Ellis, I mean. I'm in love with him.
Leo: DUH (a scoffing grunt of brotherly superiority, doesn't count)
Sadie: *angry face emoji* (emojis don't count)
Leo: *eye-roll emoji*
Sadie: Careful, I might love him more than you.
Leo: No, just differently.
Sadie: Let's hope so.
Leo: Weirdo.
Sadie: LOL (acronym, not a word, doesn't count)

Then I waited, watching the three dots flicker for a long time.

Leo: I'm going to give this one to you because I'm magnanimous like that. I don't know what happened or if any of it has to do with me, but if you are looking for my forgiveness, you have it. Permission run? It's yours. My love, respect, admiration? Done, done, and done. Unconditionally. Forever and always. But here's the thing, Shorty. I'm not the one you need to hear it from. Look in a mirror at your gorgeous face (and hopefully better-conditioned hair). You did what needed to be done, leaving Pembroke Industries. Part of it anyway. Now, *move forward. Take your time. Like Grandaddy said. We've got all there is. You've always been a builder, a maker of things. Complex, complicated, worthwhile things. Now you need to go build a life. And it should include Dutch.*

Leo's ability to read between the lines—lines of truncated texts, no less—amazed me. No, he didn't know what he forgave. To him, it didn't matter. So wise and yet blissfully ignorant. I intended to keep him that way.

Sadie: *I broke him—us. Badly.*

Leo: *Heaven forbid you should do anything half-assed. I know a fixer you can call.*

Sadie: *Hm, it might be a conflict of interest. Besides, he retired.*

Leo: *Really?! Well, it's a murky business. Or so I hear. Sounds like you're both at a crossroads. Maybe you can help each other out.*

Sadie: *Now you sound like his mother.*

Leo: *Huh?*

Sadie: *Never mind.*

Leo: *I've got to go, and so do you. Love you.*

Sadie: *XOXO (symbols representative of kisses and hugs, not a word, doesn't count)*

Leo: *Just stop.*

I allowed myself a giggle, watching the three dots flicker another second before they vanished. Still on my back, the blink of the smoke detector caught my eye until the scrape and rustle of paper brought me to my elbows. Someone slipped a large envelope under the door and it glided to a stop on the carpet. I rushed to catch the deliverer in the act.

Addie tip-toed down the hall like a character from a Scooby Doo episode. Disappointing.

"Addie?"

She froze, her shoulders about her ears. An ersatz smile showed off those years of orthodontia when she spun to see me. "Heyyy, Sadie," she said with an awkward wave. "Sorry. Didn't mean to disturb you. I wasn't sure you were here. I mean, I saw your truck was here and thought I heard you come through the lobby when I was in the back office, and you're the only guest checked-in, but still, you never can assume."

"No, I guess you can't. I didn't mean to startle you. I just thought maybe you were someone else. El—Dutch, maybe."

She looked over her shoulder toward the lobby, then back at me. "No, ma'am. Just me. Bringing you an envelope that got dropped off for you. By someone else."

"Addie? Did *Dutch* deliver this for me?" I hadn't heard from him since he walked out of our morning meeting with Tristan two days ago but figured he was far from Canaan Cove.

The poor sprite of a woman stood stock-still until I took a step in her direction. Suddenly, in her widest stance, arms outstretched, she side-shuffled a zig, then a zag, like an offensive lineman ready to tackle me rather than let me pass to catch the former quarterback. Silly, to be sure. I had a head more height, and she knew my childhood—the giant Leo I'd wrestled in my younger days. Did she seriously think I couldn't take her?

I had no interest in playing her game. Canaan Cove was a small town, and if Dutch Holland was there, I'd see him unless he didn't want me to. And if he didn't want me, then I needed to make peace with that too. And why would he? It was right, even though it wouldn't be easy. More atonement, or maybe it was karma. Either way, it was a bitch.

"Stand down, Addie. You're clear. I'm not going to chase after the man."

"Why? I mean, who? I mean, *huh*?"

I squawked a genuine laugh. "Not for nothing, but if anyone comes around asking you to join some clandestine service, you should stick to your day job." I winked, and she frowned. I hurried to amend my statement. "Because you are damn good at it, Ms. Watson. And you should drop the other name. He didn't deserve you. And he certainly doesn't deserve you hanging onto his name."

Her grin returned, a real one this time, and she might have blushed. "Why, thank you, Sadie. For all of it." She morphed from footballer to curtsying hostess in a breath and twirled to return to the front desk in a manner far more befitting her than me.

"Uh, Addie? You don't happen to know where—"

She whirled back to me with a look of panic.

"Never mind, Addie. Never mind." I fanned myself with the envelope and slunk back toward my motel room.

"Sadie, you know Dutch and Junior Ford are tight, right? Nice that even after all this time, they're still good friends." Addie scampered down the hall but gave a quick peek back at me with her own exaggerated wink.

"Thank you, Addie," I called to her.

"What for? I don't have a clue what you're going on about. I'm a busy woman with no time to stand around gossiping." She disappeared through the corridor to the lobby while I slipped into my room.

The envelope's label included the official header marking the report from the county fire investigator and my home's street address—what was left of it. The quick turnaround felt like a blessing, but that was a premature assumption. The packet hadn't been opened. I tore through the seal and emptied the contents onto the bed. Having read more than a few scientific reports in my life, I knew to skim for a bold caption that read *Conclusion.*

I sank onto the edge of the mattress, an f-bomb falling from my lips. Phrases like "outdated wiring and breaker box," "nearly one-hundred-year-old structure," "overloaded circuits," "seasonal vermin infestation," and "sudden prolonged system stress" blurred across the page. And just when I thought I had taken decent strides toward making amends for my many misdeeds, another conviction got added to my rap sheet. The fire was my fault.

Junior Ford lived closer to the Motor Lodge than I had realized—a mere block and a half on a short dead-end street dotted with huge, crooked oaks dripping in Spanish Moss. I remembered the old Southern Gothic house, not because he'd lived in it back in our youth, but because no one had. It was *the* dilapidated, scary house of Canaan Cove. Fodder for rumor and innuendo, the center of tall tales detailing late-night horrors and supposed acts of bravery. A residential Boo Radley. Now, the only thing left to whisper about such legendary gossip might have been the appropriately rusty ornate finials and wrought-iron gate decorating the end of its stone walkway. That path led to the brick home, shaded by sprawling trees and the tiny blooms on wiry stems that hung from them. Another example of old Canaan Cove made new again, and definitely for the better. The structure represented a stunning example of architecture, and that Junior Ford had salvaged it said a lot about the man.

I parked out front. The gate squeaked a welcome that would have been considered a warning so many years ago, or so I guessed. Nosing around an abandoned manor was not something I would have ever done. Still, my nerves throbbed, equal parts eager and anxious, hoping I'd find Dutch there.

"He's not here," Junior delivered the unfortunate news with kindness and stepped aside, beckoning for me to enter. "But I'm glad you are. Please, come in."

I hesitated. Despite the play-acting, for Tristan's benefit, on my porch some weeks ago, Junior Ford and I were barely acquainted. I knew he and Dutch were teammates and, I guessed, good friends in high school, but we weren't in the same class and wandered different paths even when we were both students at Canaan Cove High. Our sole connection was Dutch. And Junior wasn't someone Dutch and I often talked about.

A social visit with a virtual stranger, who was also a wildly popular former professional athlete, hadn't made it to my to-do list for the day. Then again, my to-dos had dwindled of late. Gone up in smoke, actually. I nodded, hugging the fire investigation report to my chest, and entered the high-ceilinged foyer. Considering the old home's former condition, it had to be a complete gut-job, but the attention to the architectural details and the quality of the finishings impressed me.

Gesturing with the large envelope, I admired the surroundings. "If I rebuild, I'm gonna need the name of your interior designer. This is amazing, Junior. Beautiful but comfortable—simple but stunning—it's—"

"Thank you. A bit of Canaan Cove history, huh?"

"A real gem."

"Well, I can't take much credit for the design, but the designer sure got me—I mean, she got what I was going for—what look I meant to—well, she's really good at her job." It was the first fumble I'd ever seen Junior Ford make. "And I'm sure you've met her." He recovered. "Addie Watson-Dodson." Junior's grin revealed more than I think he intended, but any attempt to suppress it failed.

"Addie, huh? You know, she and I were talking just a bit ago, and I think she's decided to drop the Dodson."

"Yeah?" The question betrayed a hint of gleeful surprise. "Oh. That'd be—that would be good." His already broad chest expanded further when he pondered the little pixie's name change. Suddenly, the combination of his hulking benevolence and Addie's woodland fairy-like sincerity came together like a perfect fit. I'd never dabbled in matchmaking, but I felt a new hobby creeping up on me.

I smiled, squinting at the goofy grin he fought to hide. "Yes, it definitely would be."

"Iced tea? Let me get you something." Junior ushered me into a library den, all books and leather, with a fireplace I could imagine snuggling in front of with a good and girthy Nora Roberts novel or maybe some old-school Austen on winter evenings.

"Thank you, no. I don't care for—"

"I happen to have an unsweetened stash," he interrupted, and I knew that even if Dutch wasn't there now, he recently had been.

"That'd be nice. Thank you."

"Make yourself comfortable." Junior trotted off deeper into the house I'd love to get a peek at someday. He left me to explore black and white photographs, beautifully bound books, and expertly framed news clippings, all softened by vibrant green Alocasia dappled in the last of the late evening sunlight. A floor-to-ceiling bookshelf held a trove of Junior Ford memories.

"I have him to thank, you know." Junior startled me with his return, despite his low, quiet tone. He offered me the iced tea and a seat in a tufted club chair in buttery cognac-colored leather. "Not that I *would* thank him, but I owe my success to him."

I didn't reply, but my eyes held all the questions.

"When he got in trouble, I had to step up to play. I led a team to a state victory that, by all accounts, was *his* team. Even though Dutch only had eyes for UGA, other college scouts came to see him. They saw me instead. I'm pretty sure I wouldn't have any of this if it weren't for—"

"Oh, I'm sure that's not true." The notion made my head spin. Maybe someday, I'll be thankful to have a positive outcome of that horrible night to consider, but not yet. I sipped my tea.

"Still. But I don't think Dutch wanted it like I did. He didn't *need* it like I did. He was—*is* smart. He'd have succeeded regardless, right? Just look at him now. Football was my meal ticket. My escape hatch."

"And yet, look where we all ended up. Funny."

"Well, it wasn't my plan, but I needed a place to recoup, and I started classes online to get my MBA, got sidetracked implementing those lessons at the Feed n' Seed, and then all of a sudden I lived here. I'm almost done with the MBA, too. Now that the new and improved store is up and going, I have more time. Not that I need it, the degree, but something about the follow-through seems right."

"That's amazing, Junior. Whatever spurs you to do it. Heck, I got lured into a Ph.D. by my love of Korean barbecue, so—" Forcing another sip of tea, I grappled for the nerve to ask where his recent houseguest had gone and whether he would be back.

"Whatcha got there? In the envelope?" Junior asked.

My instinct said to hide it like it hadn't already been seen. I had no plans to share the findings, not with Junior, so I slid the guilty verdict of my most recent bad act beside me in the chair. "It's the fire investigation report on the bungalow. Thanks again for the help there. It's pretty much a total loss, but your crew saved a few very—precious things. I can't tell you what a relief that was." Truthfully, I only meant the ring, but returning it to Tristan meant a great deal to me. "I think Ellis—Dutch had a hand in getting this completed so quickly, and I wanted to let him know I got it and maybe share the findings if he wanted to—"

"To know? Yeah, I think he'd want to know." Junior got quiet, squirming in his matching club chair.

"You think?"

"I think anything to do with you interests Dutch. Anything and everything. But I also think he's—" Junior weighed his words. "Dutch has lost enough, sacrificed enough. School. His service to his country. A long rift with his dad. Now, he's quit his security guard job that seemed like it was a great gig, but he says he wanted out of it, and well—I'm glad to have my friend back, and I'd like to see him stay. But more than anything, I'd like to see him happy. And not to stick my nose in, but you might be the key to that."

Huh. Who's the matchmaker now?

Junior stretched his burly frame in his chair. He wasn't as tall as my brother, but he was of similar width, and his long legs crackled when he straightened them in the silence that hung heavily around us. Clearly, the man had more to say.

"Dutch and I have been talking about some business opportunities. Growth prospects here locally and his talents could be helpful. He seems to be able to get things done, challenging things, *impossible* things." Junior gestured to the envelope. "And fast, too. It's a remarkable skill. Plus, he has some capital—anyway, we could do some good around here, and I know the timing sucks, with your house burning down and all, but maybe it's a sign."

"A sign?"

"A sign you—" more fidgeting and throat-clearing. "A sign you should—you know—go."

"Did you say—*go*?" Hmm, maybe not so much with the matchmaking scheme.

"Yeah." His kind eyes lost some charity.

"Go where?"

"Anywhere that's not here. Anywhere he doesn't risk seeing you. It's a small town, and I think he's carried your torch long enough."

"Wait. You think his happiness is incumbent on *not* being with me?" I staggered to my feet.

"Well, *with* you is one thing. *Near* you is quite another. And my understanding is you don't want him."

"*Your* understanding? And where did you come to that conclusion? Why would you—I don't understand." The room heated by degrees, and I guzzled what was left of my tea.

"Look, Sadie." Junior stayed in his chair. "I don't know much, and Dutch and I are dudes, but this much is true—if you wanted him, he'd be yours. If you wanted him, he'd rebuild your house brick by brick, give you a boatload of curly-headed babies, and chase you around that peach orchard until you died of old age in each other's arms. It's a life he knew he'd never have, and yet he let the idea of it get in the way of any other opportunity. No one was ever going to fill that role. No one. So, yeah, given the chance, that's the life he'd choose."

"He would?"

"Or any other version you could dream up. Anything you wanted. Dutch would want it for you. You could do anything together, see the world or settle down. See the world, *then* settle down. Hell, I don't know. He got a little drunk. I got a little drunk. My point is if you don't want—"

"I'm gonna need you to *not* finish that sentence, Junior. Where is he?"

"Dunno."

"Don't know or won't say?"

"I don't know where he is, but I expect him back."

I grabbed the envelope from the chair, hurrying to leave.

He scrambled to his feet. "Wait, Sadie. I didn't mean to—"

"You were looking after your friend. I appreciate that. Message received."

"Whoa. For the record, this was *my* message. Not Dutch's. He'd never—"

"I know, Junior. Thank you."

"Sadie, wait."

But I was out the door.

Thirty-Six

SADIE

present day

Tired of getting my ass kicked by irony, I realized I had nowhere to run. My house was a charred-out hull and the smoke smell lingered in the cooler humidity of nightfall. When I grew weary of staring at it from the tailgate of my truck, I climbed back behind the wheel. The envelope with the fire investigator's report chided me from its spot in the passenger seat.

A few blocks east, the ocean stopped me, and I was relieved to find the sand strip and small parking lot with a path through dunes that led to the water's edge—a spot I enjoyed when I was a kid. At night, that time of year, no one would see me, stop me, impinge on my search for fresh air and the relaxing crash of waves. High tide narrowed the beach but left space to sit without fear of getting wet—not that I cared. My boots dangled from my fingers, and I plopped on the soft cold sand, the day's heat long-since gone. A starry sky twinkled in sync with the *clang* of a distant buoy-marker too far off in the dark to see. When a meteor shot across the speckled blue-black canvas, I gasped like I'd never seen one before, like I'd never see one again. Silly, but somehow every time was like the first.

A *thunk*, followed by the slosh of liquid, thudded on the ground next to me. My heart skipped a beat. Midge's tiny figure emerged when my tired eyes decided to take in the sight. She didn't say a word but sat, letting the peach moonshine take center stage between us. It was all the offer she would make, and I accepted it.

The sweet booze burned like both reward and penance. My eyes watered and I took a second, then a third draw. That's when Midge snatched the bottle from my grasp with a grunt. I shivered as the elixir clawed its way down my throat, preventing me from asking my drinking mentor how she liked my ovaries now.

"Might not feel like it at this moment, but you are gonna want your gullet again someday. And your liver. And some brain cells. Then again, I'm guessing you have some of those to spare despite whatever it is you did to land yourself in this pickle." She swirled the fruity boozed inches from my nose. "This stuff is one-hundred-fifty proof."

"Speaking of pickled—" I snatched the bottle back and drank more. Too much.

"Oh, *silly* Sadie, what have you done?" She messed up the Beatles' lyric.

"It's Sexy Sssadie, Midge." I hissed out more air than sound with the peachy heat.

"Ha!" she crowed. "Seen a mirror lately?"

I drank again, but Midge was done aiding and abetting my poor behavior. Her short stature surprised again with a firm yank, swift corking, and far-flung throw of the moonshine bottle into the dark.

"Should I bother asking how you got here?"

"I drove, Sadie."

"No, I mean—"

"It's still a small town. Maybe a bit greener, crunchier, bordering on highfalutin at peak season, but it's still small. People talk."

I hiccupped with my annoyance, "People?"

"Addie Watson-Dodson."

"Ah. She's dropping the Dodson, I'm pretty sure."

"Glad to hear it. 'Bout time. Then Junior Ford."

"Gee," I huffed. "He's got *lots* to say." I rolled my eyes, making me sway where I sat.

"That right?" she snickered.

"Yeah." His suggestion to "go" still stung.

"Then Leo texted a request for a 'welfare check' as he put it."

"Oh, brother."

"That's what I said. Leo. Of course, it was Dutch who knew where'd you be. He said it was your thinking spot."

"You talked to him? Did you see him? Is he okay?"

"He loves you."

I sighed, hoping it didn't morph into a sob. "You don't know, Midge."

"That's right. I'm a daft old woman who doesn't know much, but I know *that*, and I know you love him too, have since you were kids. And yep, usually, these things have a way of petering out, but every now and again, it turns out to be the real McCoy. If you're lucky, you find your way back, and whatever's gone on in that time apart makes no never mind. Right is right, and the fact you two are smart, successful, beautiful souls who have bumbled all over the globe and remained alone? Only to fall into each other's laps this many years later? Well, there is nothing more telling than that. So, fix it, forgive it, get over it, make hot, sweet monkey-love, and eventually give me grandbabies by proxy. It ain't rocket science."

I let Midge's words sink in—almost thought they made sense, that it was the right thing to do. But like Dutch had said weeks ago, the water was so far under that bridge. And yet, the fantasy of it seemed possible. "What is everyone's obsession with babies all of a sudden?"

"Oh my. The brilliant, curly-headed beauties you two would make." The old woman's breathy sigh had the opposite effect one might expect.

Forcing myself to the reality of it, I straightened with a jerk. "I can't, Midge. I can't." I hiccupped again, and the alcohol started the numbing process. An odd euphoria washed over me like the waves several yards down the beach, and I relaxed in resignation, despite the turmoil raging inside me.

"You can."

"No, I really can't. You don't know. You don't know what I did, and there isn't enough moonshine in the world that would coerce me into telling you. I'd rather not exist than tell you, and the only saving grace I've got is that my Mee-maw died before she learned the truth. Except I don't really believe in saving graces, so there you go. This is the price I'll pay. This is my sentence, the debt I owe." I wasn't worthy of Dutch, and one day soon, he'd realize it, too.

"Oh, Sadie." Midge patted my knee, sighing into the chilling night air. "You remember how I said I was a daft old woman who didn't know much?"

I swiveled to her, closing one eye to focus on her profile staring out to sea. Her lavender hair looked whiter in the nighttime light. It glowed, distracting from the petite facial features that coincided with her petite everything else—save her personality. "You mean like just a couple minutes ago? Yeah. How drunk do you think I am?"

"Drunk enough that I can talk about you and Dutch making hot-sweet monkey love and you not—you know—*dying*."

I snorted. "Two things. One. Hot-sweet monkey love with Ellis Holland sounds awfully nice." The long *I* in 'nice' dragged on a beat too long.

"Oh, Lord, you are drunk," Midge used a quiet cackle.

"And *two*, you're right."

"Usually, I am. What about this time?"

"I love him. God, I love him. I think I've always loved him. Will always love him."

"Sadie Jane Klein, stop it this minute," Midge boomed with unexpected anger. "Stop your belly-aching, your pining, and forgive yourself. I know what you did."

"I'm sorry, what?"

"You heard me. I know what you did. I know what Dutch *didn't* do. And I swore to your Mee-maw I would never tell. Never tell you the truth or that she knew all along, but to hell with it. Fifteen years is long enough, and I'm done with other people's secrets. I'm too old for this crap."

Midge's words flew at me. The ocean noise and the moonshine buzz, coupled with her excitable way, had my head swimming. "Whoa. How? Who?"

"Aw, honey. She overheard Dutch and the other boy talking."

Sweet alcohol burned in my gut, and another round of heartache hit. "So she heard Ellis practically blackmail that poor scared kid into a lie. And I know he did it for me but still—"

"To hear your grandmother tell it, Dutch tried to figure a way to tell the truth. But the other boy wouldn't do it, and I'm guessing, just like your Mee-maw, Dutch knew the truth not only would get you into some serious trouble but also *wreck* you. I see they were right on that score. So yes, he let it happen, and so did she. And before you start thinking this conspiracy ran too deep, she *never* told Dutch what she knew. She told me and no one else. And when his life imploded, oh, the guilt that woman endured. But you were her priority. Her dead son entrusted you to her, and she couldn't see you hurt. So, she pleaded his concussion case the best she could to the judge and then kept quiet except to tell me—so I let it happen too, kid. Lots of blame, lots of guilt to go around, so don't be hoggin'."

With all that on top of the moonshine, my drinking regret started before the full force of it hit me. I pressed my palms to my temples, trying to squeeze myself to sobriety, but the stupor hadn't even peaked yet, not even close.

"Why didn't he tell me that? Why didn't Ellis say he tried to convince the kid? I stood there and went on and on, accusing him of blackmail, of scaring the poor kid into doing his bidding. I called him a liar. Why didn't he say anything? Why'd he stand there and take it? Just listened to me like—oh God, he listened to me *exactly* like I asked him to."

The old crone had the nerve to laugh. "Ain't it a thing when *your* question actually *answers* your own question? Is there a name for that? There really should be a name for that 'cause it is a big ol' kick in the bits, isn't it?"

I staggered to my feet. The flickering starry sky compounded my drunkenness. "I need to go home."

"*Your* home?"

"No, not my home. I burned my home to the ground." The liquor made me even more blunt than usual.

"Is that right? How on Earth did you manage that from the mountains hundreds of miles away?" She said it like it couldn't be true, but she was wrong.

I shrugged. "I left the goddamn lights on, Midge." I hung my head as the shame hit me again. "I left the lights on."

"Oh, Sadie." She let the crashing waves fill the void for a moment before asking, "What can I do?"

"Could you get me to the Motor Lodge?"

"You bet. Now, help me up. Criminy, I'm almost a hundred years old, and you got me sitting on my ass in the sand."

I stumbled to help her to her feet. "Oh, Midge. I'm gonna be terribly drunk."

"Gonna be?" If it hadn't been so dark, and I could have focused, her incredulous look would have shamed me that much more.

"Will you drive my truck?"

Midge snatched the keys from me. "Damn skippy, I will. Don't have to ask me twice."

We rolled right to the double doors of the Motor Lodge faster than I would have preferred. It was a short ride, and I held onto the window ledge, the night air wreaking havoc on my hair with zero help to sober me. Midge hurried around the truck bed and caught my elbow as I slid off the leather seat, boots clutched to my chest. My sand-covered feet met the pavement, and I paused to be sure Newton's law of gravitation would hold up despite the grain alcohol swimming through my system.

"Good ol' Newton and his gravity. Never lets me down," I sighed.

"Pretty sure it *keeps* you down. Kind of the point, right?" Dutch stood in the glow of the Motor Lodge entry.

"Oh, hallelujah," Midge cheered under her breath. "She's all yours, Dutch. And I mean that. No backsies, as she would say. She's a mess. She'll need water and—"

"I got it," Dutch interrupted with a reassuring nod.

"I'm sure you do." She patted his arm, and the two had a serious staring moment that I didn't have the bandwidth to interpret.

"I'm standing right here—with fully functioning ears, people."

They both snickered.

"I'm leaving you here with Dutch, Sadie."

The thought of being alone with Dutch sank into my soused brain, and nerves ricocheted as everything else shut down. "Uh, okay."

"I'll see you in the morning for breakfast at the café," she said, but I couldn't pull my wasted gaze from Dutch.

"Okay."

"Lots of water, now. You hear?" She handed me my bag, the large envelope peeking out of it.

"Okay."

"And since we left the Wagoneer at the beach, I'm taking your truck."

"Okay." I hiccupped.

The duo gave each other wide-eyed looks like they couldn't believe I didn't fight any of it. I opted to make a casual break for it, fumbling with my boots while I dug for my key card. Sand between my toes stung, and I didn't want to know what my wild windblown curls looked like. My feet did a bang-up job getting me to my door, and I thought I was home-free until I dropped the room key that kept giving me a red light. *Dammit, Newton.*

A stealthy Dutch picked up the plastic card, rotated it, and inserted it properly. The light blinked green, giving us access to my room.

"I'm coming in, Sadie Jane." It wasn't a demand or a question. It just was.

"Okay."

I opened the bathroom door, and Dutch bounded to his feet. A tightening tug on my bathrobe tie gave me the courage to wobble from the steam into the room.

"You all right?" he asked with kind but concerned eyes.

I blew out a deep breath. "Sand free, and my hair's tamed, but uh, I'm drunk."

"Yeah, I can smell the peaches from here."

"Are you flirting with me, Ellis?"

"No, Sadie." His face grew sullen. "Not even a little."

I swallowed hard, letting the snub settle. Disappointment squeaked out of me. "Oh." But the real embarrassment wouldn't land until later.

"I got you a few bottles of water." He gestured to the table and chairs. "And a turkey and cheese sandwich. Mustard, no mayo. He even found you some seedless rye."

"Who's he?"

"The night manager and I have gotten chummy. He opened the kitchen for me."

The room spun, and the thought of food and water both appealed to and terrified me, but anything would be better than a stand-off with Dutch. I swayed in the direction of the makeshift picnic he'd spread on the small table. With a faked, easy gait, I gracefully toppled into one of the armchairs and guzzled half a bottle of water before considering a bite of the sandwich.

"Drunk Sadie is a *quiet* Sadie." He joined me at the table.

I shrugged with another bite, taking my time to chew. It was true, and I imagined it had something to do with a deep-seated need for control. Drunk Sadie—this drunk—was also a rarity, but I realized Dutch Holland wouldn't have any way of knowing that, though he had seen a few nips of Scotch knock me out. This evening would be a speedy repeat of that experience. My eyelids weighed heavily while I forced more water into me.

"Pardon my manners. Please. Help yourself to the minibar."

"Nah, the other night Junior and I—well, I'm good, thank you."

"He's not a big fan of me. Junior, I mean."

"That's not true."

"Beg to differ. I stopped by today and—"

"I heard. Sorry I missed you."

"Are you?" My chin dipped, and I stretched my eyelids, lifting my brow to nearly my hairline, or so it felt. More water.

"Were you looking for me?" Dutch diligently avoided my confrontation while he kept the conversation moving. Did he actually want to know, or were the questions a ruse to keep me awake longer? Help aid in mitigating a significant hangover.

I let my head roll back as I tried to remember what my intention had been earlier in the day, but my fogged mind stumped me. Prying one eye open, I caught the white of the envelope in the bag I'd dropped on my way in the door.

"Ah-ha," I scrambled from my seat, launching toward the bureau to retrieve the fire investigation report. Dutch also flew to his feet, looking startled by my sudden rush across the room. "They've come to a *clon-clusion.* Nope. Clon-*cusion.* Nope. They got answers." I wagged the papers at him.

"Sadie, I left that with Addie to give to you."

"I *knew* it!" I exclaimed, overly excited to know my earlier suspicions were correct. "*Pfft.* I knew that." I regained my composure, certain I found my way to cool confidence again. "Addie was all—hush-hush—zip-lipped, but I knew it."

"Did you think I would leave it with you without knowing what it said?" He asked an earnest question, making me revisit the seriousness of the situation. My house burned to the ground. "Did you think I wouldn't be one-hundred percent certain you were safe, that someone wasn't trying to—"

"It says I did it," I blurted what he apparently already knew. "*I* started the fire. *I* burned down my house, my grandparents' home. *Me.* I did it." I tossed the envelope aside, officially done for the night. Even if I had thought Dutch and I could find our way, some force knocked me back with the reminder that happily-ever-afters were for romance novels. A fiction in escapist fun, but not real life. My real life burned to the ground, and I might as well have lit the match.

"No, Sadie Jane. It said the house was old and had old wiring left sitting for over a year, and then the power came back on and—it was an accident, and no one was to blame. Except for maybe some wall critters that set up camp over the winter months, gnawing on that old wiring." He took slow steps toward me as he reiterated the report's findings.

"Okay."

"It wasn't your fault."

"Okay."

Dutch's fingers found mine, and I focused on them rather than his face. The truth was, when I read the report, I thought of my parents and my grandparents and how lucky they were to die with the one they loved the most, even if it was too soon. On the other hand, I had yet to tell the man I loved how I felt about him. And what if I had been in the house the night of the fire? What if I slept through the blaze, never having said the words? I couldn't get to Junior Ford's home fast enough to tell Dutch how I felt.

But Dutch's absence had seemed like the cosmos putting the kibosh on that plan. A reminder of the debt I owed. The cost of my wrongful attempt to defend my brother. Allowing another person to take the blame. The real victim, a stranger, due more than I could ever imagine and had no way to even begin to repay. And now for burning down my family's home.

"I have to go to sleep now." I pulled away and staggered toward the bed as I tried to pry apart the knot in my cinched-tight bathrobe belt.

"*Sadie Jane,*" the whispered shout sounded a bit frantic.

My head snapped to see him, and I caught myself before making what could have been a stellar face plant in the king mattress. "Huh?"

"I'm gonna need you to keep that bathrobe on." His plea came with his eyes closed and a signature neck grab.

I stared at the tie sash at my waist, then back at him. "O-okay." Shrugging, I climbed in the turned-down sheets and nestled into a perfect bed pillow. Dutch placed a fresh bottle of water and two pain-relievers on the bedside table.

"For the morning." He brushed the damp hair from my cheek, tucking it behind my ear.

"Ellis?" I couldn't keep my eyes open any longer, but my mouth hadn't quit yet.

"*Hm?*"

"I didn't come looking for you because of the report."

"No?"

"No. I had things to say, but I'm not saying them now."

"Why's that?"

I wiggled my head against the high thread count pillowcase and sighed, "I'll tell you I love you tomorrow. When I'm sober. So you'll know it's true." I sighed. "But Ellis?"

"*Hm?*" His reply included a chuckle that drifted far away as my sleep took hold.

"I still can't—I'll never forgive—"

No more talking. No more hushed laughter. No more anything but sleep.

Thirty-Seven

SADIE

present day

THE NEXT MORNING MORPHED into afternoon, but another quick shower, along with chugged water and gulped pod coffee, put me two steps closer to flying out the door. I couldn't pull my boots on fast enough. My bag slung over one shoulder, phone in hand, I reached for a denim jacket hanging in the motel room closet while I bounced, trying to yank the shaft of the second boot up my calf. The knock at the door froze me in a hands-full, one-legged stance, arms and a leg askew, bag strap sliding to the crook of my arm. Yoga calls it Struggler's Pose, I believe.

Hopping my way to open the door, still bent over in the footwear tussle, I tried to secure my oversized purse again. Wide blue-green eyes met me, and I knew I must look my typical graceless fiasco on feet, except I only perched on one at that moment. Skipping a step and a half backward, I beckoned Dutch inside, finally securing my burdensome boot.

He'd only uttered his predictably single syllable greeting when I dropped the phone and the jacket, letting them and the bag land on the floor before I charged him, sending him stumbling into the door that had just clunked closed behind him as my mouth overtook his.

My bold hello didn't meet the slightest hint of resistance. Truthfully, Dutch met my chutzpah with a bit of his own, and it both exhilarated and frightened me, but when I withdrew, he held tighter, assuring me the kiss was right, with fifteen years' worth due. I tugged at his growing curls, and his lips skimmed my jaw; teeth grazed my neck, forcing my hands to press the door to stay upright, putting some light between us. But this kiss was wrong, a false start to something that couldn't be, something I'd never be worthy of.

"Don't." His whispered plea in my ear kept me from pulling away entirely. He relaxed his hold but spoke again. "Don't go. We can stop but—stay. Don't run away. Just be here. This close to me. Just stay, Sadie Jane."

My arms dropped to my sides, as did his; the only touching involved my head resting on his chest that rose and fell like mine, breathless from the unplanned reception. I took in his smell, felt the thud of his heart, knowing mine beat as hard and fast.

"Ellis?" Our breaths settled, and I allowed my hands to wander, finding his waist, exploring the buttons of his shirt. "Can I ask you something?"

He huffed, amused. "Yes. Anything."

"That night?"

He shrank some, his body slumping into something like defeat, but I hurried to rectify it. "No, not that part. But if that part hadn't happened—if you got to take me home like we'd planned—what then? What would have happened then?" The "what if" scenario had played on repeat in my younger years, and I wondered what Dutch's version looked like. The salt in the old wound was added torture.

Dutch straightened again, considering the question. "Well, turns out I had a pretty bad concussion, so I probably would have puked on you. Small favors, right?"

I *hmphed*, nose still to his chest, hands traveling his sides. "All right. But if you didn't have a concussion, and you took me home, then what might have happened?"

"Well, I'd have wanted to kiss you."

At the word, I lifted my chin to kiss him but knew I couldn't—shouldn't. I settled for saying, "I'd have wanted you to."

He thumped his head against the door. "Which would have been a problem because I wouldn't have."

"Wouldn't have kissed me?" I pulled back but then heeded his earlier request to stay close, not an inch apart.

"I'd like to *think* I wouldn't have. Hard to say, though. I'd have been awfully tempted. And I'm guessing you wouldn't have made it easy on me."

"I don't understand. You wanted to, but you wouldn't have?"

"I made a promise."

"Not to kiss me?" I stiffened, almost stomping my foot like that petulant teen. "I'm gonna kill Leo," I growled.

Dutch's laugh rumbled through his breastbone to my ear. He kissed my damp curls. "Not exactly and not Leo."

I pressed my forehead to his shoulder in thought, then gasped, "Grandaddy?"

Dutch only nodded, his morning stubble pleasantly rough on my temple.

"That night in the garage? When I asked about the dance?" I squeezed his hips, a reflex at the humiliating memory of his bolting from me when I brazenly fished for an invitation to the fall formal. My heart got dinged that night, but the solace from his explanation now surprised me.

"Yep."

"And you wouldn't have kissed me?"

"He wanted us to wait, is all. Until you were sixteen. I promised I would."

"I saw you shake hands on it."

"We did."

"You two should have known better," I grumbled.

"Oh, we did. Trust me." Dutch chuckled at the memory.

"Always doing right, even when right isn't easy." I felt his head shake before he spoke again.

"I don't want to think about it, Sadie. Too much got lost that night. Let's not dwell on it." He rested his chin on my head, but I broke the connection—stepped away from him as reality reared its ugliness—the reminder of what I'd done and the penalty I had to pay. He cussed under his breath as I bent to pick up my things.

"Midge will be wondering about me. I need to go get my truck and figure out what I do next. Where I go next." I gestured to the fire investigation report still lying where I'd tossed it on the bureau the night before.

"Where? What do you mean 'where?'"

I slipped into my jacket and adjusted the bag strap, avoiding his eye and his questions. I didn't have an answer, but Junior's suggestion to leave Canaan Cove echoed.

"Midge will understand. Your burned-out house isn't going anywhere, and your truck is here." He offered me my keys he'd pulled from his pocket. "I want to take you somewhere. Show you something. Will you come with me?"

I spun from him, pretending to search the parking lot for the vehicle to cover my uncertainty that I could deny him anything. "Part of me would like nothing more than to follow you anywhere, but I don't know how to give myself permission to do that. I don't know how—"

His fingers gripped around my waist, and I knew my fate had found me. He asked again, lips pressed to my curls. "For the first time since I was seventeen, I am connected to something. I'm inside and not just inside my own head. It's like finding home, and it's not just you, but it is because of you, and I don't want to let go, to lose it. Come with me. Please, Sadie Jane, let me show you something. Then maybe you can find a way—find *your* way to forgiveness."

Facing him, the morning sun played up the blue in his eyes and the silver of his scar. With my hand on his cheek, my thumb brushed the crooked line I'd left him with all these years. A constant memento, not that he could ever have forgotten. I rose to kiss it with a silent vow that the kissing stopped now. Leo's recent reprimand for the *push-me-pull-you* routine played in my head. No more of that. Instead, my cheek pressed to his, my lips moved to his ear. "I'll come with you, but—" I couldn't imagine a scenario that ended in my absolution.

He waited, eyes to the ceiling, not breathing, but his arms held me close again, and my resolve slipped that quickly. "But?"

I wrenched from him. "But I'll be the one driving."

We rode north and inland, snacking on crisp green apples we'd snagged in our hurry through the motel lobby. The rush wasn't for the destination, wherever Dutch planned to direct me, but to avoid being stopped by the Motor Lodge proprietor. No such luck.

"I see you sneaking off, you two, and I'm too busy to needle you about the details, but I had better see you back here later this evening for our Labor Day celebrations by the pool." Addie caught us halfway out the door. "I throw quite the shindig, if I do say so myself." She puffed up with pride before turning sincere. "It'd mean a ton if you showed up. I mean, if you can—it really would beat all."

Since I had no idea what my day would entail, I looked to Dutch for his reply. I hadn't packed for anything more than a day trip, but my travel companion had a mysterious streak and an air-sucking smile, so I was liable to agree to anything—if I could only—

"We'll do our level best to be back by dark. Can we bring something?"

"Just yourselves." She beamed.

Dutch's use of the words 'our' and 'we' had the *exactly right* sound to my ear, but when they echoed on repeat as I drove away from Canaan Cove, I chastised myself for blissful thoughts with the reminder of penance due.

"What are you thinking about over there?" Dutch reached for me as I hunched over the wheel, driving with a white-knuckled grip. I flinched, and he retreated to his side of the bench seat. A glimpse showed some hurt, but he forged ahead with unusual chit-chat. "You're not still drunk, are you?" His tone said he joked. "It's just Drunk Sadie is a quiet Sadie, and you're awfully quiet."

I took solace in hearing Drunk Sadie had behaved the night before. I never gave much credence to selective amnesia when it came to booze binges. As an adult, I've always owned my behavior, whether I took pride in it or not. But I didn't have too many incidents to hang my head about. Again, it was a control thing. I believe one ought to admit what she did, what she said, how she lost her panties while she did and said those things and then move on. It's the grown-up thing to do.

"Sober as a judge," I quipped, relaxing in the driver's seat, hoping to lighten the mood.

Dutch huffed, "My mom could tell you stories."

"She did." I took a quick inhale. "Oh, yeah. I talked with your mom."

"I heard." He kept his eyes front-facing. "I hope you're—pleased with the arrangement you presented to Pembroke."

"Ha. I only hope Pembroke agrees to it." And I hoped I'd find out soon.

"He will."

"Should know soon, either way."

"He will," Dutch reiterated in a way that said I could count on it. I sat with that nugget for a moment, both pleased and appalled by the implication—one more than the other. I wouldn't say which, but I hid a grin.

"Rumor has it you're unemployed now." A hint of snark came with my gossip.

"Yeah. That'll definitely light up my dating profile."

"You'd be surprised. Some women—"

"Are idiots," he interjected.

I sighed. "Yeah, some of us are."

His cheeks pinked, goading me to pile on. "I wouldn't worry about it. You'd be surprised what a woman will overlook if a guy has a big enough—"

"Sadie Jane," Dutch gasped my name as he went full red, turning to the passenger window to mask his laughter.

"Bank account, Ellis. I was going to say *bank account*. Sheesh," I huffed. "So include that on your Bumble blurb."

He couldn't hide his sweet smile. In the fun of it all, I missed him taking hold of my hand. I let it continue.

"Just trying to be a good wingman—wingwoman?" I swallowed hard, not wanting him to let go.

"You keep kissing me the way you have been lately, and I reckon I don't need a wingman."

And there it was. Fun-time was over.

"Ellis, I shouldn't have kissed you."

"Yeah." He let go of my hand. "I figured you'd say something like that."

"I mean, I won't be doing that anymore. I can't—"

"Yeah, I know, Sadie Jane." He kept his gaze to his side of the road. "You're getting off here." He lifted his chin. "This exit," he pointed. "Turn right."

I swerved two lanes to exit the highway.

Thirty-Eight

SADIE

present day

If Canaan Cove was an idyllic, quaint village by the sea, Luxton Fell epitomized the posh life with sweeping views of the Ogeechee River a half-hour inland. The recent residential development built to look historic succeeded with all the majestic southern charm of Savannah, minus the seedier elements. And while the community sparkled in the glorious late afternoon sun, something was lost without the grit—at least for me. The picturesque hamlet provided a place for old money to be new again without the worry of lead pipes and paint or faulty wiring. Of course, I appreciated that concept now more than ever.

We wound our way around the river's curves. Stately homes sat off the road surrounded by lush maritime landscape, cypress trees drooping with more ubiquitous Spanish Moss. Water flowed everywhere, and the geotechnical engineer in me couldn't help but wonder about the marshland foundation upon which the massive houses had been built.

"My God, Ellis," I gasped. "Tell me you didn't buy me a house. Tell me this isn't the grand gesture that is supposed to fix everything. How could you think—how could you possibly consider doing such a thing?"

"The grand gesture?" His question held a mix of amusement, exasperation, and, I thought, sadness. Maybe the thought had crossed his mind. Like the fantasy of a big old house with a porch swing and curly-haired basketball team had played in his head too, but then he recognized it could never be. "Yes," he exhaled. "I bought you a house. The most independent, stubborn, opinionated woman I know, and I made a million-dollar, six thousand square foot decision without so much as consulting you because that's *exactly* the way I *know* you'd like to be handled." He shook his head at my foolish question.

We coasted along the residential street at a crawl, but I hit the brake with a stomp to snap him out of his ribbing. Our seatbelts caught us. He kept up a forced but quiet laugh while I stared, then shoved him. "What then? Why are we here? Did you buy *yourself* a house? Here? Wow. 'Fixing' is nice work if you can get it, I guess." I took in the verdant Bermuda grass and gas lit lanterns flanking the entries of long driveways.

"It pays," he admitted, letting go of the last of our diversion. "But no, I didn't buy a house for anyone." He pointed ahead. "Two more bends that way to a dead end." A sternness came over him, and my stomach tightened to see it. He typed on his phone as he gave my knee a brief nudge. "It's the pedal on the—"

"On the right, yes, I know." I let off the brake, and we inched forward, but to where I hadn't a clue.

Those two bends brought us to a beautiful, white-washed brick, low country house with a sprawling front yard and cascading ferns hung along the front porch that begged visitors to come sit a spell with a tumbler of too-sweet tea. It was storybook perfect, and for a flicker of a moment, I wished he *had* bought it for me. No, not really, but kinda...

"You can park, Sadie Jane." His gentle instructions drew me from the brief daydream.

"Ellis?" I squeezed his name from my throat, wondering how I had allowed myself to get dragged all this way to who knew where for who knew what. But when I met his sweet eyes, I remembered. Love brought me here.

He opened his door, and I followed suit, sliding until my feet hit the pavement. I paused to check in with my pal Newton, but the quiet creak of hinges drew my attention to the home's front porch. A tall blond man in chinos and a polo shirt exited. He looked to be my age and held a gleeful baby upright on one arm, kissing the pudgy hand that smacked him in the face. Another man, dark and handsome, followed behind. He, too, held a tiny person; this one rested its head under the man's close-cut bearded chin, gripping his collar.

Dutch had crossed the front of the truck to me and offered his hand. In a less-than-typical move, I took it without hesitation and let him tug me toward our apparent hosts. The first man held the railing to descend the steps, and as we got closer, I noticed two things. One, he had tears in his beaming eyes, and two, he walked with a slight limp.

It seemed Newton had failed me as we drifted up the driveway—the floaty feeling seemed real as I began to comprehend the scene unfolding in front of me. It was another dream—more like a nightmare I had forced myself to endure over the years, but it never looked like this. The blond gave a tentative wave, then adjusted the baby in his arms. With a glance back, he nodded at the other man who held steady on the pillared portico before his partner continued down a flagstone path, coming straight for Dutch and me. We kept moving too, slow steps, but to what end? When the infant reached for Dutch, the blond's face cracked with an ear-to-ear smile despite his tears, and he handed over the eager baby. Dutch took her gladly, offering her a drawn-out murmured version of his usual "hi."

The man, a father I presumed, stretched his arms wide and said, "So, I'm a crier, obviously. And a hugger." He stepped closer to me.

"Oh, I'm not a crier or a hugger." My quiet reply came with a small shrug, still dazed by the strange scene.

"Well, this is about to get *super* weird for you then," he snickered and wrapped me in a bear-like embrace. "Sadie Jane Klein," he said my name in a loud whisper.

Dutch moved to intervene, protective as always, but the hugger stopped him. "She's all right."

"I'm all right," I parroted in something like awe, even believing it in the surreal exchange, but my words sounded far away.

Dutch swiveled to catch my eye. "Sadie, this is Holden Chaswell. He's—"

"Yes," I pulled from Holden, looking up to study his face. "I know who he is. We went to high school together."

He was taller and softer than he had been all those years ago, but there was no mistaking him. "Yes, we did." He held my hands. "We wandered those halls acting like total strangers for more than a year, and then you disappeared."

"I graduated early and left town." It was all a matter of fact, but we spoke with such quiet deference, like neither of us could believe the moment was happening.

Holden encouraged me toward the porch. "Come meet my family."

I stiffened; thick air swirled around me—I missed the ocean's constant breeze. My feet wouldn't move.

"Come on. I have you to thank for them, after all, so it would mean a lot to introduce you."

Dutch gestured with those curls that had started to show. He telegraphed a promise of safety, and my limbs relaxed. His broad hand splayed across the belly of the baby girl, who happily perched in the crook of his arm. Another glorious image that should have come with a *viewer beware* warning.

"Ellis, you're holding a baby," I stated the obvious, proving my anxiety.

"I am," Dutch's brows rose, and his slow smile crept to his eyes.

"He is, and he does it very well," Holden added. "I just hope she doesn't spit-up on you again. Every damn time with this one." Daddy Holden chided his daughter in a sing-song voice and tapped the end of her nose, and she giggled in a way that said she definitely had plans to barf on Dutch again soon.

"Every time?" Now I only had eyes for the little firebrand. Fingering a ruffle on her gingham dress, I remembered a greenish splotch on Dutch's shirt and his "real good day" grin the evening he'd wiped engine grease from my face.

"I've visited some, yes. Only recently, though," Dutch admitted before walking away. "Haven't I? Haven't I visited?" He asked his bundle, tickling her tummy. She let loose a gleeful squeal, and everyone but me encouraged her with more laughter. I was too gobsmacked to join in the fun.

"Marcus, this is Sadie Klein." We climbed the steps, and I took the man's offered hand. "Sadie, this is Marcus, my husband. That shy boy in his arms is Booker. I know, I know. We each got to pick a name, and Marcus, a political science historian, picked Booker. But we call him Book, and don't let this bashful routine fool you. Once he warms up, he'll be all over you."

"Marcus or Booker?" I straight-faced the joke. "I'm game for either, just preparing myself."

Everyone laughed again—me included. Dutch's posture visibly relaxed.

"And this precious handful," Holden offered to free Dutch of his armload. He reluctantly returned the girl to her father. "This is Mamie Chaswell."

Little Mamie chirped, hearing her name. My prickling eyes found Dutch's, and he squinted, trying to gauge my mood, I'd guess. Disregarding the audience, I leaped to him, grabbed his cheeks, planting a fiery kiss on his lips, brief but skirting the brink of indecent.

When I released his mouth, his grin spread wide. "Thought you weren't doing that anymore," he whispered.

"Yeah. Guess we'll have to talk about that later." I placed a chaste peck on his cheek and fussed with his collar.

"I reckon we will," he declared as our happy, wide-eyed hosts welcomed us to sit.

"*Un*sweet tea—you heathens," Holden announced, an inviting spread lay on a wicker glass-top table.

"Please sit," Marcus urged us deeper into the veranda. "I want to know all there is to know about the woman that saved my Holden's life."

And my first tear sprang free.

There was a mad scramble. I staggered onto a cushioned settee. Holden joined me with more of his own tears and additional hugs. Marcus bolted inside for a box of tissues and a bottle of wine, leaving Dutch with his arms full of two howling babies, one in joy, one—not so much. Our hosts were as kind as could be, trying to pacify me while I struggled to explain that whatever was happening with my tear ducts was definitely rare and probably a good thing. They encouraged me to let the waterworks flow, but Dutch, weighed down with two drooling infants, paled like he'd seen a ghost.

I pushed that worry aside and stood for the long overdue act I never thought the universe would make possible. "I have owed you an apology for far too long. Not only for attacking you, regardless of the circumstance, but I recently learned the truth of that night, and I couldn't be more horrified, sorrier for—You are so gracious, but you must think me a monster."

"I'm gonna stop you right there, Sadie." Holden gripped my wrist, guiding me to sit with him again. His hand moved to my chin, urging me to look all around him. "Do you see this? See this life? These beautiful babies? You made this possible. You made me live my truth. You were the wake-up call. I watched you be you without caring what others thought. You didn't hide. You didn't pretend. And the way you loved your brother with a ferocity I didn't know possible let me know there was love out there for me, too. You're kinda my hero, Sadie Klein. I don't even want to think where I'd be if you hadn't done what you did—if you hadn't woken me the hell up. The apology is due to Dutch here, making him lie and the unforeseen consequences of that fiction. That's the real tragedy."

It was too. And I couldn't find my way to exonerating myself for it. It was the end of us before we ever got started.

"Dutch and I—and Marcus, have had more than one talk about it. *Dutch* is the gracious one, an example of how to be, and we couldn't be more pleased to have him in our children's lives now. Well—we could be more pleased. If *you* would be a part of their lives too. They need a fierce, smart woman who likes to play in the dirt—"

"And change spark plugs," I added. A short-lived moment lightened in my chest, but a look at a heartbroken Dutch wiped it away. I didn't deserve the benevolent fixer or the forgiving professor. They had both lost, both paid for my feral behavior, and now it was my turn. I owed a debt. "Thank you, Holden." I patted his knee. "Marcus." I reached for him, too. "Thank you for all of this." I gathered myself, blew my nose, and sipped some iced tea before I registered Dutch's ashen face again. "Are you all right?" Concerned, I tried to stand, but Holden sat too close.

"Am *I* all right?" Dutch stared, bouncing the twins in one spot. "Are *you* all right?"

"Goodness me, Dutch. Don't stare." Holden rocked me like one of his children. "Have you never seen her ugly cry? It's called that for a reason," he sang, but when his description struck me, immediately self-conscious, I wiggled free to get to another tissue to blot my eyes and nose.

"I—I've never seen her cry. At all. *Ever.*"

"*Aww.* Hurts, doesn't it? If you hadn't known you were in love with her before, you certainly would now."

I sucked in some air. Yes, Dutch had said it. Days ago. And yes, I believed it, but I hadn't known he'd told anyone else. But that wasn't the issue. I loved him too and had told Leo and Midge, but I had yet to tell—I jerked upright, eyes locked on Dutch. *Curse you, Drunk Sadie.* When did she become such a gossip?

"Holden," Marcus scolded his partner with a warning glance across the porch while taking Booker from Dutch's arms.

"There are no secrets here." Holden employed an impish grin. "Not anymore." He squeezed my hand and stood, beckoning Dutch to hand over his daughter. "Why don't we trade one girl for another," he winked, "and Sadie can fill me in on her last fifteen years."

After some rearranging, each father sat in a rocker, a child in his lap. Dutch and I shared the settee. He leaned toward me; his mouth opened to speak, but he stopped himself. I almost blurted it again right then, but the better angel on my shoulder convinced me to wait. Besides, my loving him didn't fix anything.

Holden didn't let the quiet sit for long, asking about college and career, and other aspects of life. The new fathers were professors, Marcus, a Ph.D. in political science, and Holden in psychology. They had taken sabbaticals when the twins were born. We joked and shared highlights of the last decade, avoiding the eight-hundred-pound gorilla while I fought the distraction of Dutch's thigh touching mine and the devil on my other shoulder.

When the babies started to doze simultaneously, Holden insisted they put them down to sleep because "structure and routine were important." Marcus rolled his eyes, mouthing the question, "What routine?" as he glanced at his watch but followed his spouse inside to settle the little ones into their proper cribs.

I took the opportunity to put some distance between Dutch and me—not that I wanted any. I wanted less. Less distance, less company, less clothing. And though the late afternoon had turned into a lovely evening of get-to-know-you time with Holden and Marcus, tension strained the gathering with all that went unsaid. I couldn't be the only one feeling it. Add to that, the pull between Dutch and me crackled—in my head, at least, putting me more on edge. I had things to say, but the time and place were wrong and might never be right.

The heat of him warmed my back with his approach as the day cooled with the sun setting over the distant riverbank. He didn't touch me or speak, only kept nearby. Was he waiting for me to say something? To say *it*? I reprimanded Drunk Sadie again, then stood in the quiet with nothing but the faint muffle of a sweet lullaby coming from inside the house.

Midge's words flooded my brain. "...forgive it. Get over it..." But I couldn't. The physical pain I inflicted, the emotional havoc, the lives upended by my recklessness... how could I "get over it." Everyone made it look so easy.

"Ellis, I know what you want to hear. I know what you're waiting for me to say, and I—I can't—" Tongue-tied, I faced him.

His chin hit his chest with a heavy exhale. "Well, I don't want you saying something you don't mean." His gaze moved from the porch floor to the landscape, avoiding my eyes.

I raised my palm to his chest, and he winced at my touch. "Something I don't mean? It's not that. What good would it do? I can't—"

"What *good* would it do? It would make all the rest of it possible. It makes us possible."

"No, it doesn't. It—"

The door opened. "Sometimes it is just so dang easy," Holden sighed. An entrance line had never held more irony. "Oh, sorry. Everything okay out here?"

I bolted from the porch.

"I got her..." Dutch murmured something about me being a runner, and his feet hit the stairs as I beelined to my truck. "Stop, Sadie. Please stop. Just—"

"Just what? Act like everything is fine. Just tell you I love you. Okay. I love you. I'm in love with you. It's always been you, but now I can't—"

"I know," he barked, a doubled-handed neck grip this time. "I know. You've said. You can't forgive me. I hear you. I heard you last night. The deception, the years of lying. I get it. You can't—"

"Forgive you? Forgive *you*? What for? For protecting me? For taking the blame for my awful behavior? For shielding me from the appalling truth of it?" The questions exploded out of me, shocked at how wrongly he'd read the situation. More sadness swelled when I recognized his hurt. The next questions were practically whispered. "How could you ever think you'd done anything that warranted *my* forgiveness? Is that what you thought this was? *Me* not forgiving *you*?"

We stared at one another in the sudden quiet, letting our shouted misunderstanding float across the manicured lawns to hang in perfectly draped trees, confusion on both our faces.

"I don't understand. Then why—why can't we—I love you, Sadie Jane. Are you hearing me? I love you. Why won't you let me?"

"Let you?"

"Yes, let me love you."

My scalp buzzed like the waking katydids; a vibration rolled through my limbs. Nothing made sense. "How—"

"How? Good God, Sadie." He tilted his face to the sky, pressed the heels of his hand to his eyes before cupping my cheeks. "Give me a lifetime to show you."

I softened into his plea a moment too long.

"If Holden can forgive you—if he can forgive and welcome you into his life, into his family, why can't you?"

I shook my head. "And you?"

"I made my choice, not you. You couldn't have convinced me otherwise, and as I said in my parents' basement, I don't regret a thing because you are standing in front of me now. We are getting another shot, a do-over. I can't tell you how this is going to go. That's impossible. But this is the way. You and me. We didn't crash into each other's orbits again for no reason. And I'm not going anywhere. I'm staying. You're staying. We are not breaking this time. I won't let it happen. Find your law of physics and apply it. I love you, and you love me. The rest we tackle together." He kissed me, the sexy, chaste kind, but I fought my surrender to it. He showed a surprising grin when he pulled his lips from mine, like he knew victory was his. "You are the most *stubborn* woman. Always have been." The next kiss was softer still, and my knees threatened to give way. "Good thing I've made a career of sussing out desire." He kissed me deeper. "And weakness," he whispered before his lips grazed that magic spot in the dip of my collarbone.

I was a goner. He'd found my Achilles heel. If he'd brandished a hidden mushroom and black olive pizza, I'd have stripped out of my sundress then and there. My fingers entwined in his curls I hoped I'd get to see grow longer, our mouths colliding again, crossing the PG-13 line. We may have been saved by the door handle's painful jab into my back.

"Ellis? We should—"

"Stop. Yes." He eased up but kept close.

"It's only because there's still some daylight, and I imagine this Stepford community has a pretty strict HOA." We snickered into another kiss, then snuck a peek at Holden and Marcus's front porch. The handsome pair had their arms wrapped around one another just like I'd seen Davis and Elspeth Holland in my tail lights. The two men instantly separated, spinning in opposite directions like they hadn't been eavesdropping on the scene as it played out in their driveway.

Still pressed to the truck, Dutch and I waved. Holden waved back, and Marcus pantomimed a phone to his ear and mouthed, "Call us," before he dragged his husband inside.

Dutch turned back to me, tucking away one of my curls tugged free in our reunion. "Say it." He kissed my forehead.

"I love you," I whispered, but his head tilt said that wasn't what he wanted to hear.

His lips pressed to my cheek, then moved to my ear. "The other thing."

The breathy hum and the scruff of his days-old beard sent a delighted butterfly burst in my chest. He was officially the kryptonite to my word bank. I swallowed hard. "I told you, you've done nothing that warrants forgiveness."

"You, then. Think about Holden and Marcus and the beautiful Booker and Mamie. Look at me and forgive yourself. Then give me the rest of my life to show you how much you deserve it. Say it."

I inhaled the marshy evening air, taking note of the purpling sky. My hand slid up Dutch's chest, and eyes traveled the length of him too, meeting a serious face. "I—I forgive me." I couldn't say the transformation was complete, but it was a start—an honest start. "Now, take me home, Ellis Holland." I pressed a smiling kiss to his satisfied grin, but then he craned his neck.

"You mean, like *drive*? Me? Driving you? In your truck?" His mouth hung open in mock shock.

I rolled my eyes at his puckishness, holding the keys up for him. "It's not like you haven't driven it before."

"I know, but somehow this feels different." He lunged for the keys, missing them.

"*Uh, uh, uh*," I chirped, snatching them away again. "Are you gonna drive slowly?"

One side of his mouth quirked. "I cannot in good conscience promise you that, Sadie Jane. And I wouldn't want to lie."

"*Hm*, will you kiss me when we get there?"

His nostrils flared. "At the very least." He seized the keys. "Of course, there's no *way* I'm driving slowly now." He gathered me about the waist and pulled me close.

"You better not," I insisted with a gentle nip of his bottom lip, then slid across the bench seat to the passenger side of the truck.

Thirty-Nine

SADIE

present day

THE AGONIZING RIDE CONSISTED of eager handholding and small talk, rehashing what should have been an awkward high school reunion. But other than the beyond-shocking ugly cry, it was a net positive day. We laughed about Holden and Marcus's loveable sniping, then sighed at the beauty of the twins with their opposite personalities and the family's generous warmth. Still, the anticipation of getting back to Canaan Cove—to the Motor Lodge, in particular—simmered. My butterflies grew brazen, threatening rebellion if I didn't get closer to Dutch soon.

He hadn't removed the key from the ignition before I had crawled into his lap with grabby hands and impatient lips. A teenage dream unfolded: me, parked in a truck at night, making out with Dutch Holland. At almost sixteen, it was all I ever wanted, but at nearly twice that, I wanted more.

"Sadie?" Dutch more than lived up to my youthful imagination with the heavy breathing and quickly fogging windows rounding out the fantasy.

"Hmm?" My mouth was too busy for more than a moaned reply as I struggled to peel out of my jacket.

"Sadie, I need—" Dutch joined in the frantic denim battle I seemed to be losing to my second sleeve. Finally, freedom.

"Uh-hm, yes, me too, Ellis," I panted, holding tighter.

"No, I—I need to unbuckle my seatbelt."

"Oh." I hoisted myself inches off his thighs, banging my head on the roof of the truck cab. We *"oof-ed"* in sync with my clumsy, hard landing back on his lap. I rubbed the sting on the top of my head. "You okay?"

In the dark, his pinched face nodded with a quiet groan. "Uh-hm. You?"

I hurried to lift off of him again, ramming my ass into the steering wheel with force. "*Ouch!*" I gasped over the *clank* and rustle of the released safety belt. "That's gonna leave a mark," I snickered, gently lowering my soon-to-be bruised butt onto his lap again, kissing over his apologies. The air had grown thick in the close quarters with my sundress sticking to me. My head, backside, and more throbbed as I pried my lips from his.

Another gasp slipped from me, this one from pleasure when his tongue found its way to my collarbone soft spot. "Ellis, I'll give you about a year to stop doing that. Maybe two," I sighed, feeling his rumbled delight rather than hearing it. "But it occurs to me, we are a mere yards from my motel room—" Another sharp inhale when his teeth grazed my throat. "An air-conditioned motel room with a *very* large bed and high thread count—"

He gave a vigorous nod, capturing my mouth again. I couldn't breathe, couldn't see. Everything pulsed. When I drew back for air, his firm hands slid up my torso while his mouth grazed down my chest, and I saw stars followed by the ear-splitting honk of a classic Ford Ranger F-100. I shot upright with a squawk, shocked by the blared horn, cracking my head on the roof again.

"*Goddammit,*" I hissed before falling against him, both of us laughing. "My romance novels make this seem much more tenable and there's a joke about concussions to be made here, but I can't find my way to the punchline."

"How about we find our way inside? It might be safer in there," he hummed in my ear.

It was my turn to nod, though I had little faith that the word "safer" qualified when Dutch followed his suggestion with one of those tender, virtuous kisses. I couldn't scramble from the truck fast enough.

I'd guess the anticipation of what would come next was to blame for not noticing the unusual number of cars in the parking lot, or the music and lively fun emanating from the motel courtyard, or the smell of grilled meats wafting on the evening air. I only registered Dutch's fingers laced with mine and the want in his eyes.

The welcoming shouts of our names stopped us in our tracks, and I gripped Dutch's hand tighter, letting an f-bomb whisper out of me.

"Yeah, I think we're gonna need to put a pin in that." Disappointment oozed from his airy reply.

"The Labor Day shindig," I gritted. "Yay," I cheered with zero enthusiasm. Several yards away, Addie wiggled with a puppy-like eagerness to greet us as she tried to break free from the guest occupying her. I wouldn't have been surprised if she peed a little in her excitement. Dutch and I had only a few seconds to formulate a plan before she broke free from her imagined leash.

"Maybe we excuse ourselves for—oh, I don't know—ten minutes? Then join the party?"

Dutch's incredulous squint said, *hell* no.

"An hour?" My brows bounced, thrilled at the prospect.

His jaw clenched as he scanned the crowd. He kept his voice low. "Sadie Jane. We enter your motel room, and there's no coming out for forty-eight hours, at least. That's a promise." His hand at the small of my back glided a few inches lower for a too-brief moment.

I swallowed hard. "Oh." My knees buckled as heat radiated in every direction. "That's—that's two days. Two. Ha, my favorite..." I rasped, my focus on staying upright.

Addie was *this* close to extricating herself from her current conversation. *Tick-tock.*

"Okay. Here's the play, Ellis. We split up. You make the rounds but be quick about it." I scrutinized the gathering, strategizing my own path.

"What are you gonna do?" He leaned close to pose the question. His breath on my skin and the cooling night air sent a shiver through me despite the flames crackling in my core.

"I'm going to round up all the bottled water I can get my hands on because—we're definitely gonna need to hydrate." I kept a straight face as long as I could.

Dutch exhaled, "Good God, I love you."

"Back at you, big guy, and I'd kiss you, but it'd likely get indecent in a hurry, and the delicate Addie is on her way over here."

I'm pretty sure the man growled, and I squeezed my thighs together.

Our petite hostess scurried toward us. Her eyes were aglow. "Sadie," she peeped with a two-handed wave as she approached.

"Addie," I reciprocated, her excitement contagious.

"Dutch," Junior shouted, following behind.

"Junior!" Dutch hailed back, and the two greeted each other with broad grins and back slaps.

"Sadie," Junior included a tinge of apology in his quieter hello to me. I didn't care.

"Hey, Dutch. Glad you both could make it." Addie tugged at my wrist, clearly wanting a moment alone with me. Her furtive glances at Junior told the reason why. We shared a telepathic moment, wide smiles and silent *squeals* over the giant ex-jock keeping close behind her. What was happening to me?

"Sade!" It was like an excruciating record scratch. So many names bandied about. Why *that* one? I spun to put myself between the unanticipated Tristan and Dutch, who had jerked away from his old pal Junior.

"Tristan? What are you doing here?" I pressed my back into Dutch's chest, unsure how he'd react to the out-of-towner in our midst.

"Addie invited me, and you know I never miss a party." Tristan extended his hand and the game began again, "Hello, Dutch."

Dutch reached around me and took it. "Tristan." The two shook hands, and I didn't detect an ounce of distrust or suspicion.

"Hi, Tristan," sweet Addie chirped, maybe a bit too sweetly.

"Miss Addie," Tristan brushed his hair aside with a little extra charm.

"Tristan," Junior's greeting held some snarl, and I thought whatever Tristan-inspired skepticism Dutch had let go, Junior had scooped up and was running with it.

"Good Lord, it's Cecil Ford," Tristan cheered, eager to shake his idol's hand. Junior took it and maybe unwound some too. Yep, Tristan Pembroke could bewitch even the burliest of us.

Dutch tilted over my shoulder to whisper in my ear, "Best laid plans, huh? We're gonna be here a while, aren't we?"

I snorted at his choice vocabulary.

He squeezed my shoulders. "I'm gonna grab a beer. Can I get you something?"

"I'm good," I winked with a bit lip. "See you on the other side."

Addie made apologies, getting pulled away by hostess duties.

"I understand," I reassured her. "But I'd love to talk to you about a job."

"You need a job?" She cocked her head in confusion.

"No, I need an interior designer. I've got a house to rebuild, and I need your skillset to make it right."

Tears pooled in her eyes, highlighted by the fairy lights and sparkling votives decorating the motel party-scape.

"But there'll be none of that," I chastised the sweet pixie for her weepy display. I had my limits.

"I can't promise, Sadie." Her lashes fluttered as she looked skyward, willing the tears not to fall.

"Oh, all right," I grinned. "We'll work on it anyway. Oh, and I'll be needing the scoop on you and Mr. MVP over there." My head gestured to Junior, whose head bent in deep conversation with Dutch. But when Dutch lifted his gaze to me, the earth tilted under my feet, and he stole my breath. When he smiled, I wasn't even sure I wanted it back.

"...so, between the Chamber of Commerce, Rotary Club, and my mama at The Best Li'l Hair House in Canaan Cove, believe you me, I've got *all* the scoop."

"Huh?" I'd missed most of what Addie said in my Dutch-distraction, but I got the gist. "Oh, yes, well, let's talk soon," I said with a glance across the courtyard. "Uh, it could be a *few* days, maybe," I hurried to follow-up, intent on keeping my schedule clear for the next—ahem—forty-eight hours. She seemed to agree.

I spun to join Tristan surveying the leftovers at the tucked-away food spread. "Tristan."

He kissed my cheek, more animated than usual, and that said a lot. "I can't stay long, but I've got news." He pulled a business-sized envelope from his seersucker jacket. "Daddy agreed to your demands. Easily, even. You should have seen me, Sade. I marched right into his office and *insisted* he sign off on your attorney's proposal, and he agreed. Just like that."

"Just like that?" I couldn't help another glimpse at Dutch.

"Just like that," Tristan repeated.

"Wow, that's—"

"*And* they signed over the rest of my inheritance."

"You don't say."

"There's a caveat, of course." His hint of exasperation almost made me choke.

"*Pfft*. When *isn't* there a caveat with a billion-dollar trust fund?" I sighed in something that sounded like commiseration.

"*Right*?" He paused to ponder some unfairness but then continued. "And just so you know, I've taken over the New Project Acquisitions division at Pembroke Industries. Between you and me, any developments in the area of desalination will go straight to the *bottom* of my pile. And that pile is a deep one. No way will I get through it in two years." He gave me a pointed look, and I beamed in response. "Also, half of Trust Fund 2.0 will be earmarked for philanthropy. To be given away, so, a foundation will need to be set up, a staff hired, and there are tax implications and rules, *blah, blah, blah*, but at the end of the day, this bad seed will do some good. How about that?"

"How about that?" I mumbled with a hard look at the former fixer dutifully sipping water across the way.

Tristan noticed, and the playboy guise disappeared. "I guess I'm in someone's debt now, huh?"

"I don't know what you mean." The doe-eyed routine never worked for me.

"Come on, Sade. You know I'm not as dumb as I let on, right?"

"Yes, Tristan. I know."

"Well, I think since the man *literally* stole my fiancée off my riverboat casino, maybe that makes us square. How about you?"

"*Fake* fiancée," I corrected. "Wait, you *own* the *Sapphire Selkie*?"

"Yeah, but just for shits and giggles. Come on, who names a boat after a sea witch? Uh, *this* guy." He jeered with two thumbs to his chest. "That's just unlucky." He rolled his eyes. "All right. I'm out," he half-shouted. "See you around, Sade." He waved over his shoulder.

"Not if I see you first, *Tris.*"

The new billionaire strode off into the seaside nighttime, and I fanned myself with the glorious paperwork the rich were famous for. This version confirmed my freedom from Pembroke Industries. But I had no doubt I'd be seeing Tristan again soon.

Forty

SADIE

present day

SADIE: BUSY?
   Leo: Yep. U Ok?
   *Sadie: *heart-eyes* (face emoji, doesn't count)*
   *Leo: *Netherlands flag*? (flag, doesn't count)*
   Sadie: Lol. Dutch flag?
   Leo: ding ding ding (onomatopoeia, doesn't count)
   *Sadie: *wink emoji**
   *Leo: *eggplant*? (vegetable, doesn't count)*
   Sadie: Ewww (noise of sisterly disgust, doesn't count)
   *Leo: *5 baby emojis* *basketball emoji**
   *Sadie: *Stop sign**
   Leo: Love you, Shorty
   Sadie: Love you, Leo

I slipped my phone back into my dress pocket as a low, made-for-radio voice rumbled from speakers perched near the dimly lit gazebo that provided a dance floor for the evening's summer farewell.

"Well, it's been a rockin' summer as always, but change is in the wind, and it's time to say goodbye to warm breezes and welcome some cold freezes. Thank you for letting me be a part of this season's sendoff. I'm Mark the Shark, spinning tunes for all occasions. But now, I'd like to slow it down with a romantic blast from the past. Who doesn't remember this one from...?"

I explored the picked-over food table, but my giddiness kept me from reaching for anything other than a bottle of water that, all joking aside, I needed. But when the song's first few chords played, I nearly dropped the full bottle as I spun in search of Dutch. Water flung in an arc, splashing up his chest and onto his face.

"Oh my. Sorry." I grabbed a clump of napkins to dab him dry.

"It's okay. It's only water."

"I know. I just—it startled—"

He took my busy hands. "Dance with me?"

"Here? The dance floor's over—"

"Here's fine." After tossing the damp napkins, he held me close, the way he had that night so long ago. Somehow, I possessed more courage when the tune played back then.

"Did you do this? Request this song?" I whispered, my head nestled on his shoulder.

"No. I'm not that smart—or that dumb." He pulled from me. "Which is it?"

"Huh?"

"Do you want me to make it stop?" He twisted toward Mark the Shark like he'd tackle the DJ to stop the song from playing if I wanted him to. "Is it a bad memory for you to revisit?"

"No." I pulled him to me. "Not at all. So, you do remember."

"Of course, I remember. Until recently, it was number one on my highlight reel."

I squinted a question at him.

"It's an athlete thing—never mind. But no, I didn't ask for it. Just a well-timed coincidence. Sort of feels like part of our do-over, though. Our long overdue, do-over."

It did, too—a second chance at the brief bright moment before everything went to hell. This time I could make a different choice in the choose-your-own-adventure game. I rested my head, oddly thankful for the slowed pace from the parking lot make-out madness.

"How's my nemesis? The ex-footballer? Anything new?"

"Junior? He's fine, but you've got that all wrong, you know?"

"I know. Junior feels protective of you. I can appreciate that."

"And the delicate Addie? Maybe not so fragile after all." We both snuck a peek at the once-quarterback and Grizzly Gus. Something beyond flirty bubbled between them. "How's mine?"

I snickered. "Your nemesis? Tristan? He was the bearer of all kinds of news. Good news. I'll be thanking you for a long time to come."

"*Hm.* Don't know why you think I have anything to do with any of it, but your gratitude is very appealing."

"Oh, I think you do, Mr. Fix-it. And someday, you'll need to explain to me this power you wield."

He shrugged. "As I said, I forget names as soon as I learn them. Plus, I'm retired now. Onto my—*third* career."

"What's that?"

He glanced at Junior. "Coastal redevelopment and sustainable retail."

"Snore."

"Ha. What have you got?"

"I've got two years to build a smart house with all the latest in technology before I take on desalination."

Dutch dropped his head. "We're gonna need to find a really fun hobby."

"Oh, I've got a plan for that, too. I think you're *really* gonna like it."

He stretched his neck and cleared his throat before giving me an impish grin. "I'm listening."

May I have your attention, please? Will the real Slim Shady—

I winced, pulling the noisy phone from my pocket again. "I've got to take this."

Dutch nodded, inhaling a hefty gulp of air.

"Midge," I answered.

"I heard you're at the Motor Lodge?"

"You heard?"

"Small town, Sadie. Word travels fast. And you're with Dutch?"

"Right by my side," I smiled, tugging his belt buckle, easily lost in his sea-colored eyes.

"Just where he belongs. Stop by when you two come up for air. I'll feed you, 'cuz y'all are gonna be hungry. Bye." Midge's cackle ended the call that quickly.

I shook my head at the old woman's good-hearted check-in and the small town's high-speed gossip swap. I thought it would be a good spot to put down some roots, build my life, but when I stepped into the waiting arms of Ellis "Dutch" Holland, I knew it for sure.

"You were saying." He coaxed me back to our interrupted conversation.

"Was I?" I kissed his cheek before resting my head on him again.

"You were," he insisted. "Something about a hobby—" We swayed in the twinkling lights.

"Oh, yes. Two things."

His lips met my ear. "Sadie Jane, given a chance, I reckon I can do much better than two."

I grinned. "In that case, will you take me home, Ellis?"

"I thought you'd never ask." His gentle kiss grew needier before I forced us apart. I pressed two fresh bottles of water to his chest and scooped up another four. With a glimpse of the dwindling party, I raised my brow and shuffled quick backward steps, headed for the motel lobby doors. Dutch grabbed two more bottles and chased me. I spun to make a run for it, eager to get to my destination and never happier for Dutch to catch me once I did.

The End

Please consider writing a brief but kind review and continue Reading for a blurb of Book Five of The Found Families Series, *The Importance of Extracurriculars & Other Assumptions*.

Amelia Kanaan allows herself two fibs per day. Only two, and only fibs—nothing bigger. While not convenient, it's gotten her far in life—all the way to Vice-Dean of Admission at her southern Ivy alma mater. But lies may yet be her downfall.

Raised poor by her single mom in Atlanta, Amelia (Mimi to her friends) worked hard to achieve her full scholarship to Chastain University. Undergrad days had their mishaps, particularly a campus-wide humiliation thanks to an assumption she failed to rectify. Hence the fib rule. Now, she dedicates her structured life to paying-it-forward while surrounding herself with few people but *reams* of non-fiction.

A chance run-in with Ethan, a nomadic truth-teller of another sort, sparks attraction. But when Chastain stands accused of a ripped-from-the-headlines admissions scandal, ethics suspend the love-match, and Amelia finds herself complicit in ways she never imagined. Fighting for her place in a world that offers more obstacles than opportunities, her good intentions go horribly wrong. Amelia strives to make things right while the hijinks of a cabal of well-meaning geriatrics and the old boys' club of higher education help and hurt, and if Amelia's already lonesome ivory tower crumbles, she'll lose everything—her career, Ethan, and the already fragile relationship with her mother.